"It takes writing chops to create a women's fiction/mystery/ modern western mash-up like *Releasing the Reins*, but author Catherine Matthews does it seamlessly. Set in the wild expanses of Alaska farmland, this debut novel honors the majestic landscape, explores the power of the human/animal connection, and exposes the destructive force of family secrets. Bunny O'Kelly is an intriguing protagonist: smart-witted, strong, stubborn, and a little lost. Her journey to unravel a hidden truth is also a hard path of self-discovery—readers will love her, fear for her, and root for her to find the answers she desperately needs. An up-all-night page-turner."

- CARLA DAMRON,
award-winning author of *Justice be Done,*
The Orchid Tattoo, and *The Stone Necklace*

"Fierce, vivid, and utterly captivating, Releasing the Reins is a must-read for anyone who enjoys hidden truths, rugged wilderness, and characters who are never quite what they seem."

- S.G. PRINCE,
author of *To Poison A King*

"Catherine Matthews shines in her debut novel about a young woman taking on gender bias and tackling her past in the ranching world of Alaska. Matthews's characters are richly drawn, and the book is fast-paced with an edge of danger. A definite page turner. I highly recommend!"

- JAMES D. SHIPMAN,
bestselling author of *Before the Storm,*
Beyond the Wire, and *Irena's War*

"Evocative. Suspenseful. Lush. Matthews paints the world of an Alaskan horse ranch with unsurpassed skill, as she takes the reader deep into the tundra, and into the dangerous world of Bunny O'Kelly, a female ranch hand in a world of men. As Bunny fights to carve out a home for herself in this unforgiving terrain, she stumbles upon a mystery that she just cannot leave alone. Does a murderer walk free in this close-knit community? Readers will find themselves devouring pages deep into the night as they join Bunny on her suspenseful quest for the truth and for self-discovery. 5 Stars!"

-HEATHER E. F. CARTER,
award-winning author of *The Black Unicorn*

RELEASING
THE
REINS

THE

TUNDRA SECRETS

SERIES

—

RELEASING
THE
REINS

A Novel

CATHERINE
MATTHEWS

PACIFIC
PEAKS PUBLISHING

To Scott
Thank you for introducing me to the wilds of Alaska
and making this journey such an adventure.

Chapter 1

Bunny 1984

Bunny was crushed in the airplane's window seat next to a boisterous man who smelled of pine and sage. She scanned his wing tips, khaki slacks, and protruding belly, then put him in the same category as the guy who sold her dad the bull semen.

Though it was just after breakfast, he was pouring whiskey into his coffee. He offered her some. Bunny wanted to channel her older brother, Mick, with an angry stare, but her mother's advice sounded in her head. *You can catch more bees with honey, Bunny.* Still, when he asked her name, she hesitated. If she was leaving Bunny behind, this was the time to do it.

"Benny," she announced, setting her jaw.

"Funny name for a girl. You are a girl, right?" He smiled and nudged her with his elbow, which would have been the first salvo of battle back home.

"Yeah, I'm a girl." She took a deep breath, tugged on the hem of her jean jacket, and counted to five.

"So, what gives?"

"It's short for Benjamina. I was named after my grandfather, Benjamin."

He leaned into her and pursed one side of his mouth. "You'd think they would have called you Mina or Minnie."

"You'd think." Bunny turned to look out the window, hoping he would get the hint and regale someone else with his adventures of peddling widgets, but he was not deterred.

"What brings you to Alaska?"

"I'm going to work on a ranch."

"Oh, yeah? You must be a pretty good cook for them to fly you all the way to Alaska."

"I'm not a cook." She rolled her eyes and shook her head, a move she'd perfected at the O'Kelly dinner table. "I'm a ranch hand."

"You don't say." He pulled back and looked her over. "I bet it's hard work."

Bunny bristled. "It is." She stared out the window. What was she getting herself into?

"I didn't even know there were ranches in Alaska. Seems like it'd be too cold most of the year. There're bears and wolves too."

"I can handle myself," she said with the bravado of generations of O'Kellys. The truth was, she wasn't sure. She'd brought her rifle, but even that wasn't going to protect her from every danger, four legs or two.

"I come up here a few times a year. I know my way around pretty well. There's not much to it, but maybe I could show you around one night. Take you to dinner."

Bunny looked down at the ring on his finger, then back at him. "What would your wife say?"

"It's just a friendly dinner." He lifted his glass and his eyebrows.

Bunny gave him a fake smile. "Thanks. I'll pass." With that, she turned back to the window and rested her head on the glass.

Only when the man turned his charms on the woman in the aisle seat did Bunny relax enough to notice the city streets had turned to forests.

❧

Through the window, the wilderness stretched out forever in muted greens and grays, nothing like the emerald pastures she'd left behind. Sloughs and rivers reached their tentacles across the land. Bunny closed her eyes until the wheels hit the earth and let loose her breath when the bouncing stopped. As they taxied, she gave herself the luxury of missing home. Her reverie was broken only when a flight attendant told her there was a package waiting at the gate.

They deplaned on the tarmac. Bunny stood at the top of the stairs and raised her face skyward. As she waited her turn, she shook the sleep from her legs. Despite the sun, a chill blanketed her. She followed the herd of travelers across the pavement, hoping her intent gait and confident expression would fool them into thinking she belonged.

Though the airport was much smaller than Sea-Tac, it took a moment for Bunny to get her bearings in the terminal. At the information desk, an older woman eyed her suspiciously and checked her ID before handing her the manila envelope. She ran her fingers over the words scribbled across the top in big black letters: *BENNY O'KELLY*. Like everything else, she had fought back, but there was no way to beat the O'Kelly men. In the end, the nickname stuck. With 1,200 miles between her and them, no one would be calling her Bunny—maybe never again.

Far larger than necessary, the envelope held a set of keys and a note.

Benny—Blue Dodge pickup crew cab parked in main lot second row. Map to the ranch is in the glove box. Basement room is yours. Door on the north side of the main house. Drop your stuff off and come down to the barn when you get here. Buck

She chuckled. Buck had the same conversational style as the O'Kelly boys. That suited her fine. She grabbed her duffel and rifle case off the carousel and headed to the lot. She spotted the farm truck right off. Random dents peppered the bed. Rust speckled the grill. Cautious by nature, she did a preflight check as Mick called it. The tires were full, but two of the hubcaps were missing. Through the dusty window, the bench seat was cracked and faded. A trailer hitch jutted out beneath the tailgate. More out of curiosity than caution, she placed a boot on the bumper and hefted herself up to look in the bed, where she found two bales of alfalfa stacked near the cab. Bunny gave the tailgate a tug. Satisfied when it held up against her weight, she tossed her gear in the back.

Midnight Sun Ranch was painted on the front door, which creaked as she pulled it open. The logo was a rearing stallion in silhouette against a blazing sun. A pine tree hung from the rear-view mirror, doing little to cover up the sweat, mud, and manure that hung in the air. She pulled a dusty cassette from the tape deck. Who was the J. Geils Band fan?

The truck was a stick, which made her smile. Maybe she hadn't made a mistake if Buck assumed she could drive one. Rummaging through the glove box, she found an old map hidden beneath a pair of broken sunglasses, the owner's manual, and years of vehicle registrations. As she unfolded it carefully, in case Buck was one of those guys who lost his mind if you creased his map, a blue ribbon fell to the seat next to her. Though fading, it was otherwise pristine. A flower of fabric surrounded by gold lettering: *Alaska State Fair 1976*. On the back, someone had written *Katie Miller 1st Place Jr Barrel Racing*. Bunny put it back in the compartment, paying mind to the delicate arms.

About a mile into the trip, she realized the map was useless. The road signs were riddled with buckshot and nearly impossible to read. The highway was paved, but only barely so. Every few feet, the surface fell away as if there had been an earthquake and they simply paved over the damage. She tried to avoid the craters at first, but she looked like a drunk. So she gripped the wheel and plowed through. The suspension was old, and the truck bounced twice over each dip.

The first time, she missed the entrance to the ranch, which was marked only by an aging mailbox listing toward the driveway. Rust creeping down the sides partially obscured the address. She thought about turning around until she heard her father's familiar voice. *You made your bed. You're going to sleep in it.* Michael O'Kelly never said anything he didn't mean. She got that now. He wouldn't welcome her back home if she fell on her face. Maybe she had never been welcome.

Looking down the drive curving into the trees, Bunny took a deep breath and put the truck into gear. It was a single lane with ruts perfectly spaced for the old Dodge. Anxious to avoid reverse, she crept along in first gear. A quarter mile down the drive where the road widened, a rustic post and rail fence held back spindly birch trees. Wildflowers peeked beneath the bottom rail in thick tufts. She was beginning to feel hemmed in by the overgrowth when the sun broke through. Bunny stopped the big truck and took in the farm.

To her right was a pasture where mares grazed and foals raced around on gangly legs. To her left was an outdoor riding arena. Jumps were posted around the ring, their whitewashed rails set at different heights. In the center, a man lunged a Paint. She was a magnificent beast. Covered in huge patches of the starkest white and black, her body looked as if someone had haphazardly sewn together a wedding dress and a tuxedo. Wrapped in pearl from ears to jaw, a swath of black swirled under her head and swept along one side of her neck. Ebony covered one side of her rump. Her muscles flexed as she jogged along, strong and proud.

The cowboy was short and stocky and had an ease about him, like he knew the horse would do whatever he asked. He held a whip loosely in his left hand but never lifted it off the ground. Bunny guessed the animal was pulling by the way the cowboy leaned back on his heels. A puzzled expression crossed his face as she passed by. She checked the clock on the dash and headed beyond the pasture to the house.

Bunny followed the ruts carved into the grass and parked on the side of the house. With the sun high in the sky and no familiar landmark to guide her, she prayed she was walking through the right door. She only saw one, and as with most things in her life these days, it didn't look to be quite right. He'd called it the basement, yet it was above ground. She grabbed her bags, took a beat to brace herself, and opened the door.

The room was sparse but clean, and Bunny stood there, taking it all in. Against the far wall, a small table and lamp sat next to a bed. In one corner, a dresser rested against a closet fashioned out of paneling. In the opposite corner, unfinished sheetrock walls surrounded a bathroom that had clearly never served anyone who wore makeup. Plank stairs led to the floor above.

She smiled ear to ear. This was her place. It wasn't just her own room. She'd had that before. It was the only benefit of her gender under Michael O'Kelly's roof. No, this was more than that. It was her own home. She wanted to call someone and tell them all about her adventure, but there was no one.

She didn't bother to unpack. Tossing her gear on the bed, Bunny dug out her barn boots, tightened her ponytail under the fading Red Sox cap, and set out to meet her new boss.

"Can I help you?" the cowboy called as she strode past the ring.

Heading over to the fence, she rested her foot on the rail. "Are you Buck Miller?"

"Nope. Jake James. Buck's in the barn. He's feeding right now, but I'm sure I can help you."

He wore his hat low on his head. Like the rest of his body, his face was solid. Bunny could tell he was looking her over. She knew how this game worked, so she looked right back. Worn and dusty jeans hung from a belt with a buckle he'd earned. He wasn't that much taller than her, but his boots and hat gave him a few inches. He listed to one side, not cocky but injured, Bunny guessed. It was clear he was comfortable with the animal. The lunge line hung looped in one hand, and the mare stood at attention.

"I'm Benny O'Kelly. The new ranch hand."

She stuck her hand out, but he just stared at her. "You're Benny?" His eyes narrowed, and a smirk crossed his face.

She'd been there before, so she stood her ground.

"Something funny?" She rested her forearms on the upper rail and leaned in.

"Well, I'm pretty sure you're not what Buck was expecting."

She smiled back at him. "I'm guessing he was expecting a ranch hand."

"I guess we'll see." The glow she'd felt standing in her room faded, but she wasn't going to give Jake James any satisfaction. She pushed off from the rail, tightened her ponytail, and pulled the brim of the cap down.

"The barn, you said?"

"Yes, that way." He pointed. "The big red building with the paddocks."

"I know what a barn looks like." Bunny regretted it immediately. He would file that away and, if he was anything like her brothers, he wouldn't soon let her forget it.

The barn was long, and the energy of the horses filled the space. Bunny loved the sound of big animals stomping and snorting, talking to each other. The wash stall was empty, but the floor said someone had been bathed recently. She peeked into the tack and feed rooms through the top splits in the doors. Though well organized, both needed sweeping. She knocked on the office door. A gruff "Can I help you?" from behind startled her.

"Buck Miller?"

He was an old guy, though probably not as old as his sun-weathered skin proclaimed. Clumps of silver and white hair snaked out in fits and starts from beneath a faded black cowboy hat. Above his thin lips, he sported a walrus mustache. A patina of hay dust covered his clothes.

"Yeah. We're full up now, but I expect a couple of folks to send their horses south with their kids in the fall. Might have a stall or two open then. Leave your name and number. I'll call you." He opened the office door and sidled around her. Picking up random stacks of papers strewn across the desk, he searched for a notepad and pen. He held them out to her without looking up.

"Uh, no. I mean, thank you," she stuttered. "I'm Benny O'Kelly, your new ranch hand."

He froze. Bunny could tell he didn't know what to say, so she filled the silence.

"It's a beautiful spread you have here. I'm all set to go." She forced a smile. "Where should I start?"

A resolute scowl crossed his face. "I don't think this is going to work out."

It was the second punch in the gut this month, but she stood her ground. She wasn't going back home. She couldn't. "Firing me is a little premature. You haven't even seen me work yet. I'm strong and I work hard."

"I'm not firing you. I'm just not hiring you. Have you ever even worked on a horse ranch?"

"No. But I've been working on my dad's dairy farm since I was ten. And I've been riding horses longer than that."

"A dairy isn't the same. Here, you're going to have to haul hay bales, muck out stalls, and help train the horses. It's hard work. Worse, it's dangerous work."

"I've done plenty of hard work. This can't be any more dangerous than moving a herd of cows."

"Look, I'll be honest. I thought you were a man with a name like Benny. That's your name, right?"

Bunny ignored his question. "I don't see what difference that makes. I have experience. I'm strong and willing. Give me a chance. I came a long way for this job." She could tell it was warring inside him. Something kept him from outright sending her away, and yet she knew she was losing. Eyebrows pinched together, he stared at her.

"Look, I need someone who can muck out stalls and buck bales." He crossed his arms over his chest.

Anger rose in Bunny's chest, and tears clouded her eyes. She had flown twelve hundred miles only to end up toe to toe with her dad. "I can muck out stalls and buck bales as good as any man."

"No, you can't." He stared at her. Her dad always bragged that staring down a man was the same as staring down a charging dog. So she stared back. He blinked. "Look, there is no way you can do the work a man could on this farm. I can't afford to hire someone to cover your slack."

At least he had the guts to say it out loud and didn't wait until she'd put in a decade of blood and sweat. "You don't know that." Crossing her arms over her chest, Bunny wasn't going peacefully.

"I do know it. Look. You can spend the night. I'll drive you into town in the morning. Plenty of places are hiring summer help. You'll find something that suits you better. But you're not staying here." Buck brushed by her and headed outside.

CHAPTER 2

KATIE 1982

KATIE SCANNED THE room. There were only a few men at the meeting. Most were old cowboys, long past chaps and broncs, who walked with the measured gait of men whose ribs had been broken by the stomp of hooves or the failure to tuck and roll off a clumsy bull. She was the youngest woman in the room. Though the other ladies were friendly, they were not her friends. Her father expected her to be social, and Katie would comply if she had to. To decrease the odds of being noticed, though, she tucked her chin as if studying the folders in her arms and headed for an empty chair.

"Evening, Katie. How's your dad?"

Katie nearly ran into Mr. Rhodes, a grizzly of a man with a voice that could rock you to sleep.

"I'm so sorry. I should watch where I'm going." She gave him her hand, and he engulfed it with both of his. They reminded her of her father's, warm and thick and worn smooth by hard work. "He's well. I'll tell him you asked."

He squeezed her hand, and though his eyes were sad, he smiled before moving on.

She was shocked to see Jeremiah. Katie hadn't seen him in years. As he opened the door, he swept his hat off by the crown and tipped his head in greeting. He strutted in, stride long and chest out, flashing a big smile at all the girls. Katie found a seat in the front of the room and busied herself with the agenda. Did he remember her?

"Mind if I sit here?" he asked as he scraped a chair across the floor.

"No, please do." She forced herself to look at him.

"I'm Jeremiah Cooper," he said, as if they'd never met. Heat rose in Katie's face, blooming in her cheeks.

"I'm Katie Miller." She stuck her hand out, and he laughed. Katie jerked from his grip, dropping her papers on the floor. She was grateful for the mess.

"Katie, I'm kidding. I know who you are. Here, let me help you get those." And just like that, they were kids again and he was teasing her.

"I'm fine. I've got this. Thank you." She swept the papers into her arms and looked around for her chair. He pulled it over. As she arranged the pages, she prayed he would go away.

"Really, I am sorry." He sat beside her, leaning down to catch her eyes. She forced a smile.

Katie was spared when Mr. Rhodes called the meeting to order. He had been chairing the fair planning committee since God was a boy and wasted no time launching into the list of jobs that needed leadership. Mr. Rhodes called it leadership. The truth was, and Katie knew it because she had been going to these meetings since long before her mother died, that he meant who was going to do the work.

"I need someone to organize the campers and trailers." Mr. Rhodes always opened with that one because it was the last thing anyone wanted to do. It was a giant headache. Whoever was in charge would have to stay there for the run of the fair overnight. Mr. Rhodes was as wise as he was stubborn. No one wanted that job, but he would stand his ground until someone blinked. Katie wanted the night to be over. As the ranking female at the Midnight Sun Ranch, it was her responsibility to take on one of these duties. If not this one, she might end up with garbage collection or worse, rodeo entries.

"I'll do it." She shot her hand up. A few nights in the camper would get her out of the house. With her brother Connor gone, she needed a break from managing her dad. It would be nice to be alone and out of sight of her brother's ever-present watchdog, Jake James. Katie took control, the way she always did, by making a list of all the things she needed to do in priority order.

"I'll help with that too, Mr. Rhodes," Jeremiah announced.

"Katie, did you hear that?" Mr. Rhodes asked. "Jeremiah has offered to help you."

She looked up. Across the room, feminine eyebrows arched in disbelief. No one was more shocked than Katie.

"Uh. Yes," she stammered, returning her eyes to her notes. "Thank you." She glanced at Jeremiah, who was smiling at her like she was a deer in wolf country.

Mr. Rhodes continued down his list. Though she felt Jeremiah's eyes on her, she did not look his way. It was cruel of him to make fun of her in front of everyone. She was a grown woman, not some little kid he could string along and then hide from. When they were kids, their moms would saddle up the lot of them and take them to the river to soak away the dust and endless sun. Jeremiah didn't pay much attention to her back then, though she was closer in age to him than Connor was. Jeremiah wanted to do boy stuff. Unless that involved a horse, Katie wasn't interested. His sister Jesse and Katie played together. Sometimes they tried to tag along with him and Connor, less because they wanted to play with them and more because it annoyed the boys no end. Katie could see Jeremiah wasn't a boy anymore. He was tall and lean. His dark hair was cropped close, and there was a shadow of a beard covering his face. She found that look contrived on most men, but on him, it just looked lazy.

Katie added to her list with furious speed. Map, registration forms, insurance rider, camp rules, outhouses, gate security, signage, fees. When she would get flustered getting ready for a show as a kid, her dad would tell her to imagine she was doing it step-by-step in her head. What order would things happen in? What would she need? Radios, lines on the parking area, food truck . . .

"So, should we meet and make a plan?" he said, startling her.

"I already have a list. I think we're good." She straightened the stack and slipped it into the folder.

"What do you want me to do? I'm happy to take some of those things off your list."

He looked hopeful, which made no sense at all to Katie. "I don't think this is going to take two people. If you want to work on another project, you can."

"If I wanted to work on something else, I would have signed up for another committee. I want to work on yours." He looked her in the eyes. His weren't teasing now. They were earnest and maybe even a little hurt.

"Why?" Her dad would have chastised her for her tone.

"Why?"

"Yes, why? Why did you sign up?"

"Well, my dad wants someone from the Double J volunteering this year, so he assigned me. He expects me to do something. Since I have to do something, it seems like doing it with you would be fun." He flashed a toothy grin with a sincerity Katie could not shoot down.

"Fine. What would you like to do?"

"How about we go grab a cup of coffee and go over your list? We can decide together."

Katie hesitated but knew at once she had lost. There was something in his eyes she couldn't disappoint. She gave in.

As they walked to the diner, he rambled on about his memories of the fair as a kid. He was funny and charming, as all cowboys were. Still, he reminded her of a little boy petting a kitten a little too hard. Katie tried to put him out of his misery by asking him questions about his ranch. But he deflected, turning the conversation back on her. Grateful he didn't ask about her family, she didn't ask about his. But as he talked, Katie remembered the easygoing boy he used to be, chasing behind Connor. When had that ended? Probably when Katie's mom got sick. The Millers had closed ranks then.

Katie waited until they had their coffee before getting down to business. They reviewed her list. She had to give him credit. He had some good ideas.

"We should separate the trailers into three areas. If we gave the crew a discount on camping, more might stay over. Put them between the rodeo crowd and the 4-H families, and you'll cut down on noise complaints. It might even prevent some fights."

It occurred to her that she had dismissed him as interested mostly in beer, broncs, and babes. Clearly, he was smarter than she'd thought. "That's a good idea." She remembered how protective her dad had been when her teenage eyes had wandered to cowboys.

Jeremiah offered to bring a trailer and stay at the rodeo end. Katie had to admit she was grateful for that. She was worried she was going to have to beg her brother to come home and do it. With her luck, Connor would insist Jake do it instead to earn his keep. Jeremiah solved that problem. Katie could park her trailer on the tamer family end.

They divided up the other jobs and agreed to meet in a few

days to check in. Katie watched him walk away. Had she mis-
judged him? He still had that cocky way of walking. But when
he turned to get into his truck, he stopped for a second and gave
her a wistful smile. It made her a little sad.

Chapter 3

Bunny 1984

Bunny stood there dazed as Buck stomped out the barn door. He was worse than her father. He wasn't even going to give her a chance to prove herself. She tightened her ponytail and turned to hunt him down, running right into Jake.

"Whoa. Slow down." The Paint stuttered to a stop.

"I hope you're talking to the horse."

"Well, I am, and I'm talking to you too. You can't be rushing around here. It spooks the animals. What did Buck tell you to do first?"

She stopped and tamped down the desire to throttle him. "He said to ask you."

"You can start by mucking out stalls. The wheelbarrow and forks are leaning outside. The compost pile is out back. You can dump it in the front, and I'll move it with the Bobcat later."

"I know how to drive a tractor."

"Let's see if you can drive a wheelbarrow first."

Though she itched to argue with him, it would be pointless. It was time to put up or shut up.

"Fine." She turned on her heels and got to work.

⋙

Bunny knew she was in trouble as soon as she heard his voice. She hurried to finish the last stall.

"What the hell is she doing?" Buck shouted at Jake.

"She's cleaning stalls. What's wrong?"

"What's wrong? I told her I wasn't hiring her. That's what's wrong."

Bunny kept her head down. Between her four older brothers and her dad, she'd learned a thing or two about handling a yelling man, starting with giving him a wide berth.

"That's not what she told me." Jake was stalking toward the stall. Her stomach dropped to her feet. "She told me you said to check with me about her first job."

She braced herself for Jake, but it was Buck who unloaded.

"What the hell are you doing?"

"I'm cleaning stalls." She gripped the pitchfork and pressed it to the ground, shifting her weight to the front of her feet.

"I can see that. Why are you doing it?"

"You were nice enough to let me stay the night." She could tell the men weren't buying that. "Fine. I wanted to show you I can do this job. Look at the stalls. They're spotless. And I got them done fast."

Buck looked like he was wavering, but Jake dug in. "We don't need a liar working here." He punctuated the words with a pointed finger and walked away.

"No, you're right. I'm sorry about lying," she called after him, but he kept walking. She turned to Buck. "I work hard. You have to admit that. I can do this job. Please give me a chance."

Buck looked around the barn. "Jake's right. I can't have that here."

"It won't happen again. I promise." She held her breath.

"Cleaning a few stalls doesn't prove anything. Hell, any kid with a horse can do that." As he walked away, Bunny got on his heels.

"Hey, I'm not a child. You don't know what I can or can't do. You're not even giving me a chance to show you. This is no risk for you. If I can't hack it, you won't have to fire me. I'll quit. But I am not walking away from here without a fight." She set her jaw and braced for his reaction.

He sighed and shook his head. "You don't strike me as someone who quits anything."

"You're right about that."

"Fine. But I mean it. You don't pull your weight, you're out of here. No second chances. No notice."

"I will. You don't have to worry about that."

"Don't tell me. Show me. And no more lies." Before she could answer, he walked away.

⁂

Though she wouldn't admit it to him, Buck hadn't been wrong. The work got harder fast. After she cleaned all the stalls, he sent her to pick up a load of hay. She bumped the hitch when she was hooking up the trailer to the dually. Worse, she did it in front of Jake. He gave her an *I told you so* smile, making it clear he wasn't going to help her out. So she made it clear she wasn't going to ask for it. The more he stood watching, amused as Bunny wrenched the trailer into position, the more determined she was to get it done without him. When she finally did, Jake robbed her of the satisfaction by walking away before she could throw him a smug look.

The feed store was on the outskirts of town. Two shipping containers were propped open in the lot, and trucks were lined up, taking their turns loading. It was an efficient operation, with one hand throwing and one stacking. Buck said they were holding fifty bales for the Midnight Sun. As she sat in the truck memorizing the stacker's movements, her stomach sank. She had forgotten to grab hooks or gloves. She dug around furiously, chastising herself for worrying about Jake and not her equipment. Under the seat, she found a pair of gloves a size too large for her. She would have blisters, but at least the baling twine wouldn't cut her palms.

Her heart pounded when it was her turn to back up to the container. Though Bunny felt the critical eyes on her, she took it slow and got it lined up on the first try. She didn't stop to revel in the glory of that victory. She could feel the line of trucks filled with men, frustrated at the thought of how long it was going to take one woman to load fifty bales. Bunny stood as tall as she could muster and marched over to the foreman. She handed him the order. He looked her up and down, shook his head, and wished her luck.

Bunny loaded the first layer as quickly as she could. The bales were heavy. The only thing not aching was the hair on her head, and that was soaked. It was only going to get worse as the stack grew. Most of the other hands were leaning in pairs against their trucks, arms crossed. Through the sweat dripping into her ears, their snide remarks pelted her.

A truck door slammed. "Jesus, this is going to take all day."

"Buck must be drinking again to send this chick."

She hated that word—chick. Bunny fought back the urge to answer.

"Bring a man next time, honey."

With every word, Bunny worked harder. Her back and hips burned as she lifted and turned to throw each bale. With her head soldier straight, she stacked the first row on their edge and tied them off before starting the next level. She stopped to wipe her brow. From the corner of her eye, she watched a man push off his rig and stride over to her.

"Let me help you." He pulled on his gloves and looked back at the waiting trucks.

"I've got this," Bunny replied.

"It wasn't a question. I know you think you got this. But you don't. Nobody shows up here alone for a load."

Bunny fumed inside. Buck had set her up to fail.

"Look, you're about to be overrun. I suggest you say *thank you* and let me help you so you can get out of here in one piece with your load."

Bunny clenched her hands. As her throat constricted, she bit out, "Thanks. Do you want to throw or stack?" She was relieved when he offered to throw. Bunny picked up the pace to match the man. The snickers faded into the air as she focused on keeping up with him.

When they finished, she tied off the load and turned to him. "Do you want help with yours?"

He laughed. "No thanks. I brought a crew with me." He pointed to a pair of men staring at them.

She flushed with anger at being sent here alone. As she turned to leave, he reached his hand out to her. She looked at it for a moment, surprised to see it.

"Thank you." She took his hand. "I didn't ask your name."

"You can call me Shaw."

"Thank you, Shaw. I appreciate the help. You can call me Benny."

He shook her hand, strong and solid.

"Interesting name."

"Long story."

"Well, Benny, you're welcome. You tell Buck to send help with you next time."

She stood tall and marched over to the truck. Without looking at the other men, she drove away.

❧

The trip home took longer than the ride in. Fully loaded, the trailer rocked side to side down the uneven road. Bunny slowed and looked back after each bounce to make sure she hadn't lost the load. She ached from her feet to her head, but the worst was her neck. Reaching her hand up, she wrenched her chin to her shoulder. The muscles tensed like a truck spring. They'd given only an inch or two before her eyes registered the mossy brown mass crossing the oncoming lane. Bunny stepped on the brake. The trailer fishtailed, pulling her across the center line. Her instincts kicking in, she released the brake and geared down, narrowly missing the bull moose.

Stopped in the middle of the road, her chest heaved from the adrenaline. The animal stood as tall as the cab. Bunny had never seen one up close. Terror and awe coursed through her. She waited until he'd strode into the woods to take off her seat belt and check the load. If she lost the bales, she was sure she would keep driving until she hit the Yukon. A Canadian logging camp had to be better than pulling all that hay out of a ditch.

By the time she made it back to the Midnight Sun, the rush had subsided, leaving behind an electric sting across her shoulders. She was stretching when Jake snuck up behind her.

"You're a little late." He pulled on his gloves as he headed for the trailer. "Did you have trouble?" He smirked.

Bunny pushed her anger back down her throat. Like Buck, Jake knew full well it was a two-man job. She channeled her mother, the Lovely Sophia, and let a smile seep across her face. "Nope. There was a line." She began releasing the tie-downs.

Jake searched her face. "Right. Let's get this unloaded. There's still a lot to do today."

They worked in silence. Hiding the sharp pull of her muscles took away her ability to form words. Jake didn't seem to notice. He moved with efficiency, and following his lead, she tried to match him bale for bale. On her best day, she couldn't do it. This was not her best day.

As they stacked the last of the hay, Buck appeared to inspect it. "You were gone a long time."

Before Bunny had a chance to answer, Jake chimed in, "There was a line." He looked down and wiped the back of his glove across his mouth, concealing his sarcastic smile.

Buck looked to Bunny. "Next time, you might want to ask Jake to go with you." Bunny set her jaw to dam the curse she wanted to unleash. It held just long enough for them to get out of earshot.

⁂

In the evening, riders arrived to exercise their horses. Young riders, earnest but swift, saddled up. Bunny remembered the thrill of finally being old enough to take care of her own horse without her mother's help. An old man in faded jeans brushed the dust from a mare's hair in long, deliberate strokes. As Bunny passed by, he reassured the animal that neither was too old to hit the trail. His tender exchange made her miss the warmth of a nuzzling nose to her neck.

Bunny did her best to help the boarders, but she didn't know her way around. When she hit a wall, she was forced to ask Jake. He cured her of that by the third question.

"Look, I don't have time to do your job and mine. You're gonna have to figure it out."

About the only friend she made was the ranch dog, Ruff, who she found curled up in the wheelbarrow. She held her hand to his nose, palm down, to test the waters. He lifted his head long enough to give her a sniff but was otherwise unimpressed.

"Okay. Hop out of there," she said to him.

He lifted his eyes but did not budge.

"Seriously, I have work to do." She lifted the handles, hoping he would jump out. He did not. "Okay. You're forcing me to bring out the big guns." She put the handles down and looked around. When she came back with a small stick, he lifted his head. "You like to play fetch, huh?" Bunny chucked the stick. When he leaped out after it, she grabbed the wheelbarrow and headed into the barn.

The dog's uninspired name didn't do him justice. The enormous ball of white fur lumbered along beside her as she went about her duties. For being so large, his stealthy appearance was a surprise. Other than the periodic scratch behind the ears after cleaning each stall, she wasn't sure what she had done to instill such devotion so quickly. She guessed Jake wasn't as generous with attention. Bunny took some satisfaction in knowing the dog liked her better.

As she cleaned up the barn for the night, Ruff stretched out in front of one of the stalls. He laid his head on his front paws, a mournful look on his face. He stayed there as she swept the corridor. Refusing to move when she reached him, she swept around him. Bunny collected the tools and tack and set them neatly where they belonged. She longed for the dairy, where cleaning mud and manure was as easy as hosing it down.

As she shut the tack room door, Ruff had not moved save for his head, which was now lifted upward to meet the gaze of a big Appaloosa. Split at a diagonal from his left eye to his right nostril, a patch of white speckled in black spots covered the top of the horse's face. On the bottom half, a shiny stretch of ebony reached down to his neck and shoulders. As she neared, his rump came into view. It looked as if someone splattered him with black paint. The Appaloosa was reaching his head toward the dog. If they were people, she would have thought them lost in conversation. She approached the pair quietly, not wanting to interrupt the exchange.

"Hey there, big guy." She reached her palm toward the horse. He sniffed and blew on her hand, nostrils flaring. He bobbed his head. "Easy there." He looked down at the dog, who was now leaning against her leg and, reaching his head to her hands, nuzzled her palm with his thick, soft lips. "Sorry, pal. I didn't know we'd be meeting today. I'll bring you a snack tomorrow, I promise."

"Hey, move your hand!" Jake shouted from the end of the barn. The horse shook its head and stomped back into the stall. The cowboy stalked toward her.

"What's your problem? I wasn't hurting the horse."

"The problem is, he'll hurt you. He's a biter. Don't put your hands near that horse's mouth."

"Seemed fine to me." She stood her ground.

Jake shook his head. "Suit yourself. Don't take my advice. It's not my job to save your ass. They're your fingers. Pretty hard to move hay bales without them, though."

Bunny waited for him to walk away and then looked back at the horse. "Well, I don't think you're a biter, but I wouldn't blame you if you bit him. Hell, I might bite him." The horse nodded in agreement. She checked that the latch on the stall was closed. Next to it was a brass plate etched in two lines that read *War Horse Katie Miller.*

"Strike two." She turned to find Buck approaching. "Jake will take you into town in the morning." He reached up and secured the Dutch door.

"What did I do?" The whine in her voice embarrassed her.

"Safety. And that's all I'm gonna say. I'm done arguing with you. Jake is taking you into town in the morning and that's the end of that. You can head to your bunk, or you can start walking. It's your call." He stood like a boulder.

Bunny wanted to cry, but there was no way she would do that in front of him.

CHAPTER 4

KATIE 1982

KATIE DIDN'T WANT to go home after the meeting. She couldn't put it into words, but the emotions inside her were like a jazz rhythm, notes crashing into each other, stopping and starting in peaks and valleys, going this way and that. She wished she could keep driving, but where would she go? It was still early, and her father would be awake, though not likely coherent. She thought about heading over to Carolina's house, but Carolina would pry those feelings out of her. Katie wasn't sure she wanted to examine them yet. In the end, she steered her baby blue Chevy LUV back to the Midnight Sun.

Jake was headed to his bunk when Katie pulled in. She put the clutch in and let the truck roll, but that only seemed to slow his stride. Cursing herself for protesting far too softly when Connor insisted they hire Jake, she rolled down the window for her daily dose of unsolicited supervision.

"Hey, Katie." He rested his hands on the doorframe and leaned back on his hips. His body filled the little truck's window, repelling her to the limits of her seat belt. "Where've you been? Your dad's been worrying."

"Thanks for the heads-up." It pained her to be short with anyone, but subtle cues bounced off Jake. When she tried to crank the window, he leaned in. His eyebrows nearly linking as they pointed toward his nose, he held her eyes.

"You gotta be careful out there, Katie."

She nodded and forced a smile. Forgetting about the window, she put the truck in gear and pulled away. The cowboy filled her rearview mirror. If only he would stay there.

Parking behind the house, she slipped in through the kitchen, glad she'd stopped to wash the dinner dishes before she left. Plucking the dirty shot glass from the table, she ran it under water and set it to dry. She figured the whiskey had killed any germs.

Katie was reaching for the door to the basement when her father called out, "I'm in here."

"Of course you are," Katie mumbled.

"What?"

"Nothing, Dad." She stood in the doorway. "Do you need anything?"

"Oh, honey. You do so much."

Sad Dad, Katie assessed. She didn't love that one, but it was better than Angry Dad or Passed-Out Dad.

"Well, I'm going to get ready for bed." She waited. There was no point in leaving before he was done. He was a talkative drunk.

"Come in and tell me about the fair committee meeting." Leaning forward, he set his empty glass on the table next to him. He reached out and patted the couch, almost toppling forward in the process.

Katie rushed in to help him, but he righted himself at the last second.

"I'm fine. Sit down. Tell me what happened."

Though there was plenty of room, Ruff bounded off the couch as she approached and headed for the stairs. He wasn't the only one tired of watching out for Buck.

"The usual, Dad. It was only the first meeting, so we picked committees. I'm going to be in charge of the campground."

"The campground. That's a big job, Katie. I bet your brother might help if he's home. I wouldn't want you staying there alone." He looked around. "Or Jake. I could send him."

"No, not Jake." The words shot out before she could dampen them. Even in his state, he would wonder.

"Aww, Katie. Cut the guy some slack. He's a good man."

He was searching for a bottle, but she wasn't going to help him find it. "I'll be fine. I'm not working alone. Besides, I'll remind you, I am not a little girl. I'm all grown up. I don't need Jake James babysitting me." She said it with a smile. Though it pained her to be treated like a child, Katie had learned young that arguing with a drunk was a waste of energy. In the morning, it would be her tone and not her words he remembered.

"Who's helping you?"

"It's not finalized yet. Hopefully soon, though." She took advantage of his fog. It was a lie of omission, but a lie nonetheless. She wasn't ready to tell him. "What's on your list tomorrow?"

His eyebrows knit together like he was trying to pull up some long-forgotten memory. Katie knew better, and that hurt her heart.

"Same stuff every day, darlin'. Chores, lessons, training, feeding." With that, he pushed himself onto his wobbly legs. "I'm going to head to bed. Early day tomorrow. Don't stay up too late." He leaned in and kissed her cheek.

She gave him a hug. Her chest burned with the sadness of it all. In so many ways, she'd lost both her parents the day her mom died. As he pulled on the stair rail with each step he took, she hoped he wouldn't tumble backward.

C H A P T E R 5

B UNNY 1984

BUNNY SLAMMED THE basement door, and the weight of the day hit her. She fought back her tears, willing anger in their place. *A man wouldn't cry over this.* She took off her boots and threw them at the door. *Asshole.* Letting her hair out of the band, Bunny rubbed her scalp where the heavy auburn locks had pulled beneath her cap. It fell to her knees as she rested her face on her palms. She could not give up, but she dreaded the fight ahead. What choice did she have? Going back home to her father was not an option. The thought of the smug look on his face made her sick to her stomach. Even moving on would mean going backward.

Bunny dug through her bag for clean clothes. On leaden legs, she climbed the thirteen plank steps to the unfinished interior door at the top. She searched the knob but couldn't feel a lock. *So much for safety. And that's not all I'm gonna say. Hypocrite.* Bunny gave the door a shove. It lurched half an inch and held. She tried again. Through the slit, she saw a hasp locking her in. Dragging every bit of rage through all the fear she could not confess, she scrambled back down to the basement door and threw it open. She allowed herself two ragged gulps of air and then she set upon taking care of herself.

Tucked beneath the stairs, Bunny found four dusty boxes, and though her back protested, she hauled three of them out. She briefly reconsidered. Buck or Jake might break their neck tripping down the stairs, but she thought it a fitting consequence for breaking in on her in the middle of the night. It took all her legs and one of those grunts her brothers let out to justify their He-Man Club status to heave the first box up to the top step. Bunny didn't break the seal to check, but she was sure it contained a complete set of encyclopedias.

The second box, though the same height, could have been lifted with one hand. Unlike the first, it hadn't been taped, which Bunny took as a sign. From the rustling within, she imagined discarded prom dresses. *Were there proms in Alaska?* She slid her index fingers through the slot and pulled them apart. In the center, a stack of shirts lay neatly folded. Reaching in, she lifted one side and let them fall like a deck of cards. If the bright array of colors hadn't tipped her off, the pearl and silver buttons would have. Bunny recognized them at once—show shirts. Had they belonged to the woman who earned the ribbon she'd found? Buck didn't look rich, and these shirts didn't come cheap. Whoever Katie was, she had it good.

The third box announced Montgomery Ward Authentic Western Boots 10D. Though a smaller container, it was dense. The sides were worn and flimsy. As she set it down, some of its contents cascaded out onto the steps. *Perfect. One more screwup today. One more thing I have to clean up.* She plunked down on the step and let her back fall against the wall. The dam cracked. Bunny wished she could call her mom, but the Lovely Sophia would remind her this was a self-inflicted wound. Sympathy would only be a strategy to coax Bunny home. She swiped the back of her hand across her eyes and reached for the pile of photographs. On top of the pile, a boy stood, one hand pointing forward and one hand holding on to a little girl. Neither were looking at the camera. He was smiling down at her. She was looking at her boots. His tenderness pinched Bunny's heart.

She thumbed through the stack, each photograph a notch in the timeline of their lives together. A crooked scene captured a younger Buck, one arm around a woman and one around the boy. In another, he stood in front of a baby blue compact truck, holding out a set of keys to a very excited teenager. In every photograph, the man wore his heart in his eyes. Bunny could feel their connection. Had her dad even once looked at her like that? When had Buck lost that spark? Just looking at the pictures made her feel like a thief. She quickly straightened the stack and placed it back in the box.

Secure that she would not be interrupted, Bunny took a shower. Like the rest of the room, the bathroom was cobbled together with last chance sale items. The décor was immaterial to Bunny. She needed water. Hot water. The scalding stream washed away the layer of dust that covered her body. Her shoulders burned as she raised her arms and pressed them against the tile. The wet heat eased the ache in her muscles and melted her resolve. Letting her tears mix with the droplets, Bunny gave herself just that much time to wallow in self-pity.

After her shower, she dressed and ventured quietly toward the pasture. Perched in the grass against a fence post, she waited for the sky to dim. Growing up on the dairy, Bunny would sneak out into the stillness of the night when she was troubled. She thought more clearly in the silent moonlight. The path of the sun across the horizon was disorienting, though, and she felt lost. For a time, she tried to make a plan, but in the end, her mind emptied and her eyes focused on the field of hay in front of her. Though the sun was still high, the temperature dropped. It was well past midnight. Hearing the echoes of animals in motion across the field, she took shelter in her bunk.

In the middle of the night, something hit her door with a thump. Peeking out the window, Bunny found a mound of white fur covering the mat. Ruff was curled up. She opened the door, and he looked up at her with his big, dark eyes. "Come on."

He didn't need any more encouragement. Pushing past her, he jumped on the bed and curled into a tight ball at the foot.

"Well, okay. But you're out of here if you snore or fart." She climbed into bed, and he snuggled in deep. When she scratched his ear, he uncoiled and laid his heavy head on her belly. Bunny felt the anchor of him. Before long, her muscles softened and her jaw relaxed to the rhythm of his breathing. "I wouldn't get used to this. Your friend is kicking me out tomorrow."

A lifetime of living on a farm woke Bunny before dawn. She panicked at first at the bright sunlight, but Ruff's groan reminded her of where she was. She regretted letting him in. He had burrowed into her heart and drained her sadness and anger, if only for one night. Looking out the window, she could sense the men were up. Begrudgingly, she dressed and pulled her hair through the band in her baseball cap. She put her duffel on the bed and went to collect the evidence of her one failed day as a ranch hand from the floor of the bathroom. When she returned, she found Ruff half laying on the open bag, head between his paws.

"You're going to have to move. I need to pack." They stared at each other. Neither moved. Bunny laughed as she remembered her brother Patrick's warning about allowing a complete stranger in her bed. She reached for the bag, and Ruff let out a halfhearted bark.

A knock on the door startled her. It had no effect on the big dog, who was now covering the bag.

"Benny, time to go. Jake's waiting." Buck knocked again. "You heard him."

Ruff lay there, unimpressed.

Bunny sighed and opened the door. "Sorry. I'm having a little trouble getting packed."

Buck took a deep breath. Bunny stepped out of the doorway to reveal the white blanket covering her gear.

"Ruff, get off of there." Buck stepped in and took off his hat. He swung it in the animal's direction.

"Stop it! You don't need to hit him!" Bunny stepped between the two. She turned her back on Buck and addressed the hound. "You gotta get up, big guy. I need to pack." He groaned in response. Bunny kneeled and took his head in her hands. She kissed his forehead and lifted his jowls, so they were eye to eye. "You gotta go." She stood, and he looked at her. He looked to Buck and back again. With one motion, he leaped from the bed through the open door. Buck shook his head as Ruff brushed past him.

"I'm just gonna say, since I'm already fired, you don't have to be such an ass. I would have worked harder than any guy you replace me with. You don't listen." She began throwing her clothes in her bag. "You can call it a lie if you want. I wouldn't have had to if you'd given me a chance to show you what I can do." She stopped and looked at him. "And another thing. You can hide behind 'safety,' but the fact is that I can take care of myself. I wasn't in any danger, and I didn't put anyone else in danger. I would never do that. The bottom line is that you don't trust me. If I was a guy, you would give me a chance to earn it. Instead, you're dismissing me. Fine. Your loss. But don't blame me for failing. Blame yourself for running me off." She zipped her bag and threw it over her shoulder. Marching over to the corner of the room, she grabbed her rifle case and headed to the door.

Buck didn't move. His jaw was clenched, and his mouth set

in a hard line, but his eyes were sad. She took a step toward the door.

"Stop." He looked at the floor. In the pause through the open door, the morning birdsongs slipped through. "Put your gear down. You're going to work with me today. There's food in the kitchen. Meet me at the shed in half an hour." With that, he walked away.

CHAPTER 6

KATIE 1982

A S THE WEEKS went by, Katie and Jeremiah met every couple of days to tick off items on the list. Coffee turned to pie. Pie turned to lunch. Katie felt guilty about lying to her dad, but she told herself she wanted to spare him the agitation he felt any time the Double J Ranch came up. The truth was, she liked being around Jeremiah and she didn't want it to end yet.

They fell into an easy rhythm—the way they were as kids. When Jeremiah told her his twin sister Jesse would be barrel racing in the rodeo, his eyes lit up. But when he talked about working the Double J with his dad, Rocky, storm clouds filled them. Rocky was a grizzled old man in Katie's memory. He had a harsh way of talking, no care to the tender feelings of his kids and wife. As a kid, she'd thought him an aberration. Now that Katie was older, she held no illusions. In a land that was actively trying to kill you, tenderness was an extravagance.

Though it invited back the desolation she felt about the loss of her own mother, she broached the one topic they hadn't talked about.

"What about your mom? How's she doing? I haven't seen her since—" She left the sentence hanging there. Even a decade later, it was hard for her to say the words.

"I wouldn't know." He took a bite of his sandwich like it was nothing.

"I don't understand. Doesn't she live with you?"

"No, she doesn't," he said with a fierce finality. He had that same *conversation over* tone her dad would get when she argued with him as a teenager. It must have shown on her face, because he softened.

"Sorry." He put down his food and leaned on the table, staring out the window. "My mom left us shortly after your mom . . . passed."

"I didn't know. I'm sorry." She reached out and touched his arm.

He moved his arm away and looked at her with a pain that could be as easily from his grief as from her pity. "Well, you wouldn't." He shoved his plate away.

"I'm so sorry. That must have been awful." Katie's heart hurt for him.

"No. It's awful that your mom died. Mine was selfish and walked away. What's awful is having someone like that for a mother," he said with vehemence, but the sorrowful look on his face told a different story.

Katie knew what it felt like to lose a mom. It was a wound that tore open at the slightest touch. Though her mom didn't choose to leave, she was never coming back. Even so, his loss was worse. His mom was out there somewhere but choosing to stay away. That was a wound that never healed.

"She helped us a lot when my mom was dying. I remember she used to come over and sit with her every day." Katie did not want to remember those times, but the sorrow of telling was nothing compared to his. "She made sure we all had dinner."

He looked around the room and waved the waitress over. "Well, I'm glad she took care of somebody's kids."

She knew more than most that there was no point in dwelling on a loss you were powerless to change. Katie couldn't change that for him, but she didn't have to make it worse. She tried to shift the conversation quickly to the fair, but it was clear the night was over.

As they stood to go, Jeremiah caught her off guard when he asked her to have dinner with him.

"Somehow, I don't think my dad would like that much." Katie brushed past him, avoiding his eyes.

"You're an adult. You don't need his permission."

She stopped and turned. "I know I'm an adult. That doesn't mean I don't listen to my dad."

"Look, I didn't mean anything by it. If it will make you feel better, we'll go up the highway to the Back Forty." He looked earnest. "Say you will."

"I'm sorry. I can't." She turned and headed toward her truck.

"You didn't even think about it."

"I did. My dad would be so angry if he found out you've been helping me with the fair."

He caught up to her. "Why do you let him rule your life?"

"That's not fair. And your dad would be pissed too. Don't be a hypocrite."

"Okay. You're right. But at least think about it before you say no." He waited. "I tell you what. I'll be waiting for you at the Back Forty, Thursday night at seven. I hope you'll come." Hope grew in his eyes.

"Look, I need your help with the fair, and I don't need anything derailing that."

"There won't be. No matter what happens. I promise." He gave her the sweetest smile.

Though her heart said otherwise, it wasn't that easy. "Don't get your hopes up, Jeremiah."

CHAPTER 7

BUNNY 1984

UMBFOUNDED, BUNNY STOOD in the doorway as Buck walked away.

He must have sensed it because he stopped half-way to the barn and turned to her. "Well, get a move on. You said you wanted a job. You got a job."

Bunny pulled the door shut behind her and hustled around to the back of the house. She was relieved to find the kitchen empty and a pot of oatmeal cooling on the stove. She turned the burner on and foraged for a bowl and sugar. It wasn't much, but it would hold her over. Leaning against the counter, Bunny surveyed the room. Though decaying, it'd had a woman's touch, as the Lovely Sophia would say. A muted gold Frigidaire sat across from a stove of the same color. Next to the refrigerator, there was a door, and the padlock told her where it led. As if she thought it would open at her touch, she went over and yanked on the lock. The hasp shifted against its screws but did not budge. She made a note to bring it up if she survived the day without being fired.

Bunny scarfed the porridge down and gulped a glass of milk.

With one eye on the lookout for Jake, she walked all the way around the stables. There was a split rail gate on the road leading to the shed. Bunny preferred climbing fences over opening them, so she hoisted herself over and jogged the short distance. Buck hadn't arrived. She tried the door but found it locked. Wandering over to the old truck, she pulled down the tailgate and took a seat. Before long, Ruff bounded toward her, kicking up a cloud of dust in his path. Not far behind, Buck followed with far less enthusiasm. Ruff left the ground five feet from the tailgate, and Bunny had to duck not to catch him full-on.

"Ruff!" Buck let out a sharp whistle.

"It's fine. I have dogs back home." She sank her hands into his heavy coat and rubbed the skin beneath. "I bet you like to go for rides."

"He does. So, let that be a lesson. If you put the tailgate down, he's going for a ride. He'll sit there until you do. Good thing we're taking the truck. Hop down and help me load the fence rails."

Bunny followed him around the corner to a stack of planks on a pallet.

Buck took his keys out and tossed them to Bunny. "Back the truck up. Grab the tarp behind the seat."

"You worried about scratching the bed?" She ran her hand over the wall of the rusty bed and chuckled. The words her father said to her all too often, *nobody thinks you're as funny as you do, Bunny,* slapped her in the face. "Sorry. Bad joke."

He shook his head. "Don't be a smart ass. We use the tarp to pull the wood out."

They loaded the truck and followed a dirt road around the pasture. Bunny rolled the window down and rested her chin on her arm. The woods beyond the pasture were so different from the dense evergreen forests of home. Spindly white alder trunks tilted away from each other, making room for the wind to flick their leaves. She closed her eyes and let the air blow across her face.

Buck slowed the truck. "Time to earn your keep." He took the truck out of gear and stepped on the emergency brake. "Grab your gloves." Reaching over the side of the bed, he came out with a large hammer. "There's a bag of tenpenny nails behind the rear seat. Grab those."

Bunny wasn't sure where the lever was, but she thought Buck might be running out of tolerance for dumb questions. She groped around the side until she found it. The bag of nails was too far to reach, so she kneeled on the seat and pulled it toward her. Stretching as far as she could, she grasped a piece of hard leather. She lifted it to her and found she was holding a new pair of cowboy boots. An ornate pattern of stitching swirled across the arch and up the calf, binding cream and chocolate leather together in fat flowers.

"Did you find them?" he called from the fence line.

Bunny dropped the boots and reached around until she found the nails.

Buck was hitting the top rail of the fence when she returned. Without looking at her, he said, "We need to replace the ones that are broken or rotting. There's another hammer in the bed. Knock it off the post like this." He slammed the hammer against the wood, and it popped off the post. "Hand me a new slat." Slipping a nail between his lips, he leaned one hip against the wood and grabbed the post for leverage to pull it tight to the next one. Then, in one smooth motion, he drew the nail from his lips with one hand and cocked the hammer with the other. One stroke and it was pinned. They threw the broken pieces in the truck, and Bunny walked on, searching for the next victim.

Cocking the hammer back, she hit the next slat. It didn't move.

"Jeez," Buck hissed. Then came the unmistakable sound of an irritated man stepping on the brake.

"Not like that. We'll be here all day. How'd you work on a farm for so long without being able to fix a broken fence?" He hopped out of the truck and took her hammer. "Put your weight into it and hit it hard." Buck smacked the fence and popped off the old wood. It cracked down the center. "Go do that one." He pointed. "I want to see you do it."

Bunny hustled up to the next post. Embarrassment quickly turned to anger. She pictured Buck's face and hit the fence with all her might. The rail sprung off the fence and landed in the pasture.

"Now that's how you do it."

His praise felt about as good as getting socks for Christmas. She glowered at him, but he was oblivious.

"You keep working down the line. Come back every couple posts and load up the bad wood."

Stoked by her anger, the work went fast. They made it all the way around the field by lunchtime. When they finished, Bunny unloaded the old wood on the burn pile next to the shed while Buck put the tools away. He kept the keys on the truck ring. Why, so far away from other people, did he lock it at all?

When he was done, he took a rag from his pocket and wiped his neck. Staring at the barn, he said, "Glad that's done before it gets any hotter. Let's get some lunch."

Bunny threw the last piece of wood on the pile and headed for the house. They walked side by side through the barn.

"After you eat, go down and clean stalls. Jake's got horses to work, and I have lessons this afternoon."

"Okay."

"You did good work this morning." He said it like he was reciting a grocery list. No emotion. No flourish. Bunny didn't care. She'd take that. It was more than her dad ever gave her.

CHAPTER 8

KATIE 1982

A T THE END of the lesson, Katie walked the little girl and her horse back to the barn. She was about the same age Katie was when she'd first competed. The girl beamed down at her. Though more than a dozen years had passed, she could still touch that little girl inside of her, sitting tall in the saddle and aching to gallop away. A pang of sadness for losing that hit her.

"Good lesson?" Buck called up to the girl as he reached to pull her off the mount. She giggled, nodded, and took the reins. "Pint-sized cowgirl with a barrel-sized horse. You sure you can do that all by yourself?"

It was Katie's turn to giggle at the phrase she'd heard a million times.

Buck's eyes followed the rider as she headed to the barn. "How's she doing?"

Katie waited for him to look at her before speaking. "Great. She's not ready to drop the reins, but they're building trust. It'll be time for you to take her on soon."

"You're doing fine with her. You should keep this one."

It was less a vote of confidence than a means of retreat.

"She's got potential. She needs the best. You're the best, Dad." Her smile was sorrowful for the half-truth of it.

"Katie, you don't give yourself enough credit. You'd have beaten even your mother if you'd kept at it, and she was the best."

"*I could have* doesn't beat *she was,* and you know it. You trained Mom, and you should keep on training." Katie had no intention of letting him climb any further into the bottle, even if she had given up on trying to pull him out.

"We'll see." He pulled a pair of work gloves from his back pocket. "Feel like helping your old man stack hay?" He slapped them in his hands a couple times to knock off the dirt and soften them up.

"I'm sorry, Dad, I can't. I told the girls I would have dinner with them. I can help you in the morning, though. I promise to get up bright and early."

Buck gave her a halfhearted smile. "Don't worry about it, honey. Jake will help me. Where're you going?"

"I don't know. Probably just to Carolina's." She started for the house, hoping he wouldn't ask any more questions.

"Say hello for me," he called after her.

Katie hesitated. "I will."

⌀

Katie sat on the edge of her bed. Closing her eyes, she reached her hand out and ran her fingertips across the quilt. The fabric had been softened by time and tears. She had memorized the pattern sitting in this very spot as her mother braided her hair. She tried to conjure her from the memories. In the stillness, she could almost feel her mother's hands pulling her hair back, gentle but sure. She never used a brush. She combed her fingers through

Katie's hair, tickling her scalp, until she had the unruly strands corralled neatly in her left hand. Katie remembered the gentle tug as her mom divided the hair into three pieces, fingers weaving deftly down her back. All the while, Katie would chatter away.

It was in these ordinary moments that they talked about all the big things in life. She needed one of those moments now. Her mom had missed so many, and Katie was angry about every one of them. A million inconsequential events fueled her regret. But this wasn't inconsequential. Something big was happening between her and Jeremiah. Her mom would know what to do.

Mama, what am I doing here? I'm actually considering going out with Jeremiah Cooper. I bet you're jumping for joy hearing that. Dad, on the other hand, would lose his mind. Maybe I shouldn't go. Give me a sign. He's not the cute little boy anymore. Oh, he's handsome for sure, but he's also cocky as hell. I don't know what all happened to him since you died. I wish I could talk to Connor. Even if he was here, I couldn't though, 'cause he would scare Jeremiah away. He's already got Jake James following me everywhere. Let me tell you, the big brother thing is a pain in my rear end.

And I can't talk to Dad. He's struggling, Mama. I don't mean to make you sad, but if you could get him to stop drinking, that would be great. He's going to hurt himself, and then I really won't have anyone to talk to. Wow, I'm all over the place. Okay, first things first. Give me a sign. Do I go on this date or not? I'm going to go to the closet and grab the first thing I touch. If it's hideous, I will take that as a sign that I should not go on this date. Ready?

She took a deep breath and closed her eyes. Reaching in, her fingers collided with crisp ruffles. She pictured the red blouse and sighed. *I hope you know what you're doing.*

↫

Katie headed up the highway toward the old roadhouse. The Back Forty would be packed all weekend, but Thursday nights were slow. She searched the room and was relieved she didn't recognize anyone. She thought about walking out when she realized that didn't mean they didn't recognize her. As she turned, she saw him sitting alone in the back. When she caught his eye, he stood and gave her an embarrassed wave like a boy on his first date. It melted her heart to see him without the bravado. She got a glimpse of the person he was before life happened to him.

When she arrived at the table, he stood and pulled her chair out. "You came."

"You don't strike me as someone who has to worry much about being stood up." A smile snuck out, though Katie tried to hold it back.

"You overestimate my effect on women."

The waitress appeared before Katie even sat down. A little too enthusiastically, she introduced herself. "Hi. I'm Mindy, and I'll be waiting on you." Never taking her eyes off Jeremiah, she took their orders. Neither had to look at the menu. The Back Forty was known for its steak.

As soon as she left, Katie was staring wide-eyed at him.

"What?" he asked.

"Uh. Point made." She laughed.

"What? Her? She's just trying to make a good tip."

Katie shook her head and grinned. "She's trying to make a date."

Jeremiah furrowed his brow. "Well, I doubt that, but it doesn't matter because I already have one." He paused, holding her eyes. "I'm glad you came."

As they waited for dinner to arrive, Katie filled the space with fair planning. Everything was coming together. She loved the excitement of it all. The little kids clinging to wooly sheep—some screaming, some laughing. Blue ribbons. Rodeo. Rides. It was still magical to her.

Jeremiah's favorite part was watching his sister barrel racing. His eyes lit up as he talked about his twin. As Katie listened, the thrill of watching her mom flooded back. She remembered standing at the rail and holding her breath with her hands clasped together tight at her chest until her mom rounded the last barrel. Once she passed, Katie would start cheering. When she was little, she would run down the rail, sometimes dangerously close to knocking over a cowboy. Katie told herself she gave up racing to spare her father the pain of watching her ride. The truth was more selfish than that.

Mindy interrupted their conversation with dinner. She dropped Katie's down in front of her.

"Oops, sorry." She turned to Jeremiah and took her time placing the plate in front of him. "You let me know if you need anything else."

Mindy reminded Katie of a mosquito buzzing around until it bit you in a place you couldn't reach. She was irritated with herself for letting Mindy bother her. After all, they weren't dating and, as far as Katie was concerned, they weren't going to be dating. She had to tackle that. Since he had another fish on the line, this would be the perfect time.

"So, tell me about the Double J. It's been years since I was out there."

"Hasn't changed much. The usual stuff, I guess. We have a bigger barn. We're breeding Quarter Horses mostly now." He looked down at his plate and took a big bite of his steak.

She pushed it. "How's your dad?" Knowing he couldn't chew forever, she waited patiently.

"He's good. You know, just working the ranch."

Katie steeled herself and took a leap of faith she hadn't taken with anyone since her mama died. "That's pretty much all my dad does—work the ranch. Don't get me wrong. He loves the ranch. I do too. But since my mom died, he kind of caved in. The ranch is his whole world. I swear he wouldn't leave if he didn't have to." Her stomach turned to stone. She felt like she was betraying her dad and wished she could take the words back. But how else could she know if Jeremiah was in this at all?

He looked at her, then turned to his plate. He started to saw off a piece of meat but stopped. "Yeah, my dad too." He rested his fork on the lip of the plate. "Well, other than hitting the bars, he lives for the Double J. Since my mom took off, he doesn't do much but work and drink. He was never like your dad, though. You know, the way he played with you and Connor. My dad, he's rough. It's worse since my mom took off. I have to hand it to Jesse. She won't take it. Hell, she moved into the apartment over the barn. She's a badass."

"Why did she move out?"

"Something to do with my mom, I'm guessing. Jesse probably wouldn't let it go. My dad made it clear he doesn't want to talk about our mom. If you remember Jesse, though, she never did take orders very well." He laughed and shook his head.

Katie remembered the fits Jesse threw. When she got an idea, she was like a dog with a bone. When Jesse was seven, she decided it wasn't fair that Jeremiah got to ride the steers in the junior rodeo. They were twins, after all. As far as she could see, he only had one or two things she didn't have, and those things only made it harder to ride a bucking steer. It was solid logic to her, and she lodged her boots in the dirt until the last moment. Though unsuccessful at changing the rules, she showed the boys who was boss by winning every event she entered. She did not back down. She never did, even to a bully, and her dad was a bully. Even when Rocky punished her, Jesse stood her ground.

"My dad drinks a lot too, but he doesn't go out anymore. Connor convinced him to quit before he got a DUI, or worse.

Connor said he wouldn't go back to college because Dad was going to make me an orphan. Of course, my dad didn't want that, so now he drinks at home. I wish he'd quit, but at least he only drinks at night." Katie avoided Jeremiah's eyes.

He laughed.

"What's so funny?" she snapped.

"I'm not laughing at you. I'm laughing because they can't stand each other, yet they're the same. It's more than that. It's like they are in this standoff. Competitive. Seems like they could have helped each other through it. Can't be easy to lose a wife, whether she dies or runs off. It doesn't make sense." He shook his head. "But I quit trying to figure my dad out."

Katie felt a thread, thin but steel strong, reaching between them.

"Can I get you anything else?" The waitress picked up their plates. Jeremiah shook his head, still looking at Katie. "I'll bring your check then."

He cleared his throat and steered the conversation back to the fair. They made plans to meet later in the week. When the check came, they both reached for it. His hand covered Katie's, and he left it there. "I got this. I invited you."

The smile drained from Katie's face when she saw the check was signed *Mindy*. A heart topped the "I." She'd written her phone number below and underlined it twice.

"Told you so."

Jeremiah handed Mindy some bills without looking at her. "Keep the change." He reached his hand out to help Katie up. She took it and gave Mindy a satisfied smile.

Mindy got the last word, though. "Tell your daddy I said hi, Jeremiah."

CHAPTER 9

BUNNY 1984

THE POUNDING ON the door nearly knocked Bunny out of bed. She pulled the heavy quilt over her head, but it did nothing to block out Jake shouting through the door. "Giddy up! Time to go."

Rolling over, she searched the floor with her fingertips until they found the cold leather of her old boots. A wicked smile crossed her face. She let her irritation fuel her arm and launched the boot at the door. The pounding stopped, and she rolled over to settle back in.

"Get your ass out of bed, Sleeping Beauty. Breakfast is getting cold, and there's work to do. And bring that damn dog. I know he's hiding in there."

She heard him lumber across the gravel and regretted wasting her energy. If today was like yesterday, she was going to need every ounce.

Even with the blackout curtains, it had taken her forever to fall asleep. Her muscles screamed in the stillness. Though they'd never included her after their father laid down the law, Bunny missed the stomping, wrestling, and laughter of her brothers. She was up until the small hours wondering what was happening back home. The night crew would be getting the parlor ready for the morning milking of the first group of the herd. The twins would still be on. They were young and had a penchant for staying up all night. Her dad always joked that sneaking out the window at night gave them good practice for the night shift. He had tried the morning milking, thinking the punishment after running around all hours of the night would somehow keep them in their beds, but those boys never cracked.

Ruff groaned beside her. She looked at the furry lump leaning into the crook of her hip.

"I feel the same way, but it's time to rise and shine."

Bunny rolled out of bed, dressed quickly, and pulled her auburn nest through the back of her baseball cap. When she sat on the bed to pull her boots on, Ruff snaked his head onto her lap and pressed. "You're going to get me fired." She scratched his head. "Again."

Buck was leaving the house as Bunny stepped around the corner. A smile crossed his face as Ruff followed her out.

"I hope it's okay he stayed with me. He planted himself on my doorstep." She reached out and placed her hand on his head.

"He's famous for picking one human to stick to. I guess you're it this time." The dog strolled over to him, and Buck rewarded him with a pat. "There's chow in the kitchen. Eggs on the stove. You got an alarm? We feed at six."

The soft spot he had for Ruff did not extend to her. "Yes, sir. I had a little trouble falling asleep with the light. I won't be late again."

His eyes hit hers, and with a lift of his chin, he headed to the barn.

Bunny hustled to the main house. In contrast to the barn and riding arena, the house was plain and suffering from neglect.

Paint peeled around the weathered windows. Caulking oozed in lumps from the sill where the wood had separated. She followed a path worn in the grass to the kitchen door at the rear. As she put her foot on the first step, Jake swung the door open.

He stopped in front, blocking her path, and looked down at Bunny. "Breakfast is at five-thirty. It's time to feed the horses now. If you want to eat, don't sleep in."

Bunny liked breakfast. Her stomach growled and, on top of that, it was only six o'clock and a fire was already glowing in her chest. Her brothers usually waited until after lunch to light her up. Jake apparently wasn't going to do her the same courtesy.

"Buck told me to come up and get something to eat." She walked up the steps until she was nearly nose to nose with him.

"Of course he did." Jake shook his head and stomped down the stairs. "He has a soft spot for the girls."

&

Bunny wrapped some scrambled eggs in a pancake, a trick she'd seen her dad do for her brothers, and jogged to the feed room. Jake was filling buckets with oats. He laid each on top of a flake of hay according to the feeding schedule listed on the wall. Owners were particular about their feed. Buck handed Bunny a diagram that showed the stalls. She loaded the wheelbarrow and started hauling the first load down the aisle. As she filled each horse's trough, she got a nudge or nuzzle. Bunny repaid them with a rub on the forehead. Without thinking, she fell into her habit of talking to the animals. As she left War Horse's stall, she found Jake and Buck outside staring at her, open-mouthed.

"Sorry. It's a habit I picked up on my dad's dairy farm. The cows are calmer if you talk around them." They continued to stare. "What's wrong?"

"I told her that horse bites," Jake shot out. It seemed like he was more worried about getting in trouble for not telling her than about the potential loss of her fingers.

"Well, he seems to like me. Maybe I remind him of Katie."

"You don't," Buck growled and walked away.

"What the hell?" she mumbled.

Jake's shoulders dropped. "Nice job." He kicked his heel back, hitting a stall door and startling the animal inside. "Katie's his daughter. She's dead."

"What? Damn it. I'm sorry. Why didn't you tell me?" The eggs turned to concrete in her stomach. Though she hadn't meant to, Bunny had hurt Buck.

"Because you don't need to know. You've been here one minute." Jake stared at her. "You're passing through and the sooner the better as far as I'm concerned." Anguish peppered the anger in his tone. He put his hands on his hips and stared at his boots.

She braced for the dressing down. Her dad always said it was best to take your medicine, and he took every opportunity to let her practice. She choked back the nausea.

Jake pulled his hat down and shook his head. Looking up, he said, "Don't bring it up again." He cleared his throat and picked up his wheelbarrow.

They worked in silence. She couldn't tell if Jake was angry or sad. Either way, he made it clear he did not want to talk. Bunny was embarrassed by her insensitivity. Even more, she was tired of men who kept their feelings loaded like a shotgun until she came along and then pulled the trigger. After all their words pelted her, they walked away unburdened.

⁂

After feeding, they moved the mares and foals out to the pasture. Jake showed her how to coax the foals into the halter. Bunny was transfixed by his tenderness and patience with them. They were itching to run and play, which made them a handful on the lead. Bunny patiently walked them in circles until they moved forward with her. She caught Jake smiling as one head-butted her. The young horses were so full of joy; Bunny reveled in their playfulness. They were being what they were supposed to be—wild and free. They would be brought to bear soon enough.

As soon as they released the lead ropes, mare and foal raced off around the pasture. It was a sight to see. Manes whipping in the wind they created. Hooves pounding the earth. Stomping and bucking through the tall grass. They looked so free and unapologetic. Her heart swelled. Watching them, Bunny missed her horse, Hawkeye. There was something about racing across a field on top of a thousand pounds of muscle that made the rest of the world fade away. It was one of those elemental instances in life when she felt completely right.

Jake broke the spell by announcing the next job—cleaning the stalls and hauling in wood chips. They did the mares' end first, while they were out. Then they worked their way through the rest. Horses were locked out in their paddocks while they removed the soiled chips and brought in fresh ones.

Most of the horses were friendly. Jake moved the two stallions to their paddocks. There was one on each side, and they could not have been more different. One was a retired racehorse, a Thoroughbred named Hollywood Night Life. Tall and lean and full of energy, he knew he was a handsome beast. When anyone came near his stall, he stomped and bucked. He breathed in fast, heavy puffs. Jake and Buck were confident around him, though neither rode him. Hollywood was exercised on a lunge every day and then washed down. When he was being worked, no one else was allowed in the ring. To keep the mares from mayhem, he was always moved through the rear barn doors. When a mare was in heat, the top of Hollywood's stall was latched to keep him from seeing the mares.

The other stallion was no less dangerous. He was young and dumb, which presented a whole different set of challenges. He was a Shire named Huey Sings the Blues, elegantly colored in jet black with a vibrant white forehead and cannons. When Huey was put out to run in the pasture, his long black mane and white cannons flowed behind him, giving the impression that he was much faster than he truly was. He had a way of prancing around that didn't quite fit his heavy, round body, like a lineman in a ballet class. At two years old, he was already full-sized, which was twice the size of any other horse on the ranch. Though he was nearly full grown, he had the mind of a toddler. It took two people to safely move Huey out of the barn.

As Jake cleaned Hollywood's stall, Bunny moved into War Horse's. The paddock door was open. Most of the horses moved out as soon as she entered. Not War Horse. He stood there, staring at her. For a time, Bunny stared back. The thought occurred to her that perhaps her pride and arrogance were about to get her yet another scar. That had never stopped her before, though.

Ruff barked from behind the door, breaking the standoff. War Horse and Bunny turned his way. When she turned back, he was coming toward her. Before she could back up, he planted his forehead on her belly. Bunny reached down slowly with both hands and stroked his jowls. He nuzzled in. His coat was satin in her hands. Ruff barked again, and War Horse raised his head. He sniffed Bunny's face, then turned and walked out into his paddock. Bunny slid the stall door open to find Ruff sitting primly just outside the door. He lifted his fluffy body and raced out to find War Horse. They stood outside together until the stall was clean. As she took out the wheelbarrow, Ruff scurried behind her and out the door of the stall. War Horse wandered back in, but not until they were gone.

"You're gonna get hurt. I'm done warning you." Jake was waiting for her in the aisle.

She put the wheelbarrow down but didn't respond. What was the point? He wasn't going to give her any credit.

"Let's go, Calamity Jane. I have a filly I need your help with."

Halfway down the aisle, he opened a stall and brought out a young Morgan. She looked to be a couple of years old. Jake clipped the halter onto a lead on the wall and handed Bunny a brush.

"Her name is Whiskey. She's not fully broke yet. So brush her gently."

His condescending tone made Bunny angry, but she kept her mouth shut, hoping to make it through an entire day without being fired. This was the last job before the evening feeding. She was craving a long shower and a warm bed.

Whiskey hadn't filled out, but she was already powerful and proud. The coat across her back and neck was almost black but faded as it slid down her body to a silky chestnut. She stood, neck raised and head held high, watching and listening.

"I'll lunge her for a bit to get the piss and vinegar out of her. Then I'll need you," he said over his shoulder as he walked by her.

He led the horse out to the ring. Bunny closed the gate behind them and climbed up to watch from the rail. She'd never broken a horse. Back home, she had a Buckskin handed down from her mama when the Lovely Sophia fell in love with a golden Palomino.

Whiskey already knew the routine. She made a weak effort at resistance, but Jake quickly brought her in line with a flick of the whip and a short, sharp whistle. It was interesting to watch his transformation. With Bunny, Jake was tense, almost hostile. Even though the filly could give him far more trouble, he looked more relaxed with her. Once he took the center of the ring and brought her to a trot, he transformed, fluid and powerful and sure.

Bunny wished she had that kind of confidence. She wished she could strut out into the center of her life, sure that things would happen exactly like she wanted them to, sure that she wouldn't have to fight or defend. She was rapt watching him. Each was a thing of beauty, though Bunny would never admit that. She suspected both knew they were power and strength, embodied. Neither needed another admirer.

Jake slowed the horse to a walk and brought her in. Why did he need her? Then he walked the filly over to the steps. "It's time for her to get used to feeling some weight on her back." She hesitated, picturing being thrown on the hard ground. "You good to do this, or should I find someone else?"

"Nope. I'm good." It was a lie, but she wasn't going to admit it to Jake. She climbed up on the steps as he led the horse over. Bunny's leg was half over when he stopped her.

"What are you doing?"

"Getting on the horse."

"No. Not like that. That's too much. You're just going to lean on her first. Then you'll drape your body over the back. We do it in steps." His tone was urgent but calm. That was more about Whiskey's feelings than hers.

She put her hands on the young animal's back. The Morgan stomped away from the stairs. Bunny tried to catch herself teetering on the edge, but she was too far off balance. She shoved off to avoid breaking her fall with a thousand pounds of horseflesh.

The filly reared up and Jake pulled her lead forward, talking calmly, "Whoa, whoa, you're fine." He walked her in circles until she calmed. Jake had a skeptical look in his eyes.

Bunny dusted herself off and climbed the stairs. "Don't say it. Bring her back around. If you don't, she's going to shy away from this."

He stopped about ten feet from the stairs and stroked Whiskey's neck. "Okay. Let's do this again. You're going to be fine."

He led her to the stairs, where Bunny placed her hands once again on the horse's back. Slowly she added pressure, backing off when the animal got tense. Eventually, Whiskey let Bunny lean her forearms on her back. When Bunny stood, Jake took another lap. Whiskey's gait was stilted.

"Let's see if she'll take your weight," he called up to her.

Bunny had a bad feeling. "I think she's had enough."

"That's not for you to decide." When she didn't move, he said, "Do it or I'll find someone who will."

His tone wasn't helping the horse's disposition. It didn't feel right, but Bunny had been here before. What he meant was *I'll find a guy who will do it*. It was a strategy her father used, only he never bluffed. Still, when Jake brought the horse around again, she placed her hands on its back. Slowly, she bent down to her forearms. She leaned in and slid over until she centered her belly in both directions. Whiskey stomped.

Jake reached out and stroked her shoulder. "You're okay." The animal stilled at the sound of his voice. "How are you doing?" he asked softly.

"Fine," Bunny clipped.

"We're going to move forward a few steps and then that's it for today. Are you ready?"

He didn't wait for an answer. He began walking the horse. Whiskey stuttered, and Bunny started slipping. She grabbed at the horse's flank out of reflex and startled the animal. Whiskey bucked once, and Bunny fell backward to the ground. She rolled, narrowly escaping her hooves. Scrambling to get out of the way, Bunny spooked the horse again, and she reared up. Jake pulled hard to bring the horse's head down. After a few moments, she settled.

Without a word, he took the horse to the center of the ring and gave her some line. The horse trotted, and Jake urged her on. Before long, the filly settled into her pace. He let the horse run until she worked up a lather, then he brought her back down and walked her back to the barn.

Bunny followed them to the washing stall. Without a word, Jake handed her a sponge. He soaked the horse slowly, never raising an eye to her. Bunny seethed. Though her right hip hurt like hell, she kept her mouth shut. She wasn't giving him any more ammunition. Whiskey must have sensed her anger. She shied away from Bunny.

"Easy there," Jake said as the horse hemmed him in against the wall.

As Bunny softened her strokes to calm the animal, she really looked at the horse for the first time. Whiskey was a beautiful beast. Though not fully grown, the sheer power of her showed in the ropey muscles of her shoulders. She had a mind of her own, though, that was for sure. She wasn't going to be pushed. Bunny pulled the sponge slowly down her neck to her shoulders, cringing at the thought of hurting the horse because she couldn't stand her ground with Jake.

"Can you do this or not? Tell me now. We do a lot of training on this ranch." He talked at her from the other side of the horse.

"I can do it." Bunny wasn't going to apologize.

They finished washing her down in silence. Jake took Whiskey to her stall alone. While he got her settled, Bunny headed out to the pasture to bring the mares and foals in. She needed to be alone. She needed a win. When she opened the fence, a colt danced over to her. She stood still as he bucked and popped on his knobby legs. Eventually he wore down and let her put the halter on. Bunny rubbed his ears to thank him. His mama wasn't far behind, edging her way in between them. As she led each pair to the barn, Ruff watched with increasing interest from his perch on a bale of hay. By the time she had brought in the last of them, he was waiting by the feed room for her. Was he afraid she would go in without him?

Bunny had no interest in facing Jake or Buck, so she skipped dinner. She figured she would sneak in later and grab some leftovers. She couldn't avoid them forever, but she needed to let the memories of her screwups fade a little. After she fed the horses, she went to her bunk to nurse her aching hip and bruised ego. Ruff trailed behind her. When she opened the door, Bunny waited for him to walk inside, but he curled up in front of the door and stared out at the farm. He seemed disappointed in her. She felt the same way.

CHAPTER 10

BUCK 1982

Buck couldn't blame Katie for picking her friends over hauling hay. She'd worked so hard, taking over her mom's chores when she passed and working the ranch to help him. Loading the last bale on the trailer, Buck fired up the tractor. It was a short ride to the barn, but it would have taken five trips with a wheelbarrow. He was getting too old to let his pride rule his life. It didn't stop him from sending Jake to the bunkhouse, though. Buck didn't need his help except to lend a name to the lie. Katie would have canceled her plans to help him. Buck wanted her to hang around, but not out of obligation. He missed his little girl tagging along all day, looking at him like he was the Lone Ranger. He missed his wife even more. She'd have been able to translate Katie to him. Without her, a deep canyon of misunderstanding and regret kept them apart. So, he did what he could to make her happy, dreading the day when she wouldn't be around, even for that.

By the time he got to the barn, most of the riders were done for the night. A few stragglers were still brushing down their horses. Colt Browning was just getting started. A lawyer by day, he liked to cowboy late in the evening when the arena was empty. Sometimes Buck would even saddle up and hit the trail with him. They had a lot of history—and a tacit agreement to never talk about it.

"How goes the battle, Colt?" Buck called out to him.

"Same as always, I guess. Can't complain."

"Lone Star looks happy to be heading out. Escaping a house full of women?" Buck joked as he stacked the hay next to the feed room.

"Lord, I hope not. Carolina said the birch are killing her. Her eyes are about swollen shut from the itching. You must never see Katie these days. I heard she's heading up the campground planning for the fair."

"Yeah. That kid. She's always biting off more than she can chew." Buck laughed. "Like her mama."

"Jodie was a force of nature. God rest her soul," Colt mused. "Katie's following in her footsteps. Sounds like she's got help, though."

It made Buck's heart happy to see his wife blooming in their daughter, though he would never admit it to his buddy. "Headstrong though, like your Carolina."

"Tell me about it. There are days when I wish she would be more like her mom. Then I remember what it was like living with that woman." Colt mounted his horse. "I won't be too long. I can lock up if you want to head in."

"Thanks. I think I'll do that. I could use some peace and quiet while the girls are out."

Buck stopped in his tracks when Colt said, "Sounds like Carolina is missing out."

CHAPTER 11

BUNNY 1984

As the days wore on, the three of them eased into an awkward rhythm on the ranch. Bunny asked Buck about the lock on the basement door. He cited safety and protection. It wasn't clear if he was joking, so she stifled a guffaw and asked him to install a lock on her side. He refused, so Bunny left the boxes in place. To be fair, she warned him about the booby-trapped stairs. He didn't seem concerned. Of course, now that he knew the boxes were there, he could just kick them aside as he invaded her space.

They trusted Bunny to do routine tasks like feeding and cleaning. Mostly, Jake supervised her work. He didn't ride her quite as hard as he had when she'd first arrived. But she always felt he was waiting for her to screw up or give up. Bunny refused to give him the satisfaction. No matter how sore, scraped, or bruised she got, she kept it to herself. She wouldn't have asked him for a Band-Aid if she cut an artery. If she did something wrong, she kept her mouth shut and did it again.

One afternoon, Jake had her stacking bags of alfalfa cubes.

With each level, they slid a hair to the right until they looked like the Leaning Tower. Fortunately, Bunny caught it before Jake did. Despite the backbreaking agony of moving all those bags, she disassembled the stack and did it again. Though she was sure he knew she had taken it down, Jake's only comment was, "Took you long enough."

Most nights, they ate dinner together, then went their separate ways. Buck never asked her to cook, but after a couple weeks, they started taking turns. Bunny didn't mind it, though she wouldn't have wanted to be chained there, either. On her nights to cook, she went up early alone. Buck and Jake weren't much for talking, but they were always together except in the kitchen. Cooking was a one-man operation, Buck said. Bunny came to love the peace of it.

It surprised her how much she had picked up from her mom. Even the slightest addition of a spice or herb brought unexpected gratitude from the men. Had anyone ever looked after them? They acted as if eating was simply a utilitarian necessity. That was never the case when Bunny was a kid. Her mom made the food special because she cared to, not because she had to. Though she could have thrown some chicken in the oven and fed it to her brood plain, she never did. Three meals a day meant hours of preparation and planning. Bunny had never appreciated it until she was eating Jake's signature meal—a chicken breast, canned beans, and a slab of store-bought bread.

They ate in an old dining room. The table was long, as if the owner expected to have regular company. Half-opened mail covered one end. On the other lay three faded placemats. Bunny suspected they were homemade from the uneven stitching and irregular corners. There was a hutch in the corner that looked out of place. Gouges in the floor led Bunny to believe it had been roughly shoved out of the way of the growing pile of life's debris. It was the only thing in the room that was not dusty. Though dishes filled the hutch, they used the same three worn plates at every meal.

Bunny rang the bell and hoisted the Dutch oven onto the table. Buck and Jake waited for her to sit down before opening the pot. The gesture irritated her. The two men never waited for each other to eat. Buck pulled the lid off like he thought something was going to jump out of it. He held it in mid-air and stared at the pot.

"What's wrong? It's just chicken and vegetables." Bunny grabbed a slotted spoon and started dishing up the food.

Jake started to say something, but Buck quickly interrupted. "Nothing. It's fine. Smells great. Let's eat."

It wasn't fine. It was delicious. Bunny decided not to push the point when they dug into the food. The chicken tasted like home. She wanted to call her mom and tell her, but she knew exactly what she would say: *You went all that way just to end up doing exactly what you were running from.* She wouldn't understand. Bunny cooked because it was her turn. She cooked because they pushed her as much as they pushed each other.

"We need to pick up a horse in Anchorage. He's coming in on the barge from Seattle. It's a Quarter Horse stud."

Bunny nearly missed Buck's announcement, distracted by trying to figure out how the meat stayed in his mouth as he chewed with each word.

Jake put his fork down. "It's kind of late in the season to start breeding. How old is he?"

"Practically a colt. I want to work with him this summer so he's manageable next season."

Buck didn't seem to notice Jake's tone, but Bunny got it right away. It was the tone her brothers used when they thought their dad should have consulted them before making a big decision. She chuckled at the thought of her dad actually giving the farm to them. He was never going to be out of the picture. Her brothers had no idea.

"When are we leaving?" Jake asked.

"We aren't. I am." He shoveled another helping on his plate. "And I'm taking Benny with me."

"Benny? No offense, Benny, but she's not going to be much help with a young stud."

Bunny couldn't tell if Jake was talking about the horse or males in general. Either way, she was offended. She wanted to speak up, but she wasn't sure she could handle a young stallion, even with Buck.

"She's going." He said it with a harshness she had not heard him use with Jake before.

Bunny kept her mouth shut. She had been waiting a lifetime for someone to take a chance on her like this, and she wasn't about to let it go by. She made a silent vow to do whatever it took to make sure that horse got back safely.

He stabbed the air with his fork to punctuate his directions. "We're leaving day after tomorrow. The trailer is in the shed behind the arena. Get it hooked up and outfitted by morning. Make sure the tires are solid. Make sure you pack a couple of days of hay and water in case we run into trouble." Turning his attention to his plate, he pierced a hunk of potato. "Take the truck into town and pack the cooler with food and water for us. He'll have a halter, but I want you to pack an extra one and a couple of leads. We'll hook up the truck tomorrow night and be on the road by six. Any questions?"

Bunny felt like he was testing her in front of Jake. "No, sir. I'll be ready." She was glad she'd eaten before he made the announcement. Bunny started making a list in her head of all the things she had to do. As she cleaned the supper dishes, she prayed she wouldn't screw up.

CHAPTER 12

KATIE 1982

AFTER WEEKS OF planning, it was finally fair time. Sins of omission were piling up, as Katie failed to name the only other person on her committee whenever she updated her dad on her progress. It was risky. Even though he would not hang around like the other men, he would surely show up to see his riders compete.

Jeremiah and Katie arrived in the early morning when the sun was already high in the summer sky. He had recruited a crew to help park the trailers. Katie didn't know if it was his power of persuasion or natural charm. Whatever it was, apparently even cowboys were not immune. The rodeo crowd packed one end of the camping area. Coolers were filled and strategically placed between lawn chairs by noon.

Together, Jeremiah and Katie had convinced some of the crew to park their trailers in the middle. Though they would have to be a barrier for families from the revelry of cowboys and buckle bunnies, they did it happily to camp for free and save gas on the drive into town each day.

Katie parked the Midnight Sun trailer at the entrance next to the 4-H families. They were no less boisterous, but they stayed on the PG side of it. Her biggest challenge would be the teens sneaking off in pursuit of love and beer. It wasn't too long ago that she had tried, without success, to escape her dad and Connor in pursuit of a Bud and a cowboy. By dinner time, everyone was parked and unpacked. Livestock were in stalls, and farm kids and cowboys slid into their feeding and cleaning schedules.

Jeremiah and Katie had met for dinner several times as they planned for opening day. Each time, she became more and more at ease with him. Katie knew his reputation, but she was seeing the real man. Though she lied to her father about where she was going, she never worried too much about people's talk. There was enough gossip when her mom died to last her father a lifetime. Katie had let it hurt her heart for too long. When she told her dad about it, he said, *People are gonna talk. That doesn't make it true. You can't give your power away to them. Don't listen, and you won't hear it.* He was right, and so she toughened up.

Each time they met, Jeremiah and Katie talked less and less about the fair. The night before it opened, something shifted in her. It was like this valve in her heart opened, and he seeped into the empty spaces. When Jeremiah walked her back to her truck the last time, he kissed her tentatively, like he was afraid she might run away. Katie leaned in like a starving animal and let him know there was no need for hesitation. He grasped her shoulders, and a warm thrill rushed through her. It soon froze, though, when he pushed her away. Before he could say anything, she ran to her truck and drove away. When she looked in the rearview mirror, Jeremiah was still standing there, hands on his hips, watching.

The embarrassment bubbled through her skin, settling in hot, red blotches. Katie was halfway home when she realized she was crying. She pulled off on a dirt road and turned off the engine. Sobs wracked her body. She'd needed that kiss. It was humiliating to crave the warmth of him. As the sadness dried up, she scolded herself for letting her guard down.

⁓

On the first morning of the fair, after the ravenous and unrequited kiss, Katie searched for ways to avoid Jeremiah. That was until it came time to organize the campers. Even then, because they had been pretending so long, it wasn't hard to act like they were just doing a job. Katie retreated into her beloved list and the business of getting everyone squared away. As soon as the campers were all parked, she went in search of more work on the other projects. People were more than happy to let her take something off their hands. Katie helped the grounds crew set out garbage cans. Unfortunately, her mom was right when she'd said, *many hands make light work.*

She kept moving so she would be hard to find. Katie unpacked programs in the ticket office. She checked on her Appaloosa, War Horse. Though he didn't need it, she killed some time grooming him. She waited until it was late that evening when everyone would be settled in before she headed back to her trailer.

The 4-H dads sat in a misshapen circle of lawn chairs. The colorful webbing strained beneath the slouches brought on by a day of hard work and a night of easy drinking, Katie guessed. They would be telling tales of working their farms and crowing about their kids' blue ribbons. She remembered sliding the window open and hugging the wall of the trailer to listen to the men talk when she was a kid. She loved to hear her dad boast about her. He never told her outright, but her dad must have been proud to say it to his friends. Her mom said that made it special. Most of the men only bragged about their boys. Her dad and Rocky were competitive where Connor and Jeremiah were concerned. Rocky never bragged about his daughter. But her dad told them she rode like the wind.

Katie must have stood there watching the men a bit too long, because the conversation quieted. The flash of a white hat startled her. She recognized Jeremiah as he turned to say hello.

Ignoring him, she turned her eyes to the other men. "Hello, gentlemen. Did everyone get settled in?"

Jeremiah stood and, with a tip of his hat to the men, apologized for taking her away.

"Katie, I've been waiting for you. I had a question about something on the rodeo side. Do you mind?"

She wanted to say yes, but it would seem unfriendly, so she smiled. He took her by the elbow and led her toward his trailer.

Katie waited until they were out of earshot and pulled away from him. "What do you need?"

"Let's talk in my trailer," he said with an infuriating calmness.

"I don't think so. You can say what you need to say to me out here." She stopped in her tracks. The last place she wanted to be was his trailer.

He turned to face her. "What the hell is wrong with you? You've been giving me the cold shoulder all day."

"Nothing is wrong with me." She crossed her arms and looked him straight in the eye. "I'm sure you've noticed I've been a little busy with the fair."

"Yes. Me too. But you weren't too busy to talk to me before. So, what's the deal?"

"Nothing. Less than nothing." Katie regretted it before the last word was out of her mouth. She swallowed her shame.

"Ever since I kissed you, I've gotten the cold shoulder." He leaned into her.

Though it was the truth, she had no intention of admitting it. "Look, you're right. Let's forget about the kiss and get through the fair." She turned to walk away, but he caught her elbow and pulled her back.

She was so caught up that she didn't notice the cowboy headed their way until she felt his anger.

"Katie, are you okay?" Jake James planted himself next to her. Though he was speaking to her, his eyes drilled into Jeremiah.

She cursed her luck. "I'm fine, Jake. Thanks for checking. We're just working out some issues with camping." Katie didn't think Jake even heard her.

"Keep your hands off her, Jeremiah."

Jeremiah squared up with him. "What's it to you, JJ?"

Jake two-stepped nose to nose with Jeremiah. A snarl crossed his face.

Great, Jeremiah, light him up right now. That will make every-thing better. Katie stepped in. She had to separate them before Jeremiah said something stupid that Jake would take right back to the Midnight Sun. She didn't need him making a big deal about it, especially since she and Jeremiah were over.

"Jake, it's fine. I'm fine. It's regular fair mayhem. But thanks for checking."

He looked at her. "Just say the word and I'll be there." He turned to Jeremiah but made no move to walk away. Jeremiah stared him down.

Katie grabbed him by the elbow and dragged him toward his camper.

"Stop. I don't want to forget about the kiss. Why would I want to forget?" The force of his words threatened to bend her backward.

"Keep it down." She glared at him. "At the time, it seemed like you wanted to forget." He didn't back down, so Katie did. "Look, it's fine. I misread your kiss. Clearly, I was more into it."

He shook off her arm. "Stop! I was—I am—plenty into it." He looked at his boots as if the words were written on the toes.

"I just, I don't know. Look, I pictured our dads seeing us kiss. They don't like each other. Maybe they never did. Anyway, that hit me when we were kissing. You have to admit, the image of our dads would put the chill on any kiss, even as hot as that one was."

Katie had to give him that. His dad gave her the creeps for sure. He was right, their dads did not like each other. After Katie's mom died, her dad and Rocky never spoke again. In retrospect, they probably never liked each other. They tolerated each other like two bull moose waiting for the rut to begin.

She laughed at the thought of being caught kissing. It had been her biggest worry when she was little. When she looked up, Jeremiah was staring at her with the sweetest smile. No teeth, just a gentle grin that reached his eyes. Without thinking, she kissed him, and he leaned in. The kiss filled her heart. She prayed he wouldn't break it.

CHAPTER 13

BUNNY 1984

BUNNY LAY IN the dark, wide awake. She rolled to her right side, and Ruff filled the space she left behind, pushing her to the edge.

"Okay, that's it. Get on the foot of the bed!" He was so still. Was he even breathing? "I mean it. Move!" With a shove of her shoulder, she forced him over. He stood with a growl. "Don't you start on me. Lie down." He plopped down on the foot of the bed, and she rolled again. Even in the dark room, the ball of fur was unmistakable. Though his eyes were hidden, she sensed he was watching her. She reached out and felt for him. All she got was a wisp of an ear. "Stubborn." She bent at the waist to get closer, and he took the hint. Crawling on his belly, he slithered to her until she wrapped an arm around him. "I'm sorry."

The scene at dinner played on repeat in her head. Was Buck giving her the chance to prove what she could do, or was he afraid to leave the ranch to her for a day? Self-doubt grew in her belly like morning glory choking a field. The tendrils surrounded her, pulling her back to the dairy where she knew her place.

She drifted back to their last dinner as a family. Like a king, her father sat at the head of the table, her mother to his right. Once everyone was served, he covered her mother's hand with his and gently squeezed. Bunny still felt the ache of envy for the encouraging smile he got in return. Without preamble, he made the announcement. "I'm going to retire."

Bunny scanned her brothers' faces for evidence of a conspiracy. Clearly, it was a surprise to all of them.

"When?" Mick liked to get right down to it. The Army had honed his natural inclination for one-word questions and answers.

"No time soon, but we need to start planning. Some things I'll keep a hand in, like breeding. I'll start moving operations over to you boys."

"Boys?" It came out of Bunny's mouth and Patrick's in the same moment. Patrick always had a bit of a chip on his shoulder for being second born. He hated being called a boy.

"Don't you mean boys and girl?" Bunny could have said men, but she liked to yank Patrick's chain. Her dad's answer rubbed the smirk right off her face, though.

"No, I don't. I mean just what I said. Boys. The boys will split the farm. They'll have to keep it together until I'm gone. When one of them gets married and starts a family, your mom and I will move to one of the bunkhouses. Or maybe we'll build."

He kept talking, but Bunny didn't hear a word. The air left her lungs. Her father had thought the whole thing out, and she didn't figure into the equation at all.

"What about me?" Bunny's cheeks burned.

"What do you mean, what about you?" he replied.

"I mean, what about me? What the hell happens to me in this scenario, Dad?"

"Language, Benjamina," her mother clipped.

Bunny skipped the obligatory apology.

"Well, I assume you'll live here until you get married and then move in with your husband."

"And that's it? A lifetime of working this farm and you're giving it to the boys? I get literally nothing except the generous offer to stay on until some man comes to marry me?"

"Don't be dramatic. Nobody made you work the farm." He picked up his fork and speared a piece of meat. "No one even asked you to. That was all your idea." Michael O'Kelly saw the world in profits and losses. He knew when to cut his losses, like the prized cow who quit producing and was now dinner. Apparently, it was time to cut his losses with her too.

"And you insisted," her mother added. "You didn't have to."

There it was. The Lovely Sophia twisting the knife. No one made her work on the farm. She could have stayed cooped up, learning to play house like a proper lady. Her choices, her consequences, as her father had told her many times.

"You're right, Mom, I didn't have to. Silly of me to think my efforts were appreciated."

"This isn't about appreciation. It's about logic. I'm not leaving my farm to the man you marry." Her father raised his already booming voice.

"What the hell are you even talking about? Who said I was going to get married? Who said you would be leaving anything to my husband if I do marry?"

"Calm down." He said it in a tone that should have told her to stand down, but Bunny's fuse was lit and there was no putting it out.

"There it is. Patronizing. That's my favorite." She tossed her napkin on the table.

"Where the hell is this coming from, Bunny? This isn't about you. It's about keeping the farm going for the next generation of O'Kellys. It's a community property state. I am not leaving a farm that has been in my family for generations to some random guy." Michael O'Kelly had spoken.

"There is so much wrong with that, Dad. I don't even know where to start. First, thanks for thinking my marriage will end in divorce. Second, have you ever heard of prenups? Third, this absolutely is about me. This is about me not being a boy, one of your boys. Oh, sure, you let me play at it as long as I pulled my weight and kept my complaints to myself. But let's be honest, you were harder on me than any of them. So fine. Message received. This is not my farm, and it never will be. I'm clear on that now."

She shoved her chair back, grabbed her keys and jacket, and walked out the door. No one moved a finger to stop her.

&

She took the dirt road to the river a little too fast. Her rifle bounced in the rack behind her head. It felt good to pound through the ruts, shoulders clenched, gripping the wheel. It was dusk, and the row of trees along the riverbank made a long shadow over the old road. She didn't need lights. She could get here in the dark with her eyes closed.

Generations of bone-tired farmhands had dug a turnaround between the trees to park the truck. A single track, still muddy from the recent rain, led to the rocky shore. She found her way to a boulder large enough for her to lie on. She settled against the cold granite, rifle across her lap, and looked to the sky she had been staring at for over twenty years. The same sky her grandfather and his grandfather stared at.

Somehow, she knew she wouldn't be looking at this sky much longer. The sadness of that filled her chest. She couldn't stand alongside them all, knowing she was wasting her future on a misunderstood present. She knew what she had to do. Aiming her rifle at a log across the river, Bunny took a deep breath and let it out slowly. She squeezed the trigger and splintered a branch protruding from the front.

Bunny closed her eyes and listened for the echo of the shot to fade in the distance. The silence thickened as the crack expired. The creak of an old truck heading for the river quickly sullied the moment. It was Patrick. The twins were too self-involved, and Mick and her dad were too stubborn to drive out here to check on her. She thought about running into the woods, but he would just wait. Patrick was the patient brother.

"You okay?" He stood atop the boulder and looked over the river.

"Yeah. I'm fine." Bunny stared at the splintered log, wishing he would disappear.

Patrick crouched down and placed his hand on the rock to take his weight as he pivoted over the edge. "Talk, Benjamina."

Patrick was her favorite. He was never too cool to let her tag along. He was the one who introduced her to the magic of growing up on a farm—the cycles of life, the operation of machines, the changing of the seasons. Patrick even taught her to drive the tractor on the sly when their dad told her no. He was never too busy for Bunny. She suspected he felt like he didn't quite measure up either, though she'd never asked because asking required admitting. She wasn't ready to tell anyone she knew she was never going to make the grade with Michael O'Kelly.

"Don't call me that." Bunny knew he was trying to break the ice, but she felt like a glacier. "How would you feel, Patrick? Put yourself in my boots."

He eased himself next to her, back against the rock. "I'd probably feel relieved. Hell, apparently, I'm destined to operate this farm with the rest of the O'Kelly boys until I die. Not exactly what I had in mind." He took off his hat and leaned his head against the rock, gazing toward the sky. "I know you don't feel that way."

She saw it clearly now and felt like such a fool. He hadn't praised her—not once. Every day, she doubled down, hoping to deserve it. On time. Mouth shut. Shoulder to the grindstone. She'd always thought it was her fault, but it would never be enough. He'd never wanted her there.

"No, I don't. I love working on the farm. I know I'm not supposed to, but I do." There was no point in talking about it. As much as he loved her, Patrick couldn't understand what it meant to be less than everyone else.

He looked her in the eyes. "Who says you're not supposed to?"

"Give me a break, Patrick. You know full well Mom has not approved of a single day I have spent out here since the day I was born. And I completely misread Dad." She threw a rock into the river.

"Hey, Red. You didn't misread Dad. He appreciates your work out here."

"That's bullshit, and you know it. At least respect me enough not to lie." Bunny pulled her cap down and tightened her ponytail.

"I'll talk to him." He shoved her with his shoulder, his version of a hug.

"Don't bother. You aren't going to change his mind. And I don't want to stay, anyway." Bunny didn't want Patrick to save her. She didn't want saving at all. She had earned her spot on the farm. She wasn't going to beg for it.

"What the hell does that mean?"

"It means it's time for me to go." Bunny knew it was the truth because all the fight had faded out of her.

"Because Dad has decided that sometime in the future, he's going to retire and give the farm to us?" Patrick was getting his hackles up. He never yelled.

"Basically." There was nothing to argue about. Her mind was

made up. Bunny's Irish streak was legendary. Once her heels were dug in, they were impossible to dislodge.

"You're as stubborn as he is. What are you going to do?"

"I don't know. I do know I'm not spending any more of my time working your farm." Bunny got up and dusted off her jeans.

"I think you're making a big mistake."

"I guess we'll find out." She walked away before he tried to change her mind. Bunny knew she was disappointing him. The fact was, he'd disappointed her too. He never shied away from stepping up to the great Michael O'Kelly. But when it counted, he didn't step up for her. None of them did.

In the days that followed, they didn't talk about it again. The O'Kellys didn't waste words. Bunny bet they all believed it would blow over and she would somehow come to her senses. Then, what good would rehashing it do? She was an O'Kelly, and they might not say much, but what they did say was law. Bunny was more mule than any two of the O'Kelly boys put together.

CHAPTER 14

JAKE 1982

J AKE FUMED AS Katie led Jeremiah away. Seeing them together now, he knew he'd been right from the start. They'd been doing more than fair planning. He kicked himself for not listening to his gut as he'd watched them leave the diner after that first fair meeting. She'd been gone too long. Buck had been in no condition to notice, let alone track her down. But that was what Connor had him for. The way she'd watched him walk away that night had been a punch in the gut. Jeremiah didn't deserve her heart. Not one ounce of it. Jake had been the one who was there every day, keeping the ranch afloat with Connor while Buck was drowning in grief. He'd been the one who watched over Katie when Connor went to college. After all that, she didn't even notice him, but she mooned over that stray dog.

Standing in the middle of the aisle, Jake focused on Katie gripping Jeremiah's elbow. She was strong, an athlete like her mother. He admired that. Jeremiah would harden her tender spirit, though. If her dad had even the slightest inkling she was dating Rocky Cooper's son, he would flat lose his mind.

Jake had thought he could handle it himself. Hell, he thought he would be comforting her broken heart by now. It was a miscalculation. Now that he'd let it get so far without telling Connor and Buck, he was going to have to handle it himself. They'd be pissed he didn't warn them. Worse, he hadn't protected Katie and, for that, they would take over. No, he was going to have to be artful about this. A breakup with Jeremiah was inevitable. Just like his whoring dad, he'd never kept a woman long. When it happened, Jake would be there. He might even help speed it along.

⁓

Jake headed back to the Midnight Sun to pick up the second load of horses. Most of the boarders competed in the fair or helped with the events. By tomorrow, only a few animals would be left at the ranch. Knowing full well Buck would insist he go, he offered to stay back to run the ranch. He was manipulating the man's grief, but all this would blow over, and there was no sense in bringing him along for the ride.

"Everyone getting settled?" Buck called from the feed room. Jake shook his head. The man had ears like a hawk, but he couldn't see what was going on right under his nose.

"Yep. Just picking up the last of them and a few more bales of hay." Jake walked a Quarter Horse down the aisle.

"Good Golly Miss Molly." Buck reached out and patted the animal on her muscled rump. "I'll be out tomorrow afternoon to see this girl run. Should be a sight. Jenn's legs just barely get around her. That child's fearless, though. I'll give her that. Reminds me of Katie, before." Buck left the sentence unfinished.

"I might just stay out at the fairgrounds. We've got a lot of stock there this year. No sense in driving back and forth. Do you mind if I sleep in the truck?"

"No. Have at it. You're going to be stiff in the morning, though." Buck ran his hand along the horse's back. "I appreciate you doing it." Jake knew Buck was itching for the arena. He'd watch Jenn's run if she qualified in the morning, but he wouldn't stay to celebrate. He'd head home, open a bottle of whiskey, and remember the most beautiful rider he ever trained.

⁓

Jake got up early. At some point in the night, the jacket he'd rolled into a makeshift pillow had slipped onto the floorboard. He shook the hay off it and pushed himself up. Buck wasn't kidding. His hip was throbbing—another injury he'd gotten from not properly sizing up his opponent. Unlike the bull, he wasn't letting loose of Jeremiah.

He wiped the fog from the inside of the window. The dust of a hundred horses had settled in his mouth. He needed to piss, brush his teeth, and find some strong coffee—in that order. He hadn't slept much the night before. His mind kept jumping to Katie. Did she sleep in her trailer? Was she in Jeremiah's? He thought about sneaking over and checking, but with his luck, he would have gotten caught by some wasted bull rider still stinging from his emasculating ride lasting one bounce out of the chute and looking for a way to reclaim his manhood by chasing off a Peeping Tom. Instead, he let his mind race until it wore itself out. In the end, he only got a couple of hours of shut-eye.

The call for the first round of barrel racing came, and he quickened his pace. Jeremiah's twin, like her mother before her, was legendary. He wouldn't miss her qualifier. If Katie was with him, well, then he'd know. It would break his heart, but it was better to know.

He spied Miss Molly coming out of the barn. "Hey, Jenn. Are you up next?"

"Soon. They started at the top. The best riders get the most rest before the finals. I guess that makes sense. Still . . ." Jenn was still talking into the horse's neck as she checked her saddle when Jeremiah jogged off toward the arena.

Jesse was headed for the finish line as he arrived. He searched the rails and spotted them. Katie's feet swung a foot off the ground as Jeremiah twirled her in his arms. Jake's heart clenched at the sight. Then Jeremiah kissed her, and all the air went out of Jake. He fell against the fence, his eyes to the dirt. When he looked again, Jeremiah was smiling at him.

CHAPTER 15

KATIE 1982

KATIE GOT UP early to watch the qualifying runs of the barrel racers. As she walked through the campers, families were getting ready for the day. She missed those mornings. Her mom would help her get dressed in her show clothes. Katie loved the colorful shirts and shiny boots. Her mom would brush and curl her hair. Katie never complained about that, even when she pulled her hair. She loved the feel of her mother's hands, strong but soft even though she worked the ranch with her dad. She would let Katie wear a little makeup when she was competing, but she always told her she didn't need it. Her mother would say, *You are a natural beauty. No need to gild the lily. But we want those judges to see you from a mile away.* Katie always felt like a princess on her horse.

As she walked through the campers, the older kids were heading out to feed or getting ready to compete. Dads were leading the youngest competitors by the hand. She missed those times. Her dad didn't stay in the camper after her mom passed. He let Connor stay with her instead and only came in to watch her or a boarder ride.

The Midnight Sun had a few boarders barrel racing that morning. She was surprised her dad had not shown up yet. He had trained a couple of the riders and never missed one of their runs. A perk of being on the fair committee was an all-access pass, and Katie took advantage of it. She loved everything about the fair. Most of all, she loved the memories etched in the smells and tastes and touches of this place. If she closed her eyes, she could feel her tiny hand in her mother's. Her heart hurt thinking about it.

Katie leaned on the arena fence and closed her eyes. She took a deep breath in through her nose. The fresh dirt filled her nostrils. It would be dusty later, but they watered it down in the morning, and the scent made her feel warm and happy. She loved riding on fresh dirt. One boot propped on the bottom rung, Katie rested her chin on her forearms. She tried to conjure up her mom. Katie remembered the feel of her hoisting her up to watch the barrel racers. Her mom's hands were strong, but her fingers tickled her belly.

She told Katie stories of her glory days racing full tilt in tight serpentine around the triangle of barrels. Katie would listen, heart swelling, as her mom blossomed at the retelling. She said she was going to teach her as soon as she was old enough. Sometimes she would put Katie on the front of her saddle and race her around the ring, laughing. Her mom's laugh was like a bell, and she ached missing it. Though she trained other riders, Katie quit barrel racing. Her mom's passing ruined it. She didn't want to follow in her footsteps if she wasn't there to walk them with her.

When she opened her eyes, Jeremiah was standing next to her.

"Jesse's up next." He had told her he never missed his twin's ride.

"Is Rocky here? Maybe you shouldn't be seen with me." She took a step away from him and glanced around the arena. When she did not get even the tiniest audible response, she turned to find him stone-faced, eyes fixed on the chute.

His lips barely moved as the words slipped by. "My dad doesn't watch her ride."

That surprised her. Katie's dad never missed her rides, even now that they were just for show.

"Never?" she asked.

"No. He keeps tabs on her wins, but he won't watch."

"Is he afraid she'll get hurt?"

His eyes never left the arena. "No. I think it reminds him of my mom."

She couldn't picture Rocky caring. She'd never seen him gentle. Though, in fairness, she hadn't seen him much in the last decade, so she let it go.

Jesse started down the alley. Her hair almost matched the black horse. The only thing that separated the girl from the mount was a red shirt. Jesse was bold. Katie envied that so much. She never looked like she cared what anyone thought. Now that Katie knew her mama had left them, she was even more impressed. At a hundred yards away, she felt the energy of Jesse and her horse. River bounced sideways, begging Jesse to let him run.

The announcer boomed, "Next up, Jesse Cooper of the Double J Ranch, riding Wild River."

Jesse exploded out of the chute before he had time to finish. Jeremiah grabbed Katie's hand and squeezed. She felt the connection all the way to her heart. Jesse gave the horse his head, and they sprinted to the first barrel. As if they were one animal, she leaned back, and he dug his rear hooves into the first tight turn. Wild River catapulted out of the turn, tearing up the dirt in front of him. The second barrel was even tighter. The horse faltered, and Jesse lifted her leg to his shoulder. Jeremiah let out a gasp, but the barrel stood tall. Jesse urged River on, and he hunted down the third barrel. River lifted his chest out of the last turn. She forced her heels down and stood suspended over his neck. She spurred him on, whipping his haunches as they raced to the finish line.

Jeremiah let go of Katie's hand, lifting her in a hug and twirling her around. He kissed her hard and fierce. When he caught her eyes, though, he seemed to realize what he was doing and broke it off. He put her down, his eyes apologetic. She felt a glimpse of what could be. Though it was just a glimpse, it hurt her heart to lose it.

"Well, I should go see her. I'll see you later." He smiled, but his eyes were in the distance when he walked away.

CHAPTER 16

BUNNY 1984

BUNNY OPENED THE door and looked around for the men. She needed some time alone with the trailer. Desperate, Ruff nearly knocked her over, racing for the nearest bush. Knowing he would follow her, she headed out in the opposite direction. Bunny walked on the grassy edge until it ran out. By the time she hit the dirt and gravel, she was too far away to be heard.

Behind the arena was the shed, or what Buck called the shed. In reality, it was a three-door garage. The side door was unlocked. The building had no windows, and she had to feel around to find the light switch. Farm equipment was parked in the first bay. The second bay held the flatbed and the horse trailer. In the last bay, an oilskin tarp was draped over what looked like a small truck.

Bunny had lots of experience driving a stock trailer full of cows, but her mom didn't trust her with their horses. This was one of the few points on which her parents disagreed. Her father was always quick to point out that if Bunny could haul the cows, then she should be allowed to haul the horses because the cows were far more valuable than the horses. That comment was one of the few things against which Bunny and Sophia stood together. Bunny's father did not have the same definition of valuable.

The two-horse trailer was newer than the truck that would haul it. A rounded nose held a compartment for feed and tack, and a small door on each side opened to the interior for ease of feeding the horses in transit. The Midnight Sun logo was printed on each side. Bunny walked around the trailer. The rear door doubled as a loading ramp, not unlike the stock trailer they had at home. The tires looked low. Bunny spotted a compressor in the far corner of the shop beyond the covered truck. As she was pulling it away from the wall, the door to the shop opened and Buck called for her.

"I'm over here," she yelled back.

He stomped through the garage. "What the hell are you doing back there?"

"I'm getting the compressor. The tires are low." Bunny pulled it around in front of her for him to see.

"Give me that." He yanked the handle away from her and dragged it to the trailer. He kneeled, his back to her, and started filling the tires.

"I can do that, Buck." Bunny didn't know what his problem was, but she knew how to fill a tire. "You don't have to," she bristled.

"It's fine. I'll take care of it. Pull the truck up and let's check the lights on the trailer." He released the trigger, and his head dropped to his chest. "Before you do, throw the feed in and I'll help you pack the trailer."

She stood there a moment, staring at his back as he hunched over to fill the tires. Bunny got the impression he didn't want her to see his face.

"Stay away from that truck. Nobody touches that truck but me." His voice rumbled deeper with each word, like an earth-quake building momentum.

"I wasn't messing with the truck."

"Just leave it be."

Bunny stormed out of the garage. *What does he think I'm going to do? Steal it? Steal parts? Wreck it? What the hell is his problem?*

When she got to the house, Jake was eating breakfast. Bunny didn't say a word. She ripped the keys off the hook.

"Hey, slow down there, Red. You're going to have an accident."

"You know what? I just got my ass handed to me by Buck. Don't you start. I'm not going to steal his truck. I'm not going to wreck his truck. What is the problem with you two?"

Jake didn't look up from his eggs, flecks of which slipped from his maw as he spoke. "He can't be too worried about it. The keys are right there. He's letting you drive it to Anchorage."

"Not that truck. The one he keeps in the shed. Christ, it probably doesn't even run."

Jake's fork hit the plate and bounced, leaving scrambled egg debris in the drop zone. "Leave that one alone. It's none of your business."

"You too, huh?"

"Hey, I'm trying to save you some trouble. Keep poking the bear. Next time he fires you, you'll be hitchhiking out of here." He picked up his plate and fork and dropped them in the sink. Disgust darkened his eyes. "You can't just shut your mouth and do what you're told. Katie died in that truck."

Heat rose in her belly. Jake slammed the door before she could stoke the fire. With no foe left but herself, she lit off to get the truck.

As she tore out for the garage, Ruff yelped. Bunny slammed on the brakes, gripping the wheel. Her stomach sank to her feet. Throwing it in neutral, she stepped on the emergency brake and opened the door. Ruff was sitting on the ground, looking up at her. He scolded her with a bark. The air went out of her. As she relaxed, he leaped into her lap and settled on the passenger side. Ruff forgave her, curling up with his heavy head on her leg. Bunny scratched his ears, and he relaxed into her. When she stopped by the barn to load up some hay and oats, Ruff took his place behind the wheel. He followed her every move like a cotton-covered sentry.

Buck had the garage door open by the time she got back. Without speaking, she backed up to the trailer, got out, and hitched it up. He stood watching like it was a test. Bunny connected the lights. The only time Buck spoke to her was when he shouted directions as they tested the signals. Bunny could feel his anger but, with each passing moment, she cared less and less. She was sick of guessing what she'd done wrong. She was tired of worrying what she'd done to upset someone.

Bunny filled the feed compartment, nursing a grudge that would beat even her dad's personal best. She wasn't looking forward to the six-hour drive to Anchorage alone with him.

CHAPTER 17

KATIE 1982

KATIE URGED WAR Horse on. He was more than happy to chase after Thunderbird. She let him close the distance but always held him back a little. She loved to watch Jeremiah ride. He was a little boy again in the saddle, wild and free and fearless. They didn't have to hide on the tundra. There was no one to see or hear them. The sun was creeping lower in the sky with each passing day. It felt like a door slowly closing between them. The waning light told her she wouldn't be riding over much longer. It would be riskier by truck. Someone might catch her turning down the dirt road.

"Katie Miller, you let me win." He chuckled as he scolded her.

"Don't blame me. War Horse is older than Thunderbird. He needs a head start." She leaned over the saddle horn and rubbed his neck, whispering in his ear, "You could totally beat him."

"I heard that," Jeremiah chided.

Katie giggled and squeezed her mount. "Race you to the cabin."

They had taken to meeting at the old homestead cabin on the far corner of the Double J once the fair was over. The cabin was remote enough that they never ran into anyone. There was a tension in Jeremiah that faded when he was there, like he was taking off a suffocating mask.

"Hold Thunderbird a minute." He handed the reins to Katie and dug in his pockets for a small bag. He walked out among the trees. With a few flicks of his wrist, he emptied the contents.

"What was that?" she asked as he took the reins from her.

"Just some oats."

"Softie."

He pursed his lips to corral the smile that was trying to burst out. Without a word, he took the reins from her hands and led the horses to a stall in the back. He didn't bother removing the saddles. They wouldn't be there long. The thought tugged on her heart. With each passing day, Katie wished she hadn't insisted on the secret. Jeremiah's bold declaration that she was an adult and did not have to do what her father expected had long since dissipated. It was clear he now feared telling his own dad. That relegated them to stealing evening rides on the nights their fathers were otherwise engaged with whiskey neat or whiskey eyes.

Jeremiah had been coming to the cabin since he was a kid. It wasn't much, just one room heated by an old woodstove. He told her he liked the solitude of it. What was he seeking solitude from? Over the years, he'd outfitted the log house in the ramshackle manner that single men do. A wooden crate served as a table. Next to it, an armchair oozed stuffing. There was no electricity. In the summer, sunlight filtered through the windows, milky with age and grime. In the winter, a lantern lit the space. The kitchen was nothing more than a recycled basin that emptied into a bucket and a countertop fashioned from plywood. On one end, a reclaimed cabinet sat, filled with random kitchenware. A table large enough for two was pushed against one wall. On the opposite wall, there was an old army cot.

They held each other with the desperation of faithless youth. She lay in his arms on the musty cot as they talked for hours. Losing their mothers gave them a bond that allowed her to say things to him she could not say to people who still got to hug their moms. Though he'd told her about his mom leaving, he held back a hurt he could not confess. He talked about it like he was reading a repair manual. It was deeper than that, but no matter how much she opened her heart, his remained locked.

When they were in town, they only talked in public if there was a good reason. After the fair was over, there weren't too many good reasons. He swore he didn't see other women, though that became a worm boring into her head as he kept up the façade by flashing his smile, tipping his big white hat, and flirting with ease.

❧

She tried to hide her jealousy as the weeks went on, but it seeped out one night while she was having dinner with her best friend Carolina at the Lodge. Katie caught a flash of Jeremiah talking to a leggy blond. It was the waitress from the Back Forty who had given him her number. Though she had a wholesome glow, she was anything but in Katie's estimation. She wore her hair too big, her makeup too thick, her pants too tight, and her top too low. She'd cut off half the women in the place to get to him. He flashed his smile, like he always did, but then he made her laugh. There was something about that laugh that made Katie feel like the waitress had stolen something from her.

"Hey, what's wrong with you tonight?" Carolina asked.

Katie shook it off. "Nothing. Why?"

"Well, I'm pretty sure you haven't heard a word I've said in the last ten minutes, for one thing. And for another thing, you are vaporizing someone with your stare."

"Sorry. That new chick irritates the hell out of me. Could she be more obvious?"

Carolina looked around the room. "The one talking to Jeremiah Cooper? They're made for each other. He's such a dawg. I bet he's loving the attention."

Without thinking, Katie slammed her beer on the table.

Carolina raised her eyebrows. "Why do you care about those two?"

She caught herself. "I don't." But the truth was, she did care. And in the pit of her stomach, she wasn't sure if Jeremiah felt the same. She scanned the bar. Had anyone else noticed her outburst? She didn't need anyone reporting back to her dad. She avoided looking back in Jeremiah's direction. It was humiliating to love someone more than they loved you. She couldn't risk seeing the proof on his face, not in public.

She thought her tantrum had gone under the radar, but her stomach sank when she saw Rocky Cooper staring at her from the end of the bar. He held a beer bottle halfway to his lips, which were frozen in a sinister grin. Rocky held her eyes for a moment, then slid them in the direction of Jeremiah and the waitress. As he looked back, he tipped his beer toward her and took a long pull. She looked away quickly, willing her face to stone. When she turned back, she was staring into the plaid shirt of Jake James.

"Hey, Katie." He lifted his chin to Carolina. It was clearly a practiced move, meant to look cool but coming off awkward at best. "Do you want to dance, Katie?" He gave her a hopeful smile.

"No thanks, Jake." She turned to Carolina. "I'm getting tired. Do you mind if we go?" When Carolina didn't say a word, Katie smiled and grabbed her coat. Like the best kind of friend, she didn't ask for an explanation, and she didn't let her leave alone.

"I can take her home if you want to stay, Carolina," Jake offered.

She patted his arm. "I've got this. You go have fun."

As they walked past the bar, Katie opened her purse to search for her keys. She kept close to Carolina, hoping to miss Rocky's gaze.

"Carolina." His voice was a low hum. "Katie." He drew the word out a beat longer than it had to be. There was no ignoring it.

"Hi, Mr. Cooper." When Carolina stopped, Katie cursed her friend's good manners.

"How are you girls doing tonight?" He spoke to Carolina, but his eyes drifted to Katie.

"We're fine. Heading home now."

"Well, you be careful now. It's getting darker every day." He took a drink from the bottle. "Say hi to your daddy."

"Will do, Mr. Cooper." Carolina smiled at him.

As they walked away, he said, "You too, Katie Miller. You tell your daddy I said hello."

CHAPTER 18

BUNNY 1984

Buck was tossing a duffel bag into the back of the crew cab when Bunny came out of her bunk.

"I thought we were going down and back today."

"We are, but this is Alaska. You never know what you're going to run into. I'd advise you to pack some gear in case we run into problems. Make it quick. I want to get on the road."

The day had barely started, and already Buck was switching things up. She tossed a change of clothes into a bag and grabbed a toothbrush, cussing him under her breath. Behind the closed door, she grumbled, "You couldn't have told me to pack last night? It's like you want me to screw up. Well, I'm not some horse you're gonna break, asshole. Michael O'Kelly didn't beat me, and you got nothing on him."

She threw her toothpaste on the counter. It landed with an impotent thud. She hated the person she saw in the mirror. Taking a deep breath, she closed her eyes. His horn bellowed on the other side of the door. She refused to let him see her like this, so she turned the faucet on and filled her hands with the cold water. Slowly, she plunged her face into the well of her palms. She headed for the truck. No matter what he threw at her, she wasn't going to fold.

Bunny tossed her duffel into the back of the truck. She opened the passenger door, and as she pulled herself up, Ruff jumped over her onto the front seat.

"Uh-uh. Wrong side," Buck said.

"Ruff, out," Bunny ordered.

"Not Ruff. You. You're driving down. I want to see how you handle the trailer before I have you drive with the horse loaded."

Another test. She tamped down her temper. Without a word, she got into the driver's seat. Ruff jumped into the back seat as soon as Buck got in. Bunny put the key into the ignition. Then she remembered. This was a test. Everything was a test. She got out and checked the hitch. The lights were disconnected. She plugged them back in. Refusing to ask for his help, she turned on the flashers and walked to the back of the trailer to make sure they were working. Buck sat silently in the truck, looking forward. She walked around and checked all the doors. One of the feed compartments was not latched. She kicked the tires. It wasn't necessary, but it felt good.

Her anger choked her, so she took a moment behind the trailer to calm herself. Though she was boot-stomping mad, she was not going to let her body give it away. *You can do this. Buck Miller is an amateur next to the O'Kelly boys.* She remembered what Mick used to tell her when her anger flamed, and she felt like giving the same advice to Buck: *Don't bring a knife to a gunfight.* She pulled herself into the cab and put the truck in gear.

As she pulled out, he said, "Good job."

⤟

The drive down was beautiful. Vast glacier-cut valleys stretched out for miles. Ribbons of rivers wound on the floor. Wildflowers peppered the shoulders. They didn't talk at all, and eventually Buck fell asleep. Bunny took that as a compliment. He wasn't the kind of guy who could sleep if he was worried she might kill him.

Every once in a while, Bunny would glance over at him. He had rolled his jacket into a pillow of sorts to cushion his head on the window. His face relaxed from the perpetual grimace she had not noticed before. His hat rested on one knee, his hand loosely grasping the crown like he was frozen in the thought of putting it on. Ruff leaned forward with his giant head resting on the back of the seat, peering out the front window. Did Ruff think she might not get them to Anchorage safely? He was a stowaway of sorts. He had refused to get out of the truck when it was time to leave. Buck gave in without much of a fight. Bunny was glad to have someone along who liked her. Along the way, the small towns they passed made her homesick.

Just south of Willow, a roadside sign told her she was an hour out of Anchorage. Not sure where she was going when she got there, Bunny thought about waking up Buck. When she glanced his way, the lines in his face had relaxed as they bounced down the highway, revealing how little peace he had while awake. She decided to give him twenty more miles.

Anchorage had a lot of coastline. So when she hit Wasilla, she couldn't wait any longer. "Buck, it's time to get up. We're almost there." She looked his way when he didn't answer. "Buck!" she tried again, louder. When she saw the cutoff to Palmer, she shoved his shoulder. "Buck, you need to wake up. I don't know where I'm going."

Buck sat up straight. "What?" He scanned the windows, rubbing the sleep from his eyes. "You're doing fine. Just keep going. I'll tell you when to turn."

He navigated them to the docks. Bunny didn't know much

about shipping, but she knew a lot about tides. They were looking at a minus tide. The only ships or barges she saw were tethered out at sea in a floating traffic jam. Tractor trailers were parked on the dock. Buck got out of the truck without a word and went to the guard shack. He stomped back a few minutes later, pulled himself into the cab, and slammed the door.

"Back it up," he ordered. "The tide went out before the barge got in. They can't bring the horse off until eleven tomorrow."

Buck directed her through town to a motel on the edge. The building looked like remodeled Army barracks camouflaged with sky-blue paint. The parking lot was old and in need of painting. It was dinnertime, and her stomach was howling. She hadn't eaten since they gassed up in Healy, and Buck hadn't eaten at all.

He told her to stay with the truck as he went in to get rooms. As soon as he shut his door, Ruff jumped in the front seat. He sat arrow straight, staring out the windshield and leaning on her shoulder. When Buck returned, Ruff was still sitting guard. He refused to make eye contact with him. Bunny felt like he was taking her side in some silent argument.

"You always did like the pretty girls," Buck muttered to the dog. "Alright, that's enough. Get in back." Ruff turned slowly to face Buck. Something passed between them. Ruff gave Bunny a nudge and hopped in back. "We're around back. They only had two rooms on the first floor. I guess we aren't the only ones who didn't check the tide table."

She pulled the truck and trailer around to the rear lot, hoping she wouldn't have to back it out in the morning. She parked next to a semi caked with dirt.

Buck wrestled his bag from the back of the truck. "Get settled, and then we'll go get some dinner."

She nodded and headed to her room. Ruff followed. It had been a long day and, if she hadn't been so hungry, she would have fallen asleep right then on the scratchy cotton bedspread. Ruff hopped up on the bed and rested his head over her left shoulder. In the mirror, she watched him breathe, eyes closed, relaxing into her like an anchor. Bunny shifted to stand, and he pressed in like he didn't want her to go. She didn't want to go.

"I'll be back, big guy. Don't you worry. I'm beat. Warm up the bed for me." Bunny gave him a good head scratching and grabbed her jacket. Buck was leaning on the bed of the truck, waiting for her. Tucked into the pockets of his vest, his hands pulled the material over his chest and shoulders, revealing he had lost some bulk since he'd bought it. He stood in rigid repose, legs crossed at the ankles and heels dug into the dirt. He'd tilted his face skyward, eyes closed. Had he fallen asleep again? She considered leaving him there in peace but changed her mind when she looked across to the tavern.

"You ready to go?" she asked.

He pushed off the truck without answering and headed across the lot. The bar had the feel of a place that welcomed regulars and tolerated everyone else. Though dark, she sensed the stale air permeating every object and person in the room. Peanut shells crunched beneath their feet. Bunny suspected that if they were swept up at all, it was by someone with poor eyesight. Captain's chairs were scattered around the tables. Buck lifted his chin to the bartender. From the way he answered in kind, Bunny guessed they'd met a time or two. Buck grabbed a couple of menus from the bar and led them to a table along the wall. It was scarred and damp. Bunny's jacket stuck to it when she leaned forward.

"The burgers are pretty good. I'd avoid the soup of the day. It should be called the soup of the month." Buck looked around the room. He didn't open the menu. A few guys played pool in the back of the room. She was the only woman in the place. It was early, and she suspected it would start filling up now that the workday was over.

A waitress appeared and, without wasting time on a greeting, barked, "What'll you have?" She was older than Bunny by at least a decade, and her face showed signs of hard living. She wore her hair too long and her shirt too tight for her age. She wasn't bad-looking, but she hid it under her desire to be twenty-one again.

"Whiskey straight. Make it a double." Buck looked around the room until the waitress gave up and turned to Bunny.

She ordered a burger and a beer. "Aren't you eating?" she asked him.

"Yeah." He picked up the menu but put it down without opening it. "A burger, please."

Bunny suspected he wouldn't have ordered food if she hadn't asked.

They sat in silence, nursing their drinks. Buck blinked first.

"You did a good job hauling the trailer today." He looked her in the eyes when he said it.

"Thanks, but you were asleep, so I'm not sure how you'd know." She was disappointed despite the compliment.

"Well, that's how I'd know. I would have woken up if you hadn't. So, take a compliment, would you?"

"Sorry. Thanks." She contemplated her beer. "It was a beautiful drive."

"Where'd you learn to drive a trailer?"

"My dad's farm. I hauled the heifers. My brother, Patrick, taught me, although I'm guessing my dad thinks he did. He doesn't have much patience. Patrick always gave me lessons in the things my dad was going to teach me." Bunny didn't know why she was sharing all this, especially since Buck shared so little. He looked content to drink his whiskey and listen. About halfway through her burger, she noticed he hadn't started his.

"Aren't you hungry?"

The question seemed to surprise him, and he looked at his plate with a frown. Picking up his burger gingerly, Buck stared at it a while before taking a bite. He chewed it like it was a chore.

When the waitress asked if he wanted to take it with him, he politely declined and ordered another whiskey.

The bar filled. A few women filtered in, all wearing considerably less clothes than Bunny. Conscious of her worn jeans and work boots, she tugged at her long red hair held captive by her Red Sox hat. She hoped none of the men had noticed her. Surely, she would come up short compared to the curvy girls dancing to the jukebox.

"You want to play some pool?"

Bunny hadn't seen him approach the table, though she wasn't sure how she missed it. He was tall and thick. Bunny imagined he walked with a heavy thud of each shoe.

"Me?" She looked around the room to see if all the other women had left. "Uh, no thanks."

"Come on." He leaned on his pool cue.

"She said no," Buck slurred.

"You her husband?" He straightened and faced him.

"No. Boss."

"Then you got nothin' to say, old man," he taunted.

Buck started to get up but faltered under the weight of two doubles.

"Hey, boys. No need to argue on my account." She looked toward the exit, planning her escape. "It's time for me to hit the sheets, anyway. It's been a long day, and it's going to be a longer one tomorrow. I'll see you in the morning, Buck."

Bunny shrugged on her jacket and pushed past the pool cue. She held her head high and her hotel key in her pocket. It was a habit Patrick drilled into her. He showed her how to hold the keys between the knuckles in a fist. Bunny would never beat a guy, he said, but she could stun one long enough to get away. She pushed the heavy door open, expecting darkness. The light hit her eyes, blinding her briefly.

She was about halfway across the parking lot when there were footsteps. Picking up her pace, she clutched the keys. She was nearly to the truck by the time he caught up with her. He grabbed her arm, his fingers bruising her flesh. She reached out and caught him in the cheek with her key. She struggled, but he did not let up. He brushed his face, coming back with a handful of blood.

"Bitch," he growled.

Her face collided with the bed of the truck, and she felt his hand reach for her belt. Bunny stomped on his foot, but it had little effect. Briefly, she thought she might need a better self-defense coach than Patrick. Ruff started barking from her room. Bunny called out to him. The man had her belt undone and was grappling with the button. He released her arm and covered her mouth. Bunny sunk her teeth into the meat of his hand. He ripped it away and shoved his body against hers, pinning her against the truck. In the tight space between their bodies, she felt him reach for his belt buckle. Ruff jumped at the window. It didn't break, but it startled the roughneck. She slammed her head backward as hard as she could into his face. He let go of her mouth and grabbed her ponytail, pulling her head back. Her scalp screamed. She was sure he was tearing her hair out. Ruff jumped at the window again, bowing the glass.

"Hey, what the hell are you doing! Get off her!"

Buck was yelling. But she didn't have much hope, given his condition. It caught the man's attention, and he let loose of her hair long enough for her to head-butt him one more time. This time, his nose crunched. He stumbled backward. Buck was nearly to him when he ran away. Bunny rushed to her room. Her hands were shaking as she shoved the key in the lock. Ruff didn't stop to check on her. He shoved past her and ran, growling toward the man. Ruff nearly beat him to his truck. He lunged for the door, clawing to get in. The man peeled out of the parking lot with Ruff in pursuit. Buck called him back. Bunny gasped at the thought that she had almost gotten him killed twice now. He stopped and swung his head toward Buck and then back again to the speeding truck. In the end, he raced toward the hotel.

"My God. Are you hurt? Did he hurt you?" Buck followed Bunny into the room.

Without a word, she went to the bathroom and slammed the door. Blood welled in the scrape on her forehead. The back of her head, where she had smashed the man's nose, throbbed. Her scalp burned at the edges of her hair. She pulled off her jacket to find his fingerprints on her forearms.

"Benny, let me in. Are you okay?"

Bunny's heart was racing, and she couldn't catch her breath to talk. Silent sobs wracked her body. She tried to swallow them down, but they wouldn't stay. Sliding to the floor, she hugged her knees to her chest. She wanted her dad, but she knew she couldn't call him. They would be on the next plane, then she would be on the one after that. It would prove she couldn't take care of herself. No one would assault a man.

"Benny, please open the door. The police are here."

Shit. The police. Who called the police?

"Why did you call the police? I didn't ask for that." Her voice cracked as she yelled at the door.

"Benny, I didn't. I would have asked you. Someone saw . . . what happened. Please come out."

"I lost my cap."

"I have it."

"I want Ruff."

"Open the door. He's sitting right here."

She slid her butt around and leaned against the cabinet. "Okay. You can send him in." Ruff pounced into the room, smelling every corner like he was still searching for the guy. Then he came to her. He was gentle—first sniffing, then nudging until he curled into her. Though the door was still open, she refused to look up.

An officer got down on the floor in front of her. She asked everyone else to leave, save Ruff and one paramedic. While the paramedic checked Bunny's head, the officer asked her questions. Though she was kind, she didn't treat her like she was fragile. She was grateful for that dignity. Bunny suspected not everyone would have given that to her.

One by one, they filtered out with promises of action, until it was just Bunny and Buck. She expected him to insist she call her dad. She expected him to tell her she should go back to Washington. Instead, he sat down on the bed, put his face in his hands, and said, "I am so sorry. This is all my fault."

"What are you talking about?"

"I shouldn't have been drinking. I should have walked you home. I should have protected you." He spoke into his hands.

"If this had been Jake, you wouldn't feel this way." Bunny knew she was supposed to let him off the hook. She couldn't risk losing this moment.

"No one would try to rape Jake." He looked her in the eye. Though he spoke the truth, it still pissed her off.

"So, this is my fault because I'm a woman."

"No. Aren't you listening? It's my fault. I shouldn't have taken you to that dive. I knew the kinds of guys who go in there."

"So why did you, then?"

He cradled his head in his hands. As the silence pushed the air from the room, he said, "Because I needed a drink and that was the closest bar." It came out as a growl. He didn't look at her when he said it. "I didn't take care of you." He ran his hands through his hair. "I didn't take care of Katie."

It was barely audible, and yet, the force of his sadness hit her in the face. She wanted to ask. They wouldn't be in this place again. In so much pain, their armor had slipped off. Yet, somehow, she knew if she asked, he would want something in return that she was not prepared to admit, even to herself. He stood. His eyes were red.

"I'm so sorry. Do you want to head back tonight?"

This wasn't one of his tests, but a guy wouldn't fold. Even if she didn't have to prove it to him, she had to prove it to herself.

"No. I'm fine. Let's get the horse in the morning. Then we can go."

"You sure?" He didn't say it like he was surprised. He said it like he wanted her to know they would leave right then if she asked.

"I'm sure. Ruff is here. I don't think anyone is coming in."

He stared at her with a look of gratitude. Like she gave him a gift by not insisting they leave. "I won't drink anymore tonight. I promise," he said, hat in hand, eyes lowered to the floor, and then left her room. When he got outside, he yelled through the door, "Lock up."

CHAPTER 19

JEREMIAH 1982

ROCKY WAS STILL up when Jeremiah rolled into the drive. He sat in his truck, staring at the living room window, willing his dad to be asleep in his chair. Rocky sat motionless in the light of the old television. He had stripped off his work shirt, as if he planned to go to bed but changed his mind. He held a beer loosely over the arm of the chair. His legs were spread wide. To anyone else, Rocky would have looked deep in thought. Jeremiah knew better.

"You're home early. I thought you might be going home with Mindy." He barely moved as he spoke.

"Mindy?"

"The waitress you were putting the moves on." He took a sip of his beer. "She's a sure thing." He nodded like he had given his words due consideration and found them convincing.

"Jeez, Dad. I was being polite."

"You should save that for Katie Miller. I think Mindy might appreciate a bit more than polite."

Jeremiah searched his memory. He was sure they'd covered their tracks.

"Surely you've noticed how she looks at you, son." His words dripped with disdain. "You've spent enough time together. Hell, she looked like she wanted to slap Mindy tonight just for talking to you." Jeremiah stood stock-still waiting for impact. "I guess now that the fair is over, Katie will give up hope." Rocky set his beer on the table. He pushed himself out of the chair. Uncoiling to his full height, he stood eye to chin with Jeremiah. "All for the best, son. A girl like Katie isn't going to stick around with men like us. We need something a little tougher. Like Mindy." Jeremiah didn't flinch, so he added, "I wouldn't worry about Katie, anyway. It looks like Jake James has her in his sights. He'd be Buck's pick for his girl. Don't you think, son?" Without waiting for an answer, he turned and walked away.

Jeremiah let out his breath. His heart raced at the thought that Katie was angry with him. When his dad's bedroom door shut, he picked up the phone but then stopped himself. Though he suspected he'd be dead drunk by now, Jeremiah couldn't risk her dad picking up the phone. Even if Katie picked up, what would he say to her? He knew what she wanted him to say. Though it was in his heart, the words caught in his throat. They would ruin it. He glanced at the calendar. Two days until they were supposed to meet at the cabin. Jeremiah prayed she would show.

CHAPTER 20

BUNNY 1984

BUNNY KNEW AS soon as Ruff bounded tail up toward the door that the pounding was coming from Buck. With a groan, she pulled on her jeans. Her whole body hurt, but nothing hurt more than her head. It was clear Ruff did not share her agony as he sprinted past the open door to pee on the nearest bush. Buck pushed past Bunny without invitation. With a thud, he dropped a box of donuts on the table and handed her a coffee. Maybe it was the early donut delivery. Maybe it was his cheerful attitude. Bunny stared at him, unsure what was happening.

"Well, eat up. We need to head out soon to get in line at the docks." He said it as if nothing had happened the night before.

Bunny looked at the clock.

"Oh, shit. I overslept. I'm so sorry. Man, I never do that. This is twice now." Bunny rushed around the room, picking up her gear and loading the duffel. "I just have to finish getting dressed, and then we can go."

"Slow down," Buck said. Bunny stopped in her tracks.

Here it comes. A lecture or my walking papers.

"You have time to sit down and eat. I didn't expect you to be up at the crack of dawn after last night." He took the lid off one of the coffee cups and took a sip. "I rode rodeo for a time. Mornings were always hard after the rush the night before. I'm guessing you had one of those nights."

Bunny stared at him. She could not believe her ears.

"I'm sorry. I don't mean to say what happened to you was like riding a bull. I mean it must have got your heart pumping. Oh, hell, that didn't come out right, either." He rubbed his hands across his face like an embarrassed child.

He was wrong, though. She wasn't insulted. She was proud. The guys Bunny grew up with talked about riding a bull like they were conquering heroes. Even the ones who hit the ground walked taller. Those were the ones who dusted off their hats and strutted out of the ring. Even the losers knew they did something other people were afraid to do. Buck was putting her in that category.

"No," Bunny said, picking up her coffee. "It came out just right."

Buck stared at her like he wanted an explanation, but she didn't think he would have understood. So, she ate a donut with the slightest grin. She drank her coffee. And they talked about the day to come. Bunny had a funny feeling that something big was happening inside of her. Like all her parts were a puzzle in a box. They were finally snapping into place in the way they were meant to. Somehow, not one single piece was missing.

❧

By the time they got to the docks, the line was long, but Buck didn't seem to mind. He was different from her dad in that respect. Her dad acted like the universe purposely put roadblocks in front of him. Buck seemed to expect obstacles, and he just kind of ambled around them, taking life as it came. He worked hard, but he didn't get upset about a setback the way her dad did.

As they waited, he asked about her family and the farm. Bunny gave him the history of the dairy farm as it was told through the entertaining, but not entirely reliable, O'Kelly lore. It was one of those American Dream stories where the great-great-grandfather weathers immigration, discrimination, and poverty to build a foundation his family will grow on for generations. Hard work, wisdom, sacrifice, luck and, above all, God conspiring to provide for every branch of the ever-growing family tree. She left out the part, as her dad always did, about how his mother worked in the dairy all through the Second World War to keep it afloat for her husband when he returned. It hadn't harmed the man's ego to let her do it, but it killed him to give her credit once he came home.

Like her dad, Buck inherited his ranch. The way he said it made her wonder if he thought it was a burden more than a gift. Bunny must have gotten lost talking about home. She turned to Buck, who was staring at her.

"Sorry. It used to annoy my brothers to no end when I would get ramped up like that."

"Don't be sorry. Seems like you really loved that farm." He gave her the smallest smile.

"I did." Bunny looked out the front window. Her chest opened and her heart broke all over again.

"Then why did you leave?" His voice was quiet, like he was trying not to spook her.

"It's not my farm." It came out with an unnecessary harshness. But she didn't apologize. She couldn't explain it to him, but the failure came with a shame she felt, sharp and deep. Buck had faith in her, though only the tiniest seed, in a way her dad never did. She couldn't risk killing it. So, instead, she turned the conversation to the Midnight Sun. While he talked about his ranch, he kept to the edges when it came to his family.

"Connor loved the horses, but he wasn't much for ranching. Oh, but Katie. Katie loved it all. Never complained about a single piece of hay." The lines on his face softened. Bunny memorized the moment. Cruel twist of fate that she hadn't been born to someone like Buck. He broke the connection and rolled his window to adjust the mirror. "Can you see okay?"

Bunny nodded. How had he lost his wife and daughter? Before she had a chance to ask, it was their turn to load the truck. Buck jumped out, a bit too anxious to load the horse.

He guided her back to a parking area on the dock where a long trailer was being off-loaded from the barge. Bunny set the tire blocks and unlatched the rear door to release the ramp. As she filled the feed compartment, Buck walked over to the truck coming off the barge. The Midnight Sun was not the only ranch picking up a horse. The driver backed each animal out of the trailer. Bunny felt their pent-up energy from the long trip. The muscles on their shoulders and haunches flexed as they stomped and pulled at the leads. The driver was calm as he led each one in a circle closer and closer to the trailer. He tied each one off. They were unsteady on their feet, shifting to the right and left, bumping into each other. Bunny was in awe as each man, in turn, waded into the electricity, taking a hold of a beast and leading it away.

The driver looked over Buck's paperwork and pointed to a chestnut stallion. His coat was a rich brown. It shined in the sunlight with glints of auburn satin. He was tall. As Buck approached, the horse seemed to grow a little taller. He pulled against the lead, and when he could not back away, he turned his rump so as to keep an eye on the man. Buck spoke to him as he reached up to stroke the horse's neck. His nostrils flared as he breathed in Buck's scent. Save for the stroke of his hand, Buck stayed still. He inched his way down to the shoulders. The big animal bounced his head, slower and slower until he was still.

Buck ran his hand slowly down the horse's back to his haunches. The horse craned his neck toward his rear, making a weak effort to scoot away. Buck stayed there, stroking the horse until he stopped moving. When it relaxed, Buck moved to the other side and did the same, stroking and stilling the horse.

Bunny was mesmerized by the act. He was gruff and often impatient with her. With the animal, it was like there was nothing else in the world, just him and the beast. He never once looked back at Bunny or at his watch. He ignored the other cowboys picking up their stock. He was unmoved by the impatient driver staring at him, arms crossed at the chest, boot tapping. Bunny was not sure what was passing between Buck and the animal, but something was. An unspoken agreement. A bond of trust. She knew it for sure when he untied the lead and led the animal toward the trailer.

"Say hello to Dante's Desert Flame, Benny." Bunny reached her palm out flat for the horse to smell. His hot breath tickled her hand. With a sniff, he pulled back, head bouncing. "She's okay, Dante." Buck eased his grip on the lead and stroked him with his voice. "War Horse likes her, and that's good enough for me. So, it's going to be good enough for you."

Her stomach clenched. Jake must have told him about her War Horse encounters. Bunny assumed he would be upset with her since it was Katie's horse.

"It's a long haul back. We're going to head over to a friend of mine's place. It will give me a chance to see how he trailers. I'll work him for a bit to get the piss and vinegar out of him. If all that goes well, we'll head for home." Buck had never called it home before. It was always the ranch, the farm, the barn. Bunny hoped it would all go well. She was looking forward to going home.

It took a couple of tries to get Dante to load. Bunny expected, after a few days at sea, he wasn't much interested in going back into a trailer. They didn't have far to go to the arena. She perched on a fence to watch Buck work him. The young stallion took advantage of the lead right away, stomping and shaking his head. Buck didn't seem concerned. He gave the animal a little rope and urged him forward. It was an awkward dance at first. With every step Buck took, the animal countered, sometimes trying to turn, sometimes taking a step back until he figured out that moving forward meant freedom.

Dante tested the waters by hopping about at first. Buck slowed him to a walk when he got out of hand. If he was frustrated with the horse, it didn't show. Bunny gripped the rail, a buzz building in her chest, as the man reined Dante in, then gave him his head and let him run. It was like they were negotiating how much power they were going to give each other. Each one stood confident and tall. They weren't fighting each other. They weren't giving in either, though.

Buck slowed the horse and reeled him in. He led the animal to her. "Dante and I are going to get along fine, I think." As Buck stroked his neck, the tiniest grin stole across his face. "Let's get him dried off and head out." Bunny watched them walk away. It felt so right somehow. Like Buck was made to lead that horse. Whatever it was that he didn't want to talk about disappeared in that ring. She knew the gift of that peace. Somehow, she also knew she would be the one to pick at that wound.

CHAPTER 21

ROCKY 1982

ROCKY FELT THE worm circling his gut. Jeremiah was up to something. No one passed up a sure thing. Mindy was a sure thing. She'd strolled into town from the bush a few months back. Something was off about her. In his experience, white girls raised in the bush were pretty ignorant when it came to life in general. They spent their childhood fetching firewood, cooking, and praying. Real men scared them. Not Mindy. She was bold. Word was, she would go out with darn near anyone. She wasn't particular about the age, either. Rocky wasn't biting, though. He wanted a woman for one thing, and he was straight about that. He would come right out and say it if he had to.

Though, if he thought he had to, he usually walked away. It wasn't worth the energy. Those were the women who would try to convince themselves that every day he stayed, they were one day closer to being a real couple, maybe even a family. He was never taking a step in that direction again. Not one step. In his mind, it was kinder to walk away without a word than to string someone along with his dick until they got tired of waiting for a ring. In his mind, he was doing them a favor.

He got so he could tell, just by watching a woman, if she was still hoping for happy-ever-after. Mindy was not. He watched her night after night tending bar. It wasn't that she wasn't looking for a husband, though. He suspected she was. She treated men like she was shopping for a car. She took a test drive on every last one, and she wasn't buying until she was sure the price was right. What did Mindy think the price of marriage would be?

In his experience, the price was high, and he had no intention of paying it. Not now, not ever again. He'd dodged a bullet once and wasn't taking any chances, especially if it meant losing half his ranch to some piece of tail. He'd made sure Jeremiah and Jesse's mom had known she'd be leaving empty-handed. She didn't deserve to take anything, least of all his ranch. All she had to do was take care of his house, his children, and him. It was a more than fair trade for breaking his back to provide for her.

When Mindy had arrived, he thought he would take a shot. He doubted Jeremiah would go out with her if he had, though. So, he had bided his time as she worked her way through half the town. Now he was glad he did. Rocky was going to need Mindy if his suspicions were right.

CHAPTER 22

BUNNY 1984

Buck checked the latch on the back of the trailer. "Toss me the keys."

"I can drive," Bunny offered.

"I know you can drive, but you're not gonna." He wiped the back of his glove across his brow.

"Why not? I'm fine to drive."

Buck extended his hand, palm up and open. "Quit being a mule. You've got to be tired. Hell, I'm tired."

"I'm not too tired to drive."

"Maybe you aren't. Maybe you are." Buck took his hat off and dragged his hand through his hair before setting it back down. "Look, I'm not taking a chance with this horse. Now give me the keys and get in the truck."

Bunny tossed him the keys and stomped away, but not fast enough to hear him mutter, "Goddamn pain in my ass."

Bunny's body ached, and her head throbbed. She'd never admit it to Buck, but she was grateful for the chance to sleep. She rolled up her sweatshirt, pulled down her cap, and leaned on the door. Before long, the rocking of the truck on the uneven road lulled her to sleep.

She wasn't sure if it was the creaking of the truck door or Buck's knees, but one of them woke her up. As she stretched her neck, she looked down the highway. Other than a run-down gas station that looked days away from being boarded up and a motel that already was, there wasn't much else around. A weathered sign announced the cutoff to Cantwell. Bunny hopped down from the truck and took a minute to shake the sleep out of her legs and back. Buck was at the side of the trailer checking on Dante when she found him.

"Everything alright?" she asked.

"Yeah, I needed a stretch, and I figured he could use some water." He climbed up to the feed compartment with a groan. Bunny smiled as he talked to the horse. "You thirsty, boy? Well, I got some water for ya. Probably not what you're used to, so I put a little molasses in there to sweeten the deal. We're 'bout halfway home. We're gonna have to wait to give you a run 'til we get there. Not safe here. But we'll have a good run later. That's good. Drink that up."

Bunny perched on the fender and closed her eyes. When he stopped talking, she looked over to find him stroking the horse's head as he drank. He showed a tenderness he certainly didn't give to her or Jake. Had he been kind to his kids and wife? She was getting only a glimpse through a keyhole into his life. She didn't know what his gruff exterior was protecting, but that big animal brought down the wall.

"Do you want to drive?" he asked.

The question startled her. Bunny figured now that they had the horse, he would want to drive back.

"Are you sure?"

"I wouldn't have asked if I wasn't." He said it in a matter-of-fact way.

"Yeah, I want to drive." Grateful for his directness, she took the keys and settled in as he locked up the trailer.

They drove in silence for a while. Bunny listened for the horse. At first, she could feel his stomping as the trailer shifted on the hitch, but he settled quickly.

"I never asked. Do you ride?"

Bunny glanced over at him. He was staring straight ahead.

"Yep. My dad is not a horse guy, but my mom loves them. I rode with her mostly."

"What do you ride?"

"I have a Buckskin Quarter Horse gelding, Hawkeye. I've had him since I learned to ride." Before Buck could respond, a wave of sadness slipped out. "I miss him."

"Is he a big horse?"

"No, fifteen hands. His mom's a Palomino. She's a lot taller."

"I've seen you in War Horse's stall."

Bunny tensed at his words.

"War Horse doesn't like most people. He loved Katie. Katie was about the only person he would tolerate, in fact." He looked at his hands. Taking one in the other, he scratched under a nail. "Until you came around. Not sure why, but he seems to like you." The words came out in a pained staccato. "He hasn't been exercised much because he gets aggressive with Jake. I was thinking when we get back, I want to see if he'll let you lunge him. If that works out, maybe you could ride him. He needs to run. He misses being out there with her."

Bunny looked at him. He still faced forward. She wanted to jump up and down and hug him. He was trusting her with the horse, not just any horse. She tamped down her glee, fearing he would change his mind.

"I'd like that." She glanced his way, and he was still looking straight ahead, but she could tell he was smiling.

"Okay then." With that, he leaned against the window and went to sleep.

As she drove down the road, her heart was bursting with pride. Driving his new stallion was big, but exercising his daughter's horse was monumental.

CHAPTER 23

ROCKY 1982

IT DIDN'T TAKE long for Rocky to figure it out. Jeremiah never had much imagination when it came to mischief. Kicking himself for not thinking of it sooner, he remembered back when Jeremiah discovered the old cabin. They'd been out riding together. He must have been little because he wasn't on his own horse yet. Rocky remembered the feeling of his boy in front of him giggling like a little girl as they bounced along. Jeremiah clutched the saddle horn with both hands while Rocky hemmed him in with his arms as they rode along the perimeter of the property together. Rocky was killing two birds: checking the fence line and spending time with his kid. Rebekah was always on him to spend more time with his kids. She didn't get what it took to run a ranch. As he thought about her now, he was still as angry as the day she tried to leave.

He tied his horse up to the railing on the porch like he did that first time with Jeremiah. He wasn't as eager to go through the door as Jeremiah had been on that day. Rocky thought of the little boy pulling himself up the stairs that were as tall as his legs were long. Grabbing the post, Jeremiah had lifted one leg as high as it would go, then he pulled with all his might. Rocky could have helped him, but he believed you had to learn early to struggle for what you wanted in this life. He was raising a man, not a boy.

Rocky yanked on the knob, expecting the resistance of layers of rust. When the mechanism spun beneath his fingers, he knew the cabin was used regularly. He looked down to see the threshold, cleared of the usual berm of dirt that grew through the windswept fall. Stepping inside, he scanned the room. The place was cleaner than it should have been. Jeremiah came up here when he needed to get away, but this was too tidy for him. He walked around the edge of the room. A woodstove sat in the center facing the door, squat and heavy like a bulldog. Rocky crouched down and opened the door to find it full of ash. A pot of water sat on the cooktop. He wanted to fling it across the room.

His eyes were drawn to the corner where a kitchen, cobbled together over decades, stood. A cabinet door hung askew. Rocky opened it with a flick of his index finger. A stack of plates sat on the shelf. The garbage was empty. This cabin had a woman's touch. Anger burned in his throat and chest when he realized which one.

CHAPTER 24

BUNNY 1984

THEY GOT BACK to the ranch late in the evening, but there was still work to be done. Though Buck was fresh from his long nap, Bunny was exhausted. They unloaded the horse, and Buck took Dante to the ring to work him. Bunny could feel his energy as they walked away. Dante was a sight to see. He kicked and hopped around, thrilled to be free. Buck didn't fight him. He held the line confidently, letting him settle to a trot in his own time.

Bunny finished cleaning the trailer, stowed the broom, and climbed on the rail. Watching Dante run, mane swinging and tail bouncing, made her chest swell with joy. He had such power and grace. Bunny could tell by the way he responded to Buck that Dante didn't yet know how much power he had. If Buck ever wanted to ride him, he would have to make sure the animal never figured that out. As Dante transitioned to a canter, his hooves began to grip the earth and pull it behind him. He was made to run.

She hadn't noticed Jake approach until he was leaning on the rail beside her.

"He is something else," she said.

Jake grunted his assent. Or at least Bunny thought it was.

She looked his way and found him grinning ear to ear, silently watching the man and his horse. Had Jake ever smiled that way at a woman?

"You better get some sleep. Your vacation is over and tomorrow starts in a few hours." His words pelted her like sleet, so she turned her back on them. He walked away without another word, and Bunny turned back to the arena. Dante was like a thunderstorm—dangerous and beautiful all at once. She stayed, transfixed, until Buck reeled him in and led him to the barn.

⸙

Despite a lack of sleep, Bunny popped out of bed the next morning, nearly knocking Ruff on the floor. She regretted the jarring motion as every bump and bruise throbbed anew. Ruff was more forgiving, requiring only a quick scratch behind the ears.

"Big day. We've got to get moving, so we can spend some time with your buddy."

By the time she finished the morning feeding and started cleaning the stalls, riders filled the barn. She suspected some came by just to see the new stud. Pretty as Dante was, Bunny was only interested in War Horse.

She left his stall for last. When she got there, Bunny found a Thoroughbred tied to his door. War Horse craned his head over the door to nuzzle the gelding. A woman about Bunny's age was cleaning the big horse's hooves. She was tall, lithe, and porcelain. Save for the flowing locks of blond hair, she could have been the Lovely Sophia's daughter. She rode English and looked the part. Her breeches were clean and pressed, and her boots gleamed. She was struggling with the hoof.

"Do you need some help?" Bunny offered.

The woman looked up and smiled. "No, Sonny and War Horse are old friends, so they get a little excited when they see each other. I shouldn't have brought him down here, but he's even worse if I don't." She dropped the hoof, and the horse nodded as if to say thank you. "I'm Carolina. I've seen you around. You're the new hand."

"Yes. Benny." She wiped her hands on her jeans before taking the woman's hand. "Beautiful horse. I love the name. Sonny's Last Chance." *What an idiot. She knows her horse's name.*

"Turns out it's ironic. He was supposed to be the last offspring of Sonny Come Home. They were hoping for a natural racehorse, but Sonny doesn't have the speed. Needless to say, they kept trying. My good luck, though. Sonny does well jumping and with dressage." A loud snort caught their attention, and they turned to find Sonny and War Horse muzzle to muzzle.

"He bites," Bunny warned.

"Let me guess. That's what Jake told you?" Carolina shook her head and rolled her eyes. "Yes. He bites. He bites Jake. War Horse does not like Jake. Not sure why. Jake has such a sunny disposition." Bunny laughed along with Carolina. "I rode with Katie all the time. War Horse is as gentle as they come."

"He seems to like me," Bunny said, reaching up to stroke his head.

"I bet he does." She spoke with a note of sadness. "We should ride sometime." With that, she saddled up in one graceful leap and trotted off to the arena.

Bunny didn't know what to make of the offer. Carolina was everything she was not. The Lovely Sophia and Michael O'Kelly would have been so proud to have her as their daughter. Bunny brushed the dirt off her jeans and tightened her ponytail. Carolina struck her as the type of girl who was always socially correct. Not a hair out of place, and never unkind. Bunny would bet she always said just the right thing at just the right time. She certainly would never have embarrassed them by coming home with cow manure smeared on her boots and silage stains on her jeans.

Bunny turned to War Horse. "Well, pal. Once I get your stall mucked out, you and I are gonna to get some exercise." War Horse stuck out his neck and grabbed her hat in his mouth, pulling her ponytail out with it. Unruly hair covered her face. She quickly tried to corral it with her hands.

Jake walked by as she wrestled her locks. "I told you he was going to bite you." Jake gave Bunny a self-satisfied grin.

"He didn't bite me. He stole my hat." Bunny reached out and grabbed the hat from War Horse's mouth. He gave it up without a fight. "You never told me he was a thief. He's just being playful."

"Buck says you're going to work him today. Do you want help?" He leaned against the wall and crossed his arms over his chest. It didn't seem like a genuine offer. More like a dare.

"No, I've got this. Thanks." Bunny tightened her ponytail and pulled it through her cap. Without looking back, she opened War Horse's stall and clicked her tongue at him. He moved to the paddock and let her clean. Her work slowed as a sick feeling came over her. What if she couldn't handle the big horse? What if something happened to War Horse? He was all Buck had left of Katie.

Bunny stood there holding the pitchfork, frozen. War Horse nudged her toward the door. She took that as a sign that he wanted to go for a run rather than a sign that he wanted her out of his stall. Ruff, who was waiting outside the door, confirmed it with a bark.

In the tack room, front and center, Bunny found War Horse's gear. A western saddle perched below an English one. Bridles and halters hung neatly above them. Ribbons of every color peppered the wall. While the blue ribbons far outnumbered all the others, the rainbow told a story of someone who worked their way to the top. Not a natural, but a fighter. War Horse's gear had a layer of dust that the others did not. Had he been out of his paddock since Katie died? Bunny felt like a thief as she selected the lunge line, halter, and whip.

"Katie kept some gloves in her tack chest. I'll get them for you," Buck murmured. Bunny could tell this was hard for him.

"Buck, I don't have to do this if you're not comfortable."

"No, I want you to. She loved that horse, and it pains me to see him in that paddock. I should have done it myself." Buck scanned the shrine of awards framing her saddles. Bunny could feel his pride swelling. "She loved this life. Hell, she'd have slept in the tack room if I'd let her." With his back to her, he lifted the lid and dug around. "Truth is, I just couldn't. Every time I went in there, my heart broke again. It's been two years. Jake's tried, but that horse does not like him. War Horse holds a mean grudge." Buck handed her the gloves. "Anyway, it's time someone else tried. He's taken a shine to you. I think we should see how he does. Hell, we might even get you in the saddle."

Buck followed her down to the stall and watched as she brought the horse out. She brushed him down and attached the lunge line. They walked out to the arena slowly. Buck took a seat on the rails to watch. At first, the big Appaloosa danced around her as she tried to let out the line. Bunny wanted to avoid using the whip, but there was no way to get around it. She flicked it and he hopped.

"Settle down." Bunny kept her voice low and steady.

He turned in to listen. Bunny clicked her tongue and pointed to his shoulder. He stepped out. Like dancers fighting to lead, they took turns stepping together and away until he was trotting in a big circle. She gave him more line, and he started to canter. She slowed him, then brought him back up. He paid attention and eventually the whip hung still in her hand. He was out of shape, but it didn't hold him back. If Bunny hadn't stopped him, he would have run himself into the ground.

War Horse walked in and faced her. They stood there silently staring at each other, his black face shining with sweat. Without warning, he shook his mane and reared up with a roar. Buck jumped off the rails. But as fast as War Horse went up, he came down. He stood there for a moment. Then he reached out his muzzle to her belly and gave her a shove. It reminded her of her brother Patrick when he played a mean trick on her. His way of saying he was sorry was to give Bunny a shove and say, *Are we good?* Bunny thought this was War Horse's way of asking that same question.

"Buck, I'm fine. He's fine. Slow down or you'll startle him."

He stopped in his tracks.

She rubbed the horse's head. "You're okay. You just got a little too excited. We're okay. What do you say we go get you cleaned up?" As she turned toward the barn, Jake was on the rails watching. As soon as he caught her eye, he shook his head and walked away.

Carolina returned as Bunny was washing down War Horse. Bunny offered to move since she was a paying customer, but Carolina insisted they finish.

"He looks happy." She tied Sonny to the stall and took his saddle off. Perching on a bale of hay, Carolina stroked his head. "I still miss her. I guess I always will. I bet he does too."

"I bet Buck and Jake do too, though they haven't come right out and said it."

"Doesn't surprise me. Guys are terrible at feelings. Buck just kind of folded. Of course, his heart broke when Jodie died. Katie was always his sidekick. Her death did him in. Connor went off to college like nothing happened, but they were close. And Jake is just angry."

"Was Jake dating Katie?"

"No. He wished, though. Buck and Connor bought the big brother act, but he isn't fooling anyone else. Jake was in love with her. Katie wasn't interested in him, anyway. Truth be told, he kind of gave her the creeps."

Bunny finished cleaning up War Horse and led him to his stall. Carolina was washing down Sonny. Bunny naturally fell into helping her. She didn't have a lot of girlfriends, mainly because she preferred hanging out with the guys on the farm, but Carolina was easy to talk to. Bunny didn't get that feeling she usually got around other women that she was a hinny in a herd of Palominos.

"We should go for a ride together," Carolina offered.

"War Horse isn't quite ready."

"Oh, sure." She looked disappointed, though Bunny wasn't sure why. Carolina Browning didn't strike her as a girl who had a shortage of people to ride with. Still, she had a hangdog look on her face.

"Maybe in a couple of days. I want to ride him in the ring a few times before we go out on the trail."

A grin blossomed across Carolina's face. Bunny shook her head. What would it be like to be so free?

CHAPTER 25

KATIE 1982

KATIE WAS LATE. Buck had taken longer than normal to drink himself into oblivion. As the years wore on since her mom's passing, she quit fighting his drinking so long as he stayed sober during the day and drank at home. Losing two parents would be too much to bear, even for Katie. Though she didn't feel right about taking advantage of his drinking, her chances to meet Jeremiah were waning now that winter loomed. Not even Buck was drunk enough to believe she would go for a horseback ride alone in the late evening this time of year.

She followed Jeremiah's tracks to the cabin. His truck was much bigger than hers, so she hugged the rut on the driver's side. It was cold enough to freeze, but there wasn't enough snow for Katie to put it in four-wheel drive yet. She thought about not showing up. That might have forced him to come for her, but the possibility he might not come at all pained her. Like every Miller before her, she decided to meet it head-on. Better to end it than live in this purgatory. She parked her little truck next to his, well hidden from the road.

Katie sat in the cab of her truck watching the smoke drift from the woodstove pipe in the roof, saddened this was the place it might end. The snow crunched beneath her feet when she got out of the truck. She closed the door and stood, letting the cold air bite into her cheeks. Resolute, she headed for the door. Ten feet into the journey, a twig cracked behind her and she froze.

"Jeremiah?"

She searched the night, but nothing moved. If it was an animal, she wouldn't see it until it was on her. Halfway to the cabin, she wavered. Could she reach the truck faster or the front door? To her left, she heard the crunch of heavy footfalls. Not one but three steps broke through the silence. *Just my luck. I am smack in the middle of a bear and her cub.* All the advice her father ever gave her about wild animals turned to mist in her head. She ran for the door. As she raised her hand to knock, Jeremiah opened it. Seeing him stopped her in her tracks. He looked so relieved to find her standing there. Jeremiah reached out, but Katie brushed past him. She went to the stove and closed her eyes, letting the heat seep into her.

"There's something out there."

Jeremiah eased the door open and slipped out. She could hear him walk from one end of the porch to the other. By the time her heart had slowed, Jeremiah was back.

"Animals likely. Whatever it was, it's gone now." He closed the door and stood silently behind her. As she warmed herself, her chestnut hair fell in rivers down her shoulders. She felt safe, hidden behind the cascade.

"I'm sorry I'm late. Dad picked tonight to give abstinence a try." She flipped her hair over her shoulders.

"I was beginning to wonder if you were coming." He looked down at his boots.

She stared at him until he lifted his eyes to hers.

"Oh," he said. "I see."

"Look, I don't think I can do this anymore."

"What? This? Coming to the cabin?"

"No. This . . . us. I can't keep sneaking around. Look, Jeremiah, I love you. I wish I didn't because I know you don't feel the same. But I do. I can't watch you flirt with Mindy. I can't keep this from my dad. So, unless something has changed for you, I'm done." She rubbed her arms over her coat, more for comfort than warmth.

"Mindy doesn't mean anything. No one means anything but you."

"You can't say it. Can you?"

"Katie." He hesitated. "I love you. I do."

She pulled her truck keys from her pocket. "Then why does this have to be a secret? I don't care if my dad approves. I'm an adult. You're an adult. You said so yourself."

"You don't understand." He slumped against the wall.

"No, I don't understand. But I feel like I'm your dirty little secret. Like you're ashamed."

"You know that isn't true." He pushed off the wall and started toward her but stopped when she put her hands out.

"If it's not, then let's tell your dad about me."

"You don't understand. It'll ruin everything. And I'll lose you." He looked as if he might cry.

"I'm not your mom, Jeremiah. I'm not going to leave because your dad is an ass."

"You don't understand."

"I guess I don't. But you have a decision to make. Either we walk out of here a couple and tell our dads, or I walk out of here alone."

She held his eyes. He didn't say another word. Not as she buttoned her coat. Not when he followed her out the door. Not when she was sobbing behind the wheel. He just turned away, slamming the door behind him.

CHAPTER 26

BUNNY 1984

A s SOON AS Bunny had the door halfway open, Ruff shoved past her. She knew where he was going and wished she could join him, but she headed for the feed room. In a few weeks, Bunny had a system, and based on the whinnies and stomping, War Horse and his friends knew it. She loaded the feed cart and headed for his stall. He was the first to be fed and the last to be cleaned. Her dad would have called it discipline, but he was all about the stick. Bunny was all about the carrot.

She grabbed a flake of hay and slid open the stall door. Unlike the other animals, War Horse stood centered in the doorway.

"I have your breakfast. You want to back up?"

He gave her the chance to come clean. When staring Bunny in the eye did not move her, he put his nose against her coat pocket and gave her a nudge.

"You're going to make the other horses jealous. Back up and I'll give it to you."

He considered her for a moment, then moved from the door.

She put the alfalfa in his feed bucket, but War Horse showed no interest. He had his eye on her pocket.

"You are mercenary!" She looked around and stilled to listen to the barn. Satisfied they were alone, she pulled an apple from her coat and held it out in her flattened palm. She rubbed his forehead as he pulverized the fruit. "Eat it all. We don't need any evidence of my crime." He seemed happy to oblige.

War Horse kept tabs on her as she cleaned the stalls. The closer Bunny got to him, the more he stomped and neighed. She loved that about him. He didn't hide how he felt. Ruff, however, was more reserved in the barn. He would stand guard at War Horse's stall, monitoring her progress like he thought she might forget him. They were a study in contrast: Ruff, a compact ball of snow-white fluff, and War Horse, a tall slab of speckled ebony. Bunny could tell they were fast friends. Everything led back to Katie. Ruff and War Horse were no exception.

"It's your turn, and then we're gonna get a saddle on you." War Horse moved toward the paddock. "Jeez. You made a mess here. We may have to cut back on the apples, buddy." The snort was probably coincidental, but it made Bunny laugh. "My brother Mick would like you. Ironically, they should have named him War Horse. He's such a hardass." She shoveled the last of the manure into the wheelbarrow and dropped the pitchfork on top. War Horse approached, demanding an ear scratching for his troubles. "You remind me of him. He doesn't like everybody. Hell, he doesn't like most people. But if he likes you, you get the best side of him."

"Hey, Dr. Doolittle! Are you done with your chores?" Jake called to her.

Bunny leaned into War Horse and whispered, "He's such an ass."

"I asked if you were done." Jake stalked her way.

"I'm done as soon as I dump this load. Then I'm going to exercise War Horse."

"You know, it would go a lot faster if you didn't carry on a conversation with the animals."

"Well, Jake, turns out I can talk and shovel at the same time. It's a gift. Besides, I only really have a conversation with War Horse. All the others just get a polite greeting. You know. Good morning. How's your day going?" She rubbed his cheek and turned to pick up the load. Jake stood in the door, blocking her way.

"You think you're funny, but you're a pain in the ass, and you don't belong here."

Bunny stood her ground. She set the wheelbarrow down and prayed her face wasn't giving away her fear. "I worked for Michael O'Kelly my whole life. I never missed a day. I never backed down. So, if you think you're going to run me off, you're going to have to up your game a notch." She picked up the wheelbarrow again and took a step forward. He put his hands on the front to stop her. He leaned over the load of horse apples until his face was a foot from hers.

"Well, if he didn't run you off and you never back down, what are you doing here?" He shoved off the cart.

"I need to go dump this. You want to move?" She stared at him until he walked away. Bunny's hands were shaking when she picked up the wheelbarrow. Though she would never let him know, Jake James hit a nerve.

Bunny tied War Horse up outside the tack room. The periodic stomp of his hooves told her he was impatient. Every day, he had been getting stronger. He was a smart animal, anticipating the changes in pace from her smallest movement. It was time to see how he would take the saddle.

Bunny stood staring at the two saddles hanging on the wall.

"Katie preferred Western," Jake barked.

"Damn, Jake. Don't sneak up on me." She leaned down to catch her breath. Apparently, Buck hadn't told him about her run in when they were in Anchorage. She had no intention of sharing. He didn't need any more ammunition. Bunny realized how protected she was on the ranch. Ruff was always at her side. Buck watched over her in his own way. No strangers wandered in. She hadn't ventured into town alone since they got back. "Good thing. So do I." She flashed him a smile and pulled the saddle from the rack on the wall. When she turned back, he was gone and Ruff had replaced him in the doorway. He pranced in place, rushing Bunny along.

War Horse took the blanket with a snort. When he saw the saddle, he danced a little sidestep away from her. Ruff let out a mighty woof, and War Horse stopped in his tracks. Bunny hefted the saddle onto his back. Though it had been some time, he knew to bloat as soon as she cinched it up. She let that go.

"He's looking good," Carolina said as she brought Sonny out. "Are you riding today?"

"Not yet. I want to lunge him with the saddle first to see how he does. If all goes well, I'll ride him in the ring tomorrow."

Carolina bounced on her toes, and Bunny thought she might yell, *Give me a W!* Bunny turned her head to hide her smile as she led War Horse to the ring. After tightening the cinch, she let out the line slowly to match his pace. He didn't seem to mind the saddle. In fact, he pranced a bit as he trotted around the ring. After a few minutes, she brought him in and tightened it a little more. He was breathing too hard to fight her.

"Okay, big guy. Let's do it." Bunny let the line out a bit, and soon he was pulling it through her grip, nearly hugging the edge of the ring. He loped around the ring with such grace. It was like he was showing her what it would feel like to ride him—fast but smooth, like riding a wave. She let him lather, then slowed him to cool off. He responded without argument. Bunny felt like they were building a trust. He had already given it to her. But she hadn't given it to him. Bunny reeled War Horse in. He lumbered toward her, planting his head in her belly. She repaid him by rubbing his cheeks. When she turned to lead him back to the barn, she found Buck, Jake, and Carolina all watching her.

"What? You've never seen a horse lunged before?" she asked.

Jake turned and walked away. Buck gave her a big smile and tipped his hat to her. The gesture exploded in her chest.

Carolina let out an exuberant "yippee!" and rode off on Sonny.

Carolina was going to be a challenge to figure out. As she stood there, a smile washed across Bunny's face. War Horse broke her reverie with a raspberry to her cheek.

"Let's get you cleaned up. You need a good night's sleep. We're going to ride tomorrow."

CHAPTER 27

ROCKY 1982

ROCKY HEARD THEM fighting through the old windows of the cabin. From the pain and anger he had seen on her face in the bar, he already knew Katie was in love with Jeremiah. He was furious his son had deceived him, but even more so when he realized he loved her too. His boy had always been a little weak, like his mother. He guessed getting rid of her hadn't toughened up Jeremiah like he thought it would. Rocky was tempted to put him in his place. But he knew firsthand how a man could be led around by his dick for a woman he loved. To be sure Katie would stay away from him, he would have to scare her off. As he saw in her eyes that night in the bar, it wouldn't be too hard. She was already scared of him.

Rocky raced through the woods back to his truck. Worried Jeremiah might come after her and catch him in the turnaround, he drove out with his headlights off and his foot on the gas. His truck was invisible. He had driven the road a million times and didn't need headlights to navigate it. As he hit the gas, desperate to get on the highway, he slid around the last turn. His front tires gripped a patch of clear roadway, sending his rear out from under him. Rocky stepped on the gas, grateful it was in four-wheel drive. The snowplow blade on the front of the truck nearly bounced him out of his seat when the truck hit the highway. He gunned it.

The snow glowed in the moonlight, so it was a mile before he noticed his lights were still off. As he turned them on, she was there, half off the road. He had only a second to register her form hunched over in the front seat.

CHAPTER 28

JAKE 1982

Jake walked Dusty down the aisle. He stopped to check the latch on each stall as he passed. Buck trusted Katie, but he was blind where she was concerned. With each passing day, she was more and more distracted. He'd hoped the end of the fair would be the end of them. Jeremiah would move on.

He thought about calling Connor. He couldn't see a way of doing it that did not end in getting fired. He could find another job, but he could not stand the thought of not seeing her every day. If she could just see him, not as the guard her brother left behind but as the man he was. He was a good man, a strong man. Jeremiah never even took her out in public, like he was ashamed of her. Jake imagined their future together. If she married him, she wouldn't have to work the ranch. She could ride and teach their kids to ride. He would help Buck build the ranch back up.

He tied Dusty off and went back to close the barn door. At the big house, an engine turned over. A powder blue pickup, headlights off, creeped beneath the floodlight. Bees swarmed in his chest as Katie pulled out. The lights were out on the main floor, which meant Buck was either asleep or drunk. That had to stop. He had to find a way to get him back on track. In the meantime, Katie needed sorting out. Maybe tonight was the night for that. It was too late to be going into town. She definitely wasn't spending time at the Double J. That left the cabin. He led Dusty back out and mounted up.

✧

Jake made good time, though he had to be careful. The snow had quit falling, leaving a dusting on the trail. He'd have a hard time explaining why he was out here if Dusty stepped in a hole. He smelled the wood burning long before he reached the cabin. He came in on the back side, slowing to skirt the road for coverage in the birch stand. He stopped when a truck door shut. Slowing his breathing, he relaxed in the saddle, hoping it would still the horse. A twig snapped in the distance and Dusty's ears shifted forward. Looking into the darkness, shadows in the trees shifted. Dusty stomped his hooves, but Jake held him.

Though the words were muffled, Katie's hurt drilled him through the timbers. He wanted to break in. Then she would know, though, and she would never forgive him. His gut soured. He moved the horse closer to the cabin. When the door slammed, Dusty jumped back a step. Before he could dismount, Katie's truck came to life and tore down the road. Jake followed.

C H A P T E R   29

BUNNY 1984

S RUFF LAY snoring next to her, oblivious to her restlessness, Bunny tossed and turned. Somehow, riding War Horse seemed so much bigger than riding her own horse back home. Bunny yearned to tell her mom all about it. She wanted to tell her how he let only her work him—how Jake was afraid of him, but she walked right up to him that first day. In exchange, she wanted her mom to tell her everything was going to be fine tomorrow when she rode him, that she was strong enough and skilled enough. Bunny was ashamed of the wanting. Though that wanting threatened to spill out of her heart, it would surely become lodged in her throat. Though they shared a love of riding, it was all they shared. That just wasn't enough.

The alarm clock emitted a reproachful, red glow. It was minutes from midnight, and she couldn't take it any longer. She threw the covers off and sat on the edge of the bed. Ruff made a cursory glance her way and returned to snoring. *I'll be useless in the morning—or worse, dangerous.* Scanning the room for something—anything—to read, she remembered the heaviest box. Maybe an encyclopedia would put her to sleep.

She leaned over the smaller boxes and picked at the tape seal of the largest one until it tipped loose. Bunny pulled the flap toward her and felt around until she found the spine of a book. A musty scent preceded it. *National Velvet*—a gift from her own father she'd misunderstood. Clearly, he'd never read the book. She sank to the steps, once again toppling the boot box full of pictures. Sweeping them into a misaligned pile, she thumbed through the stack, flipping them upright and forward. School pictures of Katie and Connor, she assumed, framed the years. Snapshots chronicled the growing seasons of hay, horses, and children. In every picture, the subjects were touching each other. A hug. An arm across the shoulder. Working side by side, playing eye to eye. Envy bubbled up inside of Bunny. The woman and the girl smiling at the camera, a bale of hay passing between them. The sight of them working together gripped Bunny's heart. She had never had the chance.

The Lovely Sophia had never set one foot in the dairy. She once told Bunny her mother warned her if she milked one cow, shoveled one fork of silage, cleaned one stall, she would be working in that barn every day for the rest of her life. The Lovely Sophia had no intention of spending one minute there. She was more than happy to cook three hot meals a day for her hungry brood. Sophia didn't mind housework. She minded, very much, mud and cow manure.

Despite her best efforts to shoehorn her daughter into a dress or ballet shoes, Bunny insisted on wearing a baseball cap, jeans, and boots and chasing after her dad and big brothers. She loved the lumbering, doe-eyed cows, and the smell of tall grass. Her heart pounded when she waded into the river of snowmelt after a long day of haying. Bunny never passed on the chance to shoot cans off the fence posts. By the time she was five, her mom gave up on trying to corral her in the house when the boys headed to the barn. Bunny was fast, and Sophia couldn't watch every door. It wasn't opportunity but obstinance, on each of their parts, that separated them.

She couldn't be like her mom, though she knew it would be easier on her in so many ways. When they were little and lined up in the mudroom to shed their dirty clothes before heading for the bath, Bunny longed for the laughter and teasing Sophia gave her brothers. In the catalog of her mother's rules, the first was girls do not get muddy. She couldn't adhere to any of them, least of all this one. The list became a scorecard for how wrong Bunny felt in the world.

If her alien interior was not enough, the mirror made the image crystal clear. Her mother had a natural elegance to her that Bunny lacked. Where Bunny would stomp into the room, ponytail bobbing, Sophia would glide effortlessly across the floor like a ballroom dancer, curls flowing like water. She was tall and slender, while Bunny took after her Irish father, whose genes favored women born to thatch a roof or haul in a fishnet. Bunny had her wavy hair, but it was ginger to her mother's shiny chestnut. She'd inherited two things from her mother: her prominent bumpy nose and her short fuse. The rest was all her dad. She confounded them both.

Sometimes her father would make her spend the day with her mom.

She waited a long time for you, he'd say. *I made her give me four boys first because I knew she would stop as soon as she had you, her precious girl.*

He didn't understand what Bunny did—she was not the daughter Sophia had been waiting for. Though she tried to enjoy shopping or painting their nails together, in the end, Sophia would always give up and send her out to *play* in the barn.

The only time that wrongness slipped off Bunny was when

they were riding. When she swung into the saddle, she felt like she was a part of the animal. Bunny could not go fast enough or far enough. It was also the rare time she felt her mom let go. When Sophia was on her horse, they were majestic. She rolled with his gait like the wind across a hayfield. Her mother loved to run and taught Bunny the joy of that.

It was also the one thing her mother would not acquiesce, and so the one thing Bunny admired about her. Her dad said horses ate your hay and never gave you anything in return. Cows, on the other hand, gave you milk and more cows. And when they quit doing that, they gave you steaks. He wouldn't let them keep the horses at the dairy, so Sophia rented a pasture down the road. Bunny sided with her mom on this point. All animals were magnificent. But horses were the most magnificent of all. They were strong, wild, and free—unrestrained by their breed, unfettered by their gender.

Bunny could have picked up the phone. But she didn't. Sophia might understand the joy of riding, but she wouldn't understand what it meant to ride this horse. She wouldn't be able to see how Buck had come to count on her, like his own daughter. Missing the point would sully it for Bunny. So, she tucked herself back into bed. As she rolled over to hug Ruff, Bunny said a prayer that she wouldn't screw up.

CHAPTER 30

KATIE 1982

KATIE WAS SURE she was not alone, but she didn't have the strength to open her eyes to check. She gasped for air. Her memory came in flashes. The world spun around her. An animal half in the road. Had she hit it? She searched her chest for the seat belt but could not find it. Why had she taken it off? The animal. She couldn't leave an animal dying on the road. Even without the seat belt, she couldn't move. Reaching for the door handle, she cried out. She searched her mind. *Whose horse was it? Brown, like dirt.* A sharp pain shot through her head, the back throbbing. Warm blood trickled down her face and neck.

Somewhere in the distance of her consciousness, she knew the engine had died. A click of the ignition bounced around her head, and she reached out, grasping rough fabric. *Carhartt, brown duck. Dad?* She didn't have the strength to hold on to it. A cutting chill replaced the hot air. *Please don't let it be Thunderbird. It would break Jeremiah's heart.* With every breath, it took more effort to get air. Katie felt like she was underwater, drowning. She clenched her fists and there was a sharp pain in her left hand. Letting it fall open, she released the object from her grip.

She prayed for Jeremiah to save her. Then she prayed he would not see her like this. An engine turned over nearby, and she tried to call out, but she was too tired. As the cold needled into her skin, tears seeped from her eyes. She knew she would not see her dad or her brother or War Horse or Ruff ever again. It took all her energy to breathe. Still, it wasn't enough. She willed the pain to stop. Then she begged God to bring it back. In the last moments, she wondered if she was going to see her mom.

C H A P T E R 31

BUNNY 1984

BUNNY HUSTLED THROUGH her chores the next day, itching to ride War Horse. She hoped she wasn't too different from Katie in the saddle. She didn't know why, but she had this feeling she might somehow break the spell. Like she had this connection to him, but he was going to find out she wasn't Katie. All that good stuff would be ruined.

As she saddled him, she gave him a pep talk.

"So, today's the day, big guy. We're going to start slow, in the ring. If you're feeling good, you let me know, and we'll head to the arena. No hurry." She cinched the saddle and rubbed his belly. "You know I'm not Katie. I know you miss her. I'm sorry about that. But I know you want to ride. So, unless you want Jake to take a crack at it, I'll have to do." War Horse shook his head. She laughed.

Bunny led him out to the ring. She checked the girth strap. It was loose, so she walked him around the ring. When she tightened it, he shook his head. Bunny chose to see it as a good sign. He would sense any fear, so she pushed it out with her breath.

"We've got this." She said it to herself as much as to War Horse. Bunny put her left foot in the stirrup and, with a giant bounce, swung into the saddle. He took a stutter step forward but stopped with her gentle, "Whoa." Bunny found her seat and urged him forward. They took the first round at a walk. She could tell he was holding back. It didn't take much to get him to pick up the pace. She fell into rhythm with him and closed her eyes.

"You always ride with your eyes closed?" Buck called out, startling her.

"Sorry. I was getting the feel of him." She stopped by the rail.

"You need to ease up on the reins. Trust him a bit."

"We'll get there. He wants to run. I think I'll head over to the arena."

Buck nodded. He walked beside them, one hand on the bridle, without speaking. Bunny bristled at first but then sensed it had nothing to do with her. When they got to the arena, she leaned over and unlatched the gate. He stepped aside and let them through. In the corner of her eye, she saw Buck reach out to touch War Horse as they passed.

At one end, Sonny and Carolina circled a set of jumps, studying the practice course. She looked anything but fragile on the large animal. War Horse whinnied, and Sonny slowed to look at them. Carolina waved and brought the animal back in line. Bunny turned War Horse away. She brought him up slowly from a walk, and by the time they were loping, she had relaxed into his gait. He responded to cues without hesitation. Bunny knew he was born for this.

Buck stayed to watch, one boot on the rail, chin resting on his forearms, hat tipped back. As Bunny brought War Horse to the gate, he was staring beyond the arena, a pained look on his face.

"I think he's had enough," she said.

"I expect so." He hesitated like he was forcing himself to

speak. "He looks good. You've done a nice job." Buck had a pensive way of announcing things, like he was still mulling them over as they slipped past his lips. "Might have you exercise some other horses."

"I'd like that, as long as I can keep riding War Horse."

He patted the horse's neck and looked up at her. He didn't answer, but his mouth turned up in a smile that went all the way to his eyes.

Bunny thought about dismounting at the gate, but she wanted every last second in the saddle. Buck must have sensed it because he opened the gate before she could ask him to. As they headed for the barn, War Horse walked a little taller. Bunny believed animals had emotions and personalities. He showed her his, prancing into the barn, head high, eyes forward.

Carolina and Sonny weren't far behind them. Bunny was putting the tack away when they got to the barn. Carolina tied Sonny up next to War Horse, and they nickered at each other.

"I wish I knew what they were saying to each other."

Bunny laughed. "I was thinking the same thing. I'm not sure I want to know though, since he has to haul me around."

"You have to be kidding me." Carolina stopped to look at her. "You're perfect."

Bunny rolled her eyes. "You're perfect." She pulled the brush down the horse's shoulder. "I, on the other hand, am sturdy. I am strong. I am good stock."

"Well, that all may be true. And it's also true that you're perfect." She picked up a brush and pointed it at Bunny. "And don't roll your eyes at me. You looked great up there." Carolina beamed.

Bunny let it go. "It felt good. Better than good. It felt great."

"War Horse will be ready for the trail soon."

"I want to work him in the arena a couple more times. I think by this weekend I can at least take him out around the pastures." Bunny stopped brushing, but War Horse leaned into her, urging her on.

"A couple of my girlfriends and I are going to the Back Forty for dinner and a beer Friday night. You should come." Carolina's eyes lit up like it was Christmas, but a bar was the last place Bunny wanted to go. It must have shown on her face. "You'll love it. And you'll love my friends. Come on, you've been cooped up on this ranch for weeks. You need a girls' night out."

Bunny's stomach clenched. She couldn't tell her what happened in Anchorage. She couldn't tell her she'd never had a girls' night out. Whether it was her childlike enthusiasm or the hopeful look she wore, Bunny also couldn't say no.

"Okay. But I can't stay late. I have the morning feeding."

"Yay! Should I pick you up?"

The thought of that sent a wave of panic rippling through her. She had an overwhelming need to be in control of the situation. "I'll meet you. That way you won't have to leave early for me."

"I don't mind." She sounded hurt.

"I appreciate that, but I'll feel bad if I ruin your fun. I'll meet you there." Carolina let it go. Bunny started searching for an escape route.

CHAPTER 32

JEREMIAH 1982

THE FIRE BURNED out, but Jeremiah hardly noticed. All the heat went out of him when Katie walked out the door. He lied to himself at first. *See, women leave, even if you love them.* The words swirled in his head until he couldn't think. He stared at his boots on the graying plank floor. The aged wood and scuffed leather made him think of his dad. The bitterness of Rocky's solitary existence desiccated his heart. Jeremiah could still feel his, though. As the temperature dropped, it ached with the pain of losing her.

Jeremiah had been wrong all along. Women didn't leave. Men pushed them away. Katie had stood in front of him, willing to face the wrath of their fathers. It was he who lacked the courage. He knew what he had to do. He would go to her house and beg her to take him back, in front of her father if he had to. His dad was right. He wasn't the man Katie needed. But she was the right woman to help him become that man.

Jeremiah grabbed his keys from the table and headed out to his truck. He waited as long as he could for it to warm up, but he left before it was blowing hot air. Though the chill bit into his cheeks, he didn't care. He didn't deserve to be comfortable. The snow had begun falling again. To be safe, he put the truck in four-wheel drive and slowed as he approached the highway. With the road to himself, he turned on his KC lights.

Before long, they lit up her truck, fused to the pole, roof and bed dusted with snow. As he got closer, he saw blood splattered on the back window. Nearly sliding into her, he pulled over and jumped out, leaving the door open and the truck running. As he ran to her, he screamed her name. Jeremiah almost lost his footing. Slipping forward, he caught the door handle and pulled himself up. He leaned against the cab, staring at her hunched frame. As he opened the door, the only words he could form were "no, no, no."

He reached beneath the seat to ease her back, piercing his finger on a piece of metal. Jeremiah gave no mind to the pain. He had to see her. Easing her shoulders back, he found her mouth crusted with blood. He hugged her lifeless body to his chest, then he slid to the snowy ground, wailing. Grief ripped through him. He had to get help. He tried to close the door, but it wouldn't latch. He hefted himself into the cab of his truck and drove home.

❦

His dad sat at the kitchen table finishing a beer.

"What the hell happened to you?"

"I have to call the police. There's been an accident." Jeremiah fought the tears back. His father hated men who cried. But he couldn't talk without sobbing. "Katie Miller is dead. She had an accident on the highway. I have to call the police."

Rocky eyed him. "Think about this, son. Look at yourself. You're covered in blood."

Jeremiah stopped and looked down. Suddenly exhausted, he dropped into a chair. "I loved her, and I ran her off."

"What are you sayin', boy?"

"We can talk about that later. I need to call the cops." Jeremiah couldn't think. He started for the phone on the wall.

"Stop. Listen to me!" Rocky shouted. "You say you loved her. You come home covered in her blood. Did you hurt that girl, boy?"

"How can you even think that?"

"What do you think the cops are going to think?"

"She was in a car accident."

"Get smart. They're going to think you did this to her. They always look at the boyfriend. A moose probably ran out in front of her."

Jeremiah was stunned. "I can't leave her out there."

"What's done is done. You can't help her now. But you don't have to be a martyr for that girl, either."

Jeremiah dropped his head and shoved his hands through his hair. Grabbing fistfuls, he gripped them until his scalp burned.

"Take your clothes off and give them to me. Go take a shower," his father ordered.

"What are you going to do?"

"I'm going to burn them. You need to get your head straight. Someone knows you were dating her. Count on it. You need to brace for a visit from the cops. Now, go get cleaned up and go to bed."

In a daze, Jeremiah stripped and gave Rocky his clothes. He choked back his tears thinking of her frozen on the side of the road. It made him sick, but his dad was right. He needed to have his head straight, or he was going to look guilty. Katie's father would come after him if he found out they'd been together.

C H A P T E R 33

B UNNY 1984

B UNNY STOOD IN the doorway searching for Carolina. It was dark inside the bar, and before her eyes adjusted, someone bellowed, "Shut the door!" Scanning the crowd, she stiffened. Her dad's voice echoed in her head, telling her to get back on the horse. She willed her feet to move.

Carolina was at a table toward the back with three other women. It was going to be a long walk. She lifted her chin and looked straight ahead. Before her first footfall, Bunny ran smack into an oak with a head and froze in her tracks. It was her fault, and she wanted to apologize, but panic grasped at the words and pulled them back into her belly.

He touched her shoulder. "Are you okay?"

She jerked away from his hand. "Uh . . . yes. I'm so sorry. I didn't mean to run into you."

"No harm done." His eyebrows knit together like they were holding back a question. She flashed him a weak smile and headed for Carolina's table.

Bunny caved in on herself as she walked through the crowd.

Though she had put on a clean pair of jeans and boots, she looked every bit the ranch hand. The women she passed were every kind of beautiful, from the dewy, natural outdoor beauties to the rodeo queens. Carolina looked chic even in old boots and jeans. Her friends were no different. Bunny had been sure the one place she would fit in would be a bar in Alaska. Yet again, she felt like a penguin in a flock of flamingos. As she was turning to go back to the ranch, Carolina stood and waved at her. When she didn't wave back, Carolina whistled across the room. It stopped her in her tracks.

A leggy waitress with the biggest, blondest hair Bunny had ever seen stopped in front of her. "You must be looking for Carolina." She looked her up and down like a pawnbroker assessing a discarded wedding ring. Bunny looked down at the woman's shiny boots, wishing she had stayed home. She mumbled yes and hustled across the room. She sensed the woman watching her walk away.

"You came." Carolina swept her into a hug. Bunny stiffened. Carolina must have noticed, because she let her go just as quickly. "Sorry, I can be a bit much when I'm excited . . . or happy . . . or, well, anything. Mind my manners. These are my friends." Carolina introduced them.

Her cheerful exuberance made Bunny warm and terrified all at the same time. Though they were all nice enough, she didn't say much. She watched and listened and tried to think of something to say that wouldn't make them cringe. Having grown up together, they shared a secret language. They talked and laughed about the upcoming fair and their memories of fairs past. In the end, Bunny ate and smiled and nodded, grateful they seemed not to notice her awkwardness. She suspected they wouldn't invite her again. As the night wore on, they tired of talking about the men and accepted their offers to dance. Bunny stayed behind to hold the table. She was in awe of the easy way the women moved their bodies to the music like no one was watching. Each so different, yet equally graceful and free.

Bunny ordered a longneck, shoved her chair against the wall, and propped up the heel of her boot. The bar was a large room broken into vaguely marked sections for eating, dancing, and pool. People moved fluidly, the way they do in small towns, talking to everyone by the time the night was over.

Through the sway of people, a single cowboy came into the bar. He stopped right inside the door like she had. Whereas she had been desperately looking for a friend, he was like a gunslinger surveying the bar for his next opponent. He came her way, but she was confident he wouldn't be stopping at her table. She clearly wasn't his type. Bunny knew what guys like him wanted, and it wasn't a girl in faded Levi's and a baseball cap. She wasn't stupid. She knew clothes didn't hide the assets that a man could overlook everything else to get. Still, style mattered. Hers was Levi Strauss, not Gloria Vanderbilt. From the way the waitress made a beeline to him, she wasn't the only one who had sized him up.

With every step he took, she inched a little closer to the wall and started looking for an exit route.

"Would you like to dance?" It might have been a trick of the light, but she would have sworn his hatpin twinkled when he smiled.

"Uh, no," Bunny said with a nervous laugh.

"Not your type, huh?"

"Oh, I bet you're everybody's type. But I don't dance."

Ignoring the insult, he replied, "You don't dance? Come on, everybody dances."

"Everybody minus one, I guess." She smiled.

"Since you're just sitting here, not dancing, mind if I join you?" He pulled out the chair as if it were a foregone conclusion.

"Suit yourself, cowboy." She took a pull on her beer, curious where he thought this was going. Pushing her chair back, Bunny wanted to bolt but willed herself to stay.

"I haven't seen you in here before. Are you new in town?"

"Does that line usually work?" She looked at him dead-on like her daddy taught her to. A smile slid across her face at his confused expression.

"Have I done something to offend you?"

His sincerity softened her. "No. Sorry." Her bravado slipped. Without thinking, she introduced herself. "I'm Benny O'Kelly. I work out at the Miller Ranch."

"Well then, I'm surprised you let me sit down at all. I'm what you might call unpopular with the Millers." He extended a hand. "Jeremiah Cooper." It took a beat, but she shook his hand.

"I'm not so sure I'm all that popular at the Miller ranch, either." She raised her beer to him.

"What'd you do?" He waved to the bartender, silently ordering another round.

"I was born a woman."

"Ah. That would be Jake."

She nodded. "What'd you do?"

"I was born a Cooper."

"Sounds like there's a story there."

Before he could answer, the waitress materialized next to him. "What can I get you, Jeremiah?"

She had him in her sights, staring too long. He glanced at her long enough to order a beer. "A Bud, please."

"A friend of yours?" Bunny asked.

"It's a small town. We're all friends here." He flashed that smile again.

"I bet." She flashed one right back.

Over his shoulder, Bunny saw Jake push through the door. He didn't get two feet before someone shook his hand. He gave them an easy smile he had never shared with Bunny. She knew the minute he spotted her when the scowl he had been wearing all week washed across his face. She thought about leaving, but having it out with him here was as good a place as any. Her beer was cold and full. He might try to run her off that ranch, but he wasn't running her out of this bar. Not tonight, anyway.

With his eyes on her, Jake walked up to the table. "Benny, I know you're new in town, but I'm surprised you're slumming already."

"Jake." She tipped her beer at him. "I'm guessing you know Jeremiah already."

"Yes, I do." He crossed his arms over his chest and leaned back on his heels. "And if you want to save yourself a lot of trouble, you won't bother getting to know him."

"More of your stellar advice, Jake? I'm off duty. I think I'll pass."

"Suit yourself. Don't let the fancy belt buckle and the shiny hatpin fool you. He's a dawg."

Jeremiah didn't bother to look up. "Any time you want to go, you let me know."

Jake straightened. "You talking to me or the girl?"

Jeremiah might have several inches on him, but Bunny had to hand it to Jake. He did not back down.

"Alright, boys." Bunny stood and tightened her ponytail underneath her crimson WSU cap. "As entertaining as this little pissing match is, I'm going to head on home."

Jeremiah turned to her and stood. "Hold on there. I haven't even had a chance to ask you out yet. How about dinner one night?"

Though she was wary of his practiced charm, his dimpled smile was tempting. Just when her better judgment was about to prevail, Jake chimed in. "Well, that didn't take long. You can't help yourself, can you, Jeremiah?"

And there it is, the overbearing, arrogant ass. She gave it just enough consideration to dismiss the idea she might be using him, in light of his obvious insincerity, before accepting. "I'd like that. I'll meet you, though. No need to play out this drama again."

She leaned into him and wrote her number on a napkin. Though she felt Jake's anger, Bunny refused to look at him. She set the napkin down and walked away. And she did it chin up, eyes forward, and slow—like her daddy taught her to.

CHAPTER 34

ROCKY 1982

ROCKY HELD THE garbage bag open for Jeremiah to stuff his bloody clothes in, disgusted by his son's red-rimmed eyes. Would his boy fold? Until it all blew over, he would have to ride herd on Jeremiah. He was going to need to do some thinking. In the meantime, it was his good fortune to be handed such a valuable insurance policy.

As he walked through the fresh snow past the barn, he looked up to make sure that Jesse's lights were out. He didn't need her interfering. Like most things in life, taking care of business for your family was man's work. Women would never understand the cost of that responsibility. He grabbed the sawdust bucket. There wasn't much in it, but he wouldn't need much. Snow covered the burn barrel, but it was cold enough that he brushed the dry flakes away easily. He dropped in the sawdust and a couple of old slats of wood and lit the barrel.

Once the flame burned hot, he grabbed the garbage bag and quietly opened the rear door of the barn. It was too dark to see, so he closed his eyes and imagined the layout. Using his hand to follow the stalls, he slowly made his way to the tack room. At the rear was a locked cabinet. Running his calloused hands over the front, he felt the two small holes marring the surface where the nameplate had been ripped off. Jesse wouldn't let him get rid of it, but he didn't have to see her name every damn time he went in there.

He felt the cold metal of the keys in his pocket. Most were smoothed out from constant use. One small key still had sharp edges. The click of the lock opening reverberated in the room, and he stopped stock-still to listen for Jesse or, worse, Jeremiah. Satisfied he was still alone, he opened the cabinet. In his mind, he imagined the blue ribbons blanketing the doors. The memory of wanting her stabbed him. He lifted the footlocker lid and pulled out the saddle blanket. Opening the bag, he felt around for the rough cotton of the shirt. He slipped his knife from the scabbard on his belt and cut a swatch of the material. Stuffing Jeremiah's clothes back in the bag, he rolled it tightly and shoved it into the corner of the old footlocker. He covered them with the saddle blanket and locked the cabinet. It was fitting that the evidence of Jeremiah's betrayal would be kept with the remains of hers.

When he got back to the fire, he laid the piece of plaid on the edge of the fire. Rocky watched it burn for a while. Lifting the scrap, he placed the lid on the barrel to extinguish the flames. In the cold, without oxygen, the fire soon went out. Satisfied, he dropped the scrap in the burn barrel.

Under the light of the full moon, Rocky took a detour before heading back to the house. He followed the path around the shed. Over the last decade, the trees had grown to cover the path his plow had made that night. Still, his feet knew the way. Fifty yards in, he found the outcropping of boulders. He circled the pile, looking for evidence that the frozen earth had pushed them apart. In early days, the permafrost had shifted, and it was sheer luck his anger had propelled him to this place. He'd been lucky no animals had found a convenient meal. Just to be sure that didn't happen, he'd added a few more rocks.

Without the fire, a chill set in. He headed for the house, hoping Jeremiah would be in bed. It wouldn't do for them to all be standing around when the cops showed up. He didn't think to check Jesse's window again.

CHAPTER 35

JAKE 1982

J AKE DISMOUNTED FIFTY yards from the barn on the pasture road. It was risky to wake the stallions, but the rear door couldn't be seen from the house. He was counting on Dusty being too tired to pick a fight and Buck being too far in the bag to hear anything outside of his own head. He left the lights off, navigating by the glow of the office lamp Buck perpetually left on. The chill had left a layer of frost on them that would be hard to explain away when it turned to dew on Dusty's coat. Once he put away the tack, he toweled off the horse as best he could.

Leaving the way he came in, he skirted the pasture and headed for his bunk. The morning feeding was a few short hours away, and even Buck would notice if he didn't get some sleep. The night was playing on repeat in his head, though. This was all Jeremiah's fault. Katie wouldn't be lying to her dad. She wouldn't ever have seen the meaner side of him. With that regret in his mind, he fell into a fitful sleep.

In his dream, he was in a honky-tonk with Katie. Everyone parted for them as he two-stepped her around the dance floor.

She faded a little as he advanced. When his arms were empty, he awoke with a start. A blue light swiped across the room.

Jake was still pulling on his boots when he opened the door. Before he reached the big house, Buck was on the ground.

"No. No. No." He sat on the top stair, head in his hands.

The deputy reached his hand out to help him up, but he jerked his arm away.

"Where is she? I want to see her."

"Sir, could we go inside and talk? You must be cold."

Buck did not move.

"What's going on?" Jake asked. When Buck didn't answer, he sat down next to him. "Let's go inside."

"Are you a member of the family?"

"Friend. I work here." Questions crossed the police officer's face, so Jake added, "I live in the bunkhouse. Just over there."

"When was the last time you saw Katie Miller?" The deputy pulled a notebook out of his shirt pocket.

"Uh. I'm not sure. Dinner, I guess, before the last feeding. Maybe six o'clock. Where is she? What happened?"

"Did you see her leave tonight?"

"No. I wouldn't have. I was in my bunk."

Buck looked to Jake. His eyebrows knitted together like he was trying to work something out in his head. Jake searched his mind. Was there anything Buck would remember?

"What time?" The officer looked from him to Buck and back again.

Buck fixed his eyes on him.

Jake hesitated. "Around nine o'clock. After feeding, I worked my horse in the arena."

"Was her truck here when you went to your room?"

"I didn't notice. It probably was."

"Why is that?"

Jake avoided Buck's gaze. "Well, where else would she be at that time of night?"

"I need to see her." Buck spoke to the ground.

Jake stood and asked the question he was supposed to ask. "You still haven't said what happened. Is she ok?"

"I'm sorry, but there was an accident. Katie didn't survive. We think she hit some ice and lost control. Her truck hit a power pole. The accident investigators are still at the scene. If you could bring him to the coroner's office in an hour, he can see his daughter." The deputy handed him a card and apologized to Buck for his loss.

Jake stared wordlessly at the barn, wracking his mind. Had he left any evidence of his midnight ride?

CHAPTER 36

BUNNY 1984

RUFF ROLLED OVER, firmly planting his enormous head and one paw on Bunny's belly. It was like he knew she was going to have to face Jake and take her licks for agreeing to go out with Jeremiah.

"Boy, there is just no escaping this. Do me a favor and bite him in the ass if he gets out of hand."

Ruff groaned in tacit agreement.

"If only all men were so loyal." She scratched his ears. He sighed deeply and rolled off her. She took that as her cue to get up and face the music.

Bunny thought she would give herself a brief reprieve by going to breakfast first. She cursed her bad luck. Jake and Buck were still finishing their coffee.

"Morning," Jake grumbled.

"Morning, sunshine. You look like you were rode hard and put away wet." Buck was suspiciously cheerful.

"Late night. I'll be fine once I get some coffee." She headed for the pot. Jake gave her a warning shove as he passed her, but she was too tired to retaliate.

"Looks like War Horse is coming along. Think you might ride him on the trail soon?"

There was hope in Buck's voice, but she wasn't sure the animal was ready. She wasn't even sure she was. Stalling, she took a sip of her coffee.

"He needs more time in the ring," Jake stated definitively.

"He's ready." Bunny's mouth engaged before her brain. She wasn't going to let him tell her what to do. "I'm going to take a ride in the next day or so."

"Not smart. You've only been riding him, what? A little more than a week. He's not in shape—physically or mentally." He held her eyes, but she didn't blink. "I'm not sure you are."

"That's for me to decide, Jake. He's ready." If she learned anything from her brothers, it was never back down. She was gearing up for a fight when Buck put an end to it. Bunny couldn't tell if he was protecting Jake or her.

"Let it be, Jake. If Benny says War Horse is ready, he's ready. Safety rule, though. Let us know when you're leaving and where you're heading, in case you don't come back."

At first, it felt like a declaration of his lack of faith in her ability. But when she looked at him, he was staring out the window in a wistful way that made her heart a little sad. Somehow, she knew it wasn't about her.

"Will do," she said as she pushed past Jake.

"Hey, nobody's going riding today," he said. "No rain this week, so we're cutting. I'll mow this morning. You'll have to pick up my chores. Buck can help you with the stallions. By the time you're done, you can start tedding. We could be baling by tomorrow." Jake looked at Buck, who nodded.

"Tedding?" Bunny asked.

"I thought you said you had experience haying."

Jake's tone put her on edge. "Yup. On a dairy farm. Silage, not hay bales." She matched his tone, which apparently sent up an alarm because Buck came out of his chair just as they went nose to nose.

"It's a couple more steps. If you've driven a tractor, you can drive the tedder. Same principle, you're flipping the hay over so it can dry. Jake will go over it with you. Right, Jake?"

"Yes," he clipped, holding her stare.

"Let's get to it then," Buck announced.

Bunny took that as her cue and headed down to do her chores. Shoveling horse manure was the perfect job to fuel a slow burn.

⌘

The horses sensed her sour mood and headed for their paddocks as soon as she entered their stalls. All but War Horse. He stood his ground, staring at Bunny with his nose lowered and his ears forward, like he was waiting for some explanation. They stood there deadlocked for a few minutes before Ruff came to the door and barked at them. In unison, they looked his way.

"Fine." She put her hand out and War Horse approached. As soon as he pushed his muzzle to her belly, she melted. He sucked all the anger out of her. "We're going for a ride on the trail this afternoon after I get done tedding, which I have never done. So, that's great. If I screw that up, Jake is going to feed me a ration of crap. Man, that guy is standing on my last nerve." War Horse backed up and looked at her. Without a sound, he turned and walked out into his paddock.

"Katie used to talk to him all the time. Boy, she loved that horse."

She turned to find Buck leaning on the door.

"He's a great horse." She looked out to find War Horse watching them.

"That he is. You be careful with him tonight."

"Yes, sir. I will." Bunny knew the weight of that promise.

Buck pushed off the door. As he walked away, he called to her, "Come up when you get done there. We'll do the rest after we eat."

After lunch, Buck and Bunny finished with the stallions' stalls. He moved the animals around as she mucked out the stalls. Jake met her at the tractor to give her a tedding lesson. He acted genuinely shocked to find she could drive a tractor. Tedding wasn't rocket science. She was sure Jake would walk the fields that night to inspect her work, though. Bunny didn't care because while he did that, she was going to be riding War Horse.

CHAPTER 37

JEREMIAH 1982

"Hey, heads up!" Jesse called out.

Jeremiah stumbled back against the stall door. "Sorry."

"Jeez, Jeremiah, pay attention or someone's gonna get hurt." Jesse reached up to pull her small student out of the saddle. "You okay?" she asked the girl as she handed her the reins. Jesse hugged her and shot Jeremiah a look that could freeze lava.

He needed to talk, but it couldn't be his sister. She'd always had his back, and she always did the right thing. Jesse had the guts to stand up to Rocky, even if it meant sleeping over the barn. There was no way she could keep this to herself.

With each passing day, he knew the lie he and Rocky shared would become an anchor holding them down until they drowned. Jeremiah wanted to grieve out loud. He wanted to wail and scream, but he held it in. He was a master at that. Still, his heart felt like it might tear in half. He remembered this feeling. It was the same way he felt when he found out his mom had left them. Back then, he had to keep it inside too. Rocky made it clear there was nothing to talk about. She left them, so she no longer existed. But the truth was, her leaving felt like a break in a bone that healed but ached every time the weather got bad. Now the ache of her leaving was back, and it made losing Katie worse. Even though she didn't leave on purpose, she still left him.

Jeremiah blamed himself. If he'd only had the courage to tell their fathers they were dating, she would have stayed with him. He didn't try to stop her, though he knew she was too upset to drive. Like a coward, he just stood there, Rocky's rules ringing in his ears. *A man doesn't beg a woman to stay.* Jeremiah wished he had begged. If he thought it would bring her back, he would get on his knees right now and beg. He wouldn't care that Rocky would think he was whipped.

Jeremiah missed the early feedings, but Rocky covered for him. He didn't say a word. That was uncharacteristic. If Jeremiah had the energy to be anything but grateful for the silence, he would have noticed. When Rocky was irritated with someone, he was like a murder of crows dive-bombing an eagle. He didn't let up. Over the years, Jeremiah learned to keep his mouth shut. But no matter how still or calm he got, Rocky would keep attacking until he thought Jeremiah had learned his lesson. Though he was poised for the attack now, he knew it would never come. Much like his mother's leaving, Rocky was acting like Katie never existed.

CHAPTER 38

BUNNY 1984

B Y THE TIME Bunny got back to the barn, most of the riders were gone. Carolina was leading Sonny out of the barn as she brought War Horse out of the stall.

Bunny waved. "Hey."

Carolina responded with an uncharacteristically reserved nod.

"Something wrong?" Bunny called after her.

She stopped the horse and looked at Bunny. "Well, since you asked, yes. Why did you run off the other night?"

Bunny was taken aback. "What do you mean, run off?"

"Are you kidding me? You left, and you didn't even say goodbye."

"I'm sorry, Carolina. You all were dancing. I honestly didn't think you would notice."

"How could we not notice?"

"Look, I just mean, I was a little out of place. And I didn't want to spoil your good time."

"Spoil our good time? We were having a good time *with*

you." Her voice cracked and tears peaked at the corner of her angry eyes.

"I am so sorry, Carolina. It isn't you. It's me. Oh, God. That sounds weird." She searched for the right words, but her mouth engaged while she was still looking. "See, I have four brothers. I don't know if you noticed, but I'm a bit of a tomboy. I never had a lot of girlfriends and, frankly, I feel out of place sometimes around beautiful, bubbly women."

"I'll say it again. Are you joking? I wouldn't have asked you to come if you didn't fit in. What does that even mean?" Carolina stomped her foot. "Look, everyone liked you. We were all disappointed you left. You can just be you when you're with us. It doesn't matter if you're a tomboy or a Barbie doll."

The only place she ever felt like she fit was the farm and, in the end, her dad made it clear she did not. Bunny didn't know what to say. She had a lifetime of wearing the wrong outfit or going somewhere with cow manure on her boots. Her hair was perpetually in knots. She had long ago decided she looked like a clown whenever she put on makeup. Stunned, her thoughts raced with self-doubt. *How can they find me even slightly acceptable? What is wrong with these women?*

"Look, Benny." Carolina turned her horse. Sonny caught War Horse's eye and let out a whinny. "Whatever it is that you think about yourself, I don't think that."

Her words hit Bunny like a bucket of cold water. She was right. It wasn't about what Carolina thought. It was what she thought—what she thought about her and her friends and what she thought about herself.

"Sorry. That was too much. My mom used to say that I'm too much." Carolina dabbed the tears with her fingertips.

"No, you're not too much, and I'm sorry I didn't tell you I was leaving. I should have."

"So, you'll go out with us again."

"My God, you're like a Doberman in ballet slippers. Yes, I will," she conceded with a smile. "But right now, I'm going for a ride."

Carolina grinned as she watched Bunny saddle War Horse.

⁂

Deciding to err on the side of caution, Bunny lunged him in the ring. She wanted him as settled as possible before mounting up. Carolina was at the far end of the arena, taking Sonny through his paces. As Bunny reeled War Horse in, she took a minute to watch Carolina ride. She was regal, posting in a crisp figure eight.

Buck snuck up on her. "She's been riding since she could walk, I swear."

"You can sure tell," Bunny agreed. "I'm heading out. I won't be gone long this first time. Maybe an hour, tops. I'll stay on the road around the fields." She mounted the horse. He gave a little groan and craned his head to look back at her. "Don't give me that. I'm not so big. You're just out of shape. We're going to fix that. Aren't we, War Horse?"

Buck reached up and patted the big horse's neck. He nuzzled him in return. "You take good care of her." With that, he stepped back to let them pass.

Bunny gave him a cluck of her tongue and a little rein, and off they went. The sun was touching the treetops, and the air was still and warm. They set off at a walk. Bunny could tell War Horse wanted to run. He pulled at the reins. She held his head as long as she could. But she wanted to run as much as he did. Bunny urged him to a trot.

On the left, the fence held back billowing wildflowers. They looked as if they were trying to escape the trees, reaching out with fragile purple blossoms on spindly green limbs. Bunny kept the horse to the field side, fearing they might come upon a fallen limb. The dirt road was barely wide enough for a truck. When they got to the end of the field, they stopped. She looked around from the mount. She could see the barn in the distance. The road turned to the right and followed the field farther than she could see. Closing her eyes, she took in the silence. War Horse was still, but Bunny knew his eyes and heart were moving forward. She grabbed the saddle horn and leaned forward, stroking the big horse's neck. He was sweaty but not lathered. He could take a little more. The long stretch before them had a shoulder of grass that looked even enough to canter on.

She leaned over and whispered in his ear, "Are you in, big guy?" He gave her a whinny and a nod. "Well, alright then."

Bunny turned him to the right and gave him a squeeze. They trotted until his gait got bouncy. He wanted to run, so she gave him his head. He loped along, black mane flowing like water. Bunny kept time with his shoulders. Freedom washed through her. Her heart swelled and tears filled her eyes.

She slowed him to a trot, then to a walk, as much to recover herself as to see how he responded to the cues. As they topped a small hill, she brought him to a halt. Turning him slowly in a circle, she took it all in. In one direction, the pasture rolled farther than she could see. In the opposite, the wilderness stretched out, climbing slowly upward. Between them was one lane of dirt road that didn't seem to lead to either. It was the first time she'd ever felt completely alone. Out here, she was just a girl on a horse. She closed her eyes, the waning sun on her face. The melody of the birds and the gentle rustling of the flowers slowly drifted to her ears. She wished her mom could be there with her and see her, really see her. Just a girl on a horse.

War Horse broke her reverie with a tug of the reins. Bunny leaned forward to stroke his neck, grateful for this gift. She could tell his patience was wearing thin. Before long, they were loping down the road. War Horse picked up speed, and Bunny laughed as he broke into a full gallop. He pushed her out of the saddle with his muscled haunches. She saw the flash of gray on the grass ahead and pulled back on the reins to slow him. But it was too late. Whatever happened next would be her fault.

War Horse stuttered and threw Bunny off balance. She grabbed for the saddle horn, and he pulled the reins from her hands. She slid off the side and hit the ground. The impact knocked the air out of her, and she gasped and choked as he dragged her down the dirt road. Her shoulders and head bounced on the ground. Watching his rear hooves pound the earth next to her head, she tried to release her foot, but it was caught fast in the stirrup. Bunny thought for sure her skull was going to be crushed by a hoof or bashed in by a rock.

She screamed for him to stop. "Whoa! Whoa!"

Suddenly, he slowed and turned toward her. Her foot released, and she rolled into a ball, expecting him to step on her. When nothing happened, she opened her eyes to see Carolina leaning over Sonny's neck to grab War Horse's reins. She brought him back, tying his reins to her saddle. She slid out of the saddle and crouched down next to Bunny.

"Are you alright?" She leaned over, patting her from head to feet.

"Help me up," Bunny gasped.

"I'll go get help." Carolina was already moving when Bunny grabbed her arm.

"No. No. Please, get me back on him. It wasn't his fault. It was all my fault. He spooked," she begged.

"You're hurt."

"Get me to the barn. There's a first aid kit. I'm not hurt that bad. Just scrapes and bruises."

"Benny," she pleaded.

"No. Jake will never let me live it down. Buck will never let me ride another horse, especially War Horse. He'll probably sack me again. You've got to help me." Bunny pushed herself up and dusted off her jeans. "See, I'm fine. Where's my hat?" She spied the red cap in the hay and limped off to get it. On the way, she grabbed the discarded fence rail and threw it into the woods.

When she got back, Carolina pointed out that her limp would be hard to hide.

"I've hidden a lot worse from my brothers and my dad. Buck and Jake are never going to know I'm hurting."

They saddled up and walked the horses back to the barn. War Horse seemed contrite. He didn't need forgiveness. Bunny guessed he got carried away with the sheer joy of it. Hell, she had too.

When they got back to the barn, Carolina insisted on taking care of the horses. Bunny dug out the first aid kit and set to cleaning her wounds. Her jeans and shirt were ripped. She wouldn't be wearing them again. Scrapes covered her legs and arms. Her ponytail hid the road rash on her head, fortunately. Her clothes hid everything else.

"Get in my Jeep," Carolina ordered.

"Why? Where are we going?"

"To your bunk. If you want to hide this, you can't limp up to your bunk in ripped clothes."

Carolina was intent, and now Bunny realized she'd dismissed her as weak and dumb. She wasn't either. Following her orders, Bunny got in the Jeep. Carolina rolled toward the house but made it only halfway before running into Buck walking down to the barn.

"Crap." She searched her mind for any believable lie that would explain driving from the barn to the bunks.

"Let me handle this," Carolina said.

Bunny pressed herself against the seat, hoping the pain didn't show on her face, as Carolina steered the Jeep toward him.

"Hey, Buck."

"Hey, Carolina. Where're you two going?" he asked, leaning on her door.

"Up to the house. Benny wanted to show me something."

Bunny searched her mind for a plausible lie. She was a terrible liar, but a great confessor. She confessed quickly and often. Bunny would have confessed to being the second gunman on the grassy knoll if anyone had asked.

"Yeah? What's she going to show you?" he asked with a snicker.

"My rifle. Carolina is interested in shooting." Bunny wished she could take the words back. With her luck, Carolina was an award-winning marksman.

"Benny said she'd teach me to shoot," Carolina added.

"You better check that out with your dad. I don't want him mad at me if Benny corrupts you." Buck and Carolina chuckled.

When they got to her room, Carolina looked around for Jake before she helped Bunny out of the Jeep. She stumbled onto the bed. Before Carolina could get the door shut, Ruff loped in and jumped on the bed, curling up next to her.

"You keep your mouth shut too." Bunny gave him a half-hearted pat.

Carolina scanned the small room. "I'm a terrible liar, so you're going to have to actually get out the gun and show me how to use it."

Bunny pointed to the closet. "Thanks for helping me. You didn't have to do that."

"It's what girlfriends do for each other. Although I have to say, I thought it would be the other way around." Carolina opened the closet and searched with her eyes. At first, Bunny thought she couldn't see it but soon realized she was searching for clothes that weren't there. Carolina turned and looked at her, head cocked and brows furrowed. Then, without comment, she turned back to the closet, picked up the rifle, and shut the door.

"Me? Helping you? Why would you think that?" Bunny asked. "Not that I wouldn't help you. It's just—you don't strike me as someone who needs a lot of help."

"Well, you are way off base there. I am nothing like you. You are strong and bold. I would have quit this job on the first day. I see how those guys are. Jake never cuts you a break. Buck's kind of lost. But you show up and do your job. You never back down. I couldn't do that."

Bunny didn't know how to respond. No one ever talked to her like that.

Carolina must have seen it in her expression. "Benny, you're a warrior. I wish I was more like you. I don't ever feel like I can get my hands dirty or speak my mind or stand up to anybody."

"Well, you did a hell of a job today."

Carolina tipped her head to the floor, concealing a smile. She put the rifle back in the closet. "Maybe we aren't so different. Get some rest. You're going to feel like you got hit by a truck tomorrow. Plus, you've got to take me shooting." With that, Carolina headed out.

CHAPTER 39

ROCKY 1982

Rocky'd had enough of Jeremiah's moping around. He let it go at first, but there was work to be done, and Rocky would be damned if he was doing it by himself. His body was getting too old to carry his weight and Jeremiah's. He needed to get that boy out of the house.

His gut felt raw from the whiskey, and he kicked himself for deviating from cheap beer. Groaning, he rolled over. Giving his body a little time before forcing it upright, he thought about his day. The first thing he needed was a hot shower to loosen up his old muscles. Then, he was going to have a word with Jeremiah.

By the time he got downstairs, Jesse was making breakfast. She silently put a plate of food in front of him. He didn't know what had set her off, and he didn't care. He had bigger problems.

"Where's Jeremiah?" he asked.

She turned to him. "I assume upstairs in bed. What the hell happened to him?"

If she'd noticed Jeremiah wasn't right, it was only a matter of time before other people did too. He ignored her question. "Go up and roust his ass. We got work to do."

"Do it yourself. I have a lesson in a couple of minutes." She turned the stove off. "I'll be back later to clean up this mess."

She grabbed her barn coat off the hook by the door. With both hands, she reached under her hair and lifted the long mane out from under the jacket. He hated it when she did that. She looked just like Rebekah when she flipped her hair. Rebekah's long dark hair had caught his attention in the first place. He didn't want any reminders of it, ever.

"Put your hair in a ponytail before you get it caught in something," he hollered after her.

Jesse said nothing. She just walked out. She was like her mother that way too.

Rocky ate his breakfast and finished his coffee before he climbed back up the stairs to wake Jeremiah. He pounded on the door. "Let's go, boy." When he groaned, Rocky opened the door.

Jeremiah shielded his eyes from the light.

"Get a move on. You're done sleeping in. I'm running a ranch, not a hotel. You've got ten minutes to get your ass to the barn and get to work." Rocky slammed the door.

With any luck, Jeremiah would miss feeding and Rocky could make him spend the morning shoveling manure. Fitting punishment for him to do it alone. When he stopped at Kiona's stall, the horse stuck his head out and nudged Rocky's shoulder. Kiona was about the only animal, human or beast, that he would let push him around. They had an understanding, though. In the saddle, Rocky was the boss. He loved riding Kiona, in part because there was always the chance he would lose control. Rocky wished he was still a young stud like that—powerful, wild, dangerous. He'd let Rebekah saddle him. That was a mistake he wasn't making again. He sure as hell wasn't letting his boy make it, either. Katie was out of the way. It was unfortunate she died, but she would've had to go, one way or another. Now it was done. It was time to get Jeremiah back on the horse.

He hadn't heard him come into the barn until he called out, "I'll get the stalls mucked out."

"When you get done, saddle up. We're going to check the fence line. Weather is going to get bad. Moose will be on the move soon." Rocky didn't wait for a response, and Jeremiah didn't offer one.

⌇

By the time Jeremiah finished, Rocky was settling his horse in the arena. He saw him ride in and his chest filled with pride. His son was handsome and strong. In the saddle, he looked like a warrior—confident and bold. Now that he knew Jeremiah could be laid low by a woman, he was going to make sure it didn't happen again. He knew just the girl to take his mind off Katie. Rocky had seen Mindy looking over Jeremiah like she was trying to add up his assets in her head. She thought she was in charge, but she could be controlled. A woman like her wanted money or sex. He guessed Mindy wanted both. He was going to make sure she got them.

"Let's head south first." Rocky rode past him at a trot. Jeremiah turned T-Bird on his hind legs and caught up with him. Rocky was always cutting and running. He loved the feel of the quick pivots and lurches and knowing Jeremiah had to work to keep up with him. He was a man now. Rocky knew he had to keep a mind to that.

They settled into an easy gait. "Son, you gotta quit moping

around. I know you cared about Katie, but people are gonna start asking. You're not acting like yourself."

"What difference does it make?"

"We've been through this. The boyfriend or husband is the first person they look at."

"She had an accident."

"Won't matter to Buck. He's gotta be heartbroken about losing his baby. He hasn't got much else to lose. That makes a man dangerous."

They rode in silence. Rocky worried he might have to pull the shirt out of the locker to get Jeremiah in line.

"What am I supposed to do? Act like nothing happened?" he asked.

"That's exactly what you're supposed to do. Do what you always do. Go dancing. Go on a date. Be yourself." Rocky could tell Jeremiah was mulling it over when he slowed a bit, so he pressed. "You know who you should take out? Mindy. That new waitress in town. I hear she's fun. I've seen her looking at you. I bet she'd love to go dancing. You need someone fun."

Jeremiah didn't say anything, but Rocky'd planted the seed. He didn't think it would take much to make Mindy put on the pressure.

They rode the fence line, mostly in silence. Every once in a while, they dismounted to move some brush off the fence. In the far corner, they found a wire down and cobbled it back together. Rocky made a note to check it again soon. The horses wouldn't be out in the winter, but he didn't need to make his pasture easier for the moose to get into.

As they headed back to the barn, Rocky glanced at the profile of his son. He looked like the perfect combination of him and Rebekah. He hated seeing her in Jeremiah and Jesse. Jeremiah's face was set hard. That was his thinking face. Rocky hoped he was coming to the conclusion that he needed to move on, if only for self-preservation. He worried he was mulling over some false sense of betrayal to Katie. Rocky knew his son. He would get in line. Unlike Jesse, Jeremiah was his daddy's boy. He wouldn't go against Rocky, especially now that Katie was gone.

CHAPTER 40

BUNNY 1984

THE ALARM RICOCHETED around her skull. A stabbing pain in her shoulder stopped her hand mid-slap. It was all coming back. She wanted to get up early so she could be seated before Jake walked in. There was no chance she would beat Buck, but it was unlikely he would notice her limp, anyway. Jake, however, wouldn't pass up the chance to rib her about it. She needed to be done and gone before he came in.

Bunny hobbled to the shower. Standing under the hot spray, she stretched her muscles, trying to release the death grip they had on her joints. Satisfied she was as loose as she was going to be, she slowly turned the water to cold until the shock of it emptied her lungs. The twins called it their hangover treatment. She figured it couldn't hurt.

Buck was flipping pancakes at the stove when she limped in. Staring at the griddle, he asked, "How hungry are you? Two or three pancakes this morning?"

"Two please." Bunny grabbed her plate off the table, careful to keep her gait even on the old wood floor. He dished them up and turned his attention to a skillet of scrambled eggs steaming on the stove. She slid on the seat and dug out the ibuprofen she'd stashed in her jeans. Buck brought over a plate of eggs just as she was washing down a couple of capsules with some coffee.

"Maybe you should go to the doctor." He sat down and looked her in the eye. She held her breath. Bracing, she searched her memory, trying to figure out how he found out about War Horse. "You shouldn't still be hurting from Anchorage."

Bunny deflated in relief. He didn't know. "I'm not. Just some sore muscles from driving the tedder." She wished the twins had also taught her to cover her tracks better. She felt like she was jumping from one frying pan to the next.

"Well, it can be painful driving that for the first time. Worse, I'm sure, after what you've been through lately. You can always shut it down and get out. Stretch every then and again. It ain't a rodeo." He snapped his fingers. "I almost forgot, you've got some mail."

Reaching over to the counter, he grabbed the envelope and handed it to her. She turned it over to read the address and quickly shoved it in her back pocket. Heat rose from her chest and her face reddened. She was grateful Buck was concentrating on the pancakes and not her.

"Aren't you going to read it? Looks like it might be from home."

"I will later." Bunny jumped in to change the subject. "Can I borrow one of the trucks tonight?"

"For what?" He sat down with his plate, a mound of eggs atop his pancakes, and dug in.

Bunny halted in her tracks. "I've got a date tonight." At times like this, she wished she had a gift for half-truths and sins of omission. The whole truth slipped off her lips every damn time.

Buck looked up at her. "Oh, yeah? With who?" The chair scraped across the floor as he leaned back from the table. His eyebrows came together the way her dad's did when he knew he wasn't going to like an answer.

"Jeremiah Cooper, from the Double J."

"Oh, I know where Jeremiah Cooper is from," he shot back. "I'm a little surprised you're going out with him."

"It's just a date." She felt like a little girl trying to explain away her naughty behavior.

"It's never just a date with him. Besides, what you've been through." He pierced her with his eyes.

She blinked, like she always did with her dad. Now she was doing it with Buck. Bunny looked out the window at the ranch. The mares and foals lazed in the pasture, and she remembered she wasn't back home. She was on the Midnight Sun, and Buck wasn't her dad.

"It's a date. And *that* was not a date." It came out with a little more vehemence than she intended. "It was an assault. And I'm fine." She held her ground and stared him down.

"It's your life. You're an adult. I'm not your dad. But fair warning. Nothing good comes of dating a Cooper. Nothing." And with that, he stood, dumping his half-eaten breakfast in the trash. What could make a man like Buck lose his appetite? As he put on his hat, Jake barreled into the kitchen.

Shoveling food on his plate, he asked, "Did you give the little rabbit her mail?"

"Shut it, Jake." Buck's warning was unmistakable. He stalked to the door and slammed it behind him.

Bunny followed. Before leaving, she looked Jake in the eye and said, "Don't call me that." She didn't give him a chance to respond.

The morning didn't improve from there. Much as she tried, she couldn't avoid Jake. He caught her as she was limping around the barn. Bunny refused to meet his eyes and blew past him when he stopped in the middle of the aisle.

"Hey!" he called after her.

"What?" She stopped but didn't give him the satisfaction of turning around.

"You're really going through with this?"

Turning to face him, she bit back at him, "Why do you even care? This is none of your business."

"I'd hate to see you get hurt."

"No, that's not it," she countered. "You don't give a rat's ass about me. You have some pissing match going on with Jeremiah. It has nothing to do with protecting me."

"Suit yourself. I warned you."

"Like you warned me about War Horse," Bunny challenged.

He crossed his arms across his chest and leaned back on his heels. "Yes. Like War Horse. And I wasn't wrong about that." Jake drilled her with his eyes. Bunny didn't know how he knew, but she was sure he'd figured out she got dragged. This was one time she wasn't going to confess. She turned on her heels and stomped away.

The horses must have sensed her anger. Most backed out of their stalls before she opened their doors. They were great listeners, though, as she cursed Jake James to each in turn. One even gave a whinny when she needed confirmation that he was half mule, half jackass. War Horse snorted his encouragement as she tossed flakes of hay into his feeder. By the time she finished mucking out his stall, she had burned off most of her anger. She leaned against the wall. War Horse lumbered over and put his forehead to her belly. Was it commiseration or an apology of sorts for dragging her through the field? She took his cheeks in her hands and rubbed them softly.

"It's okay, big guy. Next time, I'll pay more mind. But don't you worry, we're going for a ride again soon." He gave her a contented sigh.

❧

Buck brought her a sandwich at lunchtime. She thought it was a peace offering until he pulled a pair of heavy leather gloves from his back pocket.

"You'll need these. Do you want to throw bales or stack them first?"

She stared at him. "Dairy farm, remember?"

Jake strolled over to them and busied himself connecting the trailer to the baler.

"We're baling hay today. I'm driving. You and Jake are stacking the bales," he explained as if talking to a five-year-old. "You've got a choice to start. You can grab the bales and throw them to Jake, or you can catch the bales and stack. What do you want to do first?"

"Got it." She jammed her hands into the gloves. "I'll throw." That would be the harder job, and she wanted her first round out of the way while she was fresh. Jake snorted. When she looked over, he was wiping a grin off his face.

"You sure?" Buck smirked.

Bunny answered by climbing onto the trailer and planting herself on one of the wheel wells.

"Well, okay then. Let's head out." Buck climbed up on the tractor, stifling a groan. Jake took a seat across from Bunny. His stare reminded her of a dog trying to find the source of a strange sound. She looked toward the house. Ruff was racing toward them. As Buck pulled away, he whistled at the loping hound. Ruff caught them by the time they hit the field and jumped on the trailer. He took his place at Bunny's feet, facing Jake. Tail wagging and panting, she could have sworn he was smiling at Jake. Bunny was grateful for the ally, four-legged though he was.

The work was backbreaking. Bunny felt every bump and

bruise from the day before. She pulled the bales from the tractor and tossed them to Jake. As the stack grew, she had to toss them higher and higher. They didn't speak. Staying upright as they bumped along took all her concentration. She wasn't sure what they would have to do if she dropped one, but she expected it would fall to her to fix it. So, she focused alternately on the back of the baler and Jake. The stack of bales pushed Jake closer and closer to Bunny until they were side by side.

They hauled the trailer back to the hay shed and transferred the bales. Jake threw them down to her, and she stacked them in the shed. They repeated this, wasting no energy on unnecessary words. Hard labor always took the chip off Bunny's shoulder, or at least that was what her dad told her. She was spent by the time they finished. The thought of going on a date made her want to turn out all the lights and hide in her bunk.

That was until Jake got the last word. "Have fun tonight. I hope he's not counting on dancing."

Those ten words gave her a second wind.

CHAPTER 41

JEREMIAH 1982

JEREMIAH DIDN'T AGREE with his dad, but he did as he was told, like he always did. He picked Friday night when a lot of the guys he knew would be at the Lodge. He waited until the dinner crowd thinned out to head over. Even then, he sat in his truck in the parking lot staring at the knots in the logs until someone pounded on the window, shattering the silence.

"Jeremiah, what the hell are you doing? You sleeping in there?" He turned to find his friends standing there laughing at him. His dad was right. People were going to wonder why he wasn't himself. Pushing the truck door open, he forced himself to smile.

"Long day." He shrugged it off and hoped they'd let it go. "The beer's getting warm. Let's go, boys. It's Friday night." He had been saying those words since high school. If he could fool these guys, he could fool anyone. They found a table midway between the bar and the dance floor. They'd decided years ago this was the best location. Pretty girls who liked to dance gravitated to the tables on the edge of the dance floor. This gave the men a chance to assess them. They had devised the three-F system in high school in which they assigned ten points each for face, figure, and flexibility. Face and figure were easy. Flexibility was another thing. That was where the dance floor came in. They had never given any girl a thirty. Jeremiah would have given Katie one, though he'd never seen her dance.

"You already set your sights? We just got here." One of his buddies set a beer in front of him.

"Nah. Just getting a jump start on scoring." He raised the bottle to his friend and took a long drink. Laughing, they turned to the growing crowd. There were a few couples, but far more groups of girls. He spotted the waitress from the Back Forty. The one his dad was so keen on.

He'd been watching girls with a growing interest since Katie tossed his favorite hat in the river after he and Connor threw mud pies at her and Jesse. She was fierce. When she was mad, the color would rise in her cheeks, and she would flip her hair back before she took off after him. Jeremiah loved making her mad just to see that fire. He knew the waitress was nothing like Katie, and that was what he liked most about Mindy. He would never confuse the two. She wasn't going to stand up to him. She wasn't going to give him a fiery attitude. Mindy was going to do whatever he wanted.

Mindy stood on the outskirts of a group of women. She was long and lean, with curves that, though understated, were far from absent. Her blond hair flowed in loose curls just below her shoulders. Though she was wearing basically what everyone else was—jeans, boots, shirt—it was anything but basic. Her jeans were skintight. Strategically unbuttoned, her blouse gave every guy in the place a hint of her breasts. Her boots were red and not cowboy by a long shot. Periodically, she looked at the other women and said something. She gave them a brief smile or laugh but didn't let it distract her from searching the room for a prospect.

Jeremiah looked away before she caught his eye. He was

about a six-pack short of being ready to flirt with any girl, let alone a pro like Mindy. He swallowed down his first one and waved the empty at the waitress. He bought a round, not to be magnanimous, but to contribute to the drunkenness of his buddies. With any luck, he wouldn't say anything stupid. To hedge his bet, he was going to make sure they were too drunk to remember if he did.

It didn't take long for Jeremiah to loosen up. He went a couple rounds on the dance floor to keep up appearances. He didn't want the girls to get the wrong idea, so he changed it up each time. In between, Jeremiah returned to the table to join in the alcohol-enhanced speculation of how the night would end. He caught Mindy watching him out of the corner of his eye. He was sure she was going to ask him to dance, but apparently, she had more pride than he'd thought. His dad was right, though. She was a sure thing. That fact was obvious when she steered her dance partner right in front of Jeremiah so he couldn't miss her moves. She met his eyes and held them as she rocked her hips, hands above her head. The poor sap she was dancing with was too mesmerized by her body to notice she wasn't dancing for him.

Jeremiah smiled at her and ordered another beer. When he turned to find her again, she was gone. He searched the bar for her, but he found Jake James staring him down from a stool instead. Jake leaned back, one elbow on the bar, the other lifting a bottle. His jaw was set, and his lips formed a straight line. Being Rocky's son, Jeremiah refused to look away. He welcomed whatever punishment Jake was going to deliver. To speed up the process, he let a grin slide up the right side of his face and, to ensure he got the point, he tipped his beer in his direction. Jake was off the stool before Jeremiah took another drink. He charged across the dance floor, bumping into Mindy, who'd found another victim. Jeremiah stood and braced himself. He was in the mood for a good fight and Jake James was a bonus.

"You asshole." Jake closed in, toe to toe with him.

"What's your problem, James?" Jeremiah shoved him backward.

Jake stumbled into the crowd but came back ready to fight with a finger in his face. "You know exactly what my problem is. It's all your fault."

Before Jeremiah could answer, the bartender came around the bar and wedged himself between them. "Not in here, boys. Take it outside, preferably into the street and not in my parking lot." With a hand on each man's chest, he gave them a shove. The practiced move was little more than a warning, but it got their attention.

Jeremiah swallowed down the last of his beer, looked Jake in the eye so he wouldn't misunderstand, and started walking out of the bar. Jake hit him in the back as he passed through the door. Jeremiah stumbled forward on his knee. He was sober enough to feel the pain but drunk enough to ignore it. He waited a beat too long to get up. Jake caught him in the shoulder with the point of his boot. Jeremiah broke another one of Rocky's rules: never let them take you to the ground. Launching himself from the pavement, he gave Jake an uppercut. To be sure he ended the fight before it really got going, he hit him dead-on, and Jake went to his knees.

He leaned over him, willing him to get back up. When he didn't, Jeremiah said, "She didn't love you, Jake. Hell, she barely noticed you."

Jake lunged and pinned Jeremiah against a truck. "She was too good for you. You're just like your old man." Someone grabbed Jake's arm as he cocked it back, but he shook him off. "I'm done. You're not worth the trouble." He picked up his hat and walked away.

Jeremiah scanned the crowd. How many of them knew the truth?

Mindy was waiting for him at his truck. "You need a ride, cowboy?" It was probably the adrenaline, but he wanted to screw her. When he didn't say anything, she offered, "Look, you've been drinking, and you just got in a fight. Why don't you slow your roll on bad decisions and let me drive you home?"

"I'm fine."

"That's what all the drunks say. In my experience, and I have a lot, drunks aren't the best judge of their abilities."

"I don't want to leave my truck here."

"Fine, I'll drive your truck. Your dad can bring me back here."

"Good chance he's already drunk too." Jake was right. The apple didn't fall far from the tree.

"Then I'll spend the night. You can bring me back in the morning." Jeremiah squinted at the offer. "Don't worry. You and your dad are safe. I don't seduce drunk men and I'm not a murderer."

Jeremiah was suddenly exhausted. He looked back at the bar. Where were his buddies during all of this? He tossed her his keys, opened the passenger door, and pulled himself up into the truck.

The truck jolted him awake when it stopped in front of his house. Stumbling out of the cab, he stood staring at the lights in the front room. Would Jesse let him sleep on her floor? Thunderbird would let him crawl in his stall and crash in the hay, but with his luck, he would get stomped by his own horse.

"Let's get you inside. It's cold out here." She put her arm around his waist to support him, but he pulled away to clutch the stair rail.

"Sorry." He hadn't meant to be harsh.

Rocky opened the door as they were coming up the stairs. "Everything okay?" he said, looking Mindy up and down.

"He had a few too many and got into it with Jake James from the Midnight Sun," Mindy offered. Jeremiah started to introduce them, but apparently it wasn't necessary.

"Did they bust up the bar?"

"Nope. Just each other. He's going to have a pretty good bump on his knee and cheek. He got in a good punch, though."

Jeremiah kept moving. He was bone-tired and sore. He wanted to lie down and didn't care much where.

Rocky called to him, "I'm gonna drive Mindy back to her car. Don't do anything stupid while I'm gone."

Jeremiah waved off his dad. Before falling asleep, he realized it wasn't a good idea for Mindy to be alone with his father, but he didn't have the energy to do anything about it.

CHAPTER 42

BUNNY 1984

RUFF TOOK TO Bunny's side and followed her to her room. Apparently, following the tractor around all day wore him out. He didn't even make it to the bed before plopping unceremoniously on the floor just inside the door. Bunny knew how he felt. As she undressed, she remembered the unopened letter she'd shoved into her pocket. She took it out and looked at it again, praying she had misread it but knowing she had not. Bunny O'Kelly c/o Midnight Sun Ranch. *Thanks a lot, Mom.* She tossed it, unopened, on the chest of drawers.

It took a while to wash the dust-caked sweat off her skin. She was a tomato by the time she got out, partially from the heat and partially from the scrubbing. Had Buck and Jake conspired to make sure she was as unattractive as possible for her date?

Bunny sat on the bed, still dripping, staring at the contents of her duffel. She had packed with work in mind. Setting the standard at appropriate for a date, she had to settle for not wrinkled. Dumping the bag out on her bed, she pawed through the clothes. At the bottom of the pile, she found her show shirt. Thanking

God for a mother who was sick and tired of ironing by the time Bunny was five, she pulled out the permanent press Western shirt in a gaudy red with black piping and pearl buttons. She prayed he wasn't planning to take her to a nice restaurant.

Resigned, she pulled on a clean pair of Levi's and her good boots. Looking in the mirror, she wished she had listened to even one word of her mother's advice on makeup. Her skin was ruddy, and her lips were cracked from the sun. Her hands felt like bales of hay as she tugged her fingers through her tangled waves. There wasn't time to let it air dry, so she dug out the dryer. With every passing moment, her hair expanded into an unruly mane. The ginger waves were ostentatious enough. Now they were expanding to a volume appropriate only on the stage of the Grand Ole Opry. Resisting the urge to pull on a baseball cap, she braided it into one thick plait down her back. Like most wild things, her hair fought being tamed. Tendrils escaped the confines of the band before she even got in the truck.

Bunny met Jeremiah at the Back Forty. The log structure was heavy and squat like a bulldog. The highway ran right by it as if it had been the end of the road once. Parking was in the back. Bunny drove around the building to find a sea of pickup trucks. Spying one with the Double J Ranch logo parked in the front of the lot, she pulled in near it. She sat in the truck. What the hell was she doing? Bunny didn't want a boyfriend. Like most of her worst decisions, she was on this date basically because Jake dared her to do it. She was putting the key in the ignition, ready to drive away, when someone knocked on the window. Dropping the keys, Bunny scrambled to grab them, hitting her nose on the steering wheel. With nose in hand, she turned to find Jeremiah standing at the window.

His words spilled out in an embarrassed rush. "Sorry. I saw you out here and I thought you were lost. I didn't mean to scare you. Are you okay?"

Bunny couldn't help herself and laughed. She opened the truck door and slid to the ground. "I'm fine, just startled."

He led her inside to a table where half a beer sat warming on a paper placemat.

"Am I late? I'm so sorry I kept you waiting," she stammered.

"You're not late. I was early." Jeremiah looked at her with a gentle smile. They made small talk until the waitress stopped by the table to take their orders.

"Jeremiah," she said, never looking at Bunny. "What can I get you?"

"I'll have a beer and a burger." He turned to Bunny. "What would you like?" He repeated her order to the waitress, who gave him a smile that looked more accusatory than friendly and then walked away.

"Another friend of yours?" It was petty, but Bunny couldn't help herself.

"Well, like I said, it's a small town. We're all friends here." With a quick lift of his eyebrows, a smile swept up one side of his face.

"Not everyone," Bunny returned. "Buck and Jake, for example."

"Well, you got me there." He tipped his head to the table.

"What's that all about, anyway?"

"It's fun to wind Jake up and watch him spin. I suspect he's been influenced by Buck. And Buck?" He paused, picking at the label on his beer. "Well, that's hard to say. Our families used to be real good friends until his wife died. Then we quit hanging around together."

The waitress arrived with their order, breaking up the conversation. She handed Jeremiah his beer and placed his plate on the table. She dropped Bunny's on the table in front of her, then smiled at Jeremiah and walked away.

"I think she likes you."

He turned and watched the waitress walk away. "Her? Nah. Wouldn't matter if she did. I'm here with you right now." Jeremiah looked Bunny in the eye and held it there. His eyes said he was telling the truth. Bunny's gut wasn't so sure.

"So, the Millers and Coopers were friends. What were Connor and Katie like?" Jeremiah quickly stiffened at her question.

"It's been about a decade since I spent any time with them." He took a pull on his beer and looked around the room, avoiding Bunny's eyes.

"I thought it was a small town where everybody's a friend," she teased.

"I guess not everybody."

His tone told her to change the subject. "So, tell me about your family."

"I think it's my turn to ask the questions. I don't know anything about you. Where did you even come from?" he asked.

She gave him the *Reader's Digest* version of the O'Kelly family. She told him about dairy farming and how it compared to horse ranching. As they talked, Bunny realized just how different they were. She had always thought she wanted to own a dairy. She wasn't so sure now. Cows were like machines you took care of so they would produce milk or babies who would, in turn, produce more milk. Horses were more like people. They had personalities and moods, and they challenged her. She loved working with them. Riding them was as close to right as she ever felt. She even liked their people. Still, maybe if she had a dad like Katie's, she would have stayed.

Jeremiah let her ramble on. She lost track of time until he said, "I'd like to hear more, but I think our food is getting cold."

"I'm so sorry. I guess my mom is right. I do not know when to shut up."

They ate in silence for a while before she got the courage to ask about his family again. "So now you know all about me. It's your turn. Do you have brothers or sisters? What are your parents like?" His face hardened, so she threw in another to lighten the mood. "What do you want to be when you grow up?"

He laughed. "Hey, I am a grown-up." He took a swig.

She bet this was his tell in poker.

"Unlike you, I have one sister. We're twins." He took another drink, but slowly, biding his time.

"Come on. Spill. What's that like?" she prodded.

"What? The twin thing? Well, it's not what people imagine. We aren't identical. We look alike, like most brothers and sisters do. Our personalities are very different. She's quiet. Well, except for when she's riding River. Then she's a maniac." He laughed and shook his head. "She loves that horse. You'll see her if you go to the fair. She's a barrel racer, and she's damn good," he said with admiration. Bunny couldn't picture any of her brothers talking about her that way.

"That must be nice."

"What?"

"Being close to your sister like that."

"You're not close to your brothers?"

"Patrick, I guess." She pictured the four of them. Her memories came back in decades as they grew into men. In every picture, she was chasing them down or trying to keep up. "But the others . . . Mick isn't close to anyone. Francis and John have the twin thing going. They'll probably live in the same house when they're married. Patrick gets me. He doesn't treat me like a girl."

"But you are a girl."

Bunny raised her eyebrows.

"Woman, I mean."

"I'm not sure you can understand," Bunny said.

"Because I'm a guy? Try me."

"I loved working on the farm." She took her beer bottle in both hands and turned it in circles on the table. "And I was good at it. I pulled my weight and then some." Looking at him for a sign of doubt, she settled the bottle and pushed her back against the chair. "It felt like Mick was always testing me. Giving me something harder and harder. Like he expected me to break." She shook her head. "Francis and John always tried to step in and take over like they didn't think I could do it. Patrick's the only one who ever just let me be me. Let me screw up and dust myself off." She took a drink and let the truth settle. "And then there's my dad who never wanted me to work on the farm. He never hid that fact, but I always thought I could live up to him and change his mind. Turns out I was dead wrong."

"So that's why you came up here."

"The sad truth is, I probably would have taken that forever. Then my dad announced he was retiring and leaving the farm to the boys. Cut me right out. That was the last straw."

"I'm sorry. I'd be angry if my dad did that to me after putting in all those years on the ranch."

"I bet it's more likely to happen to your sister."

"Still, I would give her half. Hell, she's held the whole thing together since my mom walked out on us." He said it so matter-of-fact, like it was nothing. He must have noticed her surprise, because he added, "Well, this has taken a turn." He laughed. Something over her shoulder wiped the smile off his face. "Speak of the devil."

Bunny turned to find a man approaching them. He walked bowlegged but chest out like he thought he was still a young buck. His cowboy hat had weathered more than a few winters. His clothes were dusty, like he'd come from working in the fields. The only shiny thing was his belt buckle, and even that had seen better days. Jeremiah and the man held each other's gaze without wavering. The closer the guy got, the clearer it was that they were related. Though lined and rough, the older man's face had all the same angles as Jeremiah's. He walked right up to the table like he was invited.

"Well, son, who do we have here?" He took his hat off and turned to Bunny.

"Benny, this is my dad, Rocky Cooper. Dad, this is Benny O'Kelly." He made the introductions while staring at his dad, whose mouth was a harsh line.

"Benny? Strange name for a girl." The words slithered off his tongue.

"Yes, it is." Bunny didn't like him. She bristled at the way he challenged his son. Instantly, she sized him up as one of those men who tried to put everybody in their place. And that place was always beneath him.

"I haven't seen you around before." It was an accusation.

"Dad," Jeremiah warned.

"What? I got an interest in who you're spending time with. I just expected it to be Mindy." He looked her way, like he was hoping she would be surprised or hurt. Bunny would never give him that. Her daddy taught her how to stare down a charging dog, and Rocky Cooper struck her as just that.

"Dad. That's enough," Jeremiah warned. Was he angry because his dad outed him as a player? Like she hadn't already heard he was?

Rocky turned to Bunny. "So, where you from, young lady?" The condescension dripped from his lips.

"I'm a ranch hand at the Midnight Sun." She took a pull on her beer.

Rocky shot his son an angry look. "A ranch hand? Well, that's a tough job for any man. Must be even harder for a girl."

"Well, Mr. Cooper, I do just fine. But thanks for the concern." Her Irish was rising.

Jeremiah must have sensed it. "Time to go, Dad."

"Nice to meet you." He tipped his hat. "I'll see you back at the Double J, son."

Jeremiah sat silently for a moment. He took a big drink of his beer and set it a bit too loudly on the table. Bunny jumped.

"I'm sorry. My dad was out of line."

"Mindy?" She knew she probably should have let that go since this was a first and probably only date, but Bunny hated being played. She wanted him to know it.

"There is no Mindy. I mean, there is a Mindy. We went out a couple times. We are not going out, now or ever again."

"You don't owe me an explanation."

"I do, though. It seems like people have filled your head with some ideas about me. I suspect Jake James." He said the name like it tasted bad on his tongue. "Whatever he said, I can tell you I am not. I've dated a lot of women. I just haven't found one I want to date steady."

"Seriously, you don't owe me an explanation. I'm not looking for a relationship here. I had a nice time."

He let out a breath, and Bunny wasn't sure if it was relief or anger management.

"It doesn't have to be over. What do you say we hit the dance floor?"

"I don't dance, remember? Plus, I have the early feeding tomorrow."

"Jake." He shook his head.

"Yup, Jake." She smirked. "And probably with Buck's blessing."

He walked Bunny to the truck. In that moment, he didn't come across as the player others said he was. He hung one hand from the door and the other on the bed, not caging her in but making sure she was in before he shut the door. He looked her in the eye.

"To prove what a nice guy I am, I'm not even going to try to kiss you."

"Well, to prove I'm immune to your charms, I'm not going to act disappointed."

"I had a good time. I'd like to do this again."

"Are you asking me out?"

He grinned. "You're not going to cut me any breaks, are you?"

"Nope."

"I promise my dad won't join us." He looked so hopeful.

"Then yes, I will go out with you again."

He leaned in and, as she was about to pull away, planted the whisper of a kiss on her cheek. Without a word, he shut the door and walked away. Bunny guessed that was cowboy for *I'll call you.*

CHAPTER 43

ROCKY 1982

ROCKY COULDN'T BELIEVE his luck. He took it as a sign from a God he no longer believed in that Jeremiah ran into Mindy on his first night out. If he hadn't been home, would Mindy have taken him to bed? She seemed like that kind of girl. Hell, he might just have gotten lucky too, especially since his boy was in no shape to satisfy any woman, let alone one like Mindy. Planting the seed wouldn't be the chore he'd imagined.

"Thanks for bringing Jeremiah home. He's been working pretty hard. Must be blowing off steam." Rocky turned to smile at her and caught her watching him.

"No worries. I assumed he was taking Katie Miller's death hard."

When he glanced over again, she was staring out the front windshield. She was sharper than he'd given her credit for.

"Did you know Katie?" he asked.

"Not really. I met her a couple of times when Jeremiah brought her to dinner at the Back Forty." She turned and met his eyes. Far sharper than he gave her credit for. He broke off his stare at the scream of his tires hitting the rumble strips at the edge of the road.

Time to go fishing. "They've been friends since they were little kids."

"They sure looked pretty friendly to me," she offered. When Rocky didn't respond, Mindy continued. "Must be nice to have friends you grew up with."

"Well, you can never have enough. I suspect he'll be needing a new one."

"Jeremiah's a nice guy, but I get the idea he's not too interested in me, friend or otherwise. Maybe I'm not his type."

"Well, don't give up too soon." He glanced over, and Mindy was smiling at him. "You're definitely his type. Hell, you're everybody's type."

Her grin grew. Rocky almost felt sorry for her. She thought it was a compliment.

He pulled up next to the only car in the lot. As he glanced around, he counted four guys who were too drunk or too horny to drive themselves home. Rocky was guessing a couple of them were both, and that made him envy their youth. He wished he had it in him to make it the whole night in a woman's bed.

"Thanks for bringing him home. I suspect we'll be seeing you again."

She opened the door. Before hopping to the ground, she turned to him and said, "I sure hope so." She flashed a smile that made him think maybe it didn't matter which of the Cooper men she got, as long as she got one of them.

CHAPTER 44

BUNNY 1984

BUNNY WAS DOG-TIRED the next day but determined not to show it. She rolled out of bed with the only groan she'd allow herself that day. Ruff flopped his head backward to watch her hobble to the bathroom. He'd been waiting outside her door when she got home. Clearly, he'd fallen asleep on the job as she caught him shaking himself awake when she drove up. She took his tail wagging as an invitation to tell him about the night. When she got to the part about going on another date with Jeremiah, the big dog lay down with a deep sigh. Ruff wasn't sold on Jeremiah, either.

Though her stomach grumbled, Bunny skipped breakfast. She could handle Ruff's silent judgment, but Jake and Buck wouldn't let her off as easy. With the head start, she had most of the feeding done before they came down to the barn. They came in from the door near the studs. Buck met her in the aisle as she was finishing.

"We're gonna take the stallions out to the arena this morning for exercise. Make sure no one brings any other horses out when we're moving them."

The stallions were big and unpredictable. Huey, in particular, was young and dumb. Dante was the easiest one to handle, but since coming to the Midnight Sun, even he had picked up some bad habits from Huey. Though they were at the opposite end of the barn from the mares, accidents could happen while a stallion was out of his stall.

Buck took Hollywood out first. The animal fought the lead, head straining upward and legs prancing. With a firm grip on the lead, Buck walked the animal forward like there was nothing special about him. Jake walked alongside the horse, all the while scanning back and forth between the horse and the barn door.

As soon as they got to the arena, Jake backed off and let them work. Bunny watched from the barn for a while. She had a lot to learn, and she hoped Buck would teach her. Letting the horse take the lead, he let the line out and commanded him to trot. As the big horse made his way around the circle, Buck moved toward and away but always stayed a bit behind to keep him moving. With a flash of his outstretched right hand, he kept the horse's attention when his eyes or ears strayed backward. He put the horse at ease without ever giving up any control. It was like Buck knew his place in the world was right there, and he didn't have anything to prove. Every movement was graceful and confident. He never got angry or frustrated—like he knew the horse would do exactly as he asked.

Bunny was about halfway through cleaning the barn when they brought Hollywood back in. She came out of Sonny's stall to see Jake leading the big horse in the back door. He was lathered, but they wouldn't be bringing him down to clean him up. The mares would flat lose their minds.

The clop of hooves came from behind her. She turned, and a chill ran down her spine. A boarder opened a stall to bring his gelding out. The horses saw each other, and both reared up against their leads. The lead slipped through Jake's hands. As the horse went up, Jake fell backward, slamming into the stall door. Buck grabbed the lead and got Hollywood's head under control. He turned him quickly in a circle and led him into his stall. The boarder backed his horse up and shut the stall door. Both horses stomped, but the only casualty was Jake's ego.

"What the hell, Benny? You had one job!" He pushed off the stall door and stormed toward her. The boarder backed against the door to let him by.

Bunny's stomach sunk to her feet. She froze in place.

"Buck specifically told you to make sure no one was moving a horse while the studs were being brought in or out of the barn. Did you not hear him? I could've been killed. One hoof to the head is all it takes." He slammed his fist against the wall. "You're useless."

The heat of his anger was like a blast furnace. She held her breath and tightened her chest to stop the pooling tears from spilling down her cheeks. Ruff took his place pressed against her right leg, a low rumble oozing from his throat.

"What? Nothing to say. No zippy comeback, *Bunny?*"

Buck made his way down the aisle. "That's enough, Jake. Calm down."

"No. I knew this was a bad idea. She doesn't know what she's doing. She shouldn't be here. You would never have hired her if she had been honest about who she was." He was shouting in his face and Buck stood there, motionless.

Bunny was done taking it from Jake or any other guy. "Now wait a goddamn minute. First, I never lied about who I was. Second, I didn't hear him come in or I would have told him to hold the horse. It was a mistake. The fact is, you didn't get hurt." She pointed at Jake. "If you hadn't let the lead slip, Hollywood wouldn't have gone up at all. And I have busted my ass. I've been taking everything you've dished out since the day I set foot on this ranch. Most of it was bullshit. You made it harder than it had to be because you never wanted me here. I don't know what the hell your problem is, and frankly, I don't care. You're not running me off. I earned my spot here, and I am damn well staying." She pulled her cap down and tightened her ponytail.

"It's not up to you, Bunny." He dug his heels in and crossed his arms over his chest.

Bunny did the same. "And it's not up to you, either. While we're at it, don't call me that name again."

There they stood, nose to nose, her heart pounding in her chest. She willed her breath to slow as the hound pushed against her leg.

The boarder broke the silence. "Buck, there's no harm done on my part. She was cleaning a stall when I came in. I didn't see that Hollywood's door was open. Accidents happen, man. That's all this was." He gave Bunny a pat on the shoulder and walked away.

"Thanks, Colt. Glad Star's okay," Buck called after him. Colt gave a backhanded wave.

"And it's not up to Colt Browning, either," Jake stated.

Buck stepped up to him and said, "No, Jake. It's not up to Colt Browning, or Benny, or, for that matter, you. It's up to me. And Benny's right. She's done everything we've asked, and she doesn't bitch or moan about it, either. We should have warned her we were coming in." He took off his hat and brushed some dust from the brim. "That should be standard operating procedure when moving the studs. Even if she told every boarder, they still could have passed us in the aisle not knowing when we were coming in. It was an accident. We need to make sure it doesn't happen again."

Bunny knew better than to throw it in Jake's face. She uncrossed her arms. "I'm sorry. I'll be more careful when you're out with them."

Jake said nothing. He dropped his arms and rolled up his sleeves while staring her down. Then he walked away.

"He'll get over it," Buck murmured.

"No, he won't. He doesn't want me here. I'm used to that, though."

"It's not about you."

"Sure seems like it is."

"Well, maybe partially. But the other part is that he got stomped once bull riding. He isn't anxious to repeat that experience." Buck patted her on the shoulder and looked down at the dog. "He'll come around."

Bunny wasn't so sure, but she let it go.

"Finish up the stalls. Then I need you to pick up a load of hay. Better get a move on too. Supposed to rain tonight." He dug out the keys, dropped them in her hand, and walked away.

She stood there watching him. She couldn't figure him out. He took her begrudgingly at best. This was his chance to get rid of her. For all her bravado, she knew she'd screwed up. Jake was right about that. Why Buck took her side escaped her. Whatever the reason, she was thankful and determined not to screw it up again, starting with getting the hay in before the rain came.

CHAPTER 45

JEREMIAH 1982

JEREMIAH HEARD HIS dad downstairs. Though his head pounded with every beat of his heart, he was grateful for last night's beer. It was the first night Katie hadn't haunted his dreams. Still, was she in heaven watching, disgusted that he let Mindy take him home? Perhaps that was why she hadn't come to him last night.

At the clang of pots and pans, he knew it was safe to open his eyes and face his dad. Jesse was there. Jeremiah believed that when God separated them in the womb, He did not divide their genes evenly. Jeremiah got the height and the charm genes. Jesse got all the gutsy genes and most of the brainy ones. She would have paraded Katie around like the prize that she was. She would have said *I love you* first. When it came to his boldest moves, he wasn't much more than his father's puppet.

He rolled onto his back and tried to open his eyes. Gritty salt filled the corners, forcing him to blink several times before the room came into view. His jeans still held the sweat of last night's fight, cold and damp against his thighs. He tried to muster up enough spit to clear the taste of mud from his mouth, but it was bone-dry. Jeremiah didn't have much time, but he had to wash off the night before first. Stumbling the twenty feet from his bed to the shower, he turned the faucet up to a punishing temperature. As soon as the spray hit his face, he began to sob. His tears mingled with the river of water, so he might have convinced himself he wasn't crying. But his belly contracted. His heart ripped. As he slid to the floor, the cold tile on his back and the steaming water on his front met as a shock to his core. The water pelted him in fat drops, making it hard to breathe.

Jeremiah missed Katie more than he missed his mom. She hadn't left him on purpose. Katie would have come back to him. She would have seen how sad he was without her. Unlike his mother, she wouldn't have been selfish. In the end, he hadn't had the courage to chase her down and beg her to come back. His tears flowed for the man he knew he wasn't.

Jesse pounded on the door once. "Get a move on, Jeremiah. Breakfast is getting cold." Jesse waited for no man, and she never warned you twice. Jeremiah stood and turned the shower slowly to cold. Raising his face to the water, he held his breath as long as he could. He never let his dad see him with crying eyes. That was the trigger for a *time to toughen you up, boy* moment. He despised those father-son talks.

When he got downstairs, Jesse was dishing up breakfast. Rocky sat listing to his right side. His left thumb was hooked in his watch pocket, and his right forearm lay on the table as he reached for his coffee mug. Only Jeremiah and Jesse knew this practiced move hid the pain from a lifetime of backbreaking work.

Rocky and Jesse didn't say much to each other since she'd moved out to the barn. When their mom had left, Jesse took over the cooking, which spared her from haying. She helped keep the horses fed and the barn clean. She taught riding lessons. But she drew the line at baling hay.

"What happened to you last night?" Jesse gave him a sly smile.

"Leave him alone. He just had a little fun with the new girl down at the Back Forty." Rocky winked at Jeremiah.

"She drove me home is all. Believe me, no one had any fun last night." He kept his eyes on Jesse.

"Well, just a matter of time, son. She's taken a shine to you."

"She's taken a shine to everybody. And I'm not interested." Jeremiah scolded himself for being sucked into this conversation.

"Well, that's not like you, big brother," Jesse teased, a jab at their birth order. Jeremiah didn't reply, hoping it would end the discussion.

"She left her phone number. She said she thought you might have lost it." Rocky dug out a scrap of paper from his pocket and tried to hand it to Jeremiah. He stared at it a moment before turning his eyes to Rocky.

"Thanks, but I said I wasn't interested."

"You will be. Keep the number. You never know when you might be in need of something warm and friendly."

Jesse got up and put her jacket on. "Jesus, Dad, you're talking about a woman, not a dog." She turned her attention to Jeremiah. "And you, time to get off your ass and start earning your keep around here. I don't know what the hell is wrong with you, but I'm done covering for you in the barn." Without waiting for a reply, she stomped out the back door.

"You need to call that girl and take her out. It's the only way to cure what ails you." With that, Rocky got up, leaving Jeremiah alone to contemplate the scrap of paper he'd left on the table. It made him sick to his stomach, but he picked it up, like he knew he would, and put it in his pocket. His dad was right. He left his cold eggs on the plate and headed to the barn.

Jesse was in the ring with a student when he got there. She had pulled her hair back into a ponytail, revealing his mother's face. Jesse commanded the ring with the confidence of a reigning queen. How had she managed to take all the good stuff from their mother? Sometimes, when she was riding or teaching a lesson, Jeremiah would pretend he was watching their mom. He knew it robbed something from Jesse, but he couldn't deny himself the memory of her. Without those moments, she would have faded from the photo album in his head.

Jesse caught his eye and waved. Except for Rocky, she forgave easily. He wished he could tell her about Katie.

Rocky yelled from the barn, "Get a move on, boy. There're stalls that need cleaning." He avoided the ring for the same reason Jeremiah was drawn to it. With that knowledge, Jeremiah lingered there. It was a weak rebellion. He was ashamed of the pride he took in it.

"Boy, you better get your ass moving."

CHAPTER 46

BUNNY 1984

Bunny hustled through the rest of her chores. When she got to War Horse's stall, she found him stock-still, staring at her. A big, black, speckled wall.

"Back up." She unlatched the door, but he didn't move. She looked down at Ruff. "A little help here?" He, too, was perfectly still, looking straight ahead. Bunny was weary, but she hadn't yet burned off her anger. She pushed the stall door open with a flourish, which was usually enough to get any of the horses moving. Not this time. He just stood there, staring her down.

"Come on, War Horse. Move it. I need to get done." Nothing. He didn't move an inch. She looked again to Ruff. Not one snowy hair moved. "Dammit. If you want to ride tonight, you need to move your ass, horse." He lowered his head as if taking exception to having any part of his body referred to as an ass. "I've moved heifers more stubborn than you, old man." She reached out to push on his shoulder. He reached out to hers and gave it a nip. "What the hell!" She rubbed her shoulder. It was a warning shot. She wasn't hurt.

"What did I tell you?"

Bunny cringed at hearing Jake behind her. She shivered at the thought that he was following her around, trying to catch her making a mistake. She didn't bother to turn around. "I'm fine. He was just playing."

"It's your funeral." He sauntered away.

Bunny looked back at the big horse. "Dude, you can't do that crap in front of Jake." War Horse nodded his broad head and snorted. She reached up and stroked it. He leaned in, begging her to scratch his ears. As she stroked his ebony neck, the venom drained right out of her. Ruff brushed past her legs and headed out to the paddock. He let out a mighty woof, and War Horse turned to follow him.

Carolina was brushing Sonny down when Bunny finished War Horse's stall.

"Are you okay?" she asked.

"Yeah, why?" Bunny put down the wheelbarrow.

"My dad told me about this morning."

"Oh, yeah. No big deal. I'm fine," Bunny answered quickly, not wanting to relive her mistake.

"Wow. I would be fuming if Jake dressed me down like that in front of everyone. My dad said he was completely out of line." Carolina's anger pointed to personal experience. "I couldn't have stood up to him like you did. Dad said you let him have it with both barrels." As fast as it bubbled up, the anger was gone, and her face lit up.

"Well, I might have won the battle, but the war is still on." Bunny wanted to feel proud, but she knew it was going to make Jake want to put her in her place even more. "Buck stood up for me, probably just a habit from having a daughter."

"What? No." Carolina shook her head. "She worked hard and Buck gave Katie her due, but he never let her slack off. Jake would never have raised his voice to Katie. Well, anyway, I say celebrate the victory."

Bunny tried to hold it in, but a smile spread across her face.

It was short-lived, though, as Jake's boots hammered down the aisle. "Are you ready to go? We need to get a move on," he clipped.

"Go where?" Bunny asked.

"I'm going with you to get hay."

"I don't need any help. I got it myself before." Bunny was not driving anywhere with him.

"Besides, I'm going with Benny," Carolina piped in.

They both turned to look at her. Bunny was stunned. Carolina did not strike her as the kind of woman who picked up hay. She certainly wasn't going to be much help moving it.

Jake scoffed. "You're going to pick up hay? What would your daddy say about that?"

He had a mean streak. Bunny was preparing to let him have it when Carolina responded.

"I expect he would say, have fun and be careful. He always says that. But I tell you what, Jake, why don't you give him a call, and we can ask him." Carolina stared him down. Bunny's eyes turned to platters.

"Suit yourself," he said, walking away in defeat.

Bunny turned to her. Though Carolina's hands covered her mouth, Bunny could see it was agape. "Oh, my God. I cannot believe I did that. That felt so good. Does it always feel that good?" Her eyes were pleading.

"Does what feel that good?"

"Letting a jerk like Jake have it. You know, when some guy acts like you can't do something because you're a girl."

"Yeah. It always feels that good," Bunny said with a laugh. "But sometimes, they let you have it back. That doesn't feel too good. But it's worth it."

"Well, let's go get some hay." Carolina grabbed Sonny's lead and led him to his stall.

Bunny couldn't refuse her after her triumphant moment. She threw an extra pair of gloves and hay hooks in the truck in case Carolina wanted to help. As she cleaned up her gear, Bunny hooked up the trailer. When she was through, she found Carolina waiting in the passenger seat, beaming.

As they headed up the drive, they met Buck walking back to the barn. He leaned his hands on the window.

"And where are you two off to?" he asked.

"Picking up hay," Bunny stated, holding her ground through his questioning look.

"I'm going with her," Carolina announced.

"I see that." Buck's tone was stern, but it didn't show on his face.

"I've never picked up hay before." Carolina was giddy now.

Buck looked at her, and his face softened. Something passed between them, but Bunny couldn't put her finger on it. "Well, you be careful. Both of you." He pushed off the truck and let them pass. When she looked in the rearview mirror, Buck was shaking his head and smiling.

They bounced down the road. What was it like to have guys just give into you? She wanted to ask, but she thought just saying it somehow diminished her friend. It must be a double-edged sword. People underestimated Carolina. Was the cost of getting their help having to be, or at least acting, helpless? Bunny always felt like she had to fight. Did Carolina think she never could? Two sides of the same coin.

Carolina broke the silence. "So, how does this work?"

Bunny was having some very uncharitable thoughts about pretty girls when she remembered Carolina boarded her horse. She had no reason to pick up hay. Bunny was ashamed for doing to Carolina what every man she ever worked with did to her.

She'd dismissed her as a girl who couldn't do anything for herself. A girl who was playing at the work—the adult version of dress-up.

"Don't worry about it. It's not hard. I'll show you." Bunny turned her head to look at Carolina, who was smiling. Bunny didn't know what to do with that.

Carolina broke the silence. "My dad said you remind him of Katie, but fiercer."

Bunny laughed. "I thought Jake liked Katie. I guess I don't remind him of her."

"I think you might be wrong. That could be why he's so hard on you. Jake was in love with Katie."

Bunny turned to her, veering the truck onto the gravel shoulder. They fishtailed when she corrected. Carolina giggled as she was thrown against the passenger door. Bunny's eyebrows disappeared into the brim of her hat.

"Oh, I'm not saying he's in love with you. I just think you bring back the guilt and sadness. Katie was nice enough to him, but like she was to just anybody."

"Why would he feel guilty? He didn't kill her, did he?" No one ever talked about Katie. All she knew was she died in that truck.

"No, he wouldn't kill her. You probably can't see it, but he is very protective. Katie was his best friend's little sister. She died on his watch, so to speak. I think he feels like he let Connor and Buck down. I'm guessing you're a daily reminder of that."

"I can't help being like someone I never met."

"No. And you aren't her. For sure."

Bunny stared at her, offended.

"No. Look, I loved Katie," Carolina protested. "She was my best friend. But she put up with a lot. She kept secrets from us all because she didn't want to upset anyone." She looked at her boots and shook her head. "You speak your mind. You don't back down. That's how you're different. It's not a bad thing. Might have saved her life if she had done that too. Who knows?"

"I thought it was a car accident."

"It was, but I've always wondered what she was doing out that night. I know she was seeing someone, but she wouldn't tell me who it was. She wouldn't even tell me why it had to be a secret. Maybe it was a married man. Maybe it was someone her brother didn't like. Whatever the reason, she kept it to herself. And that person never came forward when she died. That makes me wonder."

Bunny thought Buck's sadness was from losing a wife and daughter. Was there more to it? If she were Buck, wondering what happened would be a poisonous snake burrowing into her heart and mind.

That thought dissolved when they arrived at the feed store. Though the line was short, this time the foreman asked if they wanted help. Bunny suspected his offer was directed at the leggy blond in the passenger seat. To her credit, Carolina declined the help on their behalf.

She caught on to stacking easily, and Bunny's fears about her strength were unwarranted. They were about halfway done when Shaw walked over and offered to throw bales for them. Carolina was getting more brazen in declining men's help, but Bunny stopped her mid-sentence.

"Not this one, Carolina. He's one of the good guys. Shaw pitched in and helped me when I came alone."

Carolina let out a nervous giggle and put out her hand. "Thanks, Mr. Shaw."

He gave her a kind smile and shook her hand. "Just Shaw, if you don't mind."

Bunny watched the easy way Carolina shifted gears, letting go of one feeling and reaching out for another without regret. To Bunny, thanks felt more like forcing a truck into gear with the clutch half in. She followed Carolina's lead and thanked him for the offer.

Bunny jumped up on the trailer to help her stack bales as Shaw threw them. He was faster than the two of them together. Still, he would wait for them, half a smile on his face with his arms tugged low by the hay. To reward that kindness, Bunny pushed herself until her muscles screamed. When they were done, she didn't wait for Shaw. She stuck out her hand.

෯

On the way back, Carolina nursed some blisters on her palms.

"I'm sorry. I have some stuff back at the bunkhouse to put on that."

Carolina turned, a questioning look on her face. She glanced back at her palms. "It's alright. It feels good."

Bunny understood what she meant. Those blisters were evidence that you did something with your bare hands. Something hard, even painful. Feeling the hurt every time you clenched your fist or picked something up was a reminder of your power. It occurred to Bunny that keeping Katie's truck probably had the opposite effect on Buck. Seeing it must be a painful reminder of his powerlessness and loss. It seemed like a physical punishment. Evidence of his failure to protect.

"What did happen to Katie?" Bunny asked. "No one talks about it."

"No one really knows. They found her truck on a pole out on the highway. She was inside, dead." Carolina paused and cleared her throat. "It looked like she hit ice and slid into a pole. Cops said no drugs or alcohol, but anyone who knew Katie would've known that. Her head hit the windshield. They said she didn't die right away, though. No one came along to help her in time." Carolina stared out the windshield. She wiped one eye. "Anyway, that's it. Police closed the file. I doubt we'll ever know for sure. Could have been a hit-and-run. Could have been a moose. Buck prefers to think it was a moose. Nothing will bring Katie back. I think he blames himself so much that he can't share the guilt with anyone else."

They drove in silence the rest of the way home. Bunny let Carolina out at her Jeep and took the trailer up to the barn, where Jake was waiting to help. They unloaded the hay in silence.

Bunny wanted so badly to ask him about Katie, but she felt like a voyeur. She didn't know why, but it was an itch deep in her chest that she couldn't ignore. She felt sure, though, that if she poked this particular bear, she was going to regret it.

Jake muscled the last bale into place. Bunny wished it weren't so, but it took the same effort for her to speak.

"Thanks for the help, Jake."

He hopped off the pile and nodded as he walked away.

Bunny waited long enough for him to clear the trailer before she headed to the shed. She backed it into the second bay and unhooked it from the truck. Bunny looked around for Buck and Jake. To be safe, she pulled the garage door closed. She headed over to Katie's truck and lifted the tarp from the hood. The front fender was dented into the radiator. There was no paint or blood on the chrome. She circled the vehicle. The tailgate and rear fender had a crease from the bold R in Chevrolet to the license plate. Bunny knew the pole took care of the front, but it couldn't have creased the tailgate.

CHAPTER 47

JEREMIAH 1982

JEREMIAH STARED AT the wrinkled paper that lay on his dresser strewn among the other items discarded daily but not disposed of. Every morning, he picked it up and set it back down like an alcoholic testing his resolve with a sniff of bourbon. He knew he would take that drink, but he held out, knowing how much Rocky wanted him to. It was the silent war that played out between them. For Jeremiah, it always ended in defeat.

He picked the paper up and rubbed it between his fingers. It was cheap, which was fitting. He felt cheap. When he was with Katie, he'd felt like he could be more than his dad. It was the only time he thought he might escape that fate. Now that she was gone, he didn't care. Rocky was right. His buddies noticed his absence, and they generally reserved their limited perceptive powers for judging the likelihood of getting skirts into their pickup trucks. It was time for him to call the number. He dropped it back down on his dresser.

Rocky was sitting at the dinner table when he got downstairs.

Jesse kept the table clear and polished like she thought they might resume their family dinners at any time. Rocky faced the staircase, one elbow on the table propping up his beer, legs out and crossed. Jeremiah knew he had been waiting for him to come down.

"Where's Jesse?" Jeremiah needed a buffer.

"Don't know. What do you say we head down to the Back Forty and get some dinner?" Rocky held his eyes as he took a long pull on the beer. They both knew it wasn't really a question, so he didn't bother to answer. He walked over to the door and grabbed his keys off the hook.

"I'll drive." Jeremiah didn't look back, and he didn't wait. The rules of engagement were established long before this day.

He headed out before the defroster was blowing hot air. Looking at the road through the two slowly growing ovals on the windshield, he navigated to the highway. After a few moments, the ice holding the windshield wipers down melted. Jeremiah turned them on high to speed up the clearing process. Feigning focus was Jeremiah's defense against conversation. Rocky's offense was to stare at him until he felt so uncomfortable that he spoke first. Jeremiah wasn't biting.

The parking lot was almost full when they arrived. Most of the pickups were old or halfway to old. Front and center, though, there was a shiny new Ford. The chrome told Jeremiah it was someone who worked on the slope. It wasn't a working truck. He hoped whoever struck it big hadn't already moved in on the new waitress. Much as he didn't want to do it, he knew he had to. If he didn't, Rocky would only double down on finding him a girl and, while he worked on that, Jeremiah would have to listen to him bitch about dragging his feet and missing out on a sure thing. The last thing he needed was another object lesson.

There were two waitresses working, but Rocky had long perfected his ability to weasel his way to the right table. Sure enough, Mindy bounced over, pen in hand.

"What can I get the handsome Cooper men to drink?"

Jeremiah looked her over. She was beautiful, but he suspected she wasn't convinced, based on the amount of makeup she wore.

"Well, it's nice to see you again, Mindy. I don't think I properly thanked you for taking care of my boy here." Rocky gave her a wolfish smile.

"No need, Mr. Cooper. I was glad to help." Mindy turned her charm to Jeremiah. "How are you doing?"

Jeremiah wished he was anywhere but there. He wanted to walk out, head for the barn, saddle up Thunderbird, and ride until they were both out of breath and so far away they couldn't come back without a good long rest. He wanted to wade out on the muskeg and lie down on a big pillow of it until he sank into the wet earth.

"Son, she asked you a question." Rocky kicked him under the table.

"I'm doing fine. Thanks for taking me home the other night." He gave her a halfhearted smile, and it made him sad to see her blush over the morsel he offered.

They ordered beers and sat in silence until she returned to take their dinner order. Mindy stood, right hip cocked, pen resting on her lower lip, a practiced pose intended to feign attention while capturing theirs. Did she know who she was playing to? His father would capitalize on her desire to be noticed. She was an amateur compared to Rocky, who ordered, a sly grin frozen on his face, eyes drilling into her until she looked away. A tell. She turned to Jeremiah in reprieve. Though he felt sorry for her, he knew with certainty now that he would ask her out. She would go. He would use her. She would take it. When he was done, his dad would take a run at her. In the end, they would both leave her. He wanted to be a better man. Though Katie said he was, he knew she was wrong. She never got the chance to find out how much he was like his father. For one fleeting second, he was glad she was dead so she couldn't see this.

Rocky waited until they had their food to launch his campaign. "This is your chance. You need to ask her out. Quit dragging your heels. It ain't gonna get any easier than this." Jeremiah chewed in silence, staring at his plate. It didn't require a response.

As soon as Rocky finished his dinner, he got up from the table. Jeremiah watched him work his way across the bar. He stopped to talk at nearly every table he passed as he zigzagged his way to the bathroom. The way Rocky transformed, like an actor on the stage, mesmerized Jeremiah. Donning a jovial mask, he nudged the young ranch hands knowingly with his shoulder. Though it looked accidental, he stopped at every table that held a boarder. Jeremiah had heard the lines so many times: *How's that filly of yours?* Even the cowboys with fillies knew he wasn't talking about their horses. Once he broke the ice, he listened to every word they said. He cataloged it and hid it away for when it would be useful. Jeremiah knew firsthand that he would pull that information out when he needed it and lay you low with the realization that you gave it away in the first place.

Rocky's contrived path ended with Mindy. He pulled out some cash and pointed to the table. With a knowing touch of her arm, he headed down the darkened hallway to the bathroom.

Mindy took the money to the bartender. She stole a glance back at the table. Jeremiah thought about looking away but then, he wanted her to know he knew. Whatever happened, he wanted her to know he knew she was in this with Rocky. Mindy smiled briefly but turned quickly back to the bar when she saw Jeremiah watching her. She counted the money and flashed the bartender a flirtatious smile. Then she sauntered his way, hips swaying left and right like a pendulum.

"Your dad asked me to leave his change. Is there anything else you want?" She held his eyes and tapped her pen on her bottom lip. Rocky was setting them both up. Until this moment, he'd thought Mindy was an innocent bystander. As she tapped her lip, one hip cocked in his direction, he knew she wasn't.

"No. But I'm wondering if you would like to get a beer and maybe go dancing at the Lodge this weekend. I'm not sure if you're working, but we could go later if you are." *Smile.* He was surprised at how easy it was to fake it.

She looked out the window as if she were mentally checking her date book. "I have the lunch shift on Friday. I could go out that night."

"It's a date then."

"What's a date?"

Jeremiah hadn't seen his father walk up.

"Well, Mr. Cooper, your son here is taking me dancing Friday." Mindy smiled with an excitement that made Jeremiah sad. Even though he was sure she knew the score, it wasn't right to use her this way. It was obvious she was no match for Rocky. Once he decided she was no longer useful, and that day would surely come, he would cut her loose. Mindy would not see it coming, but Jeremiah already could.

"Well, that sounds like a lot of fun."

Mindy's eyes spooked and her face went cold when Rocky patted her behind. What was she hiding?

CHAPTER 48

BUNNY 1984

BUNNY HAD COMPLETELY forgotten she agreed to go out with Jeremiah again. When the Double J truck emerged from the shadows of the driveway, she rushed toward it like she was heading off a loose cow avoiding the milking parlor. He slowed to a stop before he reached the ring and waited for her. She was grateful he had the sense to stay in his truck. Bunny put both hands on the window frame of the door and leaned in. It was the containment move she used on her brothers. They would never use the door to push her away, and they couldn't drive off without knocking her over. So, they were stuck talking to her. Mick figured out what she was doing. His countermeasure was to only open the window halfway. Patrick didn't put up much of a fight at all. He always surrendered with, *Get in. Let's talk.*

"What's up?" She locked her elbows, dug her heels in, and looked Jeremiah in the eye.

"Did you forget you agreed to another date?" He tipped his head down and raised his eyebrows. At that angle, they almost disappeared into the brim of his cowboy hat.

"I didn't forget agreeing. I don't recall setting a date."

"That's why I'm here."

"You have my number."

"I certainly do have your number. I thought this might be more fun." He flashed a lopsided smile.

Though Bunny knew Jake would make her pay for it later, it felt good to poke the bear.

"I can't go out tonight."

"Why not?"

"Because the guy I'm going out with thinks he can show up and I'll drop everything to go out with him. He needs to learn I don't sit around waiting for a guy."

"Consider that lesson learned." He didn't appear offended, which was a point in his favor. "I was thinking that, since you don't dance, we should go for a ride instead."

"Great. I've been itching to get War Horse out."

The smile drained from his face. "I was thinking we could head out from the Double J. I have a Paint mare you can ride. Her name is Braveheart, which seems fitting for a second date."

"Why, Jeremiah Cooper, I had no idea you were a romantic," she teased. His smile returned, but not in full force. She quickly added, "That sounds great. I'll meet you at the Double J."

They set a date, and Bunny watched as he drove in and turned around at the barn. His timing was perfect. He waved at Jake as he passed him. He stopped next to Bunny on the way out.

"Sorry, but I couldn't resist. I don't suppose you want to light him up by giving me a kiss."

"No, I do not, and thanks a lot. Now I have to put up with his crap all day." She slapped the side of the truck and walked away.

"I really am sorry," he called after her. She gave him a back-handed wave but hid the grin that started at each ear.

When Bunny rolled into the Double J, she could almost feel the Midnight Sun truck groan. She hadn't told Buck she was coming here. Parking on the side of the barn, she found her way in. A cool breeze crossed the aisle from the open paddock doors. Save for the periodic stomp or snort, the barn felt empty. No one was in the feed room, so she headed farther down the aisle. Her footsteps seemed amplified in the silence. When she passed the tack room, Rocky was sitting there on a bench, staring at a locker.

"Excuse me, do you know where I could find Jeremiah?" His slumped shoulders jerked up at the intrusion.

Without looking away from the locker, he said, "He's out back, saddling up."

Bunny headed to the back door. She loved everything about a barn full of horses—the feel of barely contained energy, the sound of hooves, the smell of alfalfa. It was one of the rare things her mom understood about her. The excitement would well up inside of her as they drove to the barn to ride. On the way, they would laugh and talk and sing along with the country music station. Bunny felt right on those trips in a way she never did with her mom at the dairy.

Jeremiah was out back saddling up a Paint. Next to her was a Quarter Horse standing stock-still.

"Hi. She's beautiful."

Jeremiah turned to look at her as he cinched up the saddle. "Yes, she is. This is Braveheart. Braveheart, this is Benny." He stroked the mare's shoulder. "And this guy is Thunderbird. Thunder is a warrior." He walked over to the stocky horse and tipped his face down so they were eye to eye. He slid his hands down his jowls and tickled his chin. Like most guys, Thunder feigned disinterest in the tender attention, but in the end, he leaned in. Forehead on Jeremiah's chest, he gave off one of those deep exhales that, for Bunny, defined bliss in a way mere words could not. Jeremiah followed suit. His face softened. He closed his eyes for a moment.

Had her dad ever had moments like this when he let the tough guy take a rest and allowed himself to feel the joy of connecting? Jeremiah caught her staring at him, and she knew her intrusion had ruined it for him. Without a word, she turned to Braveheart and began checking her saddle.

"Don't you trust me?" he asked.

"Well, I don't not trust you. It's a force of habit. My brothers think they are hilarious. I'm in the habit of checking my gear twice. Sometimes three times." Bunny didn't mention her recent spaghetti Western experience of being dragged through the tall grass by War Horse.

"I think I'd like your brothers," he teased.

"I'm guessing you would."

She walked around the mount. A splash of chestnut exploded from Braveheart's belly across her back and chest, leaving her shoulders a shiny white. From her hind legs to her rump, it looked like she'd been dipped in cream. She had a collar of white that made her look elegant somehow. Save for her nose and forehead, a rich brown covered her head. On the other end, her tail faded into a hint of chestnut. The colors were bright and rich. The border between them, though winding, was a sharp line. Her mane was full and long, but the ends were straggly, giving her an untamed look. Her ears followed Bunny, more out of curiosity than fear. Braveheart lifted her leg without protest so Bunny could check her hooves.

"You really don't trust me?" Jeremiah asked, hands on his hips.

"I want to see if she trusts me."

Bunny didn't answer his question because she wasn't sure yet.

Maybe the truth was that she trusted him about as much as she was willing to trust any guy.

Bunny led Braveheart around in a wide circle. She checked the cinch. Satisfied, she mounted the animal. Letting the horse pick her pace, Bunny steered her to the outdoor ring. They took a couple laps at a walk, then she brought her to a trot and back down again. Satisfied she would take direction, Bunny brought her back up to an easy lope to get the feel of her gait. She was smooth and strong. It felt good to be in the saddle. She closed her eyes.

"Let's go. Daylight's wasting." He laughed at his own joke.

"Yeah, we've only got like ninety more . . . days or so."

They headed out along a field that was a few fence posts smaller than Buck's. The Double J had done their first cutting already too. Walking along the first side, they stayed in the middle of the ruts dug in by years of pickup trucks and tractors. It was flat and grassy but not broad enough to safely increase their pace. When they hit the corner, the grass faded, and a road stretched out before them. Without a word, Jeremiah urged Thunder into a trot.

"Come on, pokey," he called back to Bunny.

She brought Braveheart to a trot and felt the horse begging to run. Bunny reached forward to let her have her head. She loped past the boys, mane bouncing. Braveheart must have had a competitive spirit by the way the horse turned her head to look at them as they flew by. Jeremiah laughed behind them. From the beat of Thunder's hooves, he wasn't going to let the challenge go unanswered. He probably could have left them in the dust, but he didn't. He caught up, then eased in next to her, matching Braveheart's gait. For a few moments, it was poetic. Nothing existed except the wind hitting her face and drifting to her chest through the neck of her shirt, the sound of hooves and deep breaths, the smooth pounding of hoof to earth and saddle to butt. No one talking, or wanting, or warning. Just this one beautiful, elemental moment that could never be repeated. If she rode every day for the rest of her life, she wouldn't get this moment back. So, she let her body follow the horse's, and she gave her mind a little time off.

As they approached the next corner, Jeremiah slowed. Braveheart responded in kind. To their right, the road continued along the pasture, back toward the farm. To their left, the road narrowed to half its width and disappeared into a thin stand of trees. Jeremiah turned left. Bunny froze. He was about ten yards ahead of her when he stopped and turned in the saddle.

"Everything okay?" he called. When she didn't move, he turned around and went back. "We don't have to go that way if you're not comfortable. It's beautiful out there but, if you're scared, then Braveheart will be too."

"I'm not scared." She jerked her face to him.

"Hey, I didn't mean anything by it." Jeremiah mistook her lie for offense. His eyes widened and his eyebrows lifted. When she didn't respond, his face softened. "So far, I think you might be the bravest woman I know. And that's saying something. I don't think you've met my sister Jesse. When you do, you'll get what a compliment that is."

Bunny looked over at Jeremiah. His left hand was draped over the saddle horn. Though he must have a good grip on the reins, his right hand lay limp across the left. The reins hung with the slightest of curves down the horse's neck and snaked through Jeremiah's left fingers, disappearing momentarily until they became one as they flowed over his thumb. He looked so confident there, resting in the saddle. He wasn't afraid. No pressure on the reins.

Braveheart moved toward him, and Bunny didn't hold her back. When she got to Thunder, Braveheart touched her nose to his neck and took a deep breath. Nobody seemed to be afraid, except Bunny. She took Braveheart's lead and breathed in. Braveheart took that as a sign and took a step. Bunny relaxed her grip on the reins and let her lead them down the path. She smiled when Jeremiah exclaimed, "Well, okay then."

"Well, okay then," Bunny said as she reached down and patted Braveheart on the shoulder.

Jeremiah and Thunder came alongside. The Lovely Sophia always told Bunny to pay attention while riding. She said a horse could spook over a blade of grass. She had no intention of telling her mother she had learned that lesson the hard way, but she was going to take her advice this time.

Bunny kept her eyes on the trail, stealing only furtive glances at Jeremiah. She could see why women swooned over him. He rode tall in the saddle. The heels of his old cowboy boots fell naturally below the stirrups. His bottom half looked like he was getting ready to launch himself, while his top half gave the impression that he could stay right there all day, moseying along. She didn't know if he was brave, but he sure didn't look like much worried him.

The stretch of trees was sparse compared to back home, where ancient evergreen forests covered mountain after mountain. Before long, they slid through, and stretched out before them was the tundra. The glory of it must have struck Braveheart too, because she paused. Thick shrubs of red and green erupted from the landscape in tufts. Periodically, an icy blue pond lay across the tundra like a silk sheet disregarded on the floor. It took Bunny's breath away. The trail meandered. She was torn between the desire to stay right there until the image was etched into her memory and the urge to follow it until she touched the farthest hill. Braveheart decided for them. With a great nod of her straggly mane, she moved forward. Her gait was brisk. Not a walk or a trot, but something in between that made Bunny think she might have happy memories of this place.

Jeremiah let her get ahead. She couldn't bear to stop the horse, so she yelled back to him, "You better hustle, cowboy." He didn't move at first. Bunny knew the moment he did from the rush of hooves digging into the hardpan earth.

As he raced by, he said, "Pick up the pace."

She didn't need any more encouragement than that. Bunny spurred the horse and released the reins. The powerful animal reached out with her forelegs to grab the earth and force it behind her. Her back flexed, and her rear legs lifted Bunny out of the saddle. Confidence drowned out her nerves, though she was not sure she deserved it.

"Slowpoke," Bunny called as she passed Jeremiah. She was so focused on the road beneath them she didn't notice the old cabin growing larger in the distance. Braveheart slowed to a walk and headed for the front door.

"Whoa there, Braveheart," Jeremiah called. Bunny pulled back the reins. The horse resisted at first but stopped. "It's time to head back."

"Whose cabin is this?" She didn't turn the horse around.

"My grandpa built it. My dad owns it, technically."

"Technically?"

"He owns it, but he never comes out here. Mostly, I'm the only one who does."

"Nice. It looks like a great place to be alone. I would've loved a place like this to get away from my brothers. They're so loud."

"I guess so," he said, staring at the front door like he expected it to open. "Come on, let's get back. I'll buy you a burger at the Lodge." He turned the horse and headed back up the trail. He didn't wait for Bunny, but he also didn't hurry. They caught up with him easily and rode back in silence. The slow pass the sun took along the horizon fascinated Bunny. She was used to the constant daylight now. Would she be here to get used to the constant night?

❦

Rocky was leaning on the fence, watching as they rode back to the farm. He propped his right foot up on the lowest rung, making his jeans bunch around his ankle. Though skinny now, she could see he hadn't always been. His jeans were faded, and the hem was worn. They sagged under the weight of a belt which was no longer doing its job. His button-down shirt was dirty. He'd rolled up the sleeves, revealing the leathery forearms of a man who'd spent a lifetime working outdoors. His fingers were laced together and hung loosely over the top rail. Tipped back on his forehead was a cowboy hat that looked like it had hit the dirt more than a few times. A path of creases ran along the brim. Though he looked relaxed, the closer Bunny got, it became obvious he was not. His clamped jaw and pursed lips deepened the crevices that fanned out from the corners of his squinting eyes.

"Dad." Jeremiah pulled Thunder up parallel to the fence, forcing Rocky to turn and look up. He kept one arm on the fence. With the other, he slowly pushed his hat even farther back.

"Son." He nodded and paused. "Who's your friend?" He held Jeremiah's eyes.

"I think you remember Benny O'Kelly from out at the Midnight Sun." They reminded Bunny of a couple bulls staring at each other from across a field, remembering the pain of knocking horns but wanting to do it again so badly.

"Nice to meet you again, Mr. Cooper." Rocky Cooper gave her a bad feeling in the gut.

"Yes, ma'am. Well, I'll let you two get on with it." He pushed off the fence and stood there like he had nothing better to do than watch them put the horses away.

Bunny didn't look back, but she had the creepy feeling his eyes were on her. Jeremiah led them to the front of the barn, where they tied the horses up and brushed them down. Braveheart and Thunder seemed to like each other's company. They sidestepped, trying to get close. When that didn't work, they turned their rumps away from each other and stood there staring like old friends.

"Thank you, Braveheart." Bunny stroked her neck with the brush. "She's a smooth ride."

"That's good to hear." He said it without looking at her.

"Haven't you ever ridden her?"

"Nope. She was my mom's horse. I have my own."

"Well, somebody's been working her. She has the softest saddle, even when she goes all out." Bunny stopped brushing to look at Jeremiah. He had draped his arms over Thunder's back.

"You sure are nosy for a cheechako." He considered her for a moment, then gave her a smile.

"I don't know what a cheecako is, but what can I say? I have a curious mind. So, who is it? Your dad?"

"Oh, hell no. He would never ride my mom's horse. Hell, even before she left, he wouldn't ride her. That's a girl's horse in his mind, which is bullshit. If you saw my mom ride, you would put her up against any man."

There was something in his voice. Not dreamy like love, but maybe admiration.

"Anyway, it's my sister, Jesse. She rides Braveheart. Sometimes she even races her when River is down." He pulled his hat down and got back to work, brushing down his horse. Bunny didn't ask any more questions. Something told her he had shared all his heart could bear.

By the time they put the horses back in their stalls, Bunny was as tired as Jeremiah looked. She let him off the hook for dinner with a promise of a rain check and another ride on Braveheart. Jeremiah walked her to the truck and opened the door for her. She hopped in and cranked down the window. He held on to the door, dragging out the night, wordless. Without warning, he leaned in and kissed her softly on the lips. He tipped his hat and turned to walk away.

The unexpected tenderness of the moment stunned her, and it took a moment for her to remember she was leaving. She turned the engine over, shifted into reverse, and draped her arm over the seat to check behind her. Rocky was standing stock-still in the driveway, watching her. His face was a mask of malice. Just short of spitting gravel, she got out of there as fast as she could.

CHAPTER 49

JAKE 1982

JAKE'S EGGS CONGEALED on his plate as he watched Buck drill the last screw into the hasp. He packed away his tools, slapped the plate in place, and fixed the lock through the slot. Before standing, he tossed the key into the toolbox. Buck hadn't consulted Jake before he did it. He smoldered over it. A small thing, but it was the last in a long line of small things that eclipsed his guilt. Connor had been home. He and his dad had spread Katie's ashes on the bank of the slough that ran along the back pasture. Jake wasn't invited. *You understand, right? It's a family thing.* He'd lied. He didn't understand. Connor was never around. Then he just swooped in and froze Jake out. Decisions were made. Jake crashed into them daily. Like watching Connor clear all but a few boxes from her room. And now, a shiny piece of metal blocked Katie's room off from the rest of the house.

"The wrecker is coming today. I'm picking up a load of hay." Buck poured himself a cup of coffee. "Help him get it to the garage. You might have to pull the tractor out to push it. Lock it up when you're done." Buck didn't wait for confirmation. Jake made no attempt to give it to him.

The truck plodded down the road, dragging a flatbed trailer behind it. The powder blue Chevy Luv strained against the tie-downs. The pain of her loss throbbed with every bounce. He could not see it without seeing her. Waving the driver to the garage, he turned away and locked himself down. When the vision of her that night invaded, he wiped it away with the thought of her zipping around the farm.

The driver helped him ease the truck down the ramps and into the garage. He was still cleaning up when Jake slammed the garage door, locking himself in with the vehicle. Like a caged animal, he circled it twice, looking at the walls. On the third time, he stopped at the rear bumper. He couldn't pull enough air into his lungs. He forced himself to put one foot in front of the other, stopping after each step, searching the truck for signs. When he had worn himself out, he pulled a tarp across the top of it so he would never have to look at it again.

CHAPTER 50

JEREMIAH 1982

JEREMIAH HAD BEEN chasing girls like Mindy since he was fifteen. She reminded him of the women his dad had been bringing home since his mom left. He knew it angered Jesse, but she was smart enough to know she wasn't going to change their dad. Her disruption tactics dampened the mood. She wouldn't go to sleep until Rocky got rid of his date. He had to endure the disapproving gaze of his daughter, from eyes she shared with his ex-wife, when he walked his latest conquest to the door. So Rocky took to sleeping over, if you could call it that. Jeremiah admired Jesse for her rebellion. He was weak and succumbed to Rocky's modeling. But not Jesse. She stood her ground. She badgered Rocky until he let her move out to the barn. While she moved out, Jeremiah hunkered down. Tonight was the icing on that cake.

He was sitting across from a woman who couldn't hold a candle to Katie Miller, pretending to be interested in her ridiculous chatter. He'd picked her up like a proper date, which was more than he ever did for Katie. Mindy rented a duplex in town.

He parked in front and walked to the door. Had she shoveled the walk for him, or had her landlord? He suspected she did it herself. He imagined her in boots and a parka, shoveling the heavy snow, making it nice for him. Mindy answered the door wearing her coat like she had been waiting for Jeremiah to knock.

"Well, I'm ready. Should we go? Or did you want to come in?" Jeremiah didn't quite know what to say. He'd only had Katie and the girls before her who wanted him to come in and stay the night. He had assumed Mindy was one of those girls who knew what she wanted and knew how to go about getting it.

"No. Uh. It looks like you're ready. Let's go have dinner." He held his hand out to her, and she looked at it a moment before taking it in hers. She smiled, and a blush crossed her face. Though the heavy rouge and teased hair said otherwise, had he been wrong? He walked her to the side of the truck, and they reached for the door handle at the same time. She pulled away and looked at the ground. Jeremiah opened the door and helped her up into the cab. She forced a smile as he closed the door.

They drove in silence for a bit. "I thought we would go to the Back Forty. I know you work there, but I wasn't sure if you ever had a chance to sit down for a meal there. It's very good," he said, glancing at her. She was looking straight ahead. "Unless you'd rather go to the Lodge, which is fine. It's up to you." Jeremiah sensed he'd offended her in some way, but he didn't know how.

"I would love to go to the Back Forty," she said, still staring through the front windshield.

"Are you sure?"

She turned to look at him. "I'm sure. I've always wanted to eat there, but it's awkward without a date." Jeremiah was confused at first and started to ask. Then he realized she had plenty of dates. They drove the rest of the way in silence, one happy and one sad.

Mindy waited in the truck until he came around to open the

door for her. He placed his hand on her back as he ushered her into the restaurant. She lit up as soon as they walked through the door.

"Hello. Table for two? Oh, Mindy, I didn't recognize you." The hostess hugged her. "Well, let's get you seated." She looked at Mindy, eyes wide. Mindy giggled.

They hung their coats on the way into the dining room. He pulled her chair out, earning another eyebrow raise. The hostess handed them menus and promised to return for their drink order.

"Maybe I should pass on a drink tonight," he said. "That didn't go so well for you last time."

"Well, slugger, how about I cut you off after two? I'm a skilled professional."

He was grateful. He needed a beer. "Sold, two tops. And I promise not to pick a fight, even if Jake James walks in."

"What's the deal with you two, anyway?"

"Just stupid guy stuff."

"Let me guess, Katie Miller."

"Why would you say that?" His face hardened.

"Well, you were dating her, right? And he was in love with her."

"What the hell are you talking about?" Fear rose and he tamped it down.

"I'm sorry. It's none of my business. I assumed he knew you were dating and was jealous. It's really none of my business."

"I wasn't dating Katie. We were planning the fair."

"Well, then you were the only one who knew that," Mindy mused. "Katie sure thought you were a couple. It was pretty obvious—the way she looked at you and how angry she got with me."

"You're wrong." Panic rose in his chest. How could he have been so naïve to think no one noticed? "Look, can we not talk about any other women or men while we're on a date?"

"I'm sorry." She raised both hands in surrender. "You're right. I shouldn't have brought it up."

The waitress interrupted, dissipating the tension by reciting the beers on tap. Mindy ordered white wine. Though Jeremiah knew nothing about wine, he was pretty sure there was more to ordering it than a simple color. As she went to get their drinks, they studied the menu.

He broke their standoff. "What's the most popular thing people order?"

Mindy sat up a little taller and gave him a toothy smile. "When the tourists are here in summer, the salmon, for sure. But the regulars order the steak. You can't beat it."

"Well, alright then. What do you say we order a couple of steaks?"

She nodded in reply.

Jeremiah put down his menu and searched for the waitress.

"I'm sorry. I shouldn't have said anything about you and Katie. It's none of my business." She looked down at her hands.

He was making it worse. "It's fine. We weren't dating, but I can see why you might have thought that. But seriously, I'd rather talk about you tonight." His dad told him you could always distract a woman by getting her to talk about herself. "Where were you from before this?"

"A bush town." She said it into her menu, never looking up. Jeremiah took her in. She seemed to deflate a little. She tucked one side of her hair behind her ear and let the other side drop in a curtain shadowing her face.

"Oh, I didn't realize. I thought you were from the lower 48 for some reason."

She looked up and smiled. "No, but thank you for that."

"Why'd you leave?"

"Not much to do there, I guess." She shrugged.

He would have sworn relief crossed her face when the waitress arrived to take their orders. He wondered for a moment what she wasn't saying but then remembered this wasn't a real date. This was about appearance. This was about appeasing his dad. Jeremiah turned on the charm and made small talk until the bill came.

It wasn't an unpleasant date. They were both skilled in the art of hiding themselves behind the mask of what they thought they should be. Their masks seemed quite compatible, but Jeremiah couldn't keep his on forever. And he couldn't love her the way he loved Katie. She wouldn't love him the way Katie did without his mask.

After dinner, they went to the Lodge. Like all the other small-town girls he'd known, she knew how to dance. Maybe it just built up inside them. When they finally had the chance to let it out, it was raw and joyful. She was no exception. Mindy swayed and bounced and stomped with complete abandon to whatever they played. That was what she would be like in bed. With that thought, he knew he had to quit drinking for the night. Beer melted his resolve.

"I'm going to sit the next one out," he shouted into her ear.

"Noooo!" She grabbed his hand and tried to pull him back onto the dance floor. "One more dance. And then I promise, I'm done."

"I have to get up early to feed the horses." He held firm. Another one of his dad's rules for dating—never give in if you want to hold the higher ground.

"Okay." She pouted.

He paid the tab and helped her with her coat. As they walked out to the truck, she said goodbye to every person she knew. Jeremiah had the impression she wanted them to know she was going home with him, like she wanted congratulations for her prize.

They drove in silence for a couple of miles before she broke in. "Thank you for a nice evening." She recited it as if she'd rehearsed the words.

"You're welcome. I had fun. I hope you did too." His words were also rehearsed.

"I did. It doesn't have to end, though." She turned toward him, a hopeful look on her face. She had danced away her makeup. In the glow of the dashboard lights, she looked younger. Despite the implications of her offer, she appeared more innocent without it.

"I wish it didn't," he lied. "But I do have to get up early." He glanced her way, expecting disappointment. He saw something harsher, though.

"Well, next time, then." She turned back and stared out the windshield.

"Next time."

He walked her to the door and gave her a brief kiss, breaking it off as soon as she leaned into him. She would try to change his mind with her body. When he pulled away, she looked genuinely surprised.

"Well, thank you for dinner. I had a great time." She put her key in the lock and opened the front door. She turned back to him.

"Me too," Jeremiah said. As she paused at the door, he realized she must be waiting to be asked out again. "Well, I'll give you a call." She forced a smile and went inside without a word. He cursed his dad.

CHAPTER 51

ROCKY 1984

ROCKY TOOK A shower, something he never did in the middle of the day. He stood in front of the mirror and took himself in. He was still lean, though his muscles were obscured by the ever-increasing sag of his aging skin. Still, he smiled, knowing he could charm a woman of almost any age into his bed. He was going to need all that charm, and then some, tonight. Rocky leaned into the mirror. He inspected the shadow of whiskers on his face. A shave was in order. Unlike some men, a five o'clock shadow made him look sinister, not sexy. Years of consumer research had taught him that.

Satisfied, he put on a clean pair of jeans and dusted off his boots. He dug out a clean shirt from the pile of laundry on his dresser. It was creased from being folded for so many days. He could have asked Jesse to iron it for him, but she would have had questions. He smoothed it down and tucked it in. His old hat looked out of place, but he never went anywhere without it, so he put it on.

It was times like these he was glad Jesse had insisted on

moving out to the apartment over the barn. The last thing he needed was her sticking her nose in this situation, and she would. Of course, the real risk was her sticking her nose in her mama's tack locker, but he had the only key now. Pride and irritation warred inside him. Jesse came just short of taking after Rebekah, and she had just enough of him in her. She would notice the shower and clean clothes and not let it go until she knew exactly what he was up to. Jeremiah, on the other hand, wouldn't say a word even if he suspected, even if he objected. He had him in line, and that thought made him smile. He was never going to get Jesse in line. That, right there, was all her mother.

He headed over to the Back Forty. The dinner crowd, if you could call it that, would be thinning. If he ate slowly and left her a big tip, he was sure he could convince her to hear him out. She was still nursing a grudge against Jeremiah, but he didn't think it would cost him that much to get her to let go of it. No one was at the hostess desk, so he stood in the doorway trying to figure out which section was hers.

"Hey, Rocky. Is a table okay?"

He touched the brim of his hat in greeting. "Sure. Mind if I sit by the window?"

She grabbed a menu from the stack and headed for a table. Rocky, distracted by the sway of her hips, nearly ran into her when she stopped to place his menu on the table. "Mindy will be right over. Can I get you something to drink while you're waiting?"

Rocky smiled. He wanted a beer something awful, but he needed to pace himself. "Coffee, black."

He opened the menu and pretended to look it over as he stole glances at the waitresses. It looked to Rocky like Mindy didn't want to serve him. He would need to pay some mind to that. She was still wounded. Worse, she had moved on to the grudge stage. He kicked himself for not seeing her usefulness sooner. He should have cultivated a friendship with her.

Rocky smiled at her and lifted his coffee in salute. She gave him one back, but it was the practiced smile of a waitress, always mindful of the coming tip. It did the trick, though, and soon she headed for the table.

"What can I get you, Rocky?" She pulled out a small pad from the apron around her waist. One hip was slightly cocked, accentuating the curve of her ass. Rocky looked up at her with a grin. She might detest him, but she was still working it. He ordered a steak. As she was about to walk away, he asked for a beer. After all, he always thought a little better after a couple of beers. Besides, if he sipped them, he might be able to stay until she closed. She might say no at first, but personal experience told him she would be more pliable as the night wore on.

He watched her closely as she talked to the other waitresses and served the other tables. Where had she learned to read people so well? She was like a hummingbird flitting from flower to flower, knowing how long to stay at each one to be sure she got all the nectar. With lone men, she casually rested one hand on the back of their chair and leaned just enough in their direction that they could no longer concentrate on their meals. She gave them a big smile and threw her head back when she laughed. Did she know how that made her neck a path to her breasts? He suspected she knew very well it did. Men with wives or families got a more reserved version of Mindy. She was pleasant to them. She gave her attention to their wives. Was it smart to turn her back on the man who paid the check? Then he realized that, while Mindy gave the wife her attention, she was giving the man of the house a perfect view of her ass. He was happy. His wife was happy. And Mindy got a big tip, no doubt.

As she doled out the glancing caress of a forearm as she refilled coffee or the brush of a breast on a shoulder as she removed a plate, he thought he may have underestimated her back then. Perhaps she had hardened to the transactional nature of living in Alaska. Everything you had or could do for someone was currency. You might give it freely, but you expected the same.

He ate slowly, studying her. Every time she checked on him, he laid a brick on the path back. "How's everything tasting? Can I get you anything else?"

"A little company would be nice." Her eyes danced as she looked him over.

"Well, I'm working. But I'll try to make a few extra passes to check on you." She laid her hand on his shoulder, looked him in the eye, and walked away.

Rocky cursed Jeremiah. This was going to be harder than he thought. He might have to lay it on the table and ask her price. It would be so much more satisfying if she thought she was acting on her own. But he didn't have time for that. He needed Benny out of the picture.

"Well, you've outlasted me." She tore his check off the pad. "Is there anything else I can get you?"

"Is your shift over?" Rocky said before thinking.

"Why, Rocky Cooper, are you giving me a line?" she teased.

"No, I was thinking about ordering some dessert." He held her eyes and a sly smile spread across his face. "If you're off duty, though, I don't want to hold you up."

When she didn't answer straight away, he knew he had her. "You're not holding me up. I have a few more minutes. I'd be happy to get you some dessert."

"Maybe you'd like to join me."

"I'm working."

"For a few more minutes."

"I'm not sure that's a good idea." When he didn't respond, she added, "What is it you want, Rocky?"

"I have a proposition for you."

She shook her head and crossed her arms over her chest.

"Hear me out." He tried to look pleading, but it made him

feel pathetic, so he nudged the chair out with his foot. "If you aren't interested, I'll leave you alone."

She studied him, and he could almost feel the wheels turning. He knew he had her when she dropped her arms. "Give me ten minutes to clean up and change." She walked away without waiting for a reply.

She took longer than ten minutes, but he wasn't troubled by it. In his experience, that was a woman's weak attempt at exerting her power. His response depended on what he wanted. In this case, what he wanted was worth the extra ten minutes.

She was in jeans and a T-shirt when she returned. She had freshened up her makeup and hair. Was it for him or merely habit? She carried over two pieces of pie. She set the cherry one in front of him and took the apple for herself.

"How do you know I wanted cherry pie? Maybe I wanted apple."

She grinned. "Too bad, I like apple."

Truly, it didn't matter. He didn't care about the pie, and he could afford to give her that win.

"Look, I don't know what happened between you and Jeremiah. I don't need to know. But I want you to go out with him again." He took a bite of his pie.

"Shouldn't you be talking to your son?"

"He's got an eye for the new girl working at the Midnight Sun. I want you to get his attention off her."

She took a bite of her pie and pointed at him with her fork. Her brow furrowed as she chewed. "Why?"

"Why? Why doesn't matter. I'm going to make it worth your while."

"What are you going to do? Pay me to make a pass at your son?" she sneered.

"Is that what it will take? Money?"

She dropped her fork on the table. "I'm not a whore."

"No one said you were a whore." The look on her face told him he was about to lose the deal. "Look, I'm not asking you to sleep with him. I just want you to break them up. Benny doesn't strike me as a girl who's willing to share her boyfriend. All you got to do is make her think she is."

"How do you propose I do that, exactly?"

"Oh, I think you know how to get a man's attention." He put his fork down and leaned back in his chair.

"I don't think Jeremiah is going to be interested. Anyway, what's in it for me?"

"What do you want?" he asked. She stared back but didn't say a word. "Do you want money? A horse? What's it gonna take?"

She ate her pie in silence, staring at him. He could tell she was making a decision, and the scales were tipped in his favor. He needed to hold fast.

"I've always wanted a horse, but I've got nowhere to keep one."

"Easy, you can keep it at my place. Rent free for a year." He would have to do a little creative accounting, but it saved him from a big withdrawal he might have to explain to Jesse.

She stood. At first, he thought she was walking out on him. He started to sweeten the deal but stopped when she put her hand out to shake. "A good horse and free boarding for a year." He put his hand out and repeated the deal. It was far less than he would have been willing to shell out. But it didn't surprise him that she sold herself short. So many women did.

CHAPTER 52

JEREMIAH 1982

THE LIGHTS WERE on in the barn and the apartment above it when he drove in. He thought about Jesse up there alone. While she seemed content in her decision and the consequences, he wished they lived under the same roof, especially in times like this. He stood there, looking from the barn to the house. Through the back door, he saw a light on in the kitchen. The last thing he wanted to do was recap the evening with his dad. So, he headed for the barn. Stopping at Thunderbird's stall, he slid the door open slowly, not wanting to startle the sleeping animal. Thunder was lying down. When he saw Jeremiah, he stood in a clumsy rush.

"I didn't mean to wake you up."

Thunder ambled over and gave him a nudge. Jeremiah was well trained, so he scratched behind Thunder's ears and under his cheeks. The horse closed his eyes and leaned into him. Jeremiah got lost in the moment. Horses were so easy.

"Still sneaking in the barn to play with your horse, I see." Jesse stood in the half-opened doorway.

"I'm a grown man. I don't need to sneak." He stopped scratching for a moment and Thunder nearly knocked him over when he shook his head. Jeremiah took the hint and went back to rubbing the animal.

"Really? You're a grown man who doesn't need to sneak around, huh?" She left the door open and backed up to sit on a hay bale along the far wall. Jesse pulled her knees up and wrapped her arms loosely around them, like she had all the time in the world. She was a Cooper, for sure. Stubborn as the day was long. "Seems like you've been doing a lot of sneaking."

"Nope."

"You're lying to yourself, Jeremiah."

"What the hell are you getting at, Jesse?" It came out harsher than he meant it to.

"What would you call what you were doing with Katie if you weren't sneaking around?"

"Jesus, we were planning a fair. Why is everybody making this out to be something it wasn't?" He gave the horse a heavy pat on the neck. He kicked himself for choosing this over facing his dad. All his dad would want to know was whether he nailed Mindy. He closed the stall door and turned to face his sister.

"You're such a liar. And I can see you lying to your buddies. I can't see it with me. And before you lie to me again, I saw you with her." Her voice was soft, but the words weren't. Jeremiah searched his memory. How had Jesse seen them? Who did she tell? "You and Katie came to see me ride in the qualifiers. I had my best run ever. As I was heading back into the chute, I turned and saw you. You kissed her. Don't lie to me, Jeremiah."

He sat down across the aisle facing her. He leaned forward, forearms on his thighs, and let his face sink into his hands. Talking to the floor, he said, "I wasn't keeping it from you. We agreed not to tell Dad and Buck. We thought they would break us up." He waited for her to say something, but she sat there staring at him. Jesse's silence was like truth serum. He spilled like he always did. "Honestly? I think that was just something I was telling myself. Dad, I could handle. It was the leaving I didn't think I could."

Jesse raised an eyebrow. "Was Katie going somewhere?"

"No. I mean, not right away." He toed the floor with his boot. "But she would have."

"Why would Katie leave? I mean, I know she left, but that wasn't her choice. Why would you assume she would leave you?"

"Everybody leaves eventually, Jesse." He looked her in the eye. "Even Mom did."

Both eyebrows went up. "Mom did? That's why you kept it a secret? How does that even make sense?"

"You don't have to understand, Jesse." He stood.

"Oh, hell no. Do not walk away. You don't know what you're talking about." She put her boots on the ground and leaned forward. "Mom didn't leave, at least not like you think."

"She sure as hell did. Dad told us all about it."

"Well, he lied, and I know that for a fact." She stood, nearly matching his height. "I know you don't want to hear this, but it's high time you did." She put her hands on her hips and looked at her boots. "Dad ran Mom off, I know because I was there." When she sank back down to the hay bale, he knew she was telling the truth. All the fight was gone from her face. In its place, only pain. He sat down next to her.

"Tell me." He didn't mean it. He didn't want the story in his head to change. Though he hated the ending, it was an ending he had made peace with. It was an ending that shaped him. If he was wrong about that, it would set off a chain of explosions that he might not survive. Still, he had to know.

"I was in the barn that night. I raced that day, and River had a terrible run. She was off her pace by a lot. When I went to check on her, I ended up falling asleep in the hay." She stopped, and he could see she was searching for the words. Gruff as she could be, she always tried to cushion things for him. "I heard the door slam, which woke me up. I was going to go back to the house, but they started screaming at each other. He told her she would never take his kids from him. She was apologizing and begging to stay. I've never heard Dad so angry. Mom was crying. That only made him madder.

"Then he yelled, *you should have thought about your kids and me before you slept with him.* I wanted to go out and beg them to stop fighting, but I was scared. He was so angry. I'd never seen him that way before." She wiped the tears from her cheeks. "I didn't understand it at the time, except I knew she made a big mistake sleeping with whoever it was. I knew Dad wasn't going to forgive her or back down. He wouldn't even let her say goodbye to us. He told her to get out. When she tried to get her things, he chased her down the road. I was so scared. That was it. In the morning, her car was gone. When he told us she left, I was going to tell him I heard the fight. He looked so mean that morning. He was never a teddy bear, but he'd never looked that angry."

Jeremiah stared at her. The air left his lungs and his heart raced. "Why didn't you tell me?"

"Because he was all we had. I didn't know where Mom went. Who was going to take care of us? And you looked up to him. Who were you going to believe, him or me?"

"Who was it?"

"What?"

"Who did she sleep with?"

"I don't know. I never asked. It didn't matter. The fact is, Dad ran her off." She considered her fingernails for a moment, digging dirt out from under one of them. "Look, I saw how close you and Dad were. I was young and afraid he might make me leave too. I know that sounds ridiculous now, but I really did worry about it then. I didn't want to lose you."

She waited for him to say something. He sat there, looking at the floor, hands gripping his hair. "I missed her so much. For years, I would come down here and open her locker and look at all those pictures of her riding and all of us together. Sounds stupid now, but I would hold her saddle blanket and try to remember the feel of her." He looked at her. He didn't need to say the words. "I took her key that night and hid it. Dad thought she took it with her." She stood tiptoed on the bench and stretched up to the uncovered beam. When she came down, she had the key. "Do you want it?" He shook his head. "Well, it's here if you ever do. I should have shared it back then. When she didn't even try to come back, I just gave up on her." Jesse reached back up and set the key in its place. "Don't become him. If you keep taking his advice, you're gonna."

Jeremiah stared at the floor. Out of the corner of his eye, he watched Jesse brush the hay off her jeans.

"Don't be that guy, Jeremiah." She left him there, head in his hands, a decade of anger welling up.

CHAPTER 53

JEREMIAH 1984

THOUGH HE HAD moved out to the cabin, Rocky still expected Jeremiah to show up at most mealtimes. He resisted at first, resolving to cut all ties except for working at the Double J. That was strained enough without sharing meals, but he gave in. Jesse's cooking had a way of dissipating his resolve, and he could put up with a lot to eat that well. He made a couple of valiant attempts at cooking when he first moved into the cabin. Jesse pointed out his stubbornness was only making him skinny. Even eating crow would be better than the swill he cooked.

Every once in a while, though, when he needed a change of scenery, he would head to the Lodge for dinner and a couple beers. He tried to keep it to weeknights when he knew Mindy would be working the dinner shift at the Back Forty. Jeremiah wasn't proud of the way it ended between them. Though he didn't mean to, he was sure he'd made her feel trashy. She didn't return his calls, so he left an apology on her answering machine. Then he left her alone.

It was quiet in the Lodge. Some old guys were holding court

at a table in the back. It was a strategic position for men who didn't move as fast as they used to. They had a clear line of sight to the front door, and it was too dark for anyone to see all the way back there. Girlfriends and wives never made it to the table before their prey hightailed it out the back door. The game made Jeremiah smile every time it played out. He always wanted to ask one of the women why she didn't just wait by the offender's truck, but he didn't want to betray his team.

He ordered a burger and a beer and surveyed the room. The door opened with a flash of light that made the men sitting at the bar groan. Jeremiah sat up, curious to see what drama would unfold. Carolina Browning stood there, letting her eyes adjust to the light. Jeremiah chuckled. Apparently, dads were also stalked by daughters. When her eyes hit the back table, she sashayed up. Colt Browning stood and kissed his daughter on the cheek. One of the men pulled up a chair for her. Disappointed there were no fireworks, Jeremiah turned back to his beer.

He was halfway through his burger when Mindy walked in. Like Carolina, she surveyed the room for a few moments before zeroing in on him. She strutted up to his table. Though he couldn't figure out the how or why of it, he knew this wasn't a chance encounter.

"Mind if I join you?" she asked.

He looked around at all the empty tables, hoping she would get the hint. "I was just grabbing a quick dinner before heading back to the ranch."

"That's fine. We haven't talked in a while. I thought we might catch up." She reached across and grabbed one of his fries. She dangled it in front of her mouth before taking a bite. The sad attempt at being seductive irritated him.

"Look, I tried to call you a few times to apologize. I'm sorry if I hurt your feelings." Jeremiah hoped his wooden apology would discourage her, but she was undeterred.

"You're forgiven. I've missed you." Her smile looked forced.

"You've missed me?" Jeremiah remembered why Mindy was a bad idea in every way. "Mindy, we haven't talked in almost two years. You haven't missed me too much. Don't read anything into my apology. I'm sorry for what happened. But it's not happening again." He sat back in his chair as her eyes shifted from him to search the ceiling like she was remembering some fact for a math test.

"I don't see why not. A lot has happened in the last two years. We've both grown up some. You have to admit, we had fun together." She leaned forward, elbows on the table, like he was the most interesting thing she had ever seen.

"No, I don't have to admit that. I was practically passed-out drunk. I have no idea if we had fun." He didn't want to hurt her, but she wasn't getting it.

"Well, trust me, you were pretty pleased with yourself, as I recall." She giggled.

"Look, I'm sorry, but I don't want to go back there." He pushed his chair back and looked her in the eyes.

"Oh, you will." She grabbed another fry and pointed it at him before eating it whole.

"Mindy, I came here to eat in peace. I'm going to go use the bathroom. When I get back, I don't want you to be here." He got up, tipped his hat to her, and headed down the hall. With a glance to the side, Jeremiah saw the old guys watching him. He hoped none of them had overheard him and Mindy.

He took his time in the bathroom, hoping she had time to leave. When he opened the door, she was there, leaning against the wall. Her arms were crossed, and her mouth was set in a sharp line.

"What's your problem? Are you too good for me?" She spat the words out.

"I never said that, Mindy." He tried to quiet her, but she wasn't having it.

"I'm just as good as Katie Miller. She thought she was so special. But I guess not since we shared the same guy."

Jeremiah saw red at the sound of Katie's name. "Don't talk about her," he growled. "You don't know anything about Katie."

"Oh, I know plenty, pal. I know you were dating her on the sly. Maybe you didn't think she was good enough, either." She dropped her hands to her hips and leaned toward Jeremiah.

Her bravado was short-lived. He lunged toward her, and she crumpled against the wall.

"Shut up. Don't say her name again. You couldn't hold a candle to Katie Miller." He shoved a finger toward her face, and she flinched. "Don't say another word."

She straightened up. "Or what? Are you going to hit me, big man? Is that what you did to Katie?"

The question startled Jeremiah, and he realized how angry he was. He stepped back.

Mindy made a production of straightening her clothes. In a low voice, she said, "To think I did this for free back then. You weren't worth the trouble then and you aren't worth it now. You can tell your dad you aren't worth a horse. I'm through with the Cooper men." She pushed off the wall and turned to go. Jeremiah grabbed her arm before she could brush past him. She jerked out of his grip. "Get your hands off me."

"What the hell are you talking about? Did my dad put you up to this?" He planted his hands on the wall, boxing her in. She ducked under his arms and turned toward the bar. As she pivoted, her boots collided with Jeremiah's shin, and she fell to the ground. Jeremiah's mind raced. He hadn't meant to hurt her, but his anger consumed him. He turned to help her, but she grabbed her arm and scooted against the wall.

"No! Stay away from me," she yelled.

"Let me help you. You're hurt." He moved toward her.

"That's enough, Jeremiah." Colt Browning came down the hall. His tone brooked no argument. He leaned down to help Mindy as his cronies filled the hall. "I think we better get you to the doctor. Do you want me to call the police?"

"What for?" The air went out of him with the words.

"Jeremiah, I think it's time for you to leave," Colt returned.

"It was an accident," he pleaded.

"I said go." Colt stood and faced him. Although he was much older, he was an imposing figure. Jeremiah felt Colt's anger rising. He looked past the man to the disapproving crowd forming in the hall. At the front of the group was Carolina. Even she was staring at him with a hatred he couldn't bear. Jeremiah turned and walked out the back door. He would have to settle the bill later. He had things that needed to be settled now.

CHAPTER 54

JEREMIAH 1982

JEREMIAH ROLLED OVER at the sound of pots and pans being slammed on the stove. Jesse was in a mood. His back was stiff, so he had to rise in stages like a mannequin being posed. Every ache and pain was a reminder of the night before. He needed a shave and some sun. Closing his eyes, he stretched his neck. It came flooding back. When Jesse walked away, he had started for the house to confront Rocky. He didn't get ten feet before his resolve turned to fear. He knew his dad. Rocky had died on smaller hills. He'd kept the lie up for more than a decade, and he wasn't going to just come clean. Jeremiah wanted to force him to admit it. But his dad was right, he was weak. Instead of storming the house, he sat back down on a bale of hay, seething, and waited for the lights to go out.

Stomping down the stairs, he found them at the kitchen table, eating breakfast. Jesse's face was stone. Rocky was oblivious to her anger, but he keyed into Jeremiah's mood right away.

"Did you wake up on the wrong side of the bed, or are you pissed that you woke up in yours?" Rocky growled between bites.

Jeremiah stopped at the stove. Anger rose up. It knotted his stomach. He pictured himself throwing the pot of oatmeal at his dad. He closed his eyes and took a deep breath.

"Get a move on. We got work to do. I'm not waiting all day for you to eat breakfast."

Jeremiah was a coward, just like his dad said he was. He grabbed his jacket and headed for the barn, slamming the door behind him. It was cold and the air bit his face. The barn was empty and dark. He made his way to the tack room. He did something he had never done in the light of day. Something he had not done in years. He went to his mother's tack locker. Sitting on the bench in front of it, he stared at two holes where her nameplate had been, Rebekah Cooper. When he was little, he remembered his father vowing to get a new nameplate made every time she won a ribbon. *Rebekah Cooper, Double J Ranch, State Champion Barrel Racer.* But like so many promises, he never did. He reached out and ran his finger over the jagged holes. He could feel the age-old panic rising in him. It woke him as a child when he missed her. It haunted him when he couldn't find his dad at night. He needed to open that locker. He needed to hold something his mom had held.

"What are you doing in here? You need to get to work." Rocky's gaze rested on the locker. "Leave your mama's stuff alone. It don't belong to you."

Jeremiah stopped searching. The questions raced through his head. *Where is she? What did you do to her?* But they stuck in his throat. He couldn't force them out. Silently, he held his father's eyes. For the first time, Rocky looked away before him. Jeremiah walked toward him, and he turned to let him pass. Their shoulders touched, and he leaned in enough to warn his father he was a grown man.

⌀

They worked all day without sharing another word. As he had always done where his father was concerned, Jeremiah let the hard work drain his anger. When the horses were fed and the stalls mucked out, he worked Thunderbird. Jesse brought him a sandwich. He was grateful he didn't have to see Rocky at lunch. She didn't speak. She just handed it to him and as she walked away, he could feel the weight of her disappointment.

The afternoon wore on slowly. Jeremiah waited until Rocky was working Kiona to make his escape. He grabbed his keys from the hook and headed into town. The parking lot at the Lodge was nearly empty when he got there. He backed into a spot across from the front door. Jesse was right. He was turning into his dad. Staring at the heavy wood door, he thought about leaving. That was what Rocky did. He left Texas and never looked back. Jeremiah could do that. He could turn on the truck and head down the highway. But it wasn't his truck. Nothing belonged to him. With that thought, he headed for the door.

There were a few old guys at a table, no doubt sharing war stories of taming the wild Alaskan frontier. Jeremiah took a seat at the bar. He'd heard enough stories like that to last him a lifetime. He ordered a burger and a beer, deciding right then and there he was not going to get off that stool until he fell off.

He drank the first one slowly with his dinner. Having tied one on more than a couple of times, he knew pacing was the key to getting drunk without spending the better part of the evening hugging the toilet bowl. Jeremiah intended to get drunk, and not the kind of drunk where he danced better and laughed louder. He wanted to be the kind of drunk where he couldn't feel his lips. The kind of drunk where he had no desire to move, where his head weighed him down and the room spun him to the ground. By the third one, his buddies arrived.

Jeremiah didn't want to talk about it, so he plastered a smile on his face and responded with the odd nod or chin lift. They had their sights on the girls, so they didn't take much notice of his foul mood. By the sixth one, he was apologizing to the guys he jostled on the way to the bathroom. He made a half-assed effort to stem the sway as he took a leak. Honestly, he didn't care much as long as he didn't pee on his boots.

He almost knocked himself over opening the bathroom door and had to launch himself forward to stay upright. Just his luck, he nearly plowed into Mindy on his way back in.

"Jeez, I'm sorry. Did I spill your drink?" He grabbed her shoulders and just as quickly let them go. She gave him a sly smile.

"I was done. Looks like you might be too, cowboy." She giggled.

"I think I might have one more with the guys."

"Well, you let me know if you need a ride." She stared at him through the uncomfortable silence.

"I'll be fine, but I'm gonna call you." He looked away, embarrassed by how deftly that lie crossed his lips. He checked the bar for his buddies. They had abandoned him for warm waters. He studied the wall, which was plastered with news articles celebrating the lofty and the lowly accomplishments of men. Mindy leaned against the wall. The questioning smile on her face told him another lie was in order. "I had a nice time the other night. I'd like to go out with you again."

She put her hand on his chest. "You give me a call, and we'll see." She turned away from him. He was a little stunned. No woman had ever done that except Katie. And she was way out of his league. But Mindy wasn't. He was out of Mindy's league. Shit, he was turning into his dad. He found his way back to the bar and ordered another beer. The bartender was a burly man. His face was hidden beneath a late winter beard. Should he grow one? He thought better of it when he remembered how many girls told him how handsome his face was. The man finished drying a glass and tossed the bar rag over his shoulder. He put his hand out.

"What? I got a tab running."

"Yeah, I know. Give me your keys or you're cut off."

"Fuck." He thought for a moment and decided he wanted another beer enough to sleep in the bed of his truck, which was proof he shouldn't be driving. He exchanged his keys for a bottle and turned to watch the dance floor. It was a small enough town that you couldn't get too bent out of shape about who was dating who. Unless you got married, there was a good chance you were going to come full circle in the dating pool, or at least end up in an ex's wedding. His buddies were sidling up to a table of girls with enough variation that each of the men could find something they liked.

He scanned the room. A couple more beers and there wouldn't be an ugly girl in the place. He wasn't too drunk to kick himself for thinking it just like Rocky would. Across the dance floor, he found Mindy alone. Glasses strewn across the table suggested at least two of her friends were already on the dance floor. She raised her glass to him, and he tipped his beer in response. When his view became obscured by Jake James, who took her hand and led her to the dance floor, Jeremiah saw green and considered cutting in. He felt like an idiot. He knew he was acting like a little kid who only wanted his discarded toy when someone else picked it up. As they moved to the music, he watched her dance.

Mindy had a beautiful body. Desire welled up inside of him as she moved. He was mesmerized by her hips. Then, through the drunken haze, he remembered she had breasts. So, with considerable effort, he lifted his eyes upward. His aim was off, though, and he overshot her chest and landed on her face. She was looking right at him, a knowing grin across her face. His dad was right. She was a sure thing. Was this how his dad felt every night, confident and wanting, loose from drink, hunting for a warm body whose expectations were low and enthusiasm high?

The music ended, and Mindy hugged Jake and walked away. Jeremiah celebrated the victory in silence. He tracked her back to her table. He wished he had stopped a couple of beers ago. In his mind, he pictured himself storming over, taking her hand, and leading her out to his truck. Unfortunately, his body was not on the same page. All he could muster was an intense gaze. A satisfied grin crossed his face when she collected her coat and purse and headed his way.

"Come on, cowboy. I think you've had enough. Let's get you home." Without waiting for his agreement, she put her coat on and reached out for him. "Did he pay his tab?" she asked the bartender. He shook his head, and she opened her purse.

"Oh, hell no. You aren't paying my tab." He dug out his wallet and peeled off some bills. "Is that enough?" His words bled together so that it came out as *ssatnuf.* The bartender nodded, smiling.

"Where are your keys?" Mindy asked in a tone his mama used to use when he was little.

"I got 'em." The bartender held them out over her outstretched hand. "Don't let him drive," he warned.

"Oh, don't you worry. I'm going to take good care of Jeremiah." She smiled.

Jeremiah laughed. "I'll bet."

Mindy blushed at the bartender. "I'll take him home. Hopefully, his dad can bring me back for my car tonight. If not, I'll get it in the morning."

"Sure, Mindy." The burly man's tone softened. "Be careful."

"Let's go, cowboy." She draped one arm over her shoulder and tugged. Forgetting to move his legs, he nearly crumpled to the floor but stopped short when he felt Mindy falling into him.

He wasn't too drunk to be embarrassed, so he marshaled

whatever brain cells he had left to straighten up and walk like a man. It took considerable effort, and he was grateful for Mindy's shoulder. As he pulled himself into the truck, tendrils of disgust grew. She pulled herself into the driver's seat and leaned over to buckle him in. He didn't help. The scent of her hair as she crossed his body filled him. A few hours ago, he wanted to be numb. Now he wanted to feel every nerve in his body shooting.

"I'm sorry." He didn't want to look at her but somehow remembered you were supposed to look at a person when you apologized. So he did.

"For what? Getting drunk? You're entitled." She looked over at him and smiled. Reaching out her hand, she covered his on the seat and squeezed. "No big deal."

"Where are we going?"

"I was going to take you home. Where do you want to go?"

"No. Not home."

"Where do you want to go, Jeremiah?"

They drove awhile in silence. Jeremiah stared out through the windshield. He was jolted back to the cab when she pulled off the road and repeated her question. He couldn't face Rocky.

"I want to go to the cabin."

"I've never been there before."

"I'll give you directions."

"You sure you can get me there?"

He considered it for a moment, then nodded confidently.

He got out of the truck and was halfway to the door before he realized she wasn't following him. It was cold, and he didn't want to walk back for her, but girls liked special treatment, so he headed back to the truck. He opened the door, but she sat there staring at him.

"Aren't you coming? It's mighty cold out here."

"I'll leave your truck at the bar and let Rocky know you're up here. I'm going to head home."

"No. Please, stay." He didn't want to beg, but he didn't want Rocky to come up to the cabin. This was his place now. "Please stay. I want you to stay." It wasn't true, and he felt a pang of guilt, but he was desperate to keep this place just his. Once Rocky set one foot on that porch, he would ruin it. He would erase all the memories of him and his mom riding up here to play. He would sully the memories of him and Katie here alone. That was so much worse than having Mindy spend the night. She turned to him, and Jeremiah tried to imagine wanting her, hoping his face would show only that.

"I'll stay. But I have to work the lunch shift, so you have to take me back to get my car in time to get ready for work." Jeremiah took this as a good sign. In his experience, women who were hoping to get laid rarely worried about being late for work. He reached out for her. She took his hand and slid to the ground. When she looked up at him, he knew he had been wrong.

CHAPTER 55

BUNNY 1984

BUNNY AND RUFF were heading up from the evening feeding when Carolina sped down the dirt drive. They hugged the fence line and waited. Carolina braked hard at the sight of them, causing dust to billow up around her. Ruff stood at attention, leaning into Bunny's leg. She reached down to calm him with a rub of the ears. She was worried when the dog did not stand down.

"Jeez, Carolina. You scared me. Where's the fire?"

"I'm so sorry. I wanted to get here before he did. You know, in case he was coming to see you." Carolina jerked the Jeep door open and was halfway out when it started to roll. She quickly hit the brake and slammed it into gear. Bunny had never seen her frazzled. It was unsettling.

"Slow down. Take a breath. What's wrong?" She walked over to where Carolina stood clinging to the doorframe. Ruff was clearly still weighing his options. He stayed vigilant by the fence, looking back and forth between the two women.

"I'm so sorry." She covered her mouth with praying hands.

She crouched down. "Ruff, I am so sorry, big guy. I didn't mean to scare you. Come here." The dog, like males of all species, did exactly what she said.

"Carolina, what happened?" She and Ruff looked up at Bunny as if she were intruding. Still, she gave him one last pat and kissed him on the head.

"It was awful. I went by the Lodge to ask my dad about some papers that need to be filed with the county. He was there with his buddies, having their weekly roundtable discussion about what's wrong with the world." She rolled her eyes.

Bunny's instinct to grab her by the shoulders and tell her to get to the point was momentarily interrupted by the revelation that she had a job. It never occurred to her that she worked. She snapped out of it when Carolina took a breath.

"Carolina! What happened?"

"Well, Jeremiah was in there alone, having dinner. He was drinking too, of course." She must have caught the exasperation on Bunny's face. "Anyhow, in walks Mindy, that waitress from the Back Forty. I never did like her. She yanked Katie's chain for some reason. Anyway, she came in and sat right down with Jeremiah. Only he didn't look too happy about it. They talked for a while. It didn't seem friendly, though. He got up to use the bathroom. She followed him. Next thing, there was shouting in the hallway. By the time we all got there, Mindy was hitting the floor. I think her arm is broken. Jeremiah just stormed off. I've never seen him so angry. What he did to Mindy was horrible."

"Are you sure?" Bunny was having trouble picturing him hitting a girl. "That doesn't sound like him."

"Benny, I saw it with my own two eyes. Believe it. Anyway, I know you went out with him, and I wanted to warn you. You need to be careful."

"He broke her arm?"

"At least I think it's broken. They are at the hospital now." She reached down and gave Ruff another pat. "Be careful. Listen, I need to go pick up my dad. He went with her. I'll come by later if I can." Carolina climbed back into the Jeep and gave her one more fretful look before backing out. Ruff hugged Bunny's side.

CHAPTER 56

JEREMIAH 1982

H IS LEFT ARM was pinned under a warm body. His right arm and leg were cold and damp. Though his head throbbed, he forced his eyes open. As he tried to roll over, it all came rushing back. Mindy had driven him to the cabin, and apparently, he wasn't too drunk to get naked with her. *Shit, Jesse is right. I'm turning into Dad.* Slowly, he slid his arm out without waking her. He sat on the edge of the bed, heart pounding with regret. A chill was seeping in. He found his jeans and pulled them on.

"Going somewhere, cowboy?" Her voice was dreamy, punctuating his screwup with an exclamation point. How in the hell was he going to get out of this? He shoved his hand in his pocket, looking for his keys. "They're on the little table. Are you leaving me?" She said it with a smile, so Jeremiah assumed she was joking and left the question in the air. He pulled his jacket on. "Are you?" The concern in her voice was a sign of experience.

"Of course not. I'm getting wood for the fire. It's freezing in here." The words came out in a spray, and he knew it hurt her. "Sorry. I'm not a morning person." He left before she could respond.

He cursed himself when he opened the bin to find it empty. Searching his mind, he tried to remember if he had built the fire last night. He would have brought more wood in. *What an ass, making a woman build the fire.* The throbbing in his head made his thinking fuzzy. It came back to him slowly. When he got back to the cabin, Mindy was already dressed.

"Come on. I'll take you back to your car." He patted his pockets as he looked around the room. "There's no more firewood. We can't stay here." Jeremiah was sick at the thought that he had sex with Mindy in the spot where he and Katie shared so much that was real and beautiful. She was a stain standing there, proving he wasn't good enough for Katie. Proving he was just like his dad, a drunk, skirt-chasing asshole. He wasn't coming back here until he was a man who deserved those memories.

"What are you searching for?" Her tone gave away her irritation. He couldn't blame her for being annoyed, but he didn't care. He wanted to drive her away, and there was no time like the present.

"My wallet. Where's my wallet?" Jeremiah lifted the cushion on the chair and swept the room with his eyes.

"It's in your truck. You never put it back in your pocket after you paid your tab."

"Dammit. It's been out there all night?"

Mindy crossed her arms over her chest and glared at him. "Well, you were in a hurry to get me into your cabin. You weren't paying too much attention to your wallet."

He brushed past her. The wallet was sitting on the seat of the truck. Instinctively, he opened it to check its contents. At first, relief washed through him at the sight of his driver's license, money, and credit cards. It was short-lived, though, when he saw the unopened condom packet.

"Fuck!"

"What?" She came up behind him.

"I don't suppose you brought a condom with you?" He turned, holding the unopened package.

"No, I didn't, and you weren't too concerned about it last night." She got in the truck and slammed the door. Jeremiah did the same.

"Great." He slammed the truck into gear and headed back to the bar. Anger filled the cab from both sides. When they arrived at her car, she jumped out of the cab without a word. Jeremiah had a brief attack of conscience and followed her to her car.

"Mindy, stop. I'm sorry. I should have had you take me home last night."

"Don't be sorry. Your dad was right. I'm exactly your type." With that, she got in her car and tried to start the engine. Not even a click of the starter. She got out of the car and looked down the highway. Jeremiah could tell she was seriously considering walking.

"Get in. I'll take you home." She looked at him, breath billowing from her nostrils like an angry bull. Without a word, she got in the cab and slammed the door. They rode in silence.

Throwing the door open, she turned back to Jeremiah. "Don't call me." With that, she slammed the door and walked away. He could see he'd hurt her, but he couldn't make himself follow her. It wasn't kind, but it was right. He knew what he had to do.

When he got back to the cabin, he sat in the cab of his truck with the heat blazing from the vents. He pictured the cabin burning to the ground. The power of it vibrated in his chest. As soon as he stepped on the porch, he thought of all the times he stood there with his mom, with his buddies, with Katie. He wasn't going to let one bad decision ruin a lifetime of his best memories. He hoped that night wasn't going to hold a lifetime of responsibility.

The cabin was just as they left it. Sheets were tangled on the bed. The furniture was askew. Though cold now, he opened the woodstove door and poked the ashes, hoping for an ember. Finding none, he went to the cupboard and pulled out the matches. Jeremiah stared at the bed until the cold seeped beneath his jacket. He pulled the sheets and blankets from the bed and shoved them into the stove one at a time. When it was half full, he lit the match and watched them burn. The smoke went up the flue, but a stench like burning hair snuck out. Jeremiah hoped the stench would stay forever, a reminder of the kind of man he was.

CHAPTER 57

BUNNY 1984

Bunny held the envelope in one hand and rested the other on the pile of soft fur beside her. Ruff hadn't left her side since Carolina sped off. He must have sensed she was on edge. Rather than spending his time turning in circles, claiming the best spot on the bed, he sat at attention in the bathroom doorway, staring at the front door while she got ready for bed. When Bunny got into bed, he stretched out so close to her she hugged the edge. He laid his head on his paws and stared at the front door, muscles tensed.

She was torn between doubt and fear. Bunny didn't think Jeremiah would hit a woman. She wanted to be fair, but she didn't need an object lesson in misplaced trust. As her dad had reminded her many times, it was important to know when to cut your losses and move on. Her dad and brothers could be gruff, but they would never lay a hand on a woman. She was certain of that. And they would never stand by if another man did. Before coming here, she'd never met a man who would harm a woman. Now she had met two. Why did she have no instincts for this? Had her brothers run all the bad guys off? Bunny always suspected they scared away the boys she liked, often before she even had a chance to find out if they liked her. Her brothers never owned up, though. Lying there, she was grateful for their protection. Black and white were fading into gray. Oh, sure, the boys stuck up for each other. They stood side by side, ready to fight together. It was different with her, though. They were willing to fight for her. Too bad her dad hadn't been.

She thought about opening the envelope. Her mother had never written her a letter before. She'd never had the need to. Bunny dreaded its contents. She didn't think her heart or mind could stand another scolding, especially a long-distance one that couldn't be answered aloud. Rolling over, she shoved it in the pocket of the jacket she'd discarded on the floor. She stared at it until she could no longer keep her eyes open. It followed her into her dreams.

Ruff heard the tires before Bunny did. He nearly knocked her out of bed, leaping for the door. She scrambled to the window to see Jeremiah's truck coming up the drive. Her heart was pounding, but she was done being scared. She grabbed her rifle and pulled back the bolt. Ruff stood in front of the door.

"Move," she growled. He looked up at her but stayed planted there. "Move, Ruff, now." Bunny grabbed the door handle and yanked it open as he rushed behind her to avoid being hit by the swinging door. There she stood in front of the door, cradling the rifle against her chest, when he drove up to the house.

"Don't get out of that truck," she shouted.

He opened the door anyway. She moved her right hand to the butt and her left to the stock. That got his attention. She was prepared to aim at him. He stopped, left boot on the dirt, still. He leaned on the door. "I just want to talk."

"The time for talking is over. Get back in your truck and leave." She swung the barrel toward his truck. "Don't come back." She lifted the rifle to her shoulder and looked down the sights. "Lose my number."

For seconds that lasted forever, he stared at her. Words formed on his lips, but he didn't say them. Finally, he shook his head and lurched back into his truck. He kept his eyes on her as he slammed the truck door. Bunny willed her face to stone. He pulled out, spitting gravel, and raced down the drive. As soon as he was out of sight, all the air went out of her, and she fell against the doorframe. She slid to the ground. The rifle fell into her lap as she took her face in her hands and cried. Choking down the sobs, she feared she would wake Buck. He couldn't see her like this. Ruff nudged her with his head, snuggling in tight to her body. She reached out and pulled him in close.

Staring at the drive, the air cooled in a blanket around her. Still, she didn't move from that spot. She welcomed the cold. Closing her eyes, Bunny listened to the night. The only thing breaking the silence was birds. She took a deep breath and smelled the hay floating in the air. She felt the rough wood against her back and the ground beneath her. She felt the warmth of Ruff leaning on her arm. Her body warred with power and exhaustion. Bunny wanted to call her dad and tell him she had faced the bear, but she knew he wouldn't share her pride. He would want her to come home where it was safe, and they could stick up for her because she couldn't. He would miss the point entirely. She couldn't risk that.

The door opened at the front of the house, and she scrambled to her feet. Startled, Ruff jumped off the porch. She slipped her rifle in. It was too late to follow it.

"What are you doing out here in your pajamas?" Buck called. Ruff ran to him.

She looked down at her clothes as if she didn't know. "I was letting Ruff out. I'll get dressed and be down in a minute."

Buck laughed. "Benny, it's four in the morning. Take your time. Get some breakfast. Does he wake you up like this every morning?" He reached down to pet the dog.

"No. He must have heard something." Feeling exposed, she crossed her arms over her chest. "Well, I'll see you in a bit." Before he could respond, she disappeared into her bunk, leaving Ruff to Buck.

Bunny leaned against the door, thankful he didn't mention hearing Jeremiah's truck. She stared at the rifle leaning against the wall. It hit her, what she'd done. She pointed her rifle at a man. Her dad always said, "If you own a gun, you better be prepared to use it." Until that moment, she'd shot cans off fences and targets. She had never pointed her rifle at another living thing. Until this moment, she didn't know what she was capable of. Was this the limit or just the beginning? Either way, she was done being scared. She could take care of herself.

Her mother crossed her mind. Had she been scared? Was that the root of it? Maybe it wasn't that Bunny wanted to do things that only boys should do. Maybe it wasn't even that she couldn't keep up with the boys. Maybe she only wanted Bunny to be safe. Perhaps her dad did, too. Bunny thought she was seeing herself through their eyes, but she was looking in the mirror and blaming them for what she saw. Through the fortress of O'Kelly pride and determination, she couldn't see that until now.

Once she had decided to leave home, it was a done deal. It only took a couple of weeks to find a job as a ranch hand at the Midnight Sun. Twelve hundred miles seemed far enough away. In those weeks, she'd kept her mouth shut and did her job like any good employee would. It was painful. Each task became a last. Bunny felt like she was saying goodbye to herself, even as she knew she'd be leaving a big part of herself behind at the dairy. Not just the fence posts she pounded into the dirt or the wire she strung. Not just the calves she secretly visited at night when she was sad. It felt like there was a part of her in the very soil of that farm. It was her choice, so she had no right to be sad. She tamped it down like the hay in the silage pit, packed tight and rotting into a sickly sweetness.

She announced it the same way her father did—at family dinner, definitively, and brooking no argument.

Mick said, "When?"

Her dad said nothing.

Patrick had had enough. "You're making a mistake. Seriously, Dad, are you going to let her go?"

It pained her to see him so angry.

"Not my choice. She's an adult. If this is her way of forcing me to leave her part of the farm, she's wasting her time." And the mighty Michael had spoken. Bunny was as hardheaded as him. She knew he wouldn't beg, but she thought he might ask her to stay. As he told her on so many occasions, she was making her bed, and she was going to have to lie in it. And Bunny knew with absolute certainty, he wouldn't rescue her if it all went to hell.

The twins, John and Francis, kept their mouths shut, no doubt glad she was the center of attention for once.

And at the right hand of her father, her mother, the Lovely Sophia, sat silently. She reached out for her husband's hand and covered it with her own. A silent declaration of her loyalties. Bunny met her eyes, but she said nothing. Sophia spent the two weeks trying to talk some sense into her. "You're becoming a woman. You need to start thinking about having a family. You don't have to work out there."

It became clearer with each passing day that she did not know Bunny at all. She was clinging to this picture of a little girl in crinoline and patent leather holding her hand at Mass. She refused to loosen her grip on the dream that Bunny would spend hours in the kitchen with her, learning to bake cakes and make casseroles. In the end, she gave up. Sophia quit talking altogether. They passed each other in the kitchen with a cursory good morning. They ate in silence at night. She didn't get Bunny's dreams. Bunny didn't get hers.

Patrick offered to take her to the airport but, when the time came to fly out, her dad insisted on driving her. They had fallen into an uncomfortable silence in those weeks. He wasn't going to change his mind, so there was no point in wasting her words. The sad fact was he didn't even try. He dug his heels in too.

They were halfway to Seattle when he said, "There's still time to back down." He didn't take his eyes off the road. He had a deliberate way of doing things. When he drove, it was eyes forward, right hand on the stick, left hand on the wheel. He even talked in forward motion.

Bunny looked at him. His face, weathered and lined, always seemed rough to her, though she was never scared of him. When he said something, he meant it. He was strong, and she remembered always racing to keep up with him. He never gave her credit. One time, they were loading some cows for the fair. One got spooked and started stomping around the trailer. Bunny jumped in and leaned into the animal with all her might. She stayed there, pushing until the cow stilled, save for the breath billowing from her nostrils. Bunny remembered he said, *One of these days, you're going to get stomped.* If one of her brothers had done that, he'd have bought him a beer. That story would have been told every time three men gathered.

He looked different to Bunny on that ride to the airport. Like a stranger somehow, though perhaps he was more himself than he had ever been. He'd been humoring her all these years.

Bunny took working on the dairy so seriously, but he didn't see it. It was always going to end this way.

"You can come home anytime, you know." It was nearly a whisper.

"I know." The truth was, she couldn't go home. It wasn't her home, after all. At least up north, no one would be pretending it was.

As he stopped at the curb, he said, "We're your family, Bunny. Even when you don't agree with us."

"Please don't call me that anymore." It was petty. After twenty years of refusing to be called Benjamina or Benny, Bunny seemed wrong now too. Bunny was the little girl playing farmer, not the woman deserving respect. With that, she grabbed her duffel bag and rifle case, and she walked away. She didn't look back.

Sitting on her bed in a bunkhouse twelve hundred miles away, she was wishing she had.

CHAPTER 58

JEREMIAH 1982

IN THE DAYS that followed, Jeremiah avoided his father and Jesse as much as he could. He slept in the cabin. To stave off another unfortunate game of pregnancy roulette, he stayed away from the Lodge and the Back Forty. He figured if he didn't hear anything in a month, he probably wasn't going to be a dad. Regardless, he swore off drinking for a while. He made a list of all the jobs they normally did to prepare for spring and started working on them one by one. His dad seemed surprised when he told him to do something, only to find it done. Rather than praise him for his initiative, he said, "'Bout time you took it upon yourself to take care of shit before I had to ask."

Next to working with the horses, working on the equipment was by far his favorite chore. Jeremiah was checking the tractors to see what needed to be done before haying season. The tires had flattened in the cold air. Knowing they would plump up as it got hotter, he didn't bother with the air compressor. He hooked up a charger to the battery and climbed into the cab. Ever since he was a little boy, he loved the feel of sitting in the cab of the tractor. Despite his mom's protests, his dad let him ride in the cab on his lap. Jeremiah would lean forward, his tiny hands on the wheel next to his dad's, laughing at the bouncy feel of the rig. His mom wouldn't let him go when they were cutting hay until he was old enough to drive it. Fortunately, he was tall and strong, so that day came earlier than for most.

While the battery was charging, he changed the oil and filters and then pulled the tarp off the mower. He would wait until it was warmer to check the gear box. He felt along the line of the blades. They were due as well. Pulling the tarp back on, he mentally made a note to call about sharpening. His dad didn't like him to leave things to the last minute.

He scanned the shed for anything else that could be done now. In the corner, he noticed the snowplow on a pallet against the wall. He couldn't remember his dad saying anything about taking it off the truck. He usually left it on all winter. It wasn't hard to take off or put on, but it was inconvenient, especially if there was a storm. Driving the snowplow had been another thing his father had done with him on his lap. As he'd gotten older, he sat in the passenger seat as Rocky plowed the drive. Though he was shaking in his boots, he didn't let on the first time his dad asked if he was ready to plow alone. This wasn't the plow he had learned on. They still had that one as a backup, but it was old and dented and hard to keep trim. It was out back beneath a tarp, no doubt rusting away. For all his faults, his dad was a hard worker. The ranch was his pride and joy.

"What are you doing back there?"

"Jeez, Dad, you scared the crap out of me." Jeremiah turned to find him standing inside the door.

"I asked you what you're doing."

It was a tone he was well acquainted with. It reminded him of the drill sergeants in war movies. "I'm checking out the equipment. Charging the tractor battery so I can fire it up." He stated it without his usual apology. Being alone had given Jeremiah time to think. He was a grown man, but he didn't feel like one. He took orders from his dad at work. He slept under his roof and ate his food. He took his dad's advice in every area of his life. Katie had been the one exception. With her, he'd felt like a grown man. She'd expected more from him. What he had taken as her need to be recognized was really her need for him to be recognized, not in Rocky's eyes, but in his own. She'd already seen him as that man. She'd wanted him to see himself as she did. He faced his dad and waited.

"There's nothing back there for you to work on."

Jeremiah turned back to the plow. "Why'd you take it off the truck? Snow's still coming." He looked it over carefully. There was something his dad didn't like about him being near it.

"I don't need a reason to take my plow off my truck." He stood, legs apart, knees locked, arms crossed over his chest, daring him to ask another question.

Jeremiah pulled the plow back and surveyed the front. He glanced at Rocky, who hadn't moved. Jeremiah knew that didn't mean anything. His poker face was legendary. The only thing he saw was a dent that had been partially pounded out on the passenger side face. Dents weren't unusual on the lower edge of a plow, but this one was more than halfway to the top.

"How'd you get this dent, Dad?"

"Didn't know there was a dent. It's a plow, son. I probably hit a rock or something." He tipped his hat back.

"No. You didn't hit a rock." His heartbeat sped up. He took a breath to steady his voice. "It's too high for a rock. And I didn't pound it out. Jesse sure as hell didn't pound it out. That leaves you."

"What are you getting at, Jeremiah? Spit it out. There's a dent in the plow. Why are you making a big deal about it?"

Jeremiah couldn't believe he hadn't seen it before. Rocky was like a porcupine spraying quills to protect his soft belly. He was done ducking the quills. He wanted to know what he was protecting. "What am I getting at? I'm wondering why you're lying about denting the plow."

"Are you calling me a liar, son?" Rocky dropped his hands to his hips. Jeremiah flinched and he laughed at him.

"You are a liar, Dad." He wanted to tell him he knew all about his mother. He wanted to make him say it out loud. But he couldn't let the snowplow go. "What did you hit, Dad?"

Rocky stood there, face blank, mouth shut, staring at him. And Jeremiah knew what he hit. He charged at him. His rage carried them across the shed. Rocky went limp when they hit the wall. Jeremiah grabbed his shirt and dug into his chest. "What did you hit, Dad? What did you hit?"

Rocky was silent and still. That infuriated Jeremiah. He shoved his dad and let him loose. He choked on the question. Every muscle in his body was tensed to hit him. "Did you hit Katie's truck with that snowplow?"

"No, I did not." The words came out flat and cold.

"Where did the dent come from?"

"Normal course of plowing. I hit things all the time." Rocky leaned back against the wall. "Hell, I used that thing to move boulders in the pasture."

"No. You use the old one for that." Jeremiah's mind searched for a date. When had he had the plow on last? "The cops can tell what you hit."

Rocky pushed off from the wall and stalked over to Jeremiah. "Oh, yeah? Well, they ain't gonna find anything. How are the cops going to find out my snowplow has a dent in it, anyway? Are you going to tell them?"

Jeremiah stood his ground. He needed Rocky to say it. He needed him to admit to this, and to running his mom off, and to every other cruel thing he ever did.

"Well, I tell you what. If the cops show up at my door inquiring about that snowplow, maybe I'll let them run some tests on your bloody clothes." Rocky straightened his shirt. "I had an idea you might get a case of conscience, so I kept them for insurance. The troopers aren't gonna find her paint on that plow, but I bet they're gonna find Katie's blood on your shirt. What do you think, son?" Rocky patted Jeremiah on the shoulder as he walked by. Like he did every time, he had won the battle.

BUNNY 1984

IT WASN'T LOST on Bunny that she had wanted to be alone. She had wanted to disentangle from the knot of family and stand on her own. More than anything now, she wanted to talk to Patrick. She wanted a hug from her dad. Seeing Buck made her sad. He'd lost a daughter he adored. She'd bet he never missed a chance to hug Katie. Her pictures were proof of that. Envy disgraced her.

Bunny offered to make a feed run just to avoid Buck. When she was hooking up the trailer, she noticed Katie's truck again. She stared at the canvas tarp. Why hadn't Buck had the truck parted out or crushed by now? It had been almost two years that it lay dormant in the garage. Bunny thought it must have been some kind of penance. Every day, he had to come into the garage for something. And every day, he saw the lump of steel under that tarp. Did Buck ever lift up the tarp? It hurt her heart to imagine him standing there, staring at the place his daughter died. She couldn't stop herself from looking. Careful to remember exactly how the tarp was placed, she lifted it from the bed of the truck.

The truck was sky blue. Across the tiny tailgate, CHEVROLET was printed in big black letters. On the passenger side of the tailgate, there was a dent. Bunny shook her head, remembering Mick practicing his deep breathing so he wouldn't throttle her after she put a dent just like that in the tailgate of his pickup.

It was a delicate truck, almost a toy. She couldn't see Buck or Jake ever driving it. It wasn't new, but it didn't look old, either. Katie must have taken good care of it. The bed was smooth and shiny. There were a few scratches and dents on the inside, no doubt from hauling something. She moved the tarp up gingerly. Katie had been in the cab when she died, and though two years had passed, Bunny knew it would tell a story.

As she lifted the tarp higher, she could tell the rear window was shattered just by the first couple of inches of glass. Katie's head must have hit the window. The spider web of glass shards was speckled with brown. Bunny wanted to think they were hot chocolate or coffee, but she knew it was dried blood. She closed her eyes and imagined the accident. It had been snowing, and the roads were icy. Katie lost control and drove off the road into a power pole. It must have been terrifying. She walked around the driver's side of the cab. The front windshield was cracked. Something about it wasn't right, though. Bunny tried to imagine being her, terrified, gripping the wheel, sliding out of control. Her heart raced. Ruff let out a mighty woof.

CHAPTER 60

JEREMIAH 1982

JEREMIAH JERKED HIS shoulder from beneath Rocky's touch. He couldn't think. Anger turned to granite in his head. He pushed past his father, nearly knocking him over. When he got to the barn, he slammed the door so violently that horses stomped all the way down the aisle. Matching the beat of their hooves, he stalked to the tack room, shaking from a flood of adrenaline. Like a thousand times before, he stood face-to-face with her locker. He thought about shoving his knife in the lock until it broke loose and dumping the contents on the floor for his dad to see, but that was the act of a little boy. Jesse was right on that account. It was time to act like a man.

Just like the key that lay where Jesse left it, his mother's saddle blankets were right where she had left them. He reached out and let his fingers rest on the coarse weave of raspberry and pine stripes. Sliding his fingers around the thick folds of wool, he felt a string of beads, unmistakably hers. Before he pulled them out, the memories flooded back. The Alaska State Fair, 1972. Jesse and Jeremiah found the necklace at a table in an alley by the stock barns. They agreed their mom would love the alternating beads of dark and light wood. Rocky made them promise to do their chores the rest of the summer without any bitching or whining before he parted with the five dollars. They proudly presented it to her, and she cooed over it. Rocky ruined the moment by spilling their deal. *I paid for it. If they don't hold up their end of the bargain, it'll be a gift from me.* As she always did, she placated him while hugging them.

Jeremiah pulled the strand out and searched it for more memories. She never took it off. That nagged at him. *Why was it here if she was gone?* He drew the beads through his fingers. It hung like a line of teardrops. At the end, the clasp was broken. *Was she wearing it that day?* The beads were dirty. Red-brown stains dotted the alder wood. The thought slithered in, but he pushed it away. Shoving the necklace in his pocket, he locked the box and returned the key. Thoughts of the morning after stole his breath. Jesse silently crying at the breakfast table. Rocky listing the jobs she would have to do now their mama walked out on them. Jeremiah crying inside, hoping his father would not see his weakness.

He grabbed his tack and jogged back to Thunderbird's stall. The big horse shook his head and paced the short distance between the two walls. Jeremiah crowded him against the wall. He knew the horse might rear. He didn't care if he got a hoof in the head, but he didn't want the animal hurt. Willing himself to calm down, he took a deep breath and reached out to the horse's neck. Sliding his hand slowly down the silky hair, he rubbed Thunderbird's chest for a moment, then moved his hand behind his front leg. He closed his eyes and felt Thunderbird's pulse beneath his fingers. His heart was pounding. Jeremiah stroked his neck, slipping the halter on when the horse was distracted. He hung the bridle over his shoulder and tucked the metal bit into his shirt. The cold metal stung his chest but warmed as he saddled the horse. He worked quickly, thankful the horse cooperated.

❧

They stayed on the farm roads and took it slow. The snow wasn't deep, but even so, he didn't want to risk injuring the horse. Jeremiah wasn't dressed for the winter ride, but he didn't care. He wanted to suffer like Katie had, cold and alone on the side of the road. If he could have whipped himself, he would have. It was plain as day now. He had overlooked so much, believed so many lies—forgiven so many wrongs—all to hold on to his father. He couldn't overlook this. He couldn't believe this lie. It was a cruel irony that he finally had the courage to stand up to him, only to be shackled by his father's threats.

Of course his father hadn't destroyed the bloody clothes. He should have known that Rocky would want something to hold over him. He thought about that night and how he'd let him make all the decisions. Though the truth cut deep, Jeremiah had to be honest that he had let him take care of everything his whole life. When push came to shove, Rocky looked out for himself. He didn't know how it happened, but he was sure he had a hand in Katie's death somehow.

While Jeremiah was busy mentally flogging himself, Thunder had wandered to the cabin. He thought about going in but remembered he was out of wood. He sat high in the saddle, staring at the front door, willing it to open and spill out the memories it held. Locked behind that door were the good times. Jesse and he had picnics with their mom in there. He partied with his buddies there. He made love to Katie there. Until this moment, he hadn't realized how those good times far outweighed anything bad that had happened here. This was his place. This was where he would become who he was meant to be. Jeremiah understood why Jesse lived above the barn. They couldn't leave, but they couldn't stay.

He rode around the weathered cabin, taking inventory. He would have to build a stall for Thunder. He needed more wood. As old as it was, the place was in fairly good shape. It needed sealing in a couple of places. The porch needed replacing. He'd look at the roof when he came back. In spirit, the place had always been his, but he had never really owned it. He was going to own it now.

He pulled his collar up to shield his neck. Grabbing the saddle horn, he pulled himself forward and patted the horse on the neck. He smiled at the memory of his mom and sister doing the same after every race, no matter what the outcome. Win or lose, they thanked the horse for getting them through it. For so long, he'd been angry at his mom for leaving. It had never crossed his mind that she might not have wanted to go. That she might have felt backed into a corner by Rocky, like he did now. He saw his mom as strong and bold. Perhaps she also felt powerless like him. The door didn't open. The memories didn't spill out. But he knew they were in there. Somehow, those memories held the key.

CHAPTER 61

BUNNY 1984

THE DOOR OPENED and Bunny dropped the tarp. Fearing it was Buck, she hurried to the front of the shed.

"Hey. I thought I'd see you at the barn," Carolina called out. "Do you want to go for a ride today? War Horse is missing you."

"That would be great. I need to go to the feed store first, though." Her words stumbled off her tongue. She willed her heart to slow.

"Is everything okay, Benny?" Carolina's knitted brow told Bunny she'd failed at nonchalance.

She pulled her ponytail tight under her baseball cap and plopped down on the side of the trailer. "Everything's great. I'm just busy." For the millionth time, she wished she could fib like the twins. She stared at her boots, mustering the courage to admit she was meddling. "I feel guilty about it, but I can't stay away from Katie's truck."

"What do you mean you can't stay away from it?" Carolina

raised her eyebrows. Bunny was momentarily distracted by how perfectly formed they were.

"It's weird, I know, but I need to know what happened to her. I can't stop thinking about her and Buck. They had everything. TV show family perfect."

Carolina looked confused by her admission. "It is weird, Benny. She had a car accident. Car accidents happen every day."

"Well, you know what else is weird?" Bunny stood to face her. "Keeping the truck your only daughter died in under a tarp in your shed for two years. And that's not the only weird thing." She headed for the truck, knowing Carolina would follow her. Bunny pulled the tarp over the cab on the driver's side. "What do you see?"

Carolina looked away, as though she might cry. "I see the place my best friend had her head smashed in."

"Don't look at it like that. Look at it like a—I don't know— like an investigator. She was driving down the road. It was winter, so she probably wasn't going that fast. She lost control on the ice. It probably sped her up. She hit a pole. Right?"

"Yes. That's what happened." Carolina crossed her arms and cocked her hip, but she looked at the truck. A brief glance was all she gave it at first. The second time, she took a longer look. She reached out and ran her fingertips across the tailgate. "Katie loved this truck. She always wanted a truck. It made her feel like she belonged. It sounds funny, but I guess that's what happens when you lose your mom and you grow up in a house full of men. You want to belong." She took a tentative step forward. "But she also loved being a girl. Her dad and Connor called this her Tonka truck. She didn't care. She had the best of both worlds. She had her pickup truck, and she got to be a girl." Carolina swiped a tear from beneath her eye and laughed. "I loved that about her. You know? Like she didn't have to be one way or the other. Truth is,

I envied that about her." She stared at the front cab. Then she turned to Bunny. "I envy that about you too."

Carolina held her gaze, and Bunny knew there was something she was supposed to say, but the words stunned her. She froze like a rabbit. Bunny couldn't understand why she would envy her.

"You're wrong. Not by a long shot. My dad never wanted me to work on the farm. And I never felt I was both. I always felt like I was leaving a part of me behind, no matter where I was. I can't explain it, but I would have killed to have a dad like Buck."

Carolina gave her a gentle smile. No pity, no baseless protests. After a time, she turned back to the truck and gripped the bed with both hands.

"I haven't touched this truck since before the accident. Truth is, I never really looked at it, though I had plenty of opportunities." She looked inside the cab, continuing forward until she was standing at the front bumper. Seconds ticked by. Her eyes were a watery blue. Bunny wanted to tell her, but she needed Carolina to see too. Grief gave way to wonder. Her gaze focused on the glass like Bunny had willed it there. "She always wore a seat belt." Bunny kept still. Carolina's eyes slid upward like she was trying to calculate something in her head.

"Yes?" Bunny prompted.

"I don't think she was wearing one when she had the accident."

"No, she wasn't. She wouldn't have hit the front windshield at all, let alone hard enough to make that dent. She was too short. If she had her seat belt on, she would only have hit the steering wheel. Plus, the impact was greater on the rear windshield. She got hit from behind before she hit the pole."

Carolina put both hands on the top of the cab. She leaned forward, closing her eyes, and resting her forehead on her hands. "What are you going to do?"

Bunny had underestimated Carolina Browning. She wasn't

the benevolent Barbie doll. She had a keen mind. "Nothing, yet. And I don't want you to say anything, either."

"Benny, someone caused this accident. You don't think we should tell the troopers or Buck?"

"No, I don't, and I don't think you should do it, either. Do the math, Carolina. The police investigated, and Buck has been holding on to this truck for two years. So, either we are way off base, or someone doesn't want to find out how Katie died." Carolina stared at Bunny open-mouthed.

"You can't think Buck did this. He loved Katie."

"No, I don't. But you have to admit it's not normal to hold on to the truck your daughter died in. There's something just wrong about it."

"Fine. I won't say anything now. Eventually, we will have to. We can't pretend we don't know forever."

"Well, if someone else is responsible, we need to be careful about who we tell."

R OCKY 1984

R OCKY WAS IN the office paying for his load of hay when Benny drove up. He couldn't believe his luck catching her alone. It was time for him to put an end to this once and for all. He hadn't heard from Mindy, but he believed in covering all the bases. Push a little, pull a little. Get the job done.

The crunch of his boots must have alerted her because he could see her watching him through the side mirror of the pickup. When he reached the rear bumper, she exploded out of the cab and turned on him.

"What do you want?"

Her tone might have impressed him if she weren't a girl. It was a surprise, though. He didn't think she had it in her. He expected her to turn tail and hop away. But she stood her ground, and that stopped him in his tracks.

"Just a word. No need to get your panties in a knot." He leaned on the bed of the truck. Benny slammed the door and crossed her arms over her chest. She stood, feet spread and grounded, like a man. He scoffed at that. She was no match for him.

"You're not welcome at the Double J." His voice was low and menacing.

"Is that it? Is that the word you wanted to have with me?"

He had to give it to her. She wasn't backing down. "No. No, it's not. You need to stay away from my boy. The last thing he needs is another girlfriend from the Midnight Sun. He has a girlfriend. He doesn't need you interfering." Rocky tipped his hat back to make sure she could see his eyes. Rebekah always said he looked scary when he meant business.

"Oh, you don't need to worry about any of that." Benny dropped her hands to her hips and sneered. "I'm sure I made it clear to Jeremiah last night that we won't be going out again. Maybe you should have a word with your boy before you talk to any more of his girlfriends." With the way she said boy, Rocky knew she was done with him. "I understand you'll have to visit one of his dates in the hospital. Better get going. It's gonna be a busy day for you."

"Well, it wouldn't be his first girlfriend to get hurt." He glared at her, willing her to look away, but she didn't. She stood there, brazen.

"Hey, Mr. Cooper." Carolina bopped up to them.

Rocky wasn't going to do anything to upset Colt Browning's daughter, so he slapped a smile on his face and aimed it at her.

"Benny, we're next. They're waiting. Good seeing you, Mr. Cooper." Carolina smiled at him but didn't move.

He glanced over at Benny. A sly smile crept up one side of her face. Rocky tipped his hat to Carolina and walked away. He needed to have a word with Jeremiah.

CHAPTER 63

BUNNY 1984

CAROLINA PUT ON her work gloves. The leather was unblemished. She looked at them like a newlywed considering her wedding ring and giggled.

"What's so funny, Carolina?" Bunny wanted to be annoyed, but Carolina made it impossible. Looking skyward, she shook her head.

"That was fun. I put Rocky right off his game."

"Yeah, it's like your superpower. Men lose the ability to think in your presence. Sometimes I wish I could do that."

Carolina, incredulous, turned on the seat to face her as they began pulling forward. "Jeez, Benny. Are you truly that clueless? Men don't know what to say to you, either."

"It's not the same thing."

"No, it's not. Men defer to me because of who my daddy is. Rocky holds his tongue in front of me because he doesn't want me saying anything bad about him to my dad. It's business. Jake is tongue-tied because I'm beautiful." Bunny raised her eyebrows at Carolina, but it didn't stop her. "Don't give me that look. You're just as beautiful. There's a big difference between us, though. Guys dismiss me as nothing more than my looks. But you? You terrify them because they know you aren't going to take their crap. You're going to stand up for yourself. You don't need them to make it in this world. That's your superpower. I'd take that over blond hair and a powerful dad any day of the week."

She turned without another word and stepped out of the truck, leaving Bunny stunned. She walked around the truck and waited for her to roll down the window. "You might want to turn the truck around. It'll be easier to load." She put her hands on the loading dock and jumped up like she owned the place.

They loaded the trailer in silence. Carolina's words bounced around in Bunny's head. Every time they started to form into something solid, she would try to capture them before they faded beneath all the stories she had told herself.

"What was that all about, anyway?" Carolina had waited until they were headed home.

"Rocky? He was basically warning me to stay away from his son. I don't think he knew about Mindy."

"Interesting. I thought he and Jeremiah were thick as thieves."

"Not sure about that. He said Jeremiah didn't need another girlfriend from the Midnight Sun. Had to be Katie."

"No way. Rocky was winding you up. Katie would never hurt Buck like that. He hates Rocky Cooper."

Carolina didn't say anything else the rest of the way home, but Bunny could tell the gears were turning in her head.

When they got back to the Midnight Sun, she made a weak offer to help unload, but Bunny could tell she was grateful when Jake insisted on taking her place. He didn't say much as they stacked the bags of feed, and she doubted her beauty rendered him mute. When they finished, he slapped the side of the truck and said, "Dinner's in an hour. Buck's cooking." With a backhanded wave, he headed for the house, leaving her to put the trailer away.

Bunny intended to park it and head down for dinner, but she couldn't help herself. The shed door was still open. When she put her hand on the knob, she froze. Her dad's voice echoed in her head. *Let it go, Bunny. Why can't you just let it go?* She saw now that he was right, but she was powerless to stop. She didn't even look back. She felt along the wall to the light switch. The shed lit up. In the back, the blue tarp glistened like seawater under the fluorescent lights. Her mind raced. Someone had caused the accident. Buck must have known that by the windshields alone. Maybe he knew even more than that. Was the truck his punishment? Why weren't the police suspicious? She slid the stiff plastic over the cab. Peering in the window, she imagined Katie's head hitting the glass behind the seat. The force of the pole propelling her body forward into the glass. Why wasn't she wearing her seat belt? Had she forgotten to put it on? Was she getting out of the car?

Bunny moved to the back of the truck. Save for the one crease in the tailgate, the bed had no other damage. That could have happened anytime, but it would explain Katie's head hitting the rear window if she was hit from behind. Driving on a country road in winter was nerve-wracking. Bunny had done it more than her share of times, in more forgiving conditions. She wouldn't have stopped without a good reason. Her eyes went to the tires. They were low but not flat. The door creaked when she pulled it open. She crouched down on her knees. Someone had pushed the seat all the way back. The floor mat was damp and musty. There were a few dead leaves, but it looked like Katie had kept it clean. Would she have been frozen solid? The thought made Bunny sad. Alone, cold, and dying. The truck was a stick. Such a silly thing, but it made her feel closer to Katie. She was a farm girl too.

When she pushed herself up, something sharp cut into her hand. At the base of the seat, a small pin lay needle up. She plucked it from the carpet where the thin edges had dug into the fibers. In silver marred by wear, two overlapping *J*'s lay in her palm.

"Benny, where the hell are you?"

Jake's call shook Bunny out of her head. She clasped the pin in her hand and yelped as it punctured her again. Shoving it in her pocket, she yelled. "I'm coming." But she wasn't fast enough. He was there before she could shut the door.

"Jesus, how many times has Buck told you to stay away from Katie's truck? He's going to have a fit. What is your problem? Why can't you just leave this alone?" He was ten feet away, but they might as well have been nose to nose. His chest heaved.

"I'm sorry, Jake. But something's not right here." Bunny didn't want to anger him. She didn't want to fight, but she couldn't make herself back down.

"Well, you're right about that. Something's not right, and that something is you." He put his hands on his hips and toed the floor like a bull. Tipping his head back, he looked to the rafters and shook his head. It was a move she'd driven her brothers to frequently. "You come here and all you've done is stir the pot." His voice was quiet. His anger seeped out, punctuating his words. "You need to quit stirring this one. You're never going to replace Katie." He paused and closed his eyes. When he opened them, his face was scarred with pain. "Nobody wants to relive this. And it's none of your damn business. You're going to tear open a deep wound in Buck. I can see why you had to leave your family farm. Whatever work you can do doesn't make up for what a pain in the ass you are." He took a long look at her. His eyes were glassy. He turned and walked away.

Bunny started to call after him. She wanted to defend herself, but what was the point if it was true, and somewhere deep inside she suspected it was.

In her heart, she knew Jeremiah had caused Katie's accident.

What difference would it make to know? Katie was dead. They had grieved over her loss. Proving he caused her death wouldn't bring her back. For a moment, she thought maybe Jake was right. But only for a moment.

CHAPTER 64

BUNNY 1984

S HE COULDN'T FACE Buck. Bunny was ashamed of what she'd done. But it was bigger than Katie now. That might have been an accident. But Mindy's broken arm wasn't. She headed up to the kitchen to grab the truck keys. She was sick to her stomach. Someday, she was going to have to ask the twins how they did it. Lying made her want to throw up. Bunny wiped her palms down the front of her jeans. She held the knob a long while before she turned it—so long that Ruff had meandered onto the porch and, tired of waiting, let out a mighty woof. She looked down at him. "Nice job. I was trying to be stealthy."

She opened the door. Buck and Jake were already at the table, dishing up.

"Sit down. Get some dinner." Buck glanced at her. She grabbed the truck keys off the hook.

"I need a break. I'm going to go into town for a while." She refused to look at Jake.

"Suit yourself. More for us, I guess. Don't stay out too late.

We have a long day tomorrow." Buck glanced at her but just as quickly went back to dishing out his food.

Bunny opened the door to leave, and Ruff slipped out ahead of her. As he always did at the sound of car keys jangling, he headed for the truck and planted himself in front of the driver's side door. She kneeled and took his head in her hands. She snaked her fingers through his thick, white fur. She looked him in the eye and said, "You might not want to be a part of this. It could be considered treason." She rubbed behind his ears, and he groaned in pleasure. "Well, you've been warned." She stood and leaned over him to open the door. He turned and leaped in one graceful move that was surprising for a beast of his girth. He climbed over to the passenger seat and planted himself like a sentry, staring out the window. Pulling herself into the cab next to him, she said, "Just so you know, I have no idea what I'm doing." He looked her way and then turned forward again. She took that as direction.

Driving cleared her head. There was something about a cool breeze through an open window and an open road ahead that made the rest of the world fade away. She headed down the highway with no real plan. She thought about the hatpin in her pocket. As the truck jostled down the permafrost-addled two-lane, it hit her. He'd kept the secret for two years. If it was a random accident, why hide it? If it wasn't, why do it at all? There was bad blood between Rocky and Buck. That was for sure. But she'd seen bad blood between plenty of men. No matter how bad, it always stopped short of murder. It had to be an accident.

Lost in her head, she ended up in front of the wrought-iron gate of the Double J Ranch. She pulled off to the side of the road. She tried to pry the pin from her pocket beneath the seat belt, but it was too tight. With a click, she let it loose and it retracted. By the time she had learned to drive, her dad was a staunch seat belt advocate. That might have had something to do with raising four boys before her. Whatever it was, she never felt safe driving without it. Even sitting here on the side of the road without it made her nervous.

She pulled the pin from her pocket, watching the rearview mirror for oncoming traffic. The two Js in her hand matched the logo on the fence. The pin was tiny, silver, and shiny, the exact opposite of the logo on the gate. But unmistakable in style all the same. When there came the rumble of a truck coming up the drive, Bunny put the truck in gear and pulled out onto the road. She wasn't sure which way they'd go, so she picked up the pace. It wasn't until she hit a rut that bounced her out of her seat that she remembered the seat belt. She tried pulling it on, but it was stuck. Not wanting to cross paths with Jeremiah or Rocky, she pulled onto the first dirt road she saw. She was hemmed in, so she backed into the brush. Praying she wasn't going to get sucked into the muskeg, she turned the truck around just in time to see Jeremiah drive by.

Bunny pulled on her seat belt and headed back on the road to follow him. He was heading into town. She slowed, half hoping she would lose him. There weren't too many places he could go this time of evening. She doubted he would be welcome at the Lodge. That left the Back Forty. Sure enough, his truck was in the lot. Her disdain for him grew at the thought that he was chatting up some chick while the one he assaulted was still in the hospital. She didn't particularly like Mindy, but nobody deserved what she got.

Bunny backed into a spot as far away from the Double J truck as she could get. Ruff, who had given into the rocking of the truck and fell asleep, woke when she killed the engine. He popped his head up and looked around. Apparently satisfied, he lay back down on the bench seat and closed his eyes. She stared at the door, watching people go in. It was an eclectic mix. Back home, bars attracted one type of person. Bikers wouldn't hang out in a cowboy bar. Here, everyone seemed welcome. As time wore on, she played her options out in her head. None of them included walking into the bar and confronting Jeremiah. Hunger hit her. It was time to give in, eat cold leftovers, and go to bed. She leaned over and patted Ruff on the head. "Thanks for coming along and not judging me for being an impulsive idiot."

"Talking to the dog now, are you?"

Bunny jumped against the seat belt at the sound of Jeremiah's voice. "I told you to stay away from me."

"Well, that's pretty hard to do with you following me." He put his hand on the top of the cab, and she felt trapped. Ruff stood, nearly filling the cab. He wagged his long tail against the side window and reached across her chest to crane his head out the window at Jeremiah.

"No, Ruff. Back." Bunny tried to push him back with her forearm, but he wouldn't budge.

"He's fine. He likes me."

"He must not know you very well."

"Actually, he does." He rubbed Ruff's head. "Let him out. He wants to see me."

"Are you out of your mind? I'm not letting him out. We're leaving."

"Jesus, let him out. Can't you see he misses me?"

Ruff was nearly all the way out the window anyway, so she pushed him back and opened the door. Before she got her seat belt off, he leaped out of the cab. Jeremiah crouched down, scratching Ruff as he wound himself in tight circles.

"See, this dog loves me." Jeremiah looked up at her. "Why wouldn't he? We're buddies. Right, Ruff?"

"I don't know. Maybe I thought he was more protective than that." Bunny crossed her arms and backed up.

Jeremiah tipped the dog's face up to meet his eyes. "Why would you have to protect Benny from me?"

"Not me. Katie." Bunny took another step back. He stopped petting the dog and stood.

"Why would Ruff have to protect Katie from me?" The dog

groaned. Jeremiah's brow furrowed. "What would make you think that?" He took a step toward her. She put a hand out to stop him.

"Get out of my space, Jeremiah." Ruff looked back and forth between them before taking up his post at her knee.

"No. Tell me what you mean." He moved to the left, cutting off her only forward escape. She would be forced into the woods behind her if she wanted to get away. "Why would you think Ruff had to protect Katie from me?"

Bunny hoped someone would come out of the restaurant and see them. Steeling herself, she reached into her pocket and held the hatpin out in the outstretched palm of her hand. He stared at it, confused.

"Where did you get that?" He barked at Bunny. Ruff stiffened at her side.

"On the floor of Katie's truck." He reached out, but she closed her palm and slipped it into her pants pocket.

He put his hand out. "Give it to me."

"No. Tell me how it got there." She knew she was lighting his fuse, but she couldn't put out the match. "Were you and Katie dating?" When he didn't answer, she added, "Were you there when she died?"

Anger turned to wonder on his face for just a moment. He turned on his heel and slammed her truck door. "I'll kill him." He stormed away.

Bunny melted against the side of the truck. Ruff crouched down next to her. If only she hadn't gone out with Carolina and her friends. She should have known from the way he and Jake went at it that it was a bad idea to get mixed up with Jeremiah. But she had to poke the bear. She couldn't just let Jake be. He was right. Jeremiah was trouble. Jake had warned her.

"Goddamn Jake James."

CHAPTER 65

BUNNY 1984

BUNNY SKIDDED TO a stop in front of the bunkhouse. Jake's lights were out. Ruff sat up and turned to stare at her. "I screwed this up good." Her hands were shaking as she opened the truck door. That was when it hit her. Ruff never lied.

She ran up the stairs and pounded on the door. "Jake, open the door." She hoped she wouldn't wake up Buck. She might be able to stop this train without hurting him. "Jake!"

"Hold on. I'm getting dressed." He opened the door as he pulled a T-shirt over his head. "What the hell's the problem?"

She pushed her way into his bunk. "I know you're going to be angry at me, but I need your help." He leaned against the door and crossed his arms over his chest, a reluctant and tenuous agreement. "I followed Jeremiah to the Back Forty tonight and confronted him about Katie's death."

He pushed himself off the door and dropped his arms. His rage oozed like lava. "Why would you do that?"

"When I was looking at Katie's truck, I found this stuck in the carpet under the seat." She dug the pin out of her pocket and handed it to him. He held it in his palm and stared open-mouthed. "When I showed it to him, he lost it and stormed off. I thought he had caused her accident, but I was wrong. I don't think Jeremiah hurt Katie."

"Oh, yeah? Why is that?" He glared at her.

"Ruff. Ruff loves him."

"Ruff loves him? That's convincing."

"It is convincing, Jake. Listen to me. Ruff loved Katie. Ruff loves me. He is very protective. He didn't attack Jeremiah; he went right to him. How would Ruff even know him if Katie hadn't introduced them?"

Jake turned and grabbed his jacket off the hook and his shotgun from the closet. He threw the door open and headed for the truck. Bunny searched her pockets. She knew as soon as he fired up the truck that she had screwed up again.

"Where are you going?" she called, heading for the truck.

"To clean up your mess." He sprayed gravel as he pulled away from the bunkhouse. When his tail lights flashed red, she had a glimmer of hope. But Jake didn't come back. He leaned across the cab and Ruff pushed his way out. Jake didn't look back.

CHAPTER 66

JEREMIAH 1984

JEREMIAH LIT OUT of the parking lot. Braking hard on the loose gravel, the heavy truck fishtailed onto the pavement. A horn blared, but it didn't slow him down. Long overdue anger bloomed in his chest. The suspension yelped under the bed as the rear axle hit the ruts. He should have slowed, but he was long past caring about damaging his truck.

When he got to the driveway, he pulled over. The Double J brand was perched proudly on the gate in black, not a welcome but a warning. He creeped down the drive and stopped in front of the house. There was no need to go in. Rocky's parking spot was empty. The house was dark. He hit the steering wheel with his palm. Even when he was ready to stand up, his dad pushed him back down. He looked to the barn, where warm lights glowed in the windows, a lighthouse he would ignore, even knowing the peril of the rocks below.

He headed back to town, looking for Rocky's truck in front of a willing door, but he was nowhere to be found. He had a habit of disappearing every once in a while. If he didn't want to be found, he wasn't going to be found. Jeremiah bottled up his anger like he always did and headed back to the cabin. In the months before, he had made a habit of avoiding the stretch of road where Katie died. Tonight, he made a point of going that way. He wanted to feel that pain again. He slowed as he approached the pole. Pulling off across from it, he turned on his flashers, put it in neutral, and stepped on the emergency brake.

There he sat, staring at the pole, conjuring the image of her truck grotesquely embedded in the wood. The baby blue metal reminded Jeremiah of Katie's personality. She was open like the sky. The hood had crumbled like a hand clutching the pole. He pictured her there, head leaning on the steering wheel, arms hanging lifeless. Blood splashed in the shards of glass. He didn't have to touch her to know she was gone, but he needed to feel her. He wanted to pour his heat and his breath into her. The anger, which had died to a simmer, boiled over. Tears started to fall, but he shoved them back, choked them down. Now, the pain was sharp and focused. Now he could go home.

Jeremiah stopped halfway up the drive when he saw Rocky's truck parked in front of the cabin. It was a risk, but he parked behind the truck, blocking him in. It wouldn't stop him, but it would slow him down. He climbed the stairs, hoping the words would not be stuck in his throat. He wasn't surprised to find him there. Rocky favored a direct attack to an ambush. He said most men didn't have the guts for it, so it gave him the upper hand. Jeremiah opened the door. How had Rocky known he was coming for him?

He had pulled a chair into the middle of the room. There he sat like a sated king. Legs splayed, gripping the arms, back erect. Rocky was perfectly still. Save for the drinker's blush that speckled his face, he might be mistaken for dead. Jeremiah closed the door behind him. Without a word, he pulled a chair across the plank floor and sat opposite his dad. He wiped his palms down the thighs of his jeans. He knew it was a mistake by the grin that washed across Rocky's face.

"Something on your mind, Dad?" He stilled himself.

"You having woman trouble, son?" His left eyebrow raised and hung there.

He shook his head. "What makes you say that?"

"I ran into Benny O'Kelly today. She didn't seem too enamored with you, which is fine by me. She's not your type. Anyway, she mentioned one of your other girlfriends was in the hospital. She thinks you had something to do with that."

Rocky was trying to control the conversation. He saw it clearly now for what it was, a way to keep the spotlight on Jeremiah and leave his transgressions in the shadows.

"I didn't hurt Mindy. She had an accident. It wasn't my fault, but I'm sure she's not telling my side of that story." Jeremiah kicked himself for engaging. "But while we're on the subject of accidents, tell me again how the snowplow got dented, Dad."

"Christ, that again. Spit it out. What do you want to know?"

"Did you kill Katie?"

"No, I did not kill Katie."

"Did you cause her accident?"

"What? Because I dented my snowplow? That's pretty weak thinking, son. If all your suspects have dented snowplows, you're going to have to bring in half this town." He laughed at Jeremiah. That was his tell. When he was right, he fought like a bear. He laughed when he wanted him to scurry away, feeling small and stupid. Jeremiah decided right then and there, he was done.

"No, Dad. I'm wondering because Benny showed me the Double J hatpin she found under the seat of Katie's truck. You, me, Jesse. We're the only people who wear that pin."

"You can see mine, plain as day," Rocky warned. Jeremiah looked at his hat. He felt himself backing down. The longer he pushed this, the worse it would be when Rocky won. "What? Got nothing to say? How about I'm sorry for accusing you of murdering my girlfriend?" He pushed himself up from the chair.

"Sit down." It came out flat.

"You better watch yourself, boy." Rocky stopped and sank back down into the chair. "You'll find out what happened to the last person who crossed me."

"You have that pin on every hat you own, except one now, I'm guessing. I bet if I looked, I'd see you're missing one. I think you ran Katie off the road. You checked on her. Your hatpin dropped in the truck."

Rocky glared at Jeremiah, but he refused to look away. "Well, I don't think the troopers are going to be too impressed with your theory. I think he'll find mine more believable. Katie has a fight with her secret boyfriend. She wants to tell the world. He doesn't. She drives off angry. He follows and runs her off the road to prevent her telling her father about the affair. He checks on her, drops his hatpin in the cab. His clothes get covered in blood, which he saves in his missing mama's tack locker because he's a sicko. Hell, they might even try to find your missing mama."

Jeremiah's stomach filled with acid. He had been there. He couldn't figure out how, but Rocky'd been at the cabin that night.

Rocky smiled. "Or maybe you dropped that hatpin while you were planning the fair all those months ago and forgot."

"You're such a liar. You killed Katie. Why?" Jeremiah's muscles tensed. "Why did you take her from me? Just like Mom. You took her from me."

"Your mom was a whore. Getting rid of her is the best thing I ever did."

"Where is she?"

"Where you're never going to find her."

Jeremiah uncoiled. He lunged at Rocky and pinned him against the wall. He pressed his forearm into his neck. "I should leave you bleeding in the woods, like you did to Katie."

"See, son. We aren't so different." The words slapped Jeremiah in the face. For once, he leaned in.

CHAPTER 67

BUNNY 1984

DREAD SETTLED IN her gut. Legs shaking, she sank to the top step as he sped away. She looked out across the farm. The ring was empty. The horses were locked up for the night. The sun was dipping farther toward the horizon with each passing day. She loved this place. She hadn't set out to. She had set out to find the place that demanded nothing more than a hard day's work. Going back home wasn't an option. She would never hear the end of it. Bunny could take that. It would be the subtle things that would slowly kill her. They'd remind her she was just a girl, therefore deserving less voice, less respect, less O'Kelly. None of that mattered. She had found her place. She had proven herself.

She closed her eyes and tried to memorize everything about the farm. The smell of timothy waving in the wind. The rough edges of an alfalfa bale. The horses stomping in the morning as they awakened for breakfast. A field of mares grazing while their foals played tag. War Horse. Buck. Ruff. *I found the place, and I ruined it.* She was certain Jake was going to do something that would get him arrested or killed. That would be one loss too many for Buck. This wasn't just a job for him. It was his life. Bunny feared she had done what the death of a wife and a daughter had not.

She wanted to fold. Half hoping the letter was an invitation to come home, she reached in her pocket and pulled out the envelope. The letter was short and written in graceful strokes.

Bunny,

I hope you are well. I miss you. The farm really is not the same without you. Riding horses is not as fun without you. Please don't misunderstand. I'm not asking you to come home. I would not have chosen this path for you. But I can see now I was wrong. I realize that it's because I would not have chosen that path for me. But we aren't the same person, are we? I wanted you to know how proud I am of you—all of you, exactly as you are. I have always felt you have all the good things from your father—his determination, his fearlessness, his love for growing things. I hope that you got some of the good things from me too. I know you think you had to leave. Please believe me, with all my heart, I hope you found that place that feels like home for you. But I wouldn't want you to think you had to stay away if you haven't found that place yet.

I love you,

Mama

The tears built. Months of anger about her leaving seeped out in three tiny drops. She wiped her eyes and put the letter back in her pocket. She knew what she had to do. Painful as it was going to be, there was no other choice.

She pushed herself up and headed for her room, Ruff on her heels. She grabbed her rifle and dug deep for what little courage she had left. The lights were out upstairs. Bunny tried the back door, but it was locked. She considered breaking a window, but she never knew a man who didn't sleep with one ear open, so she banged on the door instead. "Buck, get up. It's Benny."

The light from the upstairs bedroom went on, and she heard him swearing. She took a deep breath and braced for impact. He threw the door open.

"What's wrong?" He was pulling on his jeans and looked at the buttons as he spoke. "Is something wrong with the horses?"

"No. It's Jake. I need to borrow your truck to go find him." She tried to push her way into the kitchen to get the keys, but he blocked her out.

"Hold on there. Tell me what's happening. Why do you need my truck? You have a truck."

"Jake has my truck. Just toss me the keys and you can go back to bed."

"I'm not giving you my truck until you tell me what this is all about. You're sure as hell not driving it in your condition. And why do you have your rifle?"

Buck wasn't going to let this go. "I know you're going to be pissed, and you have every right to be, but please hear me out." As she told him about searching the truck and confronting Jeremiah, he stood smoldering. He didn't wait for her to finish before storming into the kitchen and yanking his boots on. Buck searched through a pile of clothes in a basket and pulled on a shirt. He grabbed his jacket and keys, pushing past Bunny and heading for his truck. She had to jog to catch up.

"Where do you think you're going?" he said, one hand on the door.

She rounded the truck. "I'm going with you."

"Like hell. You've done enough." They stood staring at each other from across the hood of the truck.

"I'm going, Buck." She threw the door open and stowed her

rifle in the rack. He stood there watching her through the glass. Resolute, she pulled herself up into the cab. Before she could shut the door, Ruff jumped up, pinning her against the seat as he passed. Bunny was never more grateful for the furry white barricade. Buck waited a beat before giving in.

"I told you to stay away from that truck. Dammit. Why did you do it? Why couldn't you leave it alone?" He closed his eyes for a moment, and when he opened them, his anger had turned to pain.

"I don't know. I just couldn't help myself."

"That's bullshit. And you know it. You're the most determined person I ever met."

His words stopped her cold. The muscles tightened in her throat, choking down the words. The cab of a pickup truck had always been her confessional. It got so she knew what was coming if her dad suggested they go for a drive. It was a brilliant strategy. She was captive, and he had a knack for driving long enough to wear her down. Bunny and Buck didn't have that kind of time. She needed to get right with the world, as her dad would say, and right quick.

"I don't want to hurt you. I thought I was doing something good." Buck groaned at her words. "Hear me out, please. I didn't know Katie. But I can tell you were close. Every time I saw the truck, my heart hurt for you. I couldn't imagine how bad you hurt seeing it. I couldn't figure out why you would keep it. I thought maybe it was because you didn't know what really happened to her, so you couldn't let her go. I thought I was helping." She looked out the side window. She had hurt him in a way that he might never be able to forgive.

"You don't have kids, so you can't get it. I'm never going to let her go." It came out in a warning growl. "And no one's ever going to replace her."

It was a wound she deserved. "I know I'm never going to do

that. To be replaced, you would have to be worth something to begin with. It's messed up, but I thought figuring out who caused the accident would somehow fix things for you."

"You can't fix this. You made it worse." He was right. She had made it worse. She hoped she could still stop Jake and Jeremiah from hurting each other. Buck slowed the truck. "I didn't hire you to fill in for Katie."

"I know. You can send me packing when this is over. Just help me stop Jake and Jeremiah." Ruff leaned into her, and she buried her hand in the fur at his neck, memorizing the feel of the big hound. Her heart missed him already. When she looked up, Buck was watching them. He nearly missed the turn, and she crashed into Ruff as he took the corner. They bounced down the driveway, kicking up dust in their wake. He slammed on the brakes as soon as the house came into view. The trucks were gone.

CHAPTER 68

JEREMIAH 1984

THE SCUFF OF the door against the rough planks registered in his mind. Still, Jeremiah searched Rocky's face. He hungered for his fear. He stood on the edge. A pound or two forward and he would feel his throat crush. He imagined Rocky's chest heaving as he fought for air.

"Put him down, Jeremiah."

"Get out, Jake. This has got nothing to do with you." A boot dropped behind him. "I mean it." Before he could turn around, the butt of the shotgun collided with his head. Jeremiah crumpled in a daze. Rocky propelled him to the floor and landed in the tangle of his arms. Jake stood over their twisted embrace, gun raised. Rocky scrambled across the floor to the far wall. Jake backed up in time with him, giving himself room to maneuver the long gun back and forth between the two men until he settled on Rocky.

"You bastard," Jake said, shouldering the shotgun.

"You're making a mistake. You already got the guy." Rocky glanced at his son.

Jeremiah's face turned to stone. His eyes darkened with hate. His breath was fast and deep, like a bull trapped in the chute.

"Yeah, I got the guy. You. Get up." Jake motioned with the barrel to Rocky.

"Jeremiah, did you know that Jake James here was pining for Katie?" Rocky kept his eyes on the gun as he spoke.

"Shut it, old man," Jake said.

"Yeah, followed her around like a puppy dog." Jake lifted the gun, but Rocky continued. "I wasn't the only one there that night. Was I, Jake?"

"What are you talking about, Dad?"

"You want to tell him, or should I? No? Okay. Jake took a little midnight ride out to the cabin. He made her spin out."

"Shut up. Get him on his feet. We're going for a walk. We'll see who comes back."

Rocky scurried over to Jeremiah, but he kept his eyes on Jake. He snaked his arm under Jeremiah's shoulder and heaved. Leveraging his body weight, Jeremiah felt Rocky's knee press against his back, but Jake was faster. Rocky stopped dead still when the barrel came to rest against his forehead. Jeremiah didn't want to die, but he deserved it.

"Do that again, old man, and I'm going to drop you right here." He gave the gun a shove, pushing Rocky to his knees. "Pick him up."

Jeremiah could tell his dad was looking for a way out. He doubted Rocky would be successful. He hadn't lost enough fights to have much of a chance of winning this one. Pulling Jeremiah's arm over his shoulder, Rocky pushed him upward. With a groan, he got his knees under him. Jake moved aside and motioned to the door.

"Where are we going?" Rocky asked.

"You'll know when we get there. Just start walking." Jake's voice was dead. He stayed back and watched the pair make their way. The weight of Jeremiah pulled Rocky off course every few yards. Whenever they slowed, Jake prodded them along. When he directed them into the woods, Jeremiah knew it was over.

CHAPTER 69

BUNNY 1984

BUCK SLAMMED THE truck into reverse and spun around, nearly taking out the fence. He headed for the highway.

"I don't think they're in town." Bunny checked the clock on the dash. How far ahead was Jake? Should she jump out of the truck and walk away?

"They aren't," he answered. He gave the old truck some gas. Bunny strained against the seat belt with each rut in the highway.

"Where are we going?" She looked at Buck. The lines in his face deepened, and he leaned toward the windshield, as if urging the engine to speed up. "Where are we going?" She gripped the door handle and wedged her foot against the floorboards.

"Jeremiah has a cabin off the highway."

"I've been there."

He whipped his face to her. Grimacing, he hissed, "Of course you have."

"I didn't go in. We rode by." She should stop talking, but the need to defend herself overruled her better judgment.

"Well, it was just a matter of time."

"What the hell is that supposed to mean?"

"Just what it sounds like."

"It sounds like you're calling me a whore."

"I'm calling Jeremiah a whore. He preys on women. I tried to warn you off. I assume he did something to make you dump him. Most women cling to him. It's humiliating."

"Did you know about him and Katie?"

"Yeah, I knew."

"Why didn't you stop her?"

With a wounded look, he said, "Probably for the same reason your dad didn't try to stop you coming to Alaska alone."

"No. You don't know anything about that. Don't make it her fault. The least you could do is own it."

"You don't know what you're talking about. You need to shut your mouth for once." He slammed his hand against the dash.

"Why do men always do that?" She slapped the dash. "You know what I think? I think I'm cutting a little too close to the bone. This isn't just about Katie. It's about you."

Buck steered the truck around a bend and onto a dirt road, slowing just enough to keep the rear wheels from kicking out from under them. Three trucks were parked in front of the cabin. He parked his perpendicular to the others, blocking them where they stood.

Buck didn't wait for her. He sprinted to the door and flung it open. Bunny knew right away they weren't there. Buck turned and scanned the property for a sign of them. Without a word, he headed into the woods. Bunny grabbed the rifles from the rack and chased after him.

"Where are you going? Can you see them?" she called out.

He stopped and waited for her to catch up. When she did, he yanked a gun from her arms and jogged away. The terrain was spongy and uneven. Snow-felled trees littered their path. Every ten yards or so, Buck stopped to listen. When he stopped, so did Bunny. The signs were faint at first and could have been a moose or bear. As they zeroed in on their target, they could tell the predator was a man. Buck broke into a run, stopping only when he came to the edge of a clearing. Through the trees was the highway. Her first inclination was to make a run for it, but it was unlikely she'd be able to flag down a trooper. Then came a pump sliding a shell into place.

Buck shouted, "No!"

Bunny froze in her spot.

CHAPTER 70

JEREMIAH 1984

JEREMIAH LOOKED OVER at his father. He saw him, maybe for the first time. Rocky's eyes were darting around, searching for an escape. They never rested on Jeremiah. It was an exclamation point punctuating his self-preservation. He was weary from hiding the pain in his heart.

"Jake, did you kill Katie?" He stopped and turned toward his dad.

"Keep moving," Jake barked.

Jeremiah ignored the order. "No, I don't think you did. But you were there. You know what happened."

"You're going to take his word over mine? You're a traitor, just like your mother."

"Be a man, Dad. Isn't that what you always say? Be a man." Jeremiah blocked Rocky's path.

"Get out of the way, boy." He set his jaw and narrowed his eyes. His chest heaved.

"Don't call me that." Jeremiah clutched the tattered cotton at Rocky's neck and shoved him to the ground.

"Stop it." Jake shoved him with the barrel.

Jeremiah came back swinging, but the sound of the pump stopped him cold.

"Get him up." Jake aimed the twelve gauge at Rocky's chest.

"Before you blow a hole in me and have two souls on your conscience, tell Jeremiah how you made Katie lose control and run into that tree."

Jake struggled to hold back his tears. "That's not true. She was fine when I left."

Jeremiah heard Buck yelling, and from the snap of branches, he was closing in on him. They were almost out of time, though.

"Tell Jeremiah the truth or I'll blow a hole in you big enough to drive Katie's truck through."

"Tell me!" Jeremiah screamed.

"Shut up!" Jake boomed.

"No, Jake. Don't do this." Buck held an arm out to stop Benny, who was standing next to him.

"They killed Katie. They need to pay for that." Jake kept Rocky in his sights.

"Tell Buck the truth, Jake," he taunted.

"I didn't hurt her, Buck. She was fine when I left." The rifle shook as he spoke. "I should have stayed and brought her home. I swear she was fine. A moose spooked her. But she kept it on the road. When she didn't come home, I couldn't tell you. If I'd just stayed. But she would have hated me for following her out there. It's their fault. I want to hear them say it. I want you to know what happened to her."

"Katie's gone. Nothing's going to change that. Don't let them do this to you," Buck begged. No one moved. "Jake, I knew Katie was seeing Jeremiah. It's my fault she hid it."

"Why him? He's a dawg. She was special." Jake's words came out ragged, like the sound of a wounded animal.

"Who knows, Jake? We make stupid decisions sometimes.

And sometimes we make the right decision and everyone else thinks it's wrong." Buck's words slipped out with thick sorrow.

"You asshole!" Rocky screamed. "You took my wife from me." He lunged at Buck before Jake could get a bead on him. They hit the ground, struggling for control of Buck's rifle. Jake and Jeremiah stood by, watching.

"Stop it. Stop it, you two!" Benny fired into the air. One shot and then another. The crack of the rounds echoed upward. "Nobody's dying today."

"You're wrong about that. Get out of the way, Benny," Jake ordered.

She stood with her back to him, reminded she was not the only one with a weapon.

"Don't make me hurt you!" he shouted.

"I can't make you do anything!" Benny yelled. "You've made that clear. But I'm sure as hell not moving, Jake. I know you loved Katie."

Jake looked to Buck and a wave of sorrow passed between them.

"Did you kill my daughter, Rocky?" Time creeped by. The air seemed to cool. Everyone froze where they stood. Buck reached out and wrestled the shotgun from Rocky's grip and turned it on him. "Did you kill my baby?" He choked the words out. The barrel shook in his hands.

"It was an accident. She was sideways in the road. I clipped her bumper, and she spun out and hit the pole."

"You left her to die out here alone."

"She was too far gone. She would've been dead by the time I got back with help."

"You don't know that."

"I do."

Buck turned on Jeremiah. "Were you with him?"

"No. We had a fight. She took off to go home. I didn't find her until it was too late."

"You left her out here all night long. She loved you. She wanted to marry you." Buck raised the gun to his chest. "You didn't deserve her."

"I know." Jeremiah gasped as the tears escaped.

Buck reached into his pocket and pulled out his keys. He tossed them to Benny. "Go find a trooper. We'll be waiting here." She hesitated. "Go."

Benny stood her ground. "I'm not leaving."

Buck turned the rifle on her. "I said go."

CHAPTER 71

BUNNY 1984

For the first time in her life, Bunny wished some tree hugger had heard her shots and called the police. They needed help, but she wasn't going to leave to get it. Bunny knew in her heart Buck wouldn't shoot her. She couldn't say the same for Rocky. Much as she wanted Buck to be just her boss, she'd come to care about him. Though he was gruff, he respected her as she was. For that alone, she couldn't stand by.

"Don't do this, Buck. He's not worth it."

"You don't get it. You can't. You're not a parent."

"No, I'm not. But I wouldn't want this for my dad." Bunny could see the pain of being a father in his eyes. "Katie wouldn't want this for you."

"He needs to pay!" Jake bellowed.

Bunny had almost forgotten he was there. "He will. He admitted to it in front of all of us. It's a hit-and-run and Katie died as a result. He'll go to jail."

"Juries don't always convict."

"They will with four witnesses to the confession."

"Three," Rocky stated with a grin. Bunny could feel Buck and Jake raise their guns.

"Four." Everyone turned to Jeremiah, who stepped up to face his dad. "Four."

"You don't have the guts," Rocky said.

"Try me," he said, turning from his father to Buck. "Please don't shoot him, Buck. He deserves it. But Benny's right. Katie loved you. She wouldn't want this for you. I failed her and I'll never forgive myself for that. I'll testify that he confessed. He will go to jail."

"You're a traitor, just like your mother."

"A traitor? Jesse heard you fighting with Mom that night. She didn't walk away, did she, Dad? I will dig up every last rock on the ranch until I find her." Jeremiah pulled a string of beads and dangled them in front of Rocky. "I wondered why such a cheap man would spend good money on a new plow when he had a perfectly good one in the shed."

Rocky sprung toward Bunny, who stumbled backward to the ground, losing her grip on the rifle. Jeremiah lunged for it as shots rang out.

"Everybody, guns on the ground. Hands on your heads." The trooper scanned the group, sighting the gun on each one as he passed them. He moved them to the center of the clearing and ordered them to the ground as he called for help. Bunny fought the urge to explain. In time, another trooper came. The rifles were all collected and stored in his truck. When only Rocky was cuffed and loaded into a trooper's car, Bunny knew Jeremiah must have told the truth.

"I'm sorry. I was wrong about you." Bunny waited for absolution, but it didn't come. "Well, I just wanted to say that before I left."

"Where are you going?" Jeremiah asked.

"Home. I suspect tomorrow." She headed for the trucks,

hoping Jake would give her keys back so that she would not have to suffer the agony of riding with either of them back to the Midnight Sun. She needed time to plan. It would be tricky going home. Even with Sophia's letter, Bunny knew nothing had changed at the dairy. So much had changed in her, though. Maybe she would move on. Try again somewhere else. Going back to the dairy felt like defeat.

With every step through the woods, she tried to memorize the place. The alders' white bark peeling. Leaves rustling in the breeze. The fireweed. The spongy feel of the earth beneath her boots. She hoped Ruff would stay with her tonight. She was going to miss him. She would call Carolina and say goodbye. She was sure that was what girlfriends did.

When she saw the trucks, she stopped in her tracks. Buck was speaking to Jake, both hands on his shoulders. Though she could not hear them, she knew forgiveness when she saw it. With a slap on the younger man's back, Buck turned and looked toward Bunny.

He leaned back against the grill of his truck, arms crossed at his chest, looking down at his feet. He glanced back at Jake and nodded. Jake fired up the engine and backed away. It was time to take her punishment and go. The silence stretched out between them. Buck looked up and tipped his hat back so that his eyebrows sneaked out from beneath the brim. He closed one eye and raised one side of his mouth.

"I didn't want to know." Buck looked toward the tree line. Bunny waited for the impact. "I thought anger would be so much worse to bear than sadness. And I was so damn angry when my wife died. I did things I'm not proud of. I hurt Katie and Connor along the way. But I thought those things would take away my anger. Drinking. Sleeping with Rebekah. They planted a wedge between me and my kids. When Katie died, I felt like it was my fault. Moose or man, I brought it down on her somehow. For that, I deserved nothing short of despair."

Bunny searched for words to comfort him and instead found her arrogance for thinking she had the right to take his pain away at all.

"You've been a pain in my ass since you got here."

She took a deep breath and waited for the next blow.

"You talk too much, and you're nosy as hell." He shook his head and kicked a rock with the toe of his boot. "But you were right. You work as hard as anyone. You never complain about that, even when Jake is dishing it out." He pushed himself away from the truck. "Let's go home."

"Look, I'll pack up and head out in the morning. But before I leave, I want you to know I never meant to hurt anyone. I thought I was doing the right thing, but I see now I was wrong. I'm going to miss the ranch. And you, and even Jake." She swallowed hard, not wanting to cry. "I guess I just want you to know I appreciate all you did for me." She looked Buck in the eye, like her daddy always told her to.

He stared back at her with a furrowed brow. "Why are you leaving?"

"To go home."

"I said *let's go home* as in the Midnight Sun. Not *go home*. Jeez, Benny, you need to listen more and talk less." He put his hand out. "Give me the keys and get in the truck." A smile crossed his face.

Bunny handed him the keys but didn't move. He rounded the cab and opened the door. She held her breath when he paused there.

"Benny, you better hustle up. Your friend's getting cold there." He tipped his chin to the white ball of fur sitting by the headlight. Ruff let out a sharp bark and stood, keeping his eyes on her.

She opened the door, and the dog jumped onto the seat. Bunny hopped in the truck after him. Ruff sat at attention, focused on the road ahead. He leaned into her. Buck reached out and rubbed the dog's neck.

Bunny wanted to talk. She had so many questions, but for once, the silence spoke to her. All she cared to say was, "You can call me Bunny."

"Well, okay." Buck turned to her and nodded. "Bunny it is then."

She knew she was home.

ACKNOWLEDGEMENTS

It is a long road from idea to published novel. Fortunately, I did not walk that road alone. First and foremost, I am grateful to my husband, Scott Matthews, for the encouragement and support that fueled this fire and all the ones before it. My daughter, Shannan Browning, inspired me, through the courageous pursuit of her passions, to realize my own dream. Thank you for lighting the match, fierce girl.

Writing is a magical combination of art and craft. Both must be honed. I have been blessed to learn from the best. My critique partners, James Shipman and S.G. Prince, provided invaluable feedback and encouragement through many revisions. I am a better writer for having worked with them. This novel also benefited tremendously from the expertise and experience of my editor, Virginia McCullough. An exceptional author, I am grateful for her mentoring in the craft and business of writing. The Women's Fiction Writers Association, especially the Write-InMates, welcomed me into the writing community and generously shared their expertise, resources, and inspiration. I grew exponentially with their nurturing.

Half the battle of getting a novel out into the world is persistence. I owe a debt of gratitude to Amy Sue Nathan for inviting me to join the Early Birds who show up 365 mornings a year to write together. I am inspired daily by the talents of these authors. I must thank author, Heather Carter, who is up even before the Early Birds for a daily pre-dawn well-author check. She is an indefatigable accountability partner and advisor who challenged me to dig deep as I brought the story to life. Thank you for your friendship and for loving Bunny as much as I do.

To my sister, Judy, thank you for always being there to listen and give me your honest opinion. Thank you for the laughter and all the trips that have provided the fodder for many plots to come.

To my sister, Angie, thank you for noticing in my writing what I could not yet see. I would not have taken the first step without your words.

Thanks to the Wolf Pack, Shelley Boten, Shannon Koehnen, Donna Kapustka, and Becky Ballbach, for the decades of support that led up to this moment. I can always count on you to cheer me on, hug me through the hard parts, and give me a push when I stall. I write about strong women who have faced the storm. I do not know four stronger women than you. Thank you for facing the storms with me.

To my mentor and friend, Carol Whitehead, you have inspired me from the moment I stepped into your classroom some thirty years ago. I am forever grateful for the lessons you've taught me and your unwavering belief in me. Thank you for cheering me and this novel on.

To C D'Angelo and CJ Noble, thank you for reading my earliest drafts. You helped me to see the story from different angles and sharpen the corners. You are truly Queens.

Thanks to my Beta Readers, Jamie Edson, Carol Whitehead, Ann Burns, Shannan Browning and Heather Carter. I was blessed to have your insightful feedback. Thank you for helping me get to THE END.